77 DAYS IN SEPTEMBER

77 DAYS IN SEPTEMBER

A NOVEL OF SURVIVAL, DEDICATION, AND LOVE

RAY GORHAM

77 Days in September
Copyright 2011 by Ray Gorham

Comments on this work can be sent to: raygorham1@gmail.com.
All characters in this work are fictional, and any resemblance to
actual persons is completely coincidental.

ISBN-13: 9781499616019

*This book is dedicated to my indescribably
patient, loving, devoted and helpful wife, Jodi,
and our five wonderful children,
Geoff, Tyler, Jessica, Nate, and Andrew.*

*A huge thank you also goes out to all those who have
helped shape the story and characters and who have plodded
through the various manuscripts as this project evolved.
I couldn't have done it without you.*

FOREWORD

On July 9, 1962, residents of the Hawaiian Islands became unwitting eyewitnesses of the latest scourge to escape from Pandora's nuclear box. At just after eight o'clock in the evening, thirty electrical circuits powering a total of 300 streetlights overloaded, power lines melted together, burglar alarms sounded, dozens of car ignitions were rendered inoperable, TVs and radios malfunctioned, and microwave phone service to the island of Kauai was disrupted. At the exact same time, 930 miles southwest of Hawaii and 248 miles above sea level, the United States military had just detonated a 1.3-megaton nuclear bomb. The blast was an exercise by the Defense Atomic Support Agency (DASA) and the Atomic Energy Commission (AEC) to determine and measure the effects of high altitude nuclear detonations for potential military applications.

This test, nicknamed "Starfish Prime," was, and still is, the highest altitude, highest yield, atmospheric nuclear test of this type ever performed. It involved a bomb measuring just 20" in diameter, 54.3" in length, and weighing a little less than 1,700 lbs. A number of phenomena were observed as a result of the blast: an aurora was formed that lasted for over seven minutes and extended from Hawaii to New Zealand; seven satellites were immediately disabled, and, within a year, one-third of all low earth-orbiting satellites would fail (including Telstar 1, the world's first communications satellite); radiation from the blast was trapped by the earth's magnetic belts for seven years; and a previously theorized, but never studied, phenomenon called an Electromagnetic Pulse (EMP) was observed, the direct cause of the problems in Hawaii.

The year 1962 saw significant nuclear testing by both the United States and the Soviet Union, the world's two superpowers. The American tests, of which Starfish Prime was just one in a series, were conducted in response to the Soviet Union's failure to renew a nuclear test ban a year earlier. Late in 1962, during the height of the Cuban missile crisis, the Soviets performed Test 184, code named "Operation K." Carried out on October 22, Operation K involved the detonation of a 300-kiloton bomb 170 miles above a sparsely populated area of Kazakhstan. As with the American test, the most eye-opening consequences of the test resulted from the EMP phenomenon, including 355 miles of overhead telephone lines being rendered useless and 620 miles of underground power cables fusing together. In addition to the destruction of the cables, the power plant that was connected to the underground power line, unable to handle the corresponding electrical surge, caught fire and burned to the ground.

As scientists studied the data recorded during the 1962 atmospheric detonations, they determined that a single nuclear bomb detonated 300 miles above Kansas would create an EMP effect that would impact the entire continental United States. Indeed, the electrical devastation from such an attack would extend north and south of America's borders, affecting every major Canadian and Mexican city as well. The result of this would be a continent of twenty-first century people forced to survive with nineteenth century technology.

Less than one year after Operation K, the United States, the Soviet Union, and the United Kingdom, the nuclear powers of that period, signed the Partial Test Ban Treaty (PTBT) which, among other things, outlawed all atmospheric nuclear testing.

Since the signing of the PTBT in 1963, our world has changed significantly. Almost extinct, except in museums and time capsules, are the hardy vacuum tubes and electronics that were the standard of the early sixties. These have been replaced by the tiny, inexpensive, and amazingly fragile microchips of our day. These microchips, the source of so much convenience in our world, are many thousands of times more vulnerable to the effects of an EMP device than anything that was in service in 1962. Combine this technical vulnerability with nuclear proliferation and our world teeming with hostile countries and terrorist groups, and it quickly becomes obvious that North America, and all modern economies, face the potential for a catastrophe of unimaginable severity.

Fast forward forty-five years from the signing of the PTBT to September 2, 2008 and an article in the *Washington Times* titled *Invisible Nuclear Threat* by Dr. William R. Graham, Chairman of The Commission to Assess the Threat to the United States from Electromagnetic Pulse (EMP) Attack. In his article, Dr. Graham laments the unwillingness of the United States to adequately address the threat posed by rogue nations and their ability to launch such an attack. Instead, he laments, the government has focused its efforts almost exclusively on a dirty bomb or conventional strike that can only be carried out by a bomb smuggled into the country. Dr. Graham writes as follows:

> ...this other nuclear threat is potentially far more catastrophic; instead of a single city, it could threaten the entire nation's survival.

> ...Our vulnerability to EMP attack is increasing daily, as our dependence on electronics continues to grow.

...One scenario of special concern is an EMP attack against the United States launched from an ordinary freighter off the U.S. coast using a short or medium range missile to loft a nuclear warhead to high altitude (such missiles are readily available on the world's armaments black market).

While *77 Days in September* takes some dramatic license, it is based on realistic assumptions and is an attempt to entertain while putting into perspective the impact such an attack would have at a national, as well as an individual and family level, should the unthinkable happen.

Ray Gorham

CHAPTER ONE

Kyle worked his way down the aisle of the airplane, squeezing past the other passengers as they struggled to jam their oversized carry-ons into already too-full overhead bins. "Excuse me…pardon me…thank you," Kyle mumbled as he passed, irritated that his flight was already thirty minutes behind schedule. Kyle re-checked his boarding pass for his seat assignment, 26F, then scanned the numbers above the seats. 23… 24… 25… 26. A balding man in his late fifties who, by his tan face and comfortable attire, looked like he'd come directly from a golf course, sat in the aisle seat, the two seats beside him empty.

"I'm sorry to bother you," Kyle said, making eye contact with the man and motioning to the seat by the window. "I need to slip by. I'm in that seat."

The man nodded and rose, and Kyle squeezed past and dropped into his seat, then pushed his carry-on into the cramped space in front of his feet.

"Guess I won't be lying down for my nap today," the man said warmly as he settled back into his seat.

"Not unless you plan to put your head on my knee," said Kyle.

1

"I'm pretty particular about whose knee I lay my head on, and you're not nearly pretty enough. Guess I'll just have to lean the chair back this flight."

Kyle laughed. "My name's Kyle Tait. It's nice to meet you."

"I'm Ed Davis," the man said, extending his hand. "I guess we're neighbors for the next couple of hours."

"I guess so," Kyle said as he shook Ed's hand. "You headed home?"

"No, I'm heading out. I've got business meetings next week in Denver. Heading up early to visit my daughter and her family. You?

"Heading back home to Montana"

"Montana? You're a long way from home. What brought you to Houston?"

"Hurricane Elliot."

"You came for the hurricane?"

"No," Kyle said, shaking his head. "I came because of it. I work for Western Montana Power. It's a slow time of year, so they farm a few of us out to help in other areas."

"Hmm. Well thanks for helping. How'd things go?"

"Overall, pretty smoothly. As you probably know, the damage didn't end up being quite as bad as they'd anticipated, but the utility companies like to keep us around so the local folks can take care of their families. I helped in Louisiana after Katrina; it was my first time working out of town. Now that was an experience!"

"I'll bet. We were affected by Katrina here too, but more by the refugees than the weather. Can't imagine what it must have been like over there."

"It sure made me appreciate Montana more. The occasional blizzard doesn't seem so bad anymore."

"I don't know about that. I'm not one for the cold. I think I'll stick with the annual hurricane."

"The cold's not that bad. You get used to it after awhile."

"Have you lived in Montana long?"

Kyle nodded. "My whole life, except for a couple of years in Oregon when I was little. I love it there."

"I've heard it's nice, but I think I'd miss the city. Doesn't Houston have about five times the population of your entire state? I don't know if I could adjust."

"Sure you would. We lived in Missoula for a few years, but even that started to get too big for us. You begin to appreciate your space when you have it. This past spring we moved about fifteen miles out of town to a newer community with lots of space. We still have neighbors, but you don't hear them, and the kids have plenty of room. As long as you've got a four-wheel drive for the snow, it's great."

Ed gave an exaggerated shiver. "I think I'm too old for a drastic change like that." He turned his attention back to his magazine and the conversation lagged. Kyle checked his watch, wondering why the plane still hadn't moved from the gate. All of the passengers appeared to be on board, and the attendants were busy preparing themselves for the flight, but the jet hadn't moved.

Kyle pulled his novel out of his carry-on just as the pilot's voice came over the PA, offering apologies for the late departure and a promise that they would be underway as soon as possible. Kyle wanted to hear an estimate of when they would actually be getting underway, but the captain didn't offer any specifics.

Digging his cell phone out of his carry-on, Kyle pressed the speed dial for home. After four rings he heard Jennifer's voice. "Hi. You've reached the Tait family. We can't get to the phone but leave a message, and we'll call back."

Kyle waited for the tone. "Hi, Jenn. It's me. Just wanted to let you know that I'm late getting out. It's about quarter to three Houston time, and we're still waiting to take off. I'll call you from Denver and let you know if there are any problems with the connection. Talk to you soon."

Kyle turned off his phone and dropped it into his carry-on, then opened his book and began to read.

Atlantic Ocean, 175 miles east of Cape Hatteras, North Carolina 15:42 EST

Clouds hung low over the water, and the flags on the mast snapped out a slow, steady rhythm in the light wind as *Carmen's Serenade* rolled ever so slightly in the swells of the North Atlantic. Captain Jibril Musef, Jim to the crew, stood on the bridge of his container ship and stared down at the body of his first officer. Blood had stopped pumping from the deep gash in his neck and the body was already beginning to take on a waxy, artificial look.

"I'm sorry, my friend," Jibril muttered as he knelt down and wiped the blood from his knife onto the carpet. "Your life won't have been taken in vain; I promise you." He stood, slid the blade into the sheath that was strapped to his side, and stepped towards the forward window of the bridge. In the center of the main deck below him, four members of his crew worked feverishly to open the oversized container that had been carefully located in the center of the ship.

Jibril heard the door to the bridge open and he turned in the direction of the sound. His chief mechanic, Amman, stood at the door. His eyes moved from Jibril to the body on the floor, and then back again to Jibril.

"Is it done?" Jibril asked, noting the streaks and splatters of red on the man's arms and hands.

Amman nodded. "They are all dead. We can proceed without interruption."

Jibril nodded but showed no emotion. "That is good. Help the others on the deck. I'll be there shortly."

Amman turned obediently and left the bridge, the door clicking behind him as it closed. Jibril walked over to the computer terminal and quickly began to type. *The container will be delivered today as scheduled.* He clicked on the transmit button and watched as the computer indicated the status of the message. When the message had been sent, Jibril exited the bridge for the last time and began a rapid descent of the stairs.

Taking the steps two at a time, he reflected on the past decade. Two long years as the engineer's assistant had finally been followed by a rapid rise through the relatively few positions that exist on the large container ships. After two years as a first officer, Jibril's handlers had been comfortable with his progress and promoted him to captain of a ship they had purchased the same month he made his first voyage as the engineer's assistant. Patience marked their efforts in every way, and after thirty-one long months as captain, a courier finally informed Jibril that the mission for which he had trained and waited for twelve years, four months, and twenty-two days was ready.

Since taking the command of this ship, Jibril had slowly transitioned his crew, gradually bringing on the experts he knew were essential to the mission's success. From the stairs he could see his brothers working at the container that would change the world. He paused for a minute to admire the sight, said a prayer of thanks, and rapidly descended the final flight of steps and hurried to where his men were working.

"Any problems?" he asked.

Amman was working at a control panel and didn't look up as he replied. "No. It is all proceeding as planned. We will be ready early."

Jibril stroked the smooth, cold skin of the missile. "Today is a good day, my friends. Allah is watching. Be faithful." A motor whirred and gears engaged with a thud. Jibril stepped away as the nose of the rocket began to lift into launch position.

Pacific Ocean, 40 miles
west of Newport, Oregon 16:00 EST

Dae Hyun checked his watch. Five seconds, he thought to himself, then silently counted the time down. At exactly 4:00 PM EST, Dae's fishing boat began to shake, and a deafening roar pounded his ears. At the far end of the boat, orange flames erupted from the opening in the deck as the rocket it had previously concealed leapt skyward. His crew watched with pride, but no one on the boat cheered. They all knew the world was about to change.

CHAPTER TWO

George Bush International Airport, Houston, Texas 16:00 EST

Kyle tipped his seat back and closed his eyes. He hadn't taken a day off the entire two weeks he'd been in Houston, and between work and the uncomfortable motel bed, he was finding it difficult to keep his eyes open. The airplane still hadn't moved and with his watch showing 3:00 P.M., Kyle could picture himself missing his connecting flight and spending the night sleeping on the floor of the airport in Denver.

As his head bobbed sleepily, Kyle heard the whine of the engines pick up and then felt a bump as the brakes released and the plane lurched backward away from the gate. A weary smile registered on his face.

Atlantic Ocean, 175 miles east of Cape Hatteras, North Carolina 16:00 EST

Jibril stood on the deck of *Carmen's Serenade*, watching the glow of the missile disappear into the thick, gray clouds. His men spoke in quiet, reverent tones, their preparations and efforts of the past decade culminating in that moment.

A sense of loss unexpectedly swept over Jibril as the clouds swallowed not only the rocket, but his entire life's focus as well.

Everything he had worked for, the sole purpose of his life since his wife and son had been killed in Iraq, had been accomplished. Every sleepless night, every trip across the ocean, every obstacle overcome was now, finally, worth it.

A melancholy-laced laugh escaped his lips as he thought about how the American leaders would be reacting this very instant. His leaders in Iran had played negotiations to their maximum effect, agreeing to dismantle their own weapon's program only because Pakistan had already sold them what they needed. Now, with the American President being hailed as a hero for shutting down the Iranian's nuclear program, all while having provided Iran with the materials to build enough power plants to double its electrical output, Iran was set to dominate the Middle East and the oil and power that came with it, for the next century.

Jibril regretted that he would not live to learn of the impact his efforts would have on the Americans, nor to witness Israel's destruction and the fall of the Jews, which, with America crippled, would surely come in a matter of weeks.

The missile faded from sight. Jibril turned to Zahir, a trusted fellow warrior, and nodded. Zahir, with drops of sweat falling from his scarred brow, swallowed hard and knelt in front of a small digital display mounted on a now charred steel case and punched in the code to begin a new countdown.

Sighing with satisfaction, Jibril reflected on the past years. He had proven himself so dedicated that he had been trusted to lead the most radical strike ever attempted against the Americans. He understood that there were others attempting the same thing, but in the future, his name would be spoken in the same hushed tones as those martyrs who had died in New York City so many years before. His only living son would beam with pride, knowing what his father had sacrificed himself for.

A tear of joy formed in the corner of Jibril's eye, building slowly until it broke free and streaked his cheek.

NORAD Headquarters, Peterson
Air Force Base, Colorado 16:00 EST

Air Force Colonel Alan Gagnon sat at his desk keying an email to his wife at the end of another uneventful week.

It was 16:00:05 EST when the alarm sounded. In the nine years he'd been in his current position this particular alarm had never gone off without him knowing about it beforehand, and until this instant, he had expected it never would. Alan jumped from his desk and was in the main control room in five rapid strides. Officers were responding as they had been trained, and for all they knew this was just another drill. With his heart racing, Alan quickly assessed the situation. Rows of glowing monitors at the front of the command room showed two missiles in American airspace, relaying their locations and projecting their flight paths with faint orange cones that took in much of the continent. It was too early to pinpoint where they were headed but was obvious from their flight paths that the missiles had not traveled from foreign soil.

"What do we know?" Alan barked as he strode to the center of the room, dodging underlings who ran in every direction. "There are no scheduled tests, correct?" He already knew the answer but asked anyway.

Lieutenant Rodger Olsen, one of his most capable assistants and the only other person who would know ahead of time if a test had been scheduled, sat with his eyes locked on the screen in front of him, processing the information. "There are no tests or drills scheduled, sir. These are real, and they're not ours. Both missiles were launched simultaneously from areas with no identified military vessels, foreign or domestic. Tracking shows they are not headed directly inland at this point. They're just gaining altitude."

Alan picked up the phone on the closest desk. "Give me General Doss!" he shouted into the mouthpiece, then waited anxiously for the connection to be made. At the sound of the General's voice, Alan cut him off. "General, this is Alan. It's bad. We show two missiles, both launched from international waters, one off each coast. Both are in American airspace with indeterminate targets and unknown payloads."

Monitors filled the front wall of the room, and Alan's eyes darted from screen to screen as he continued to relay what little information he had to the General. The largest screen showed two separate lines tracking the flights of the incoming missiles. It was now seventy three seconds since they had launched, and tracking showed the missiles to be at an elevation of just over eighty-two miles.

As Alan scanned the monitors, another alarm sounded and the screen flashed as the line tracking the missile launched from the west began to blink. He covered the mouthpiece and shouted at Lt. Olsen. "What just happened?!"

The lieutenant shook his head. "I don't know, sir. That one seems to have disappeared."

"What do you mean disappeared? Did it detonate?"

"Negative, sir. Or if it did, it wasn't nuclear. Our satellites indicate some kind of explosion, but at this point, I have to assume malfunction.

"Sir?" Alan spoke into the phone. "No, I don't think so. I don't think any cities are targeted, but I can't say that with any certainty. Listen, one of the missiles has just disappeared from radar. Looks like it malfunctioned. That leaves just one, but it's gaining too much elevation for a direct strike to make sense. I think the intent is to detonate in space. It's likely that the second missile was meant as a backup. I think the country is the target, sir, not one of our cities."

Alan caught his breath as the meaning of his last statement sunk in, knowing there wasn't anything that could be done. The missile defense budget had been all but eliminated years ago, probably to make room for some government handout designed to win votes for a senator up for re-election in a tight race. Even if missile defense had not been shelved, the chances of an American missile launched from this close being accurate enough to knock out an incoming missile at an altitude of hundreds of miles were slim. But with the current situation, and no response beyond crossed fingers and desperate prayers, Alan would have liked to have had something to throw at it, proven or not.

Alan finished his conversation with General Doss and hung up. They both had calls to make, and he didn't have much time – five, maybe six minutes at the most, before all hell broke loose and America was turned on its head. The military had war-gamed this scenario for years, and every outcome was bad. How severe the results would be depended on three things: the location of detonation, the tonnage of the missile, and the efficiency of the weapon.

In the military's planning it always came down to the fact that once the missiles were in the air, there was almost no way to stop them. That was why they worked so hard to keep these weapons from getting into the wrong hands. This was America's Achilles heel, the proverbial knockout punch that any rogue nation could throw if they had the money, the resources, and the willingness to weather the inevitable retaliation.

George Bush International Airport, Houston, Texas 16:03 EST

With the captain's announcement that their plane was cleared for takeoff, the flight attendants rushed to get trays put up and seats returned to their upright positions before strapping themselves in.

Kyle folded down the top corner of the page in his book, set it in his lap, and glanced out the window. The plane had taxied down the runway and was now in line for takeoff. Kyle could see another plane ahead of them and three stacked up to land.

"I guess we're going to miss our free tickets," Ed commented. Kyle looked at him, puzzled. "What free tickets?"

"I was starting to hope we'd get stuck a little longer. If you have to wait too long, sometimes the airlines will give you a couple of free tickets so you don't hate them too much. Happened to my daughter last time she visited. Now, we just get put behind, and the airline doesn't do anything, barely even an apology."

Ed spoke with a grin, so Kyle guessed he wasn't too serious, but the thought of free tickets intrigued him. His anniversary was coming up, and surprising Jennifer with something more than their traditional dinner out would have been nice.

"What are you reading?" asked Ed, changing the subject.

"It's a mystery. I bought it at the airport on the way down and am trying to finish it before I get home. There never seems to be enough time for reading at home, and I'd like to see how it ends."

"Is it any good?"

Kyle thought for a second. "So far so good, but you can never be sure until it wraps up. If I finish before we touch down, I'll give you a full review."

Deer Creek, Montana 16:06 EST

Jennifer Tait struggled into the house from the garage, her arms loaded with a week's worth of groceries. The day's mail was shoved into one of the bags, and a corner of an envelope had torn a gaping hole in the side, threatening to dump an assortment of canned goods onto the kitchen floor. As the door swung closed, she heard a wail from the small figure struggling along behind her.

"You okay, Spencer?" Jennifer called out.

He didn't answer.

She could hear him fighting with the door, so hurried and swung the bags in her arms onto the table. A can of tomato soup, hanging part way out of the hole opened by the envelope, caught the corner of the table and extended the gash, dumping the contents onto the linoleum floor. Jennifer muttered under her breath. It had been a bad day, and this was just one more item to add to the list of things that had gone wrong. Kyle had been gone for two weeks, and she was looking forward to finally having him home again. She loved their kids, but being a single mother wasn't what she had signed up for.

As she bent to pick up the cans scattering across the kitchen floor, she heard Spencer's voice from out in the garage.

"Mom!" he called.

"What is it, Spencer?" she replied, gathering the cans.

"I need some help," he called back.

"I'll be right there. Just give me a minute."

"No, Mom! Not just a minute. I need help now," he said, irritation evident in his voice.

Jennifer giggled at his demand, marveling to herself how quickly he was growing up and reflecting on the joys of being able to watch her kids as they matured. Spencer was her baby, but he wasn't so much a baby anymore. He had been attending kindergarten for three weeks now, and she already missed having him home with her on those days she didn't work.

"Alright, I'm coming," she answered as she grabbed a can of mushrooms that had come to stop against the leg of a chair.

Setting the can on the table, Jennifer went to the door and pushed it open for Spencer, who was still struggling to get in. He smiled as she carefully opened the door wide enough for him to enter.

"That's a pretty big box," she said, tussling his hair. "You sure you have it alright?"

"I'm fine," he answered, a look of determination riveted on his face.

"Thanks so much for being such a good helper, big guy. You sure are growing up."

"I'm not big guy. I'm Spencer," came the terse reply.

"Yes, you are. You're my Spencer, aren't you?" Jennifer kissed her son on the forehead as he marched by.

Spencer grinned and reached up with his free arm to give her a hug, dropping the box of Corn Flakes on the floor as he did so. "Oops, sorry Mom," he said. "I'll get it."

Jennifer straightened back up and heard the beep of the answering machine in the bedroom, making a mental note to check the messages once the groceries were put away. "Can't have the ice cream melting while I listen to some sales pitch," she told herself.

She grabbed the remaining bags of groceries from the trunk and slammed it shut. Noticing that Spencer hadn't closed his door tight, Jennifer fixed that, waved to the neighbor working in her garden, and went back inside.

She was putting away the cereal when Spencer stomped into the kitchen from the playroom. "Mom, the TV just turned off!" he whined.

"Just give me a minute," she replied. After putting the rest of the cans away, Jennifer took Spencer by the hand and led him down the hall to see what was wrong.

NORAD Headquarters, Peterson Air Force Base, Colorado 16:07 EST

Alan watched with a cold, technical detachment as the remaining missile tracked across the screen, the speed and elevation numbers on the bottom of the screen registering the details of the rocket's flight. He was shocked by his lack of emotion, something similar, he assumed, to an Emergency Room doctor forced to treat his own child. *You should be a wreck, but the technical side of the brain takes over and you simply do what you've been trained to do.*

During the seven minutes of the missile's flight, Alan had already spoken with three of his superiors and knew, by the sound of their voices, they were in a state somewhere between panic and unbelief.

Monitors now showed that the missile had been airborne for just under eight minutes, the longest eight minutes of Alan's life, and its altitude was 306 miles.

When the missiles had first been detected, Alan had hoped that specific cities were targeted because, relatively speaking, that would have been easier to recover from. This, he knew, was going to be much, much worse.

Everyone around him was outwardly calm, and considering that the country to which they had pledged their lives was under attack, it was unnerving in a way. A few spoke on the phone, calmly relating to some unseen person the information displayed on their monitors. Others sat at their desks, watching wide-eyed as the missile tracked over Missouri towards the center of the theoretical bulls-eye. Tears streaked down more than one face.

Alan felt the room spin around him and reached for a chair to steady himself. Never had he felt so helpless. For the fifty-nine long years of his life, Alan had always known the appropriate response and could find a way out of every situation. This time he couldn't. The only hope the country had was another failure, a failure like the one that had happened to the missile launched from the Pacific.

Alan held his breath and prayed, too scared to blink in case something happened in that instant. As the missile tracked farther than expected, the possibility that NORAD was the target flashed through Alan's mind just as the largest screen in the room flashed red, and an additional alarm sounded. Detonation.

For a brief moment the room went totally silent, as if all the air had been sucked out of the building. When the lights flickered, someone cursed, and then the roar of voices began to swell as backup generators kicked on and the room brightened again.

Alan knew they would have power for months. The rest of the country wasn't going to be so lucky.

CHAPTER THREE

Lawrence, Kansas 16:08 EST

High above the sun-baked prairies of Lawrence, Kansas, the missile reached its target. No one on the ground even noticed the blast. Perhaps had someone been looking at precisely the right location, at precisely the right time, they might have noticed a tiny, momentary spark in the bright afternoon sky. Had they seen the flash, it likely would have been attributed to the glint of sunlight reflecting off a passing airplane. From any vantage point below the detonation, there was no sense of the destructive capacity contained in that tiny speck of light. More than 300 miles above the earth, a nuclear explosion impacts nothing with the force of its blast. It is merely a large bomb going off in a vacuum, creating no shockwaves, no fireballs, no radiation, not even any sound.

Despite the lack of explosive destruction, this was now the most lethal weapon to be unleashed in the history of the world, but it was a weapon that would have had absolutely no discernable effect on mankind 200 years ago, other than creating a more colorful aurora. Upon detonation, the bomb expelled an intense wave of gamma radiation in every direction. The gamma rays traveling earthward interacted with the upper levels of the atmosphere and created a chain reaction of displaced electrons that rushed towards the surface of the earth at the speed of light. Most of these displaced electrons passed rapidly through the atmosphere and grounded themselves harmlessly in the earth.

A small percentage, however, encountered conductive materials: metal, antennas, copper wiring, and silicon chips. As these conductors absorbed untold billions of free electrons, they experienced sudden surges in both voltage and current. In simple items, like a garden rake, this surge was manifested as a harmless static electricity-like spark. But in larger networks and sensitive objects, the consequences of the electron overload were devastating.

Across the country, millions and millions of miles of power lines absorbed these displaced electrons and delivered them to every home and power plant in the country, melting the electrical lines in the process. Safety systems designed to arrest voltage spikes were unable to react to the overwhelming size and speed of the surge, allowing this massive wave of power to flow unchecked throughout the grid.

In Akron, Ohio, Kevin Leishman was using his computer to look up driving directions as he prepared to head out for the long weekend. He watched in dismay as his monitor suddenly flashed brighter, then faded to black, with the smoke of his cigarette masking the smell of the melting electrical components.

Erika Smith was sitting at a traffic light in Winnipeg, Manitoba when the engine of her new Honda Accord simply shut off. Confused, she glanced up and noticed the traffic lights were no longer operating, then watched as a semi-truck turning across the intersection in front of her seemed to lose control of its steering and brakes and crashed into a corner gas station, knocking over two gas pumps and causing an explosion that hurled pieces of burning debris across the intersection and onto her car.

Jefferson Harris was reading an old issue of *Sports Illustrated* during his break at Northern Sierra Power when the safety alarms went off. He ran to the control room and watched in horror as one monitor after another flashed warnings or shut down. Then the generators went offline and he heard an unfamiliar sound from the turbines across the compound. Jefferson knew that if something went wrong, the computers were programmed to shut down the plant in a safe, orderly fashion. What he didn't know was that the system designed to handle the shutdown had also failed, and the control that maintained lubrication for the turbine was offline. In the thirty seconds it took Jefferson to determine the telephones weren't working, the temperature in the turbines rose from 300° F to just under 1,100° F. Holding the dead phone in his hand while trying to decide what to do, he heard new alarms go off, alarms that drowned out the sound of shrieking metal as the ground rumbled beneath him just moments before the generator building exploded. Shockwaves from the blast blew out the window behind Jefferson and propelled shards of glass in every direction. As he turned to run for the exit, he slipped in a pool of his own blood, pumped from a deep gash in his thigh, the first indication he had that he'd been mortally wounded.

Officer Greg Henninger was issuing a ticket on the shoulder of Interstate 70, just east of the Hays, Kansas exit. Traffic was busy, and the driver of the red Mustang he'd pulled over was voicing her displeasure. As Officer Henninger explained the details of the citation, he sensed that something was wrong and turned just in time to see a semi-truck smash into the back of his patrol car, launching it into the Mustang. Greg tried to run but was hit before he could move, leaving his boots where he'd stood on the road as his body hurtled through the air.

Frank Lunde sat in a booth at a McDonalds in Boise, Idaho, nursing a diet Coke while his grandkids played on the slides. Their mother was getting her hair done, and Frank had volunteered to watch the kids for a couple of hours. When the lights in the restaurant went dark, his attention turned briefly from the play area. The kids, oblivious to the problem, continued to climb through the giant orange and purple tubes. As he looked around the restaurant, Frank felt an ache in his chest and rubbed just below his sternum in an effort to relieve the pain. Through his shirt he felt the scar where the doctors had inserted a pacemaker the year before. He hadn't experienced any problems since his surgery, but now he didn't feel well. Frank's fingers started to tingle, and sweat broke out on his forehead. "Lexie," he called out, "don't shove your brother! Be a good girl, and come here and help your grandfather." Lexie turned towards her grandpa just as he slumped forward onto the table, then fell sideways off the bench.

George Bush International Airport, Houston, Texas 16:08 EST

Kyle looked out the window at the ground rushing by. The engines roared as they pushed the airliner down the runway, the acceleration pressing Kyle firmly against his seat. Kyle enjoyed flying, but the takeoffs and landings always made his heart pound a little harder. He'd read once that the two most dangerous times for an airplane were takeoffs and landings, and that fact lingered in the back of his mind every time he flew.

The whine of the engines increased in pitch as the plane continued its race forward, rattling and jarring down the runway. Kyle could never figure out why airplanes rode so rough on the ground, like being towed down a city sidewalk in a wagon at 50 miles an hour, bouncing and rattling on every joint in the sidewalk. For a quarter of a billion dollars, or whatever outrageous sum an airplane cost, Kyle figured that the manufacturer should have throw in a set of shock absorbers. The nose of the plane lifted off the ground, and Kyle knew it would only be another second until the rough ride would be over.

Then, without warning, the pitch of the engines changed drastically and Kyle felt himself thrust forward against the restraint of his seatbelt. The nose of the airplane plummeted back to the ground, striking the runway with a spine-wrenching crack. Overhead storage bins burst open and spilled their contents into the aisle and onto the heads and laps of the passengers, eliciting a panicked chorus of screams that rose over the rumble of the airplane. Kyle heard a child screaming hysterically a few rows behind him and her father trying to calm her.

Kyle saw his seatmate lean forward and wrap his arms tightly around his legs. Ed's face was turned towards Kyle, the terror evident in his eyes.

Frozen with fear, Kyle tried to remember the instructions the flight attendants had given just minutes earlier.

"Grab your legs!" Ed shouted.

Ed's voice was barely discernable over the uproar, but Kyle picked out the words and did as Ed instructed.

"Please, God, don't let me die," Kyle whispered as he thought of his wife and three kids. The idea that he might never see them again raced through his mind, and he again repeated the words of his abbreviated prayer.

Kyle could feel the plane slowing, but it wasn't like a typical landing. The engines weren't thrusting, and it didn't feel like there was any actual braking. He wondered how much of the runway was left and what might be at the end of it, then wrapped his arms even tighter around his legs.

The chorus of sobs and shouts blended with the roar of the airplane, creating a deafening wail. The plane had barely slowed when it ran out of runway. The front wheels bit into the soft ground, causing the plane to shudder as the landing gear snapped and the airplane collapsed onto its belly. With no perceptible slowing, the airplane continued its forward rush, tearing a deep furrow in the ground and throwing clouds of dirt high into the air.

Traveling at nearly 140 miles an hour, Flight 17 struck a large, earthen berm a hundred yards from the end of the runway and launched into the air like a wounded bird. The crippled craft made a feeble attempt at flight, hanging in the air for a moment before twisting and falling defeated back towards earth. This time the tip of the right wing made contact with the ground first and pitched the plane to the right, where the body of the plane struck with an earsplitting crash. The fuselage bounced and skidded for another 200 yards before finally coming to a stop in a cloud of dirt and smoke, the nose of the broken airplane protruding through a chain-link fence that marked the boundary between the airport and an empty two-lane road.

Screaming inside the cabin ceased briefly, and for a moment, all that could be heard was the twisting, scraping and groaning of metal as the airplane settled into the dirt.

A baby's cry was the first sound that Kyle heard and was quickly followed by a renewed chorus of wails and moans. Soon there were dozens of voices, some calling for help while others cried out in panic, pain, and fear. Above the din, a single, authoritative voice yelled instructions to open the exits.

Stunned and disoriented Kyle sat up and looked around, noticing that most of the overhead bins were open and their contents strewn around the cabin. He caressed a spot on the back of his head where he'd been struck but didn't feel any blood. Ed was hunched forward with his head on his knees and wasn't moving. A thin trickle of blood ran down the side of his face "Ed! You alright?" Kyle shouted as he reached out and shook the man.

Ed didn't respond.

Kyle clawed at his own seatbelt and managed to unhook it, then slid to the middle seat, grabbed Ed by the shoulder, and shook him again. "Ed! Ed! You all right?" he shouted, straining to be heard over the surrounding chaos.

He looked for someone to help, but people were fighting their way to the exits, shoving the slower ones out of the way, desperate to save their own lives. Kyle could smell smoke and his eyes began to sting. Glancing quickly out his window, he noticed that the wing had been sheered off, and the stump that remained was engulfed in flames. The rear of the plane glowed orange, and he could see flames licking around the windows a few rows back.

A shrill voice rose over the chaos of the cabin, and Kyle looked up to see the flight attendant who had welcomed him onto the flight pushing her way to the back. "Someone open the rear exit!!" she yelled, trying to be heard. Gone was the pleasant smile and perfect grooming. Instead, her face was bruised and swollen, and strands of hair hung limply in front of her eyes. The right sleeve of her uniform was torn, and a crimson stain was spreading around a three-inch gash. "People! Let me through!" she yelled, desperately fighting her way to the back, her eyes wide with panic and determination.

Kyle watched her as he continued to try and rouse Ed. Now at the back, the flight attendant helped a man force the door open. Kyle watched the proceedings and could make out the rush of air as the emergency slide deployed.

"We need to get out of here!" Kyle shouted at Ed. Receiving no response, Kyle pushed Ed up and felt for the seatbelt. His fingers found the steel of the latch and he yanked it open. Thick smoke made it hard to breathe, and Kyle gagged as he called for help. One man stumbled by carrying a child. Across the aisle an older woman sat in a daze, dabbing at blood running from her mouth and watching the scene around her through glassy, distant eyes.

As flames danced outside the windows, Kyle continued to shake Ed with no effect. With no one to help him, Kyle stepped past Ed and hurried towards the exit at the rear of the airplane. Three rows back the aisle was blocked by on older woman struggling with a girl about the same age as his daughter. The girl was screaming and holding onto the unconscious body of the man beside her. "Daddy!" she screamed. "Daddy!"

"Come on, sweetie. We need to go!" the woman shouted, pulling on the girl's arm. "Your dad will have to come later. Let's go find your mom."

Watching the scene unfold, Kyle could see the light of the exit marking his way to life, and he fought the urge to force his way past the woman and child. Kyle reached forward and pried the girl's hands loose from the lifeless man and pulled her into the aisle. He took a deep breath and again choked on the thickening smoke. "Get off the airplane!" he ordered, shoving the girl down the aisle.

CHAPTER FOUR

Boston, Massachusetts 16:12 EST

Senator Christine George stood behind her over-sized, mahogany desk and stared out the office window. Her staff was gone, most having left at lunchtime in order to get a jump on the last weekend of summer. She had stayed to contact a few more donors and review some committee reports, but was now anxiously waiting for the power to come back on. Irritated by the delay and worried about what she might have lost on her computer, Senator George noticed that traffic forty floors below had come to a stop and people were getting out of their cars in the middle of Hanover Street. It was a puzzling sight – motorists wandering through the knot of vehicles, not at all concerned about the traffic. As she reached for her cell phone, one of the telephones on her desk rang, the shrillness of its ring in her silent office causing her to jump. She reached for the receiver, then realized the ringing wasn't coming from the office phone, but from the secure line that had been installed four years before when she had become head of the Senate Intelligence Committee. This black, ugly paperweight didn't ring often, but when it did, it usually meant the CIA was calling to warn her about some crisis before the reporters started calling.

She stared at the phone, trying to decide whether to answer it now or put the headache off for a couple of hours. Curiosity won out, and she picked the receiver up on the fifth ring. "Senator George," she said, using her most official tone. She recognized the voice on the other end of the line instantly. "Yes. Hello, General Fletcher. What's so urgent?" She checked her reflection in the mirror on the wall and adjusted her hair while the general spoke.

"Senator, I'm required to inform you that we have an extremely serious situation. America has been attacked." His tone was even more sober than usual, if that was possible.

The Senator's hand fell from her hair, and she reached out for her desk as she dropped into the imposing leather chair that dominated the space behind it. "Was it one of our embassies? Please tell me that people haven't been hurt."

"No, Senator, I wish it was that simple. The country has been attacked. The entire country."

"What are you talking about, the entire country? Was there another terrorist strike? I haven't seen anything indicating any new threats in my reports…"

"Christine!" The general cut her off, uncharacteristically calling her by her first name. "Senator," he corrected himself." Do you remember the briefing we gave Congress back in January, the one we give every January after an election? One of the things we discussed was an electromagnetic pulse, an EMP. Do you remember?"

"That's been a while, but yes, I remember. Why?"

"Look out your window, Senator. What do you see?"

"Not much, just cars and people. We're having a blackout right now, so traffic lights …" she paused as the dots connected inside her head. "Michael?!"

"That's right, Senator. We've been hit, and hit hard." The general spoke in rapid fire staccato, a trait completely foreign to him, but that only served to give added weight to his words. "Missiles were launched off both coasts at exactly 1600 hours. There are also unconfirmed reports that there might have been a third missile down in the Gulf, but we've yet to see firm evidence on that. Of the two that we know about, it appears that one malfunctioned and broke up before it detonated. The other was successful. It's only been a few minutes, but it appears that things will be as bad as we were told to expect. The assessment could change, but there isn't going to be a positive way to spin this."

Senator George struggled to maintain her grip on the telephone. "Just how bad is it going to be? Where was the military?" she asked, her tone already assigning blame. "How could this happen?"

"We had no warning on this," General Fletcher barked into the phone. "It was a complete surprise. As things stand, there is nothing we could have done. Perhaps if there had been some warning, or if we had other weapons in our arsenal, we could have tried. As for how bad it's really going to be, we don't know, and we're not going to know the full extent of the damage for years. One is all it takes to bring everything down."

"Why wasn't there any warning? I'm the head of the Intelligence Committee and I've heard nothing. How could this happen?"

"Like I said, Senator, there was no warning. They kept this one quiet. It had to have been years in the making, but it wouldn't have taken many people to pull it off, a couple dozen at most. It's likely that none of the perpetrators ever set foot in our country, and there's only so much we can know. NORAD picked the missiles up just after they were launched; that was the very first indication we had. Both missiles were launched from non-military boats off our coasts. We didn't have a chance to react."

"We couldn't shoot them down? I thought we had systems to protect us. That's what we spend all that money on the military for, isn't it?" Senator George spat the words into the phone, her temper rising as the magnitude of the problem sank in.

"We've been working on some systems, Senator, but you know what's happened to our money. Those things aren't free. Thanks to our elected officials, everything that can be cut has been, and then some. If we'd had even a day's notice, we could have attempted something, but on this one, there was no time to get a shot off, let alone two."

The senator sat in silence, contemplating General Fletcher's words along with her role in diverting money the military had said it needed. The scenarios the military had talked about, had even threatened Congress with, seemed so remote, so unlikely. How could they justify spending billions on weapons that, in all probability, would never be needed? Surely the voters wouldn't hold her accountable for this. At least fifty-seven other senators had voted with her on each measure to reduce weapons money.

"Senator," the general said, interrupting her thoughts. "I've got other calls to make. I need to go."

"Michael," she said, barely able to choke out the words. "How bad do you think it's going to be?"

"It's hard to say, Senator," the general answered in the steady, cold monotone that she was used to, the anger from seconds ago already dissipated. "Everything before today has, for the most part, been theory. My guess is that casualties will be around fifty or so. I might be wrong, but some of our estimates range up to five times that."

"Fifty thousand?" Senator George gasped. "You're kidding, right?" It was more of a plea than a question. "You can't be serious. It's just electricity. People will adjust."

"Senator, the United States, Canada and Mexico have all been affected, and that's close to half a billion people. By the time this is over, I think we are looking at fifty million casualties. I hope it's much less, but that will all depend on how people react. The first wave is today: accidents, loss of medical care, fires, airplanes and such. Next will be weeks of chaos and lawlessness while people adjust to the realities of having no power, no functioning government, and no civic control. It will be much worse in the cities, so if you have someplace to go to, out of town, I highly recommend that you leave quickly. In this stage we'll also lose everyone who depends on doctors and medicine to stay alive. That will be followed by a relatively quiet period of starvation as people run out of food and no longer have the energy to cause trouble and contribute to the chaos. In the north, people will freeze once winter hits. In three or four months, maybe not until spring time, we'll be faced with large-scale anarchy as those who do have food and weapons try to piece together some semblance of tribal order."

"I just hope there's a country worth saving after all of that," the general continued. "I truly hope I'm wrong, but I don't think I am. We've game-planned this one over and over. It never turns out good." The general paused to let his words sink in then continued in his gravelly monotone. "Have a good day, Senator. You know how to get in touch with me if you need to, assuming this phone system that we've spent so much money on manages to hold up."

The line went dead, and Senator George let the phone drop from her hands. She knew General Fletcher didn't care for her, that he'd been obligated to call because she was the head of the Intelligence Committee. She didn't particularly care for him either. He didn't appreciate the difficult job politicians had of trying to keep constituents happy and making things work in Washington, all while working to get reelected. But despite her opinion of the general, she knew he was honest – blunt, but honest and not one to say things just for effect. As she spun in her chair to stare out the window, Senator George tried to imagine how the chaos that General Fletcher threatened would descend on her beloved city. The images that came to mind sent shivers down her spine. Then she noticed a dark plume of smoke ascending skyward from an older neighborhood to the north.

George Bush International Airport, Houston, Texas 16:12 EST

Kyle returned to the row he had been sitting in and gripped the shoulders of the lady across the aisle who was still dabbing at her face. "Get off the airplane!" he yelled as he shook her and pointed to the exit. She stood and slowly began making her way forward. He then turned to Ed, slumped over and unmoving. After confirming that Ed had a pulse, Kyle grabbed him under his arms and heaved him into the aisle. Dragging Ed behind him, Kyle backed down the aisle a half dozen steps before bumping into someone concealed in the thickening smoke. He turned to see the flight attendant attempting to rouse the unconscious man who had been traveling with his daughter.

"Do you need help?" Kyle yelled.

The attendant shook her head. "I can get him. You get off now!" she directed, jerking her head towards the flames outside the window.

Kyle felt the heat from the fire on his face and nodded in agreement, then continued dragging Ed towards the rear exit, his lungs burning from the strain and the smoke. Kyle guessed that Ed weighed less than he did, but with Ed's body as dead weight in the narrow and cluttered aisle, he was having a difficult time making it to the exit.

After a short struggle he worried might be his last, Kyle finally reached the exit. He let go of Ed, then thrust his head out of the smoke-filled cabin. The outside air was hot and thick with humidity, but free of the dense, suffocating smoke that filled the airplane. Inhaling deeply, Kyle didn't think he'd ever prized a breath so much in his life. He took a quick second breath, lifted Ed and gave a powerful tug, and they both plunged out the door. The two men tumbled down the yellow emergency slide, coming to a stop at the bottom.

With the roar of the fire and the heat of the flames pushing him forward, Kyle rapidly scrambled to his feet and shook Ed, but he just moaned and mumbled incoherently. With all the strength he could muster, Kyle draped Ed across his shoulders and set off toward a crowd of survivors who had gathered a hundred yards from the wreckage. He struggled with his load and stumbled on the uneven ground, twice falling to his knees, then rising again, until finally making it to the cluster of passengers.

Three men from the crowd came forward and helped him lower Ed to the ground, then Kyle collapsed in a heap, coughing and completely spent. His whole body felt limp as he lay on his side and struggled to catch his breath, but his eyes stayed locked on the airplane, which was now almost entirely engulfed in flames.

Through the smoke he could see the flight attendant and the unconscious man at the bottom of the emergency slide. The attendant leapt to her feet and pulled on the motionless body, dragging it only a few feet before stumbling and falling to the ground. Two men from the group started to run towards her just as a massive explosion rocked the area and knocked them, and others standing nearby, off of their feet. Kyle turned away from the explosion and shielded his face with an arm, the heat from the fireball burning the skin on the back of his neck. Debris hit the ground around him, and people, already deep in shock, screamed and ran further away. Too tired to run, Kyle crawled to Ed and knelt over him, using his body as a shield against the debris.

A scrap of smoking metal landed a few feet away and bounced past. Exhausted, Kyle reached up with his arms in an attempt to cover the back of his head. When the sounds of the falling debris stopped, Kyle turned back towards what, just minutes before, had been a modern jet aircraft but was now just a heap of burning wreckage with smoke billowing in black, oily clouds from its twisted skeleton.

Ed stirred and looked towards Kyle, but his eyes were empty and far away.

"Ed, you with us?" Kyle asked, his voice weak and dry.

Ed stared blankly, like he'd been roused suddenly from a deep sleep, but didn't answer. When he tried to get up, Kyle grabbed his arm and held him down.

"Just relax," Kyle said. "You were hit hard. There should be an ambulance here soon. They'll want to check you out."

Ed briefly resisted, then relented and sat back down while Kyle scanned the wreckage of the airplane for any sign of the flight attendant. She had been just a few feet from the bottom of the slide when the explosion happened, but that area was now a smoldering pile of rubble with no sign of survivors. The body of the airplane was broken in half just behind the wings, causing the tail portion to fall backwards onto the ground. Jagged, twisted openings covered the plane's body, as if someone had ripped away the skin of the airplane to peer inside, the exposed seats suspended precariously in the air. A few scorched pieces of fabric dangled limply below what remained of the rear emergency exit. Dozens of small fires burned in the grass surrounding the wreckage, twisting ribbons of smoke the only movement Kyle could make out in the vicinity of the plane.

Kyle turned away, wondering how many people had died and what loved ones they had left behind. Instinctively, he reached into his pocket for his cell phone to call home and let his wife know what had happened, but it wasn't there. Then he remembered tossing it into his carry-on after making his last call home.

"Ed, you got a phone?"

Ed's eyes were still vacant, but he seemed to be slowly coming around. "I do," he said groggily, then gingerly pulled his phone from his pocket and handed it to Kyle. "Where do you think the fire trucks are?"

Kyle took the phone and flipped it open. "I don't know. They should be here by now; we're not that far from the terminal." As

Kyle dialed his number, he stood and strained to hear sirens. "You don't have service," he said, handing the phone back to Ed. "I want to get a hold of my wife before she sees the news. This is going to freak her out."

Ed took his phone and looked at the screen. He pushed a couple of buttons and tried to make a call, then put it back on his belt. "How'd I get off the plane?"

"You were a little out of it, so I helped you."

Ed rubbed his head, and Kyle dropped to the ground beside him. "I don't hear any sirens, Ed. I don't know what's going on." Kyle looked towards the airport but could see only the tops of the buildings from behind the berm of dirt. "They should be here. There are a lot of people hurt."

Looking around, Kyle noticed several other people trying in vain to use their phones. "There must be some kind of jamming device. No one's phones are working," he observed.

"My phone worked earlier," Ed said matter-of-factly. "How'd you get me off the plane?"

"I had to drag you. Figured your family might want to see you again."

"Do you think everyone made it?"

Kyle shook his head. "I don't." He paused. "I think we were about the last ones. There were still a few people in there when we got off, but I don't think they made it."

Ed looked at Kyle, his eyes becoming more alert. "Thanks for helping a stranger. I hope I would have done the same."

"Don't be too grateful. I almost left you behind. I was pretty scared." Kyle stood back up. "Wait here. I'm going to see if I can tell where the emergency vehicles are. It's like they don't know we're here."

Kyle walked as quickly as his worn-out legs would go back towards the berm that had launched the airplane. It was some distance away and required him to climb to the top in order to see the buildings of the airport. Another man from the airplane was already on top of the berm, frozen, one hand shielding the sun from his eyes as he stared into the distance. Kyle crested the short hill and as he reached the top he felt the air suck from his lungs as the scene unfolded in front of him.

The other passenger turned when he heard Kyle gasp. "Is this real?" he asked, his voice cracking.

Kyle recognized the man from the boarding area. "I don't know," he replied, barely able to speak. His head swung slowly from side to side. "I've never seen anything like this in my life. It doesn't seem possible."

Deer Creek, Montana 16:20 EST

Jennifer pressed the power button on the TV one more time, then gave up and went back to putting the groceries away. As she carefully squeezed the eggs onto the crowded bottom shelf of the fridge, it dawned on her that the fridge light was out. She looked at the stove and saw that the clock was blank as well.

"Hey, Spencer," she called out, "I think I know what's wrong with the TV."

Spencer was sitting on the floor in the corner of the kitchen, hard at work on a large dinosaur puzzle. A pterodactyl's eyes peered from the piece he was using to scratch his head. "Are you done with the groceries? Are you going to fix it now?" he asked excitedly.

"No, not yet," she answered. "Mommy can't fix it. I think the power's out." She gave him an exaggerated frown. "Can you do me a favor?"

"Sure, Mom. What you need?"

"Go turn on the lights in the bedrooms and tell me if any of them work."

"You bet," he yelled over his shoulder as he lumbered to his feet and ran down the hall towards the bedrooms.

George Bush International Airport, Houston, Texas 16:30 EST

The two men from the stricken airplane stood on top of the berm, trying to make sense of the scene that spread out before them. Between where they stood and the far side of the airport they could see the burning wreckage of three other airplanes, all with thick, oily plumes of smoke billowing skyward and casting a gray pall over the area. In a neighborhood further to the east, no more than a mile from the end of the runway, Kyle could see another black column of smoke.

After a long silence, Kyle finally spoke. "I don't think that they're coming for us." It sounded like a completely inadequate comment considering the circumstances, but he could think of nothing else to say.

The man merely nodded, but his expression spoke volumes. After a few more moments of observation, they returned to where the survivors from their flight, along with some airport employees who had come from nearby buildings to offer assistance, had re-gathered.

Kyle found one of the pilots giving aid to an injured passenger on the outskirts of the group and pulled him to the side. The pilot was young, in his thirties, and his face was smeared with dirt and sweat and smoke.

"What do you need?" the pilot demanded, glancing back at the older woman he'd been attending to.

A gold pin on the captain's chest had "K. Hansen" printed on it in black letters. Kyle swallowed and was about to speak when the man from the top of the berm took the initiative. "There's something seriously wrong, sir," he began.

When their conversation was over, the pilot strode back towards the group, cleared his throat and called out to the survivors. "Attention everyone! I need you to gather in here closer, please. Quickly!" He waited as people moved towards him, then addressed the group. "As you can see, there's smoke on the other side of that bank of dirt." He motioned towards the airport, and people turned in that direction. "I'd thought the smoke was from our crash, but I've just been informed that there are other planes that have crashed as well." A murmur went up from the group. "It appears likely," he continued, "that emergency vehicles won't be coming to our assistance, at least not for awhile. I recommend that we start moving towards the terminal where we can hopefully find some help. Those who are able, please help those who are not."

"What's going on?" someone shouted.

"I have no idea," the pilot answered, his voice shaking. "I just know what I've been told, but help should have been here a long time ago."

NORAD headquarters, Peterson Air Force Base, Colorado 16:32 EST

As the ranking commander at the time of the attack, Alan had the unenviable responsibility of communicating what little was known to those who ranked high enough to be informed.

General Glenn Young, chairman of the Joint Chiefs of Staff, was on the line. "We don't know," Alan responded into the phone. "There were no military vessels in the areas the missiles launched from. We have two small navy vessels within one hundred miles of the launch on the East Coast, but that's as close as we get."

"Do we have any idea how effective the missiles were?" General Young asked.

"Preliminary indications are that this is a worst-case scenario," answered Alan. "Obviously information is still limited due to communication failures, but that in and of itself is an answer. All communication on the civilian networks is down. Our power supply has switched to self-generation. Satellite communication is no longer effective. NORAD has contact only through our military fiber optic networks. General, it's bad. We just don't know how bad yet."

"The power's out at my house in Virginia," the general mused. "We were getting ready to head to the lake when everything went dead. I thought it was local until this phone started ringing." General Young paused, his mind filtering rapidly through what he knew about a nuclear EMP. "If it's as bad as the professors told us it would be, may God have mercy on us. I'll contact the President once I figure out where he landed." The general paused a second, then added quietly, "Alan, this may sound out of place, but I hope you find some time to pray. That may be our best hope for awhile."

The solemnity in General Young's voice reverberated in Alan's ears. The general was typically a jovial individual, always upbeat and encouraging and one of the truly decent ones that Alan worked with, but today there was none of that. He sounded like a man who'd been told he only had weeks to live. "I will, sir," promised Alan. "I'm sure I won't be the only one."

George Bush International Airport, Houston, TX 17:10 EST

A handful of survivors from Flight 17 moved slowly through the concourse, tired, bloodied, and shocked by the scene surrounding them. Kyle and Ed had helped an overweight college student with a swollen ankle and knee abrasions into the terminal, along with a retired school teacher from Oklahoma who was physically fine, but suffering from shock.

After getting their two charges settled and finding a security officer to take responsibility for them, Ed and Kyle found two empty seats and dropped into them, exhausted and frightened.

Everywhere they looked it was chaos. People were pressed against the windows, watching the burning airplanes on the runways. Around the boarding counters frightened, unruly crowds gathered, demanding information but receiving none. Occasionally a police officer or airport security personnel ran through the terminal, looking worried and official but with no apparent plan of action. Parents stood guard over their children, hovering over them and protecting them from some unknown danger.

Kyle noticed that the monitors that usually displayed flight information were blank and that the terminal was lit with sunlight and emergency lighting. "This looks like a war zone, Ed. What on earth is going on?"

"I don't know, Kyle, but I need to sit for a while. Between my feet and my head, I'm about ready to pass out."

Kyle nodded. "Wait here for me. I'm going to see if I can find someone who knows what's going on."

***

Ed's eyes snapped open at the sound of Kyle calling his name. "I thought you might have abandoned me," he said. "What'd you find out?"

"I learned where there's an emergency first aid office I can take you to, but that's about it. I'll tell you what I found out while I help you get down there." Kyle helped Ed to his feet and, as they worked their way through the airport, he described his 30-minute ordeal to find answers.

"So you're saying they're clueless?" Ed asked when Kyle finished.

Kyle nodded. "Total confusion. Practically on the verge of a riot. Security has no idea what's going on, and everyone wants answers, which no one has. When I forced my way into the security office, some guy threw a punch at me before his wife pulled him away. I did get directions to where to take you to get looked at though. They were shocked to hear there was a crash that had survivors. The other planes that crashed were all airborne or landing apparently, but no one really knows for sure."

At the end of a short hallway past the car rental counters, Ed and Kyle found a medical room that was bursting with people in a worse state of panic than they had seen at the gate area. Kyle recognized a handful of passengers from their airplane, but the most seriously injured hadn't made it there yet, and most of those in the room seemed to suffer more from the stress of witnessing the crashes than from any physical injury.

"Do you want to find a chair?"

Ed surveyed the room from the doorway and watched the four overwhelmed medical personnel working frantically to help the crush of patients. "This is insane," he said, shaking his head. "I feel half dead, but if I stay here, I think I might get all the way there. Let's go find a seat somewhere else where we can rest a minute and figure something out."

They found seats in the luggage claim area and Ed dabbed sweat off his face with his shirtsleeve, making a dark patch on his forearm to go along with the growing circles of sweat under his armpits. "This is some kind of a nightmare," he mumbled as another police officer ran by.

Kyle shook his head. "It's beyond anything I've ever seen. It's unexplainable. I don't know if the airport was hit by some cosmic force, or a terrorist strike, or who-knows-what. If someone told me UFOs caused this, I'd be hard pressed to argue."

They sat in silence, lost in their thoughts and watching the pandemonium. Ed spoke after a long period of silence. "I don't think we'll be flying out of here today, even if we wanted to. I don't think anyone is. This is completely different from anything I've ever seen or heard of. With all those crashed airplanes, there should be hundreds of emergency vehicles from all over the city out there, but I didn't see a single one. There should have been enough help for us, even with the other planes down. I bet we'd still be waiting out by that airplane if we hadn't come in on our own. Something is wrong at a level I can't fathom."

Kyle nodded. "I've been thinking the same thing. I think everyone is. You can see it in their faces; there's a fear and helplessness I've never seen. Of course, how are you supposed to act when you've seen an airplane fall from the sky?"

"It's not just one plane wreck, Kyle. It's multiple wrecks. It's no emergency assistance to our flight, and no response for those other planes. It's no power in the terminal. It's total confusion with the airport employees. You saw them. They had no idea what they should be doing. Some of the smart ones are faking it, but most of them look like they want to cry. And the passengers…they're freaked out bad. There's a deeper fear there than just the power being out, more than a plane crash. Have you noticed that no one is using their cell phone? We tried mine, but it's dead. They're all dead. In a situation like this, everyone would be on their phone. It's like…I know this doesn't make any sense, but it's like we've been attacked." Ed paused a moment before continuing. "You remember 9/11?"

Kyle nodded. "Who doesn't? I'll always remember it. I was listening on my car radio 2,000 miles away from New York when it happened, but I'll always remember it."

"It feels like that, but ten times worse. Remember how unreal everything felt that day? How you couldn't believe it was happening, even as you watched it on TV? This feels the same way. I don't know why, but it does."

Seated across from them, a young mother tried to console a crying baby while her husband attempted to cheerfully read a book to a child of two or three. Kyle's eyes wandered the area as he digested what Ed had said about 9/11. Then he remembered some training he'd gone through years before. A cold chill ran down his back, and he physically shuddered. "I think I might know what's happened," he said, swallowing hard and staring down at the tile floor. "But I hope like hell I'm wrong."

CHAPTER FIVE

**George Bush International Airport,
Houston, Texas 18:15 EST**

"So you're saying that a nuclear bomb might have caused this?" Ed asked, his expression and tone failing to conceal his disbelief.

Kyle nodded as his mind continued to race, trying to remember the details.

"Why don't I see a huge mushroom cloud, or buildings being sucked over? Shouldn't we all have been burnt up in the explosion?"

"Ed, you didn't hear what I said. The bomb, assuming that's what caused this, wasn't detonated at ground level. If it had been, I'm sure it would have destroyed the city. The deal is this: if a nuclear bomb is detonated in space, the resulting electrical storm, or discharge, or whatever you want to call it, will wipe out everything electrical below it. Depending on how high the blast was, it could have impacted just the Houston area, or all of Texas, or even the entire country."

Ed sank back into his chair, struggling to grasp the information. "How sure are you about this?"

"I'm sure about the effect of a bomb, but I'm not sure at all that this is what's going on. I did some training with my company a few years ago. At the end of the sessions they were talking about worst-case scenarios, and the nuke in space was the ultimate. It fries everything. It's like lightning hitting every power pole in the country at the same time but worse. The discussion was more of a curiosity than anything, but it was frightening, almost unbelievable. The big thing I remember is that it's 'end of world as we know it' bad. I hope there's some other explanation, and I'm open to it, but I can't think of one."

Ed looked at Kyle, trying to find something in Kyle's expression that said "just kidding," but it wasn't there. "I want to get out of here," he said, his voice pinched and dry. "I feel like crap, I'm not going to get on another airplane today, and I don't think the FAA or CIA or CNN or whoever it is that investigates plane crashes is going to be showing up any time soon to interview us."

"You should get your head looked at," Kyle said as he reassessed Ed's wound. "You were out for awhile, and that cut was bleeding pretty badly. It probably needs some stitches."

Ed looked at Kyle and laughed out loud. "You just told me that a nuclear bomb in space might have sent us back to the stone-age, and you're worried about a cut on my head? I think I'll be fine."

"Just the concerned citizen coming out. It's probably not a bad idea for you to get home. Probably safer than hanging around here."

"What are you going to do, Kyle?" Ed asked.

"I hadn't really thought about that. I was planning on being home tonight."

"Do you have someplace to go?"

"No. I checked out of my hotel and turned in the car. Guess I'll sleep here tonight and see if I can get some more information if things settle down. Who knows, maybe everything will be back to normal in the morning." There was no conviction in his voice.

"Why don't you come and stay at my house? You saved my life. I'll never be able to repay you, but at least that would be something. Besides, I probably shouldn't be driving alone with a head injury."

Kyle took another look around the airport, taking in the panic and chaos, and slowly nodded his head. "I'd like that. I don't feel like staying around here any longer than I have to…this place could get dangerous."

"If things get better, I'll bring you back down tomorrow. If not, well, we'll figure it out then."

"It's a deal," said Kyle as he stood and helped Ed to his feet. "I really appreciate this."

Deer Creek, Montana 19:30 EST

Jennifer walked the fifty yards across her vacant horse pasture to the next-door neighbors' house, swatting mosquitoes as she walked and trying unsuccessfully to recall the first names of the older couple who lived there. She still hadn't gotten to know the Andersons very well. It had been just over five months since she and Kyle had moved in, and most of their spare time had been spent making their new house a home, but the few times she had visited with the Andersons, they had seemed quite nice. Usually when Jennifer went for her morning walks, Mrs. Anderson was outside tending her yard, the flourishing garden and flowerbeds testifying to the attention they received. The two women would wave and exchange greetings or chat for a minute, but between Jennifer's job and a busy summer, their relationship hadn't progressed much beyond that.

Jennifer knocked on the door and heard a noise from inside the house before Mr. Anderson swung it open. He smiled warmly at Jennifer, and she returned the smile, noticing his t-shirt that proudly proclaimed him to be "The World's Best Grandpa," a title that seemed to fit with his pleasant smile, round face, and gray hair combed carefully over the top of an otherwise bald head.

"Hello, Neighbor," he said, his voice cheerful and friendly. "What can I do for you today? Lookin' to borrow a cup of sugar?" His eyes twinkled as he spoke.

Jennifer was surprised by how friendly he was. "No. Thanks. I've got lots of sugar," she answered. "I'm sorry to bother you. I'm your neighbor, Jennifer Tait."

"Oh, I know who you are. I see you all the time, and it's no bother. It's always nice to have people drop by. You're the one with the three adorable children, correct?"

Jennifer nodded. "I live next door with the children – not sure how adorable they are, but you're right."

"My wife's told me all about your family. It's so nice to have children around. Kids just make the world a better place. We've got ten grandchildren of our own, so we like to have little ones nearby. I'll have to show you their pictures sometime. But enough about them, what can I do help you with, Jennifer?

"I wanted to see if I could use your phone, if it's working. I only have cordless phones and the power's out. I'd like to call my husband. He's supposed to be home tonight, and I haven't heard from him yet."

"I'd love to let you use our phone, but ours are dead too, even our cell phones." Mr. Anderson said this just as happily as if he were announcing the birth of a new grandchild. "Grace was talking to our daughter in Spokane when the line went out. She thought she'd been hung up on but figured it out when she couldn't call her back. I bet a car hit a transformer or a power pole because our power seems to be out too. Someone at the power company is going to be having a rotten Friday, don't you think?"

Jennifer agreed.

"We sure get spoiled, don't we? We always have power and never even think about it. Then it goes off for a couple of hours, and we can't hardly seem to function."

"Kyle, my husband, works for the power company, but he's not back or I'd send him down to check things out."

"Oh, that's right. Your husband mentioned that when you moved in. I thought I hadn't seen your husband for a little while. Is everything okay?"

Jennifer nodded. "Everything's fine. His company sent him down to Texas to help with recovery after the last hurricane. He's been gone for a couple of weeks but should be back later tonight."

"Two weeks is a long time. I hope you know you could have come over if you'd needed anything."

"That's very generous, Mr. Anderson. If anything comes up, I'll be sure to call."

"Oh, please, not so formal. I'm Charles, and my wife is Grace, but I think you know her already. She's taking a nap, or she'd come and say hello. And please, just call me Chuck. Everyone calls me Chuck, except for Grace. If she's mad at me then it's Charles Irwin, but I don't need to air our dirty laundry to you, do I?"

Jennifer chuckled. "Don't worry, Chuck," she said. "Your secret's safe with me. Thanks so much for your help. I'd better get back home and figure out something for dinner. It looks like it's going to be sandwiches tonight, or maybe we'll find something to barbeque. It was a pleasure talking to you again, Chuck. Please tell Grace hi for me."

CHAPTER SIX

**George Bush International
Airport, Houston, TX 20:30 EST**

"This is it," Ed said with great relief as he approached a sparkling, cherry red Jeep.

"This your toy?" Kyle asked as he inspected the vehicle, noticing that the Jeep's canvas top was worn, but the rest of it was in excellent shape.

Ed smiled and nodded. "It's a '78 Jeep CJ7. You like it?"

"I do. It's nice," Kyle said while running his hand along the polished chrome bumper.

Ed pulled the keys from his pocket and unlocked the door. He swung it open and pulled himself inside, then leaned over and popped the other lock. Kyle climbed into the Jeep and they both sat in silence, relishing the fact that they had reached the vehicle, but uncertain as to whether or not they'd be able to go anywhere in it.

"Do you think she's going to run?" Ed asked as he fidgeted nervously with the keys. "Because if she doesn't, it's a long way to walk to my house." He eyed the ignition, trying to muster the courage to try.

"There were some cars running as we walked through the parking lot. Hopefully yours will work, too."

"Yeah," Ed said, "but there were fifty dead vehicles for every one that worked. They were stalled everywhere, and people were still just sitting in them, not knowing what to do. Probably waiting for a tow truck to magically appear. You'd think they'd figure out that the tow truck is either dead too, or that there might be five hundred other vehicles to get to first." Ed paused. "Even if I do get her started, I don't know how we're going to get across town. The whole city could be a parking lot."

Kyle's feet hurt, his head ached, and he was tired, and anxiety had been building in him for the last few hours to the point that he was nearing the tipping point. "Just try the stupid thing, Ed! Then at least we'll know," he blurted, the words sounding harsher than intended, but Ed didn't react. Ed just sat there staring out the front window. Kyle took a deep breath to calm himself. "Ed? Sorry. You still there?"

Ed's head jerked, and he looked at Kyle. "Yeah? I'm here," he replied. "What'd you say?"

"I said try it, and let's see what happens. It's going to be dark soon. I don't know how far away you live, but the sooner we head that way, the better off we're going to be."

Ed put the key in the ignition, and they held their breath as the engine turned, resisted, coughed hesitantly, and then caught, roaring to life with a deep guttural growl that echoed off the concrete roof above them and shattered the eerie silence that had marked their journey across the streets and parking lots. Ed tapped the accelerator and the engine raced in response. Smiling, he leaned forward and rested his forehead on the steering wheel. "That's my baby," he said, the relief evident in his voice.

"I think you need to get your muffler fixed!" Kyle shouted over the noise of the engine, hardly able to speak he was smiling so much.

Ed shook his head. "That's the way I like it."

Both men leaned back and buckled their seatbelts. "I have to admit, that's about the most beautiful noise I've heard in my life," Kyle said, still grinning. "Your head alright to drive?"

Ed nodded. "Yeah. Let's get going. I've probably got an anxious wife at home. If I start to feel bad, I'll let you know."

Deer Creek, Montana 22:55 EST

Jennifer leaned down and kissed her daughter. "Goodnight, Emma. The power should be back on in the morning."

"Will Daddy be home then, too?" Emma asked, looking up at her mother with innocent, blue eyes, her long blonde hair spilling across the pillow. "He could fix this if he was here."

Jennifer smiled, pleased that for her nine year old the world was still simple and safe and that mom and dad could make everything right. "Daddy will be home in a couple of hours, and yes, I'm sure he could fix this if he was home. I'll tell him to come in and give you a hug and a kiss if it's not too late. Alright?"

"Alright, Mom," Emma answered. "I'll try to stay awake so I can say hi, but if I'm asleep, tell him I missed him." She told her mother goodnight and rolled over to face the wall.

"He probably already knows, but I'll be sure to tell him," Jennifer reassured her daughter. "Do you want me to close your blinds? It's Saturday tomorrow; you can sleep in if you want."

"No, that's okay, Mom. I don't want to."

"Alright then, sleep tight." Jennifer pulled the door closed behind her and went to the family room where her fourteen year old son, David, sat on the couch reading a book in the fading light. His earphones were on, and his head bounced lightly to the beat of the music that played on his iPod. The family room was bathed in the pleasant, warm glow of the fading sun, and Jennifer flipped on the switch for the kitchen lights just as she remembered that the power was out.

"Power's out, Mom!" David said, his voice louder than normal due to the earphones.

"Thanks for the information," she said to her grinning son. "I'm going to get the dishes done before it's too dark. You should probably get ready for bed now so we don't waste our flashlight batteries."

David pulled the headphones from his ears. "I missed that. What'd you say?"

"I said get ready for bed. It'll be dark soon. I'm going to do the dishes."

"But it's early," David protested as he looked at his watch. "It's only 9:00."

"In twenty minutes or so it'll be dark," replied Jennifer. "I guess you can stay up if you want, but there won't be much to do other than help with the dishes. I was wondering, did you have any problems tonight with your iPod?"

David shrugged his shoulders and shook his head. "No. Why?"

"I can't get mine to work. I thought the battery was charged, but it won't turn on and with the power out I can't check it on the computer."

"I keep mine locked in Dad's old gun safe in the basement so Spencer can't mess with it. That way I don't have battery problems anymore."

"Well, aren't you the smart one? Maybe I'll have to start locking mine in there too. So, are you going to help with the dishes or go to bed?"

David scratched his head as he made a show of thinking deeply and then sighed. "I guess I'll go to bed, but it was a tough decision. Maybe tomorrow night I'll stay up and help, if you're lucky. Oh! Hey, I almost forgot to ask. Can I go to Matt's house tomorrow? He's a new kid at school that rides our bus. Lives in that big, brown house that just got built over the summer."

"You have a few chores, but once they're done you can go if you want I suppose."

David grimaced. "Is there a big list?"

"Just the usual: mow the yard, clean your room, say hi to your father. Maybe a couple more things once I take a look around."

David rolled his eyes and muttered something Jennifer couldn't make out.

"I heard that," she lied. "Just because you're fourteen doesn't mean you can cop an attitude with me, young man," she scolded with a grin. "I still have the receipt for that iPod your dad got you for your birthday. It's only been three weeks, so I'm sure the store will take it back. And don't forget to brush your teeth," she reminded.

David flashed a dimpled grin at his mom as he got up and disappeared down the basement stairs to his room. Jennifer went to work on the dishes, scraping them off and stacking them on the counter, musing about how much David was starting to look like his father. He was already three inches taller than her and was starting to fill out in the shoulders. Another year, she guessed, and David would be as tall as Kyle, maybe even a little taller. The fact that girls were starting to call David at home and that he liked the attention indicated her firstborn was rapidly growing up.

Anxious to finish cleaning before the daylight was gone, Jennifer hurried to fill the dishwasher, then wiped the bread-crumbs off the table and swept the floor, finishing as the last direct rays of sunlight disappeared behind the mountains to the west.

Her watch showed a quarter to ten, giving her a little over thirty minutes before Kyle would be home, if his flight was on time. Jennifer lit a candle, checked on Emma and Spencer, then went to her bedroom and found the red, silk teddy Kyle had given her for Valentine's Day the year before. Securing the bathroom door behind her, she lit a second candle and placed it by the first one on the counter in front of the mirror before stepping back to look at her reflection in the flickering light. She turned to the right and examined her profile, sucking in her stomach and pushing out her chest. She was pleased with how she looked, having lost five pounds while Kyle was gone and coming so close to hitting her target weight.

Jennifer quickly changed into the teddy, then pulled out her make-up and sat down in front of the mirror. It was difficult to see clearly in the candlelight, but she managed by leaning in close to the mirror and adjusting the position of the candles. Kyle often commented on how pretty her brown eyes were, so she played them up with mascara and eyeliner, drawing her lashes out as long as possible. Next she warmed her cheeks with some blush, then picked out her lipstick and carefully applied it, accentuating the curve of her mouth to make her lips look as full as possible.

Finished with her makeup, Jennifer stood up and looked at her reflection in the mirror again. She liked how the cut of the lingerie complemented her figure, the neckline dipping temptingly in front and the sides cut high enough to reveal the full length of her legs, making her feel enticing but not cheap. She rested her foot on the edge of the tub and rubbed lotion on one leg and then the other. As she stroked her legs, she noticed, with satisfaction, the firmness of her muscles and the pleasant shape of her thighs, the result of hav-ing walked fifteen miles every week since moving into their new home.

Removing the elastic band from her ponytail, Jennifer let her dark brown hair cascade over her shoulders and began to brush it, slowly drawing her hair down in front of her with each stroke. Her hair was getting longer, reaching almost to the middle of her back, the natural wave giving it just the right amount of body.

By fifteen minutes after ten, Jennifer had finished getting ready for Kyle's homecoming, retrieved her robe from the closet, and was sitting on the couch in the family room waiting for him to arrive. While she waited, she read the newspaper in the dim candlelight, then moved on to the newest *Readers Digest*. When she finished that and Kyle still wasn't home, she started on a novel borrowed from a friend at work. A little before mid-night, with her eyes hurting and the room too dark to see well,

Jennifer found a blanket and pillow and lay back on the couch. Around two in the morning and too uncomfortable to sleep, Jennifer scooped up the blanket and staggered down the hall to her room where she tossed and turned for an hour more before finally drifting off to sleep.

Houston, Texas 23:45 EST

"What do you think I should do, Kyle?" Ed asked as the four figures on the side of the road desperately waved their arms. When they'd had to force their way through the exit barrier at the airport parking lot, both men had known the drive home was going to be much more difficult than they wanted. The foot traffic of airport workers and stranded passengers walking into town, along with a snarl of abandoned vehicles, had clogged the road. Most of the pedestrians, their expressions filled with confusion, fear and exhaustion, had moved out of the way to let them pass as the Jeep approached, but every so often a person had blocked the road in an attempt to catch a ride, and Ed had been forced to try and avoid hitting them.

They had picked up a couple of older ladies and dropped them off near their homes, but the reputation of the surrounding neighborhoods and the worsening conditions had kept them from straying too far from their intended route. Gunshots had rung out just as the second of the two women was getting out of the Jeep, and Ed had sped off with a squeal of his tires, not sure if the shots had been intended for him, but unwilling to find out for sure. Since then, they'd done everything in their power to avoid people while trying to take a direct path home. These efforts had required driving down medians, hopping curbs, weaving through stalled traffic, and violating every rule of the road but the speed limit.

They were on the freeway and making as good a time as could be expected when the four individuals had appeared in front of them. A young mother with three small children, the oldest no more than seven, huddled beside a car that was pulled into the median. There was plenty of room for Ed to avoid them without slowing down, but his foot instinctively went to the brake.

"It's your call," Kyle replied, "but if you're going to stop for them, let's get them loaded quick. It's not like they're the only people around that'd like a lift."

Ed grunted, and Kyle felt the Jeep slow. They pulled alongside the family, and Ed rolled down his window. The mother wiped her eyes and cheeks with her free hand. Her other hand clung tightly to the wrist of the youngest child. "Get in quickly," Ed said in as kind of a voice as he could muster.

The woman mumbled a "thank you" and pushed her children into the backseat.

Kyle looked at her in the darkness and his thoughts immediately went to his wife, sending a chill through him.

"Where are you going?" Ed asked, twisting around to look at his passengers.

The woman sniffed and tried to regain her composure. "Thank you again. We've been waiting for hours for someone..." The youngest child, who appeared exhausted to the point of passing out, began to cry, and the woman leaned down and kissed her on the forehead. "It's alright, Courtney," she whispered, "We're on our way."

Ed put the Jeep in gear and accelerated away from her vehicle, too afraid to stay stopped any longer than he needed to. "Where's somewhere safe I can take you, miss?" he asked again.

"My ex lives in League City. That's where we were headed when everything went bad. That's the closest place I've got." She paused, and her eyes glassed over as she tenderly rubbed her youngest child's head. "We left Huntsville as soon as Jonathan got out of school. Their father is supposed to have them for the weekend." Her voice was faint and she seemed to be in another place. "I've never had car problems before; do you know what's going on?"

Kyle shook his head, "We don't know anything for sure, and there's nothing on the radio but static."

"Someone said there was a war going on, that we've been attacked." The woman was fighting to control her emotions, but tears rolled down her cheeks and her voice halted every couple of words.

"Who said we were attacked?" Ed asked, looking in the rearview mirror, even though it was too dark for him to see into the backseat with the only light coming from the glow of his headlights.

"I don't know," she answered. "Just some guy who walked by us a couple of hours ago. It scared Jonathan, and me too, I guess. What are you going to do with us?"

"I guess we're going to League City," Ed said. "I can't very well throw you out on the side of the road."

The woman let out a sigh of relief, and Kyle heard her crying softly. After a short silence she spoke up again. "Thank you so much. I didn't know what we were going to do. Everyone just kept walking past us. Things are just so crazy. I suppose we could have walked somewhere, but I don't know this part of town."

"Just relax, miss," Ed said, sounding tired. "No one knows what to do right now, and I imagine being stranded with three children makes it that much harder."

"No. It doesn't. My name's Stephanie; my friends call me Steph."

"Okay Steph. I hope you can get us to your ex's in the dark. Keep your arm around your kids. I'll probably be doing some off-roading, and I'm going to keep my speed up.

***

It was four hours before Ed finally swung the Jeep into his own driveway. The Jeep's headlights, the only light in the eerily dark neighborhood, splashed across the front of his house, lighting up a brick bungalow with an attached, oversized garage. He engaged the emergency brake, shut off the ignition, and killed the head-lights, immediately plunging them into a thick, all-enveloping darkness.

"I think you might want to leave the lights on, Ed," Kyle sug-gested. "I'm guessing your security light isn't going to kick on, and there's not much for moonlight."

Ed flipped the headlights back on. "Let me go find a flash-light. I'll just be a couple of minutes." Ed jumped down from the Jeep and hobbled off towards the garage on tender feet, spot-lighted like a performer on a stage by the piercing beams of the headlights.

After a short wait, Kyle saw a small light coming from around the side of the garage. He leaned over, found the knob for the headlights, and pushed it in, the darkness swallowing them again except for the thin beam of Ed's flashlight.

"A penlight?" Kyle asked.

"It's all I could find. Did you want to wait out here longer?"

"No, I guess not."

"Then quit complaining and follow me," Ed instructed in a tired, but good-natured voice. "I'll let us in, but you wait by the door. My wife is going to be scared to death. I'm not supposed to be back until next Friday, and she's all alone without any power. I hope she doesn't shoot me with everything that's going on."

Ed let them in the front door then called out to his wife in a soft shout. "Virgie? Virgie?" Receiving no response, he continued to call her name as he walked down the hall.

Kyle stood in total darkness by the front door and listened. He heard a door open and then the muffled sound of a woman's voice. After a short exchange, he saw the glow from Ed's flashlight coming back down the hallway.

"I'm going to put you in the guestroom," Ed said as he returned. "Virgie wasn't exactly expecting company, but the room's not in bad shape. Can I get you something to drink before you go to bed?"

Kyle nodded and followed Ed to the kitchen, where they sat at the table eating slices of Wonder bread and sharing a six-pack of Budweiser in the dimming glow of the flashlight, neither having much to say. As Kyle finished off his second beer, he heard a door open and footsteps slowly approach from down the hallway. Kyle turned and, in the dim light, saw Ed's wife approach, rubbing her eyes.

"I didn't understand what you said in the bedroom, Ed. I was too tired," she said, forming her words carefully. "Why are you home? You're supposed to be gone for a week."

Ed looked at Kyle and appeared embarrassed by his wife's presence.

"Virgie, I told you I'd explain it all in the morning. Why don't you go back to bed? I still don't understand everything myself, and I'm tired."

"But I'm awake now," she said, trying to stifle a yawn, "and I wanted to meet your friend. What did you say his name was?"

"His name's Kyle, dear. I met him on the airplane." Ed stood and reached for his wife. "Let me help you back to the room."

Virgie turned away from Ed and leaned towards Kyle. "Hi, I'm Virgie," she said, extending a chubby hand as she leaned down close.

Kyle took her hand and introduced himself, trying not to recoil from the powerful smell of liquor on her breath. Initially she looked like a doting grandmother, pleasant and plump with curly, gray hair, but the bloodshot eyes and alcohol-induced redness in her cheeks ruined the grandmotherly effect. Kyle smiled and wished Virgie a goodnight, thanking her for allowing him to stay, then Ed escorted his wife back down the hallway to their bedroom, assuring her that everything would be all right.

Kyle swallowed the rest of his drink and set the can on the edge of the table.

Ed returned minutes later, using a damp washcloth to wipe at the patches of blood on the side of his face. "I'm tired," Ed said. "I'd offer you another beer, but I think I'd fall asleep at the table."

"That's fine. I'm struggling to keep my eyes open myself."

Ed motioned for Kyle to follow, so Kyle trailed him down the hall to a small room with a computer and fax machine on a desk against one wall, and a single twin bed pushed up against the opposite one.

"It's not much," said Ed. "We don't usually have company, and I'm redoing the bedroom in the basement."

"This is more than good. At this point I think I could sleep on the garage floor."

Ed smiled weakly as he gathered a couple of folders from the bed and stacked them onto the desk. "The bathroom's next door. I'll try to find you a flashlight."

CHAPTER SEVEN

Saturday, September 3rd
Katy, Texas

Kyle awoke in a small bed in an unfamiliar bedroom, the bright sunlight shining on him through the window of the bedroom. Outside the sounds of a typical Saturday morning could be heard--birds singing, dogs barking, and a lawn mower in a neighbor's yard. From the kitchen he could hear the clinking of dishes and the occasional sound of a chair scraping on the floor. He lay in bed for half an hour, trying futilely to go back to sleep but kept awake by the outside noises, the temperature of the bedroom, and a deep, nagging worry about his family as the nightmare of the day before played over and over in his mind.

Finally he got up, put on his only clothes, and headed to the kitchen. Virgie sat at the table drinking a glass of milk and eating a slice of bread covered with a thick layer of butter and jam. She looked startled to see Kyle coming down the hallway.

"Good morning," Kyle said, sounding more cheerful than he felt. "I'm Kyle. We met last night, or technically this morning I guess. Either way, it was late."

Virgie looked confused and covered her mouth as she swallowed. "I'm Virgie," she said, pausing to think. "It's starting to come back. Yesterday was a weird day, and then Ed came home in the middle of the night. I'm still trying to figure out what's going on. Did Ed say something about airplane problems?"

"Yeah, you could say that," Kyle replied. "There are a lot of things going on right now."

Virgie's look changed to one of concern. "Oh, I'm sorry," she said. "Please have a seat. Can I get you something to eat? I'm sure you must be hungry."

"That would be nice, but don't go to a lot of trouble."

"Well, we usually just have coffee and toast in the morning, but nothing is working, so I can't get you either of those." She got up from the table and opened the fridge. "Let's see," she said as she scanned the contents. "We've got some apples, orange juice, milk. Most of it's not very cold anymore." She closed the fridge and looked in the small pantry. "There's some cereal, bread, peanut butter, …"

"Just a sandwich would be fine," said Kyle. "Peanut butter and jam sounds good, maybe with some milk?"

"The milk's warm," she reminded him. "But I can get it for you if you'd like. It still tastes good."

"Warm milk is fine," Kyle answered. "I take it the power is still out?"

Virgie nodded. "It went out yesterday afternoon. I was at a friend's house. Couldn't even get my car started to come home. Strangest thing. I ended up having to walk over two miles."

"It was like that at the airport, too."

Kyle watched Virgie prepare his sandwich. She was dressed in a pair of sweatpants and an old t-shirt and she hummed to herself while she worked. The small kitchen, devoid of any furniture other than the little table and its two chairs, reminded him of his grandmother's kitchen from when he was young, minus the pictures and wall hangings that his grandmother had lovingly covered her walls with.

"So where is it that I am?" Kyle asked, attempting small talk as he waited for his food. "Ed told me, but I don't remember."

"This is Katy," Virgie said as she poured milk in his cup. "We're not too far from Houston, just a few miles west. With Houston growing so much, we're more like a suburb." She set the sandwich down in front of Kyle. "Now, what's going on. What happened with your airplane? I'm still trying to understand why Ed's here and not in Denver."

Kyle related most of what had happened. He described the failed takeoff and their escape from the airplane, how there had been no emergency response, and that other airplanes had crashed at the same time. He told her about the chaos at the airport and why he and Ed had decided to come to the house. He described the drive from the airport, how there were cars stalled all over the city blocking the roads, and that they had seen only a few other operating vehicles. He told Virgie about the accidents, the people walking home, the lack of a police presence, and how overwhelmingly dark the city had become once the sun went down.

Virgie sat across the table, her bloodshot eyes open wide, shaking her head as she listened to Kyle. By the time he was done talking, Kyle had finished two sandwiches and three glasses of milk, and Virgie was nearly in a state of panic.

"So why did it take you so long to get back here?" she asked. "It should just be an hour's drive if traffic's not too bad."

"Ed," Kyle answered. "There was a lady with three little kids on the side of the highway. Ed couldn't drive by. She was headed somewhere on the far side of the city, and it was a lot slower going because cars were stalled everywhere. We could easily have been much later because there were a lot of people who needed help, but the Jeep was getting low on gas."

"Sounds like Ed," Virgie said. "He's got a big heart, too big sometimes. So what do you think is causing all of this?"

Kyle hesitated before he spoke. "I was telling Ed, the only thing I can think of that could have done this is something called an EMP, a nuclear bomb detonated in space. It doesn't blow things up but basically cooks everything that uses electricity.

"I'm not an expert," Kyle added. "It could very well be something else, maybe a huge solar pulse or something, but even then, depending on how intense it is, the effects are pretty similar."

"If it is that EMT thing you described, how long until we get our power back?"

"Well, if it was an EMP," said Kyle, annunciating clearly, "we're probably looking at six months or more. More likely a year or two."

Virgie's eyes bulged. "Six months until everything's back to normal? We'll never survive for that long!"

Kyle shook his head. "No, you don't understand. If it really was an EMP, normal is years away, maybe a decade. Six months is how long it will be until we might get some power plants operating, and that's if things go well."

Deer Creek, Montana

Jennifer was busily working around the house, the silent television and telephone making for a productive Saturday morning. The kids had cleaned their rooms. Emma had swept the kitchen and helped pick up toys in the basement with Spencer, and David had mowed the yard and swept the garage. When his chores were done David left for his friend's house, and the two younger ones were now playing in the backyard.

By all outward signs, it was a perfect, late summer Saturday morning. The sun was shining in a brilliant, cloud-free sky. Birds were singing, the kids were getting along, and the house was clean. Even their neighborhood of homes spread out on multi-acre lots, which was usually peaceful anyway, was unusually quiet. Jennifer knew she should relax and enjoy the day, but something gnawed at her instead. She had experienced power outages before, and Kyle had been held over at work more times than she could remember, but this was different. She tried to convince herself that the power, the phones, and Kyle being late were all a coincidence, that Kyle was probably trying to reach her to let her know he would be delayed by a day or two. It wouldn't be the first time he'd been held over out of town.

Still feeling unsettled, Jennifer found her book and went outside to read in the backyard, hoping a good story would help take her mind off of Kyle and the power situation. Finding a lounge chair, she set it up on a sunny corner of their fenced in section of lawn, adjusted the headrest, rolled up her shorts, and sat back to both read and take advantage of the sunshine.

She had only read a few pages when she heard David's distressed voice shouting for her. Not expecting him to return home until closer to dinnertime and with nerves already wound tight, Jennifer jumped up from her chair and hurried around to the front of the house. David was cutting across the neighbor's property and running fast.

"Mom...you gotta...listen...to the...radio!" he said, trying to catch his breath as he came to a stop in front of her. He took a couple of deep breaths then continued. "Matt's dad...he listened on the radio...the Vice President ...he said we've been attacked... and that people have been killed."

Katy, Texas

Kyle sat in the front seat of Ed's Jeep, slowly turning the radio dial and scanning for any station that was broadcasting, while Ed searched the garage for batteries, flashlights and candles. Ed and Virgie had scoured their house that morning but only found a handful of candles, two flashlights, and several AA batteries, which were useless for the larger flashlights. In the backyard, Virgie was cooking up the meat from the freezer. Steaks were on the menu for lunch, along with barbequed corn-on-the-cob and rapidly melting ice cream for dessert.

Kyle strained to catch any hint of a signal as he patiently tuned the radio, likely the Jeep's original, an old-fashioned dial tuner that made his wrist cramp but allowed him to carefully creep through the frequencies. On the second scan through, as he was about to give up and go help Ed in the garage, Kyle found a signal. He turned the volume up and fine-tuned the station until he could hear an intermittent beeping followed by a voice announcing an emergency broadcast.

"Ed, come over here! I got something!" Kyle shouted, waving his arm to get Ed's attention.

Ed put down the box he was carrying and hurried over to the Jeep. "What'd you find?"

"I'm not sure, but it's the only signal I've detected. It says there's going to be an emergency broadcast."

They waited in silence for the broadcast to begin, with Ed adjusting the rubber seals around the door of the Jeep and Kyle chewing on his fingernails as the seconds ticked by. The announcer's voice came back. "We have an urgent message from the Office of the President."

There was a brief pause, then a voice. Kyle and Ed strained to hear over the static of the radio.

"My fellow citizens," the broadcast began. "This is Vice President Brent Hamilton. On Friday, Sept. 2, at approximately 4:08 P.M. Eastern Time, our country was attacked by enemies we have not yet identified. President Stewart was traveling at the time of the attack and is currently en-route to Washington. The target of the attack was the continental United States and, by extension, the entire North American continent. A nuclear missile was detonated approximately three hundred miles above our country. The result of this detonation was an electrical storm that appears to have crippled our electrical infrastructure. This type of attack is referred to as an EMP, or Electromagnetic Pulse."

"Damn," said Kyle. "That's really bad news."

"No one was directly killed by the blast, and there is no danger to the population from radioactivity, but the consequences of the attack are exceptionally serious and will be felt by everyone. The power generation and transmission capabilities of our utility system appear, at this point, to have been destroyed or at best severely diminished. Telephone and communication systems have also been destroyed. Transportation systems will be greatly limited due to our inability to pump and process fuel, control air traffic, and because of the direct effect of the EMP on the electronic components of most motor vehicles and airplanes. We have received word of dozens of airplane crashes and of stranded motorists, as well as inoperable train and subway systems. The full degree to which our government and military have been affected is yet to be determined."

"This is a threat for which we have been preparing for over thirty years, and many critical systems appear to have survived the attack, allowing the government to function in a limited but effective capacity. The military is also intact and is prepared to restore order and defend the United States from any military threats. All available military units have been recalled and will return stateside as quickly as possible. We ask that all members of the National Guard report to their assigned locations as soon as possible. We have been in contact with our allies throughout the world, and they have pledged to do everything in their power to help us work through these challenges."

"This is a time for the citizens of this great country to come together and display the nobility of character that has helped make this the greatest nation in the history of mankind. Every effort is being made on your behalf to restore critical systems as quickly as possible, but even under the best of circumstances, it is a process that will take months and potentially years to complete."

"The bulk of the recovery is dependent on the determination, ingenuity and efforts of you, the American people. As citizens, there are things you must do to help. Do not panic. Continue to respect and obey the laws of the nation and your communities. Be judicious with your use of food and water. We are aware that there are uncontrolled fires burning in a number of communities across our nation. Use caution in your activities as it is likely that medical, law enforcement, and emergency services will be unable to provide assistance. We encourage you to gather in your neighborhoods and communities and to organize yourselves to help take care of each other. Finally, we encourage you to remember our Maker and to call upon Him for mercy and protection."

"America, of the many challenges our country has faced, this is the greatest one of all. It will take the determined efforts of every man, woman and child for us to recover and regain our status as the leader of the free world. It is an effort that will not be without obstacles and difficulties, but there are no other people on the face of this planet who are more able to deal with such a challenge. It is a challenge we must face and from which we must never shrink.

"We will continue to broadcast information for you each day on these same stations. May God watch over us all. Thank you."

The station was momentarily silent, then the beeping resumed.

CHAPTER EIGHT

Deer Creek, Montana

After hearing about the radio broadcast from David, Jennifer had hunted frantically for a radio that worked. Getting no response from the home stereo or car radio, she'd finally found an old emergency hand crank radio in the basement and was now sitting, winded and stunned, on the front porch steps. She flipped the radio's power switch off, then reached out and braced herself against the house as a wave of nausea washed over her. There were so many questions she wanted answers to, so many details that had been left unsaid. She rubbed her temples with her fingers, pushing hard to dull the pain and to avoid getting ill. Tears welled up in her eyes as the possibility that Kyle might never come home swirled around in her head. She struggled to her feet and felt David's hand on her arm, helping her up.

"Mom, what does all that mean?" David asked, his voice more frightened than she'd ever heard before. "When is Dad going to be home?"

Jennifer fought to maintain control. "I'm not sure, Dave. I don't understand everything. I'm sure your dad will be home soon. He's a pretty tough guy," she said, as much in an attempt to convince herself as it was to convince her son. "Will you go get me a paper and pen? I want to listen again and write some things down."

David ran off, then returned with a pen and some sheets of paper he'd ripped from a school binder.

The broadcast was repeated after a five-minute break, and as David steadily cranked the radio, Jennifer jotted notes down with a hand she couldn't quite manage to keep from shaking. When the broadcast ended, she ran inside to get Kyle's flight information from the front of the refrigerator, sending magnets bouncing across the floor as she tore it down. She scanned the page to find the information she needed. His arrival time in Missoula was circled with a yellow highlighter, 9:45 P.M. He was to have left Denver at 7:45 P.M. after arriving there at 5:10. Her eyes flew to the next section. The flight from Houston was scheduled to leave at 2:08 CST. Jennifer did the math, adjusting for the time zones, and realized that Kyle's flight would have been in the air for an hour when the attack occurred.

Breathing was suddenly difficult, and Jennifer's breaths began to come in short, erratic gulps. She felt her knees weaken and stumbled over to a chair at the kitchen table. Her mind raced. What had they said about airplanes crashing? Did they say all of them?

"What is it, Mom?" David asked, his face ashen. "Has something happened to Dad?"

"David...I don't know. Let me listen to the broadcast again so I can remember the exact words. You wait inside for me." Her words felt hollow and meaningless, but she felt she had to be strong for her son.

Jennifer gathered her strength and went back outside to the radio. She switched it on and began turning the handle. The Vice President was talking about electrical power as the radio groaned to life. She turned the volume up with her free hand, hoping that somehow there would be more information this time around. Vice President Hamilton's words crackled from the speakers, as calm as if he were relating the weather report. "...*we have received word of dozens of airplane crashes...*" The words were clear and hit her as hard as a kick in the stomach. She dropped the radio and burst into tears. "Kyle, no! Please, no!" she cried under her breath, her voice quivering. The Vice President's voice droned on about the military, then the volume gave out as the small charge the radio held began to fade.

Hearing footsteps, she looked up to see Emma coming towards her.

"What's for lunch, Mom? Me and Spencer are hungry." She paused when she got close to her mother. "What's wrong?"

Jennifer wiped the tears from her eyes, swallowed, and fought to compose herself. "I'm not sure, sweetie. Can you wait a few minutes?" she said, her voice cracking.

"Why are you crying? Are you hurt?"

Jennifer's throat ached, and her head hurt so badly she could barely see. "There was some bad news on the radio, Em. I'm not sure what it means, but it's got me worried. I'll be all right. I just need to lie down for a few minutes."

"Okay, Mom," Emma said, turning to leave. "Can I go to Lindsay's house after lunch? Her mom says it's alright."

Katy, Texas

Ed, Virgie and Kyle ate their lunch on the back patio in silence, their thoughts consumed by the speech on the radio. They had listened to the Vice President's broadcast twice, and both times it was the same horrible news.

"I don't get it," Ed said, breaking the silence. "If the Vice President said they've been preparing for this for thirty years, then why's it so bad… and why haven't they ever let us in on their little secret? It would have been nice to be able to do something to prepare! With that much time to get ready, I'd damn well be prepared for it if I was in charge. They should be able to just turn the power back on." Ed's face was turning red, and he pounded his fist on the table as he spoke.

Kyle took a sip of warm water. "I agree with you, Ed. There should have been more warnings, but you don't understand how vulnerable the electrical grid is, and there's no practical way to protect all of it. I don't know a lot about communications and the other systems, but I know about our power system. The only way to maybe protect it would be to bury every power line ten feet underground in a steel tube, and even then it wouldn't protect much because ninety-nine percent of the stuff that runs on power would still be exposed. The problem is that almost everything in our country depends on electricity in one way or another. An EMP... it's like..." Kyle paused, searching for a way to explain and noticing that Virgie's worried eyes were locked on him. "Virgie, I was telling Ed this yesterday... it's like lightening hitting every power pole in the country at the same time, but fifty or maybe a hundred times worse. We don't know exactly what it'll do, but we know it will be bad."

Ed began to calm down as Kyle spoke. "They should have warned us instead of letting us find out after the fact. It seems like the government was keeping secrets from us. Maybe they didn't want to cause a panic, but now the situation is worse. "

"Are you sure it's going to be so bad?" Virgie interjected. "I didn't see or hear a thing. I was at my friend's when it happened, and everything just went dead. There wasn't any noise or anything. Everything just shut off all of a sudden, and then there was nothing but silence."

"Virgie, the Vice President said the bomb went off three hundred miles above us," Ed reminded her. "You're not going to see or hear that."

"It's the electrons that do the damage, not the impact of the explosion," Kyle reminded her. "They overload everything. Once they find a conductor, they build up and things start to melt, even the copper in the power lines. The best-case scenario is that just sensitive things, like computer chips, get cooked. The worst case is every wire and electrical appliance in the country will need to be replaced."

"But look around, Kyle," Virgie said. "Everything looks fine. I don't feel any different. If you ask me, I think the Vice President is just trying to scare us so they can raise our taxes or make some new law. I don't want some politician telling us a bunch of lies. You can't trust them, you know?"

"Virgie, I don't trust them much either," Ed said. "But you weren't at the airport, and you didn't drive across town with us. Something real bad has happened. Cars were dead, airplanes had crashed, and the whole city was stopped. People were walking, just leaving their cars and walking home. I was afraid to stop. Thought someone might kill us for the Jeep. I don't think the Vice President is lying to us, at least not this time."

Virgie shook her head in dismay and looked at Kyle. "How long do you think it'll be until things can be fixed?" she asked Kyle matter-of-factly. "The Vice President said months. He doesn't mean it, does he? It'll just be a week or two, don't you think?"

Virgie and Ed watched Kyle as he thought about his answer. "I think a year would be best case. If the power lines are damaged, it could be a decade before everything everywhere is back to how we know it, if that even ever happens, and that's assuming other countries are going to do all they can to help us. Obviously someone who doesn't like us did this, and if they send their military against us, or against our allies, who knows how long it might take. It might take a lot longer than what I'm guessing. There are just too many things I don't know to give a reasonable estimate."

Ed rocked forward and bumped hard against the table, knocking his cup to the ground and causing Virgie to jump in her chair as the glass exploded on the ground. "What are you talking about?" Virgie asked, ignoring the broken glass. "A year? A decade? If ever? You're joking, right? I can hear someone mowing their lawn as we speak. If a stupid lawnmower works, why can't they fix the power?"

"It's not a joke, Virgie. There's nothing I'd like more than for this to be a joke, but I'm completely serious," Kyle replied, trying not to let his own frustration and fear show. He understood how dire the situation was and was beginning to grasp the overwhelming challenge he had ahead of him to get home, yet Virgie and Ed seemed stuck on how long it would be until they could use their coffee maker. "Virgie, something simple, like a lawnmower, will work because it's just a spark plug on a short wire. No electronics involved. I would expect basic things, like generators, old farm equipment, and a lot of older cars will be alright because they use cables and mechanical systems, but at some point, even if they work, all those things are going to run out of gas. Our refineries and gas stations, all that stuff, require electricity and computers to operate. We are in an unbelievably bad situation, and getting mad at the government isn't going to put food on the table. I've been going over this in my head ever since the airport. Think about it, how long did it take us to get our country to where it is?"

"Since 1776, if you go all the way back, even before that, isn't it?" replied Ed.

"That's right, the better part of two hundred and fifty years. During most of that time other countries left us alone, didn't even pay us much attention until we were too big for them to do too much about us. Add to that the fact that we've developed most of the world's technology, so we've always been ahead of all these countries that've resented us. Over time, a lot of countries have come to hate everything we stand for. Hell, half of our own citizens don't seem to like what we stand for. Now, in the blink of an eye, we've been put in a position where we're third world, and they've got the power. I don't see a lot of them doing much for us.

"Sure, we've got a few allies: Australia, England, Canada, maybe some others like Israel. But Australia is an ocean away with only a tenth of our population, Britain is tied tight to Europe and most Europeans barely tolerate us, and Canada's likely been crippled by the EMP just like we have. I don't know that we've ever been in a position this serious. I hope I'm missing something and that you're right, but I'm trying to be as honest as I can. I guess it probably depends on where you live, but I think it's likely a year before we see any power coming back, and that's just the first step."

"How are we supposed to survive for a year without power?" Virgie asked. "We won't be able to do anything, and our food will go bad. And we're supposed to go through a summer without air conditioning? I don't think so," she said, crossing her arms across her chest, her defiance on display. "This is America, not the third world. There's got to be something that can be done."

"Virgie!" Kyle said, raising his arms and voice in frustration. "An EMP destroys everything! It's not like it just trips a big circuit breaker that can be turned back on. Power plants will need to get new computers and new turbines, and most will need to be rewired. And that's if they haven't burned down. Transmission lines will need to be replaced, and we'll have to do all of it with most cars and trucks needing to be fixed first. We don't keep spare parts for every piece of equipment a power plant needs, just a few critical pieces scattered around the country. We have millions upon millions of miles of power lines that might need to be replaced. Who's going to do that when no one can get to work and everyone is busy trying to find food? Your fridge, your computers, your vehicles are all dead, and all the wiring in your house likely needs to be replaced. Anything in a grounded metal box might be safe, but the rest is toast. You guys are amazingly lucky to have a vehicle that doesn't rely on computer chips to operate, but how are you going to get gas once the tank is empty?"

"You don't make very pleasant dinner conversation, you know," Ed said, his expression blank and his voice lifeless.

"It's never been my strong suit. How much food do you have?" Kyle was all business now, his patience having worn out.

"I cooked all the steaks," Virgie answered. "There are still three left."

"No, Virgie, not for lunch. I mean in your house. How much food do you have if you can't buy anything from the store?"

"I've got a little bit in the pantry. Why?"

"I'm thinking that we need to find a way to get some food and as quickly as we can. Think about it. Vehicles are dead, so nothing is going to be delivered. Power is out, and there are a whole lot of people in an area that isn't very big. How's anyone going to eat?"

"Are you saying we're going to starve to death?" Ed asked, his voice steady and matter-of-fact, his brown eyes darting back and forth between Kyle and his wife.

Kyle wasn't sure how to read the look on Ed's face, but he could see that his own sense of urgency was having an effect. "I'm saying that things are going to get bad in a hurry. People are going to start panicking, if they haven't already. Anyone that knows anything about an EMP realizes how bad of a situation we're in, and everyone else will figure it out soon enough."

"So what do you recommend we do?" Ed asked. "Rob the grocery store?"

Kyle nodded. "I don't know what else we can do. What are we going to do in a week or two when we've eaten everything in your house? I'd gladly pay, but my wallet burned up in the airplane along with everything else I own. I don't think anyone will be at the store to take your credit card, but we can take it with us if it makes you feel better. If people haven't started looting yet, they will soon enough."

Ed rolled his eyes and let out a snort. "I bring you to my house, and now you try and get me to rob the supermarket? You're insane, Mr. Montana cowboy. We don't do that kind of thing in Texas. Maybe you do in Montana, but not here," he said, his voice rising as well. "I don't even know your last name, and you want me to go on a crime spree? You are out of your stinking mind!" Ed emphasized the last sentence.

"I don't do that either, thank you very much," Kyle said sharply. "I can't believe that I'm suggesting such a thing, and under normal circumstances, I can guarantee you I wouldn't. But these aren't normal circumstances, Ed. We should have parted company yesterday in Denver and never seen each other again. I just want to survive and figure out a way to get home. If you have some generous neighbor who'll provide for you, then you're good. But if not, then we need to figure something out."

Ed leaned forward, resting his face in his hands and rubbing his forehead. Kyle could hear him breathing heavily, but he wasn't saying anything.

"Ed," Virgie said softly as she reached out and rubbed his leg. "I think Kyle's right. I'm scared. If it's half as bad as he says, we won't make it a month. You know we don't cook much. We're going to be getting hungry in a few days, maybe a week, then what'll we do? I want to survive."

Deer Creek, Montana

Grace patted Jennifer on the knee. "Jennifer, I'm sure things will be alright. We don't know anything for sure." The two ladies had been sitting on the Anderson's couch for twenty minutes, ever since Chuck had answered the door and found his neighbor sobbing on their doorstep.

After finding Jennifer a box of Kleenex, Chuck had sat quietly in a chair on the other side of the room, ready to help if needed. "I'm sorry to be a bother," Jennifer managed to get out, wiping her eyes and pausing to blow her nose. "I just needed someone to talk to. I don't want to worry the kids any more than I already have, and I can't call anyone on the telephone."

"Jennifer," Grace reassured, "don't be silly. We're glad to be here for you." She took Jennifer's hand. "Everything's going to be fine."

Jennifer smiled weakly and squeezed Grace's hand.

"You said that the President had a speech on the radio," Chuck said. "Can you remember what it was he said?"

Jennifer nodded and pulled a crumpled piece of paper out of her pocket. "It was the Vice President. I took some notes." Jennifer smoothed out her notes and read them to Chuck. "He said that there was a nuclear missile, he called it an EMP, and that they don't know who did it. He said that power and phones for the country have been destroyed, and then he said that a lot of air-planes had crashed..." she trailed off again as fresh tears streaked down her cheeks.

Grace rubbed Jennifer's shoulders. "Let's not talk about it, Jennifer. You can worry about that later," she said as she shot her husband a dirty look.

Chuck shrugged his shoulders and mouthed "sorry" to his wife. "I'm sorry, Jennifer," he said. "I didn't mean to make things worse for you. Do you mind if I look at your notes?"

Jennifer shook her head and handed him the tear-stained paper. "My writing's messy," she mumbled.

Chuck took the paper from her and scanned it. ...4:08 P.M. EST...all North Amer...nuclear 300 miles up...destroyed elect system...EMP... comm...trans...planes crashed/dozens...30yrs prep...govt/ltd function...military protecting...months/years to fix...don't panic/obey laws...organize in communities...PRAY... more broadcasts.

Chuck handed the notes back to her. "Do you remember what radio station it was on?"

Jennifer shook her head. "I don't. It was an AM station. I'll check for you." She was forcing herself to breathe deeply in an attempt to calm down.

"Did he say that every airplane crashed?" Chuck asked, trying to sound hopeful.

"No, he said dozens that they knew of. Not sure how to take that,
but Kyle's flight had probably been in the air for close to an hour."

"Well, there are thousands of flights in the air all the time, so
odds are he made it. He's probably worrying about you as we speak
and likely tried to call, but the phones are down," Chuck said, his
tone still upbeat. "He'll be back before you know it, and until then,
you're welcome to come over here as much as you need to."

Katy, Texas

Ed wove in and out of cars on the street, seeing his neighborhood with new eyes. It hadn't changed physically since he'd driven
to the airport the day before. The sun shone, leaves fluttered in
a light breeze, and kids rode their bikes down the sidewalks or
played in their yards. The neighborhood hadn't changed, but the
perspective Ed saw it with had reset 180 degrees. He scanned the
faces of the people he saw, worried not only for them, but because
of them. How would things be in a day? A week? A month? He
wondered. Would those people survive? Would he? When they
got desperate, how would they act? Was he looking at someone
who would help him or someone who would hurt him?

"Kind of creeps me out a little bit," Ed stated, almost in a
whisper. "Notice how everybody stares at us as we drive by?"

"Yeah, I was thinking the same thing," said Kyle. "Probably wondering why your car's working and no one else can go anywhere."

"I was wondering that too. Why do you think that is?"

"I'm pretty sure it's because of how old your Jeep is, and partly
due to the fact it was parked on the bottom level of the garage at
the airport and had several layers of concrete above it. You said
it's what, a '78?"

Ed nodded.

"It wasn't until the mid eighties that everything in cars went computerized. Now everything is run by computer chips, and they are extremely sensitive to any kind of power surge. That's why, when you handle computer boards, you're supposed to wear rubber gloves or ground yourself, because even a simple static electric spark can ruin them. Your Jeep is all mechanical, no computer chips to cook."

"Guess it's a good thing I bought this. When I was a kid I always wanted a Jeep. Finally picked this one up about five years ago and have been working on it ever since. I was close to being done, but it doesn't look like I'll get there now."

Ed swung the Jeep into his driveway and pulled forward into the garage. Kyle jumped out and lowered the garage door as Virgie appeared in the doorway.

"Did you have any problems?" she asked Ed as he climbed out of the Jeep.

"No," he replied, shaking his head. "It was the perfect crime. We killed all the witnesses."

Kyle laughed uneasily, knowing how hesitant Ed had been about the whole affair. "It went okay, Virgie. Others were already there, but the store was still pretty full. We squeezed as much as we could into the Jeep, and Ed watched for police the whole way home. He was sure that even though the Jeep was about the only thing on the road, the police were going to pull up behind him and haul him off to jail. I don't think you need to worry about him turning to a life of crime."

Virgie didn't laugh at either of their attempts at humor.

CHAPTER NINE

Sunday, September 4th
Deer Creek, Montana

An unexpected knock at the door startled Jennifer. After an endless night with little rest, she'd awakened only a short while before. What little sleep she had managed to get had been filled with dreams of Kyle: dreams where his airplane fell out of the sky, dreams where he walked through the door as if nothing was wrong, dreams where he stood alone on the edge of a deserted highway. Whatever the dream, they all resulted in tears.

Jennifer cinched her robe and opened the front door, allowing the muted, gray sunlight to illuminate the entryway. The weather had turned stormy during the night, and the ground was covered with puddles from rain that had been falling for most of the morning. She swung the door open and found a man in a sheriff's uniform standing in front of her. He appeared to be in his early thirties with a similar build to Kyle's, but was maybe a couple of inches taller. His hair was short and dark, and he had brown eyes that were open wide and bored intently into hers. He smiled pleasantly as Jennifer greeted him.

"Can I help you?" Jennifer asked, pushing a loose strand of hair behind her ear. The fact that the man was wearing a uniform, along with the recollection that law enforcement had the duty to inform people when a family member died in an accident, made her heart skip two beats before assuming an accelerated rhythm with an intensity she'd never experienced. She glanced around to see if a minister had accompanied him.

"Hi, sorry to bother you," the officer began, an authoritative expression seemingly chiseled on his face. "My name is Doug Jarvis, Officer Doug Jarvis actually, and I'm here because of the situation that's occurred. Are you familiar with it?"

"That depends on if there is more than one situation," Jennifer replied, barely able to choke out the words, sure that he was preparing to tell her that Kyle was dead.

"The terrorist attack," Officer Jarvis said with an earnest look. "Have you heard the Vice President's message?"

"Yes. I heard it yesterday." Jennifer swallowed hard, her throat aching, tears percolating just below the surface. "What, in regards to the situation, are you here about?"

"Well," said Officer Jarvis, "the Vice President said that we need to work as communities to get through this. I thought it would be a good idea to get as many people together as we can, to come up with some ideas. I know it's quick, but I thought the sooner the better, before things get desperate."

Jennifer smiled weakly and let out a huge sigh of relief while gripping the door with both hands to steady herself. "Sounds like a good idea, officer."

Officer Jarvis seemed very enthusiastic. "Please, just call me Doug. I wore the uniform because I thought it might help people take me a little more seriously. You know, in case they hadn't heard about the situation."

Jennifer nodded. "Sounds like a good idea, Doug. What are your plans?"

"I thought we could meet this afternoon at 2:00, while there's still plenty of light. We'll meet at my house, just a few streets over." He gave Jennifer directions and a description of his house, then thanked her and headed in the direction of the Anderson's just as the light rain started up again.

Katy, Texas

Kyle and Ed worked in the garage packing the Jeep for their trip. The "looted food," as Ed described it, along with items Virgie had gathered from the house, was carefully boxed and loaded into the Jeep. The driver's seat was clear of any supplies, but every other inch of space that wasn't needed for Kyle and Virgie was packed tight with food and other essentials. Kyle was tying a gas can to the front bumper while Ed worked on stacking boxes in the backseat.

"Are you sure that's what you want to do?" Ed asked. "It seems like you're putting your life at risk."

Kyle's hand slipped from the rope he was tugging on and banged hard against the grill of the Jeep. "I'm positive," he said, shaking his hand to ease the pain. "You're the one who needs to decide if you want to do this for me. Besides, everyone's life is at risk right now, not just mine."

After returning from their run to Wal-Mart the day before, Kyle, Ed, and Virgie had spent the rest of the day discussing how they were going to survive. It had been a long, emotionally exhausting conversation, but before going to bed, they had decided on a plan and were now in the midst of carrying it out. Virgie and Ed's son had a large home on a couple of acres near San Angelo, an area that Ed thought would be safer than Katy. Kyle would ride with them to San Angelo, then start out for Montana from there.

After a night of packing, Kyle had spent the morning siphoning gasoline from cars that were stalled in the streets. He'd run into a couple of threatening neighbors, but the only real problems had involved spilled and swallowed gasoline. Kyle smelled of gasoline, his mouth tasted like a carburetor, and his head ached from inhaling the fumes, but he ignored it all, glad to finally be doing something that would get him closer to home.

"So, have you refined your plan any more?" Ed asked as he adjusted his seat to make more room behind it for another box of food. "Last night you were pretty vague."

Kyle shrugged. "Well, the goal's still the same. I'm just trying to figure out the best way to accomplish it. The drive today will tell me a lot."

"You could wait things out in Texas, you know, till things get working again." Ed jammed the last case of soup into the backseat. "The weather's warmer. It would be easier to survive."

"We talked about that last night," Kyle said, tying the last rope on the gas can. "Nothing's changed. I have a wife and three kids in Montana who probably think I'm dead and are looking at going through a winter without electricity or heat. What kind of man would I be if I waited it out safe and warm in Texas while they struggled up there." He thought a minute. "If I didn't make an attempt to get back, I don't know that I could face them when this is over."

Ed smiled understandingly. "I know, but what you're talking about is dangerous. It's more than fifteen hundred miles from San Angelo, and you don't know how you're going to do it. What good would it do them for you to die on the road?"

"What good would it do me to go home next summer and find my family dead?" Kyle replied coldly. "The pioneers did it. They walked to Oregon and to California without roads or real maps. The worst case is I walk if I can't come up with anything better."

Kyle handed Ed another case of food, and Ed worked it in behind his seat. "I'm not trying to talk you out of it. I would just hate to see you die."

"Is your Jeep going to be able to handle the weight?" asked Kyle, changing the subject. "It's already riding pretty low, and there are still three people to get in."

"We'll be fine," Ed said as he glanced at the suspension. "Besides, I can go as slow as I need to. I don't think I'll be holding any traffic up. They made these old things pretty sturdy, not like the plastic cars we're used to today."

The men finished loading the last few boxes and went back inside the house where Virgie was busy closing and securing windows.

"Did you talk to Maria or Carlos?" Ed asked.

Virgie nodded. "I just got home a few minutes ago. I gave them a key and they agreed to keep an eye on the house. I told them they could have the food we don't take."

"Did they say what they're planning on doing?"

"No, and they're pretty scared. They don't have a car that works, and Maria said they don't have much food. She didn't say anything about their family, so I don't know that they can go to anyone for help. I'm worried about them."

"Did you tell them to get to a grocery store?" asked Ed. "There was a lot of stuff there yesterday. Not sure how much might be left, but it would be something."

"I told them you had gone down there. Couldn't tell what they thought of the idea. I suppose they'll figure something out," Virgie said with little conviction in her voice.

Virgie stood in the middle of her kitchen, surveying her home and taking inventory of what she was leaving behind. She was preparing to leave most of her worldly possessions behind, and the emotions of the past day and a half caught up with her. It started with a few tears running down her cheeks, which she tried to hide from her husband, but soon heavy sobs shook her body, and she gave up wiping at her eyes. "I think this is too much for me to handle," she offered as an explanation.

Ed took Virgie in his arms and pulled her tight. "We're together, sweetie," he said as he patted her softly on the back. "We'll be alright. I promise."

"I'm scared, Ed," she said when she caught her breath. "I'm really scared. I'm not used to running from things. No hurricane's ever even scared us off."

Ed leaned forward and kissed her on the forehead. "I'm scared too," he said. "How could we not be? But at least we've got each other." He gave her another squeeze, then they held each other, not saying a thing.

Kyle turned silently and headed out to the garage to wait.

Deer Creek, Montana

David looked up as his mother opened the door and came in the house. She had a concerned look on her face, one that he usually only saw when he was in trouble at school. "How was the meeting?"

Jennifer glanced up as she took off her boots. "Well," she said, "we didn't accomplish much, but it was good to have it I suppose"

"Did you learn anything more about what's going on?"

"No, someone at the meeting said they figured it was terrorists, then they got all worked up about the government. That led to a big argument about politics, which was a waste of time. There's going to be another meeting on Wednesday, and we're supposed to inventory what we have for food, weapons, and a few other things. I wrote down a list of stuff. Then we'll try and come up with a plan to help each other survive through the winter."

"You say that so calmly – 'survive through the winter'. How bad do you think it's going to be?"

Jennifer tried to smile at her son, but she could feel her lips start to tremble so she looked away, hoping he wouldn't see the fear she felt. "I don't know, David. I don't think anyone does. That's what makes this all so difficult. But we'll make it."

"Mom, where do you think Dad is? You haven't said much since yesterday. We're going to need him."

Jennifer's stomach sank. She had avoided talking about Kyle and had tried to stay busy with the kids to keep Kyle off of all of their minds, but it hadn't worked. "Well, David," she started, choosing her words carefully. "We don't know where he is. He was supposed to leave Texas just before this thing happened, and now we don't have any phones, so I can't call him. I'm sure he's fine. He just isn't going to be home when we thought."

"Do you think he's dead? The guy on the radio said that airplanes crashed." David's voice cracked, and Jennifer turned to see that he was fighting to control his own emotions. Her son was so much like his dad, she thought. Not just in the physical sense, but also with his direct way of dealing with situations and not finding any value in trying to hint his way around things.

"I don't think he is," Jennifer said, reaching out for his hand. "I worry about it too, but we really don't know. The broadcast didn't say every plane crashed, just that there were reports of airplanes crashing. I choose to think that he's alive, and that he'll be home to help us as soon as he can. That's how we need to face this, so we've got to be sure and be here for him when he gets back, whenever that is. You understand?"

David smiled at his mom and nodded. A tear ran down his cheek, but he didn't wipe it away. "I miss Dad," he said, his voice quivering. "He's been gone for a long time already. I hope he gets back soon."

"I'm sure he wants to be here. He really loves you kids. He told me…," she caught herself and changed her wording. "He tells me that all of the time." Jennifer paused and looked at David until his eyes met hers. "You know, until he gets home, you're going to have to be the man of the house." She waited and let the statement sink in. "Am I going to be able to count on you?"

David nodded. "I'll do what I can." He thought a minute, then added with a half smile, "Does that mean I've got to get a job?"

Jennifer laughed. "No, not for the time being at least. But you never know what tomorrow might bring. Speaking of which, I told Mrs. Anderson that we would come over and help her with her garden in the morning. She thinks she can get some more things planted before the season's over."

David rolled his eyes and laughed as he wiped away his tears. "Farming me out already, huh. I hope you're getting good money for me."

Katy, Texas

Riding low and sluggish, Ed's Jeep backed down the driveway and onto the street, the suspension straining under the load. Kyle looked at Ed and raised his eyebrows.

"We'll be fine, Kyle. Your worrying isn't going to help us get there."

"I didn't say anything."

"But you were thinking it. Just sit back and relax. Enjoy the sights of Texas. You never know when you'll be back."

Kyle grinned and tried to resituate himself to find more comfort, but the boxes of food stacked around his feet made that difficult. "This should be interesting. I hope the freeways are passable."

Ed mumbled a reply, and Kyle could see Ed's knuckles go white as he gripped the steering wheel tighter. After a couple of turns they approached the intersection where the Wal-Mart they had visited the day before sat. Kyle turned towards the building as Ed slowed to make the turn onto the freeway on ramp.

"Think there's much food left?" Ed asked, glancing over his shoulder at the store.

Kyle peered at the building. "I don't think so. It looks like all the doors are wide open, but I don't see many people. I can see a couple of guys coming out, but it doesn't look like they are packing groceries. I think they're carrying a TV or something."

"A TV?" Virgie asked from the backseat.

"Yeah, it looks like a TV. Either the foods all gone or they don't understand the situation. Hope they don't have a long walk home."

"Maybe they know something we don't," Virgie volunteered. It was obvious from her tone she was questioning their decision to pack up and leave.

"Let's just do this, okay, Virgie?" Ed caught his wife's eyes in the rearview mirror. "I'm scared too, honey, but I think we're doing the right thing. If I'm wrong, we'll come back home as soon as we can. Is that a deal?"

Kyle heard Virgie agree as they accelerated onto the highway. A mass of cars filled the road, looking normal other than the fact they were frozen in place. Kyle let out a low whistle. "This looks worse in the daytime. You can really see the extent of the disaster."

"It's not any worse than the airport. At least there's no one being burned to death." Ed shifted gears and angled towards the center lanes where there were fewer cars. "This all had to happen on a long weekend at rush hour. Not that there'd ever be a good time for it, but there are sure a lot of vehicles."

"Watch out for that man up there!" Virgie yelled, pointing at a figure thirty yards in front of them, her voice on edge.

Ed slowed and steered the Jeep to the extreme left side of the roadway. The man waved his arms over his head, so Ed slowed even more.

Kyle rolled down his window and leaned towards the man. "Can we help you?" he asked as Ed drew to a stop.

The man wore denim shorts, a Rockets t-shirt and a faded Longhorns ball cap that was wet with sweat. His neck was sunburned and red, and he wiped the sweat from his face with the back of his hand. "Do you have any room in there? I'm trying to get home."

Ed motioned towards the boxes stacked to the roof in the backseat. "We're stacked full. I'm really sorry. Where are you headed?"

"Columbus. My wife's home with our two little girls. I need to get back home." He scanned Ed's Jeep. "Could I ride on the hood or something? It's going to take me all day to get home otherwise."

Ed bit his lower lip. "Alright, I'll give you a ride, but I'd rather you stood on the back bumper. It'd be too hard to see with you on the hood."

"Thank you so much," the man said, relief washing over his face. "You saved me a day of walking." He hurried to the back of the Jeep and climbed on, then tapped on the side window to indicate he was ready.

"Don't drive too fast," Virgie directed from the backseat. "He could fall."

Ed ignored the comment and shifted back into gear. They covered the 33 miles in just under an hour's time and let their rider off at the highway exit. Ed was watching him in the rearview mirror when Kyle spoke up.

"Heads up, Ed. There's another guy flagging us down."

Ed swore. "At this rate we're never going to make it. When do we quit stopping to help?"

"That's your call. I'm just along for the ride."

The man stood in the middle of the highway fifty yards in front of them, blocking the road and waving his arms over his head. "I've got a bad feeling, Kyle. Open the glove box and get my gun out. Hurry!"

"What was that?"

"I said get my damn gun out of the glove box." Ed came to a stop about ten feet in front of the man and leaned out his window. Kyle opened the glove box and grabbed the handgun. His heart was pounding, and he could hear Virgie breathing hard in the backseat. "What can I do for you?" Ed called to the man.

"I need some help. My girlfriend's over there in our car, and it isn't working. We need a ride." Kyle glanced in the direction the man indicated and saw a large, blonde woman emerge from a beat up Ford wagon.

"I'm sorry, but we're too full. There's a town back there. Maybe someone there could help you."

The man shook his head. "We need a ride." He moved alongside the Jeep.

"I said I'm sorry," Ed continued, "but we're too full." Kyle pressed the gun against his leg, keeping it out of sight. Ed eased off the clutch and began to inch forward.

The man grabbed hold of Ed's door. "I said stop!" he shouted as he pulled a gun from the waistband at the back of his pants.

Ed stopped the Jeep. "Don't do anything crazy, alright?"

"Or what? Cops going to arrest me? I'm tired of asking. Everyone just ignores you. Now I'm telling. Get out of the car!"

With the gun tucked under his leg, Kyle held his hands up. "Don't shoot anyone, okay? I'm going to get out. I don't want anyone hurt." He opened the door and started to climb out, concealing the gun as he did so.

The man's attention was on Ed. "See old man. It's not so tough. Turn off the car and get out."

Ed turned the Jeep off and opened his door while Kyle helped Virgie from the backseat, all of them watching the man intently.

"Ashley! Get in!" the man shouted.

Kyle watched the man's girlfriend lumber around to the passenger side of the Jeep.

Ed stepped away from the Jeep and looked at Kyle. Kyle barely nodded and watched the man tuck his gun in the back of his pants before climbing into the driver's seat. Ed came towards Kyle.

"Hey, I need the keys! You think I'm stupid?" came a voice from the Jeep.

Kyle swung the gun up and ran to the window. "Keep your hands on the steering wheel and lean forward!" he ordered. "We're taking the Jeep back."

The man seemed to weigh something in his mind, then closed his eyes and leaned forward. Kyle grabbed the man's gun and handed it to Ed. "Now get out of the Jeep!"

The two groups switched places in less than a minute. As soon as the passenger door closed, Ed punched the gas and the

Jeep lurched forward. "Just so you know, we're not stopping anymore. Kyle, keep my gun in your lap and check the other one to see if it's loaded. If anyone else tries to flag us down stick a gun out the window and make sure they see it. Our next stop is San Angelo."

Kyle and Virgie nodded mutely in agreement.

Seven hours later, with daylight rapidly draining from the sky, Ed's Jeep slowed as it approached an older, one-story house on the western outskirts of San Angelo. The vehicle smelled of antifreeze and made strange noises as Ed downshifted. "We made it," Ed announced, beads of sweat rolling down his forehead.

"I guess I can let my breath out now." Kyle's shirt was soaked in sweat and stuck to his chest. He pulled it away from his skin to let the air circulate. "And I guess that means we can turn the heater off now."

"At least it got us here, and that's all that matters. Thank heavens we had water and an extra gallon of Prestone."

Kyle nodded. "Hopefully we didn't do any permanent damage to the engine. What's the temperature gauge reading?"

"Just below the H. Once we got over that last hill, it started to drop again. It'll cool down once I get it shut off."

They turned into a driveway lined with two-dozen tall trees, their branches arching across the driveway to create a thick canopy. The headlights illuminated a collection of children's toys and bicycles scattered around a well-maintained front yard, as well a red pickup and an old lawnmower parked under a carport. Coming to a stop, they climbed out of the Jeep, and Kyle heard a screen door swing open, followed by the shouts of young children. A small girl, about six years old and dressed in a pink flowered sundress, came running towards them, followed closely by her younger brother, dressed only a pair of light colored shorts. Their shouts of "Grandma!" and "Grandpa!" filled the air as they danced excitedly next to the new arrivals. Not far behind the kids followed a tall, skinny man who appeared to be in his early thirties. His clothes, a blue Nike t-shirt that was faded and stained and an old pair of cut-offs, reinforced his surprised expression. He threw his arms around Ed and Virgie and gave them a long hug, squeezing his parents tightly and kissing Virgie on the cheek. He released them and stood beside his father, the resemblance between the two men, even in the dim light, obvious to Kyle.

Ed was the first to speak. "It's good to see you, son. How's your family doing?"

"We're doing pretty good, all things considered," he replied. "It's such a relief to see you."

"Son, I want you to meet Kyle Tait," Ed said, motioning for Kyle, who was still standing by the Jeep, to come over. "Kyle saved my life on Friday. Kyle, this is my son, Donovan Davis."

Kyle and Donovan shook hands. "And these two little munchkins," Ed said, reaching down to tickle the kids who were hanging on his legs, "are Cheyenne and Logan. But they're trouble, so you'd better watch out for them." Ed grabbed his grandkids and wrestled them down onto the grass, causing them to laugh wildly and scream for help.

The three adults watched Ed wrestle with his grandkids for a moment, then Donovan turned to Kyle. "Sounds like there's a story to how you met my dad."

Kyle pursed his lips and nodded slowly. "Yeah, I can't say it was under the best of circumstances, but we're both here, so that's what counts."

As the men unloaded the contents of the Jeep, Kyle gave Donovan a quick rundown of the events of the past two days. When the Jeep was empty, they gathered in the kitchen and assessed the stacks of food. "Doesn't look like much, does it?" said Ed, a note of disappointment in his voice.

"Well, it's more than we had an hour ago," responded Donovan, sounding genuinely happy. "We've got a fair bit plus a couple of fruit trees out back, so we'll make things work. Don't worry about it. I'm just so glad you and Mom are here."

"Where's Wendy?" Virgie asked from the living room. "Is she stuck somewhere?"

"No. She's working at the hospital. She was there Friday when the thing happened; she had me worried to death because she stayed there Friday night and didn't get home until last night. She rode a bike back in this morning and doesn't think she'll be back home until sometime tomorrow. I guess a lot of people didn't come in to work on Saturday, and there are a lot of folks showing up who need help. It's a pretty bad situation."

"Do they have power?" Virgie asked.

"Wendy said they have generators and enough fuel to run them for about a week. After that, they're in trouble. She said that even with the generators, most of their equipment wasn't working. No one can figure out what's going on."

They settled in the living room and continued their conversation. "So how was your drive out here?" Donovan asked.

Virgie shuddered at the question, and even in the flickering candlelight, Kyle could see her tear up.

"It was real bad, son," Ed replied. "I guess I didn't know what to expect when we left, but there's nothing that can prepare a person for what we saw. The road was covered with stalled cars, and people, sometimes entire families with little kids, were walking down the side of the road like third world refugees. We gave away half our water in the first hundred miles before we decided we couldn't help anybody else. I think your mother rode most of the way here with her eyes closed. She couldn't bear to look at the people we were driving past. I know I'm going to have nightmares about that for the rest of my life."

"Then the Jeep started overheating," Virgie added. "The last three hours we've been nursing it along. I was sure we weren't going to make it, but your dad pulled off a miracle."

They spent the next few hours sharing more details of the past two days and discussing plans for the next few while a single, flickering candle kept the darkness at bay, both in a literal and a figurative sense. Kyle noticed relief in Ed and a significant upswing in Virgie's mood since their arrival. For all of them, it felt as if some small victory had been achieved. And while they knew there would be plenty of struggles ahead, they savored the sweetness of that feeling late into the night.

CHAPTER TEN

Monday, September 5th
San Angelo, Texas

Images of Jennifer and the children again came to Kyle in his dreams. Some were of good times spent together; in others, all of his worst fears played out. When morning finally came, Kyle woke up poorly rested, but with a renewed determination to make it home to his family.

After a hearty breakfast celebrating the Davis family's reunion, the four adults sat around the table avoiding difficult subjects. Kyle was the first to broach the topic they'd dodged all morning. "Donovan, thanks again for the breakfast. I haven't eaten that well since I left Montana... and speaking of which," Kyle smiled, putting on a brave face, "I'm going to start for home in the morning."

Ed looked down at his feet. "Kyle, I was thinking about your plans, or lack thereof, last night. Let me try and drive you home. I can have you there in a week."

"Ed," Kyle watched and waited until Ed looked up. "I can't let you do that. We barely made it here."

"But you saved my..." Ed began to protest before Kyle cut him off.

"Ed, please. I've thought long and hard about that. It's too dangerous."

"How is it dangerous?" Ed asked.

"Besides the obvious, tell me you weren't scared to death yesterday every time we drove past someone walking down the road."

Ed half shrugged. "It's just the whole situation. The world's been flipped on its head."

"I know. Yesterday was barely 48 hours since the event, and we were scared then. The longer this goes, the more desperate people are going to get. You think someone won't try and kill you, or us, for your Jeep?"

"We'll take a gun – for protection."

"How many people are you willing to kill to keep your Jeep? Besides, I know you've put a lot of work into it, but your Jeep's old. What if we break down, or can't get gas, or wreck, or have a flat tire or two. We don't even know if we can get what we need to fix it now. There won't be any mechanics or tow trucks to help us out."

Ed was fighting to find a rebuttal to Kyle's arguments, but Kyle pressed on. "You don't know how much I'd like it to work, but I don't think it will. It's too big a risk to have you take me."

Donovan had been listening in silence and spoke up when Kyle paused. "So you're just going to walk?"

Kyle nodded. "I've got a pack from the store. I think it's the best option."

"You'll never be able to carry enough supplies, Kyle. Just carrying the water you'll need to get through Texas will kill you."

"It's the only option I've got, unless you've got a second vehicle I can take. I'm in decent shape, and I can refill my water jug at the rivers."

"This isn't Montana, Kyle. A lot of our rivers are dry in the summertime. You'll die before you get out of the state."

"Well that's a risk I'm going to have to take. I'd rather die on the road than go crazy doing nothing."

Virgie reached out and squeezed Kyle's arm. "Kyle, we can't just let you walk off and die. Surely we can come up with a plan that will get you there in one piece. Donovan, don't you have a suitcase with wheels or something?" She looked from her son to her husband and then back to her son again, her eyes pleading.

Donovan thought for a minute, then smiled, his eyes lighting up. "Mom, you've given me an idea. I'm not sure if it'll work, but it can't hurt to try. Let's go for a drive first. If we can find you something to ride, I think we can build something that'll improve your odds of making it home alive. How important is it for you to leave tomorrow?"

"I'd prefer that, but an extra day probably isn't going to kill me."

***

Donovan pointed out an old brick building on the opposite side of the road, and Ed eased the jeep across the street, pulling to a stop in front of it.

"Dad, why don't you wait out here and guard the jeep. I'll go in with Kyle and talk to the owner."

Kyle noticed the business name stenciled on the glass front door: Texas Two-Wheelers. He guessed the name had also been on the large, plate glass windows on the front of the building, but now the window was in shards and scattered all over the sidewalk.

"I don't think we're the first ones here," Kyle said as Donovan pushed the front door open.

Donovan shook his head. "Doesn't look like it, does it." He stopped in the doorway and looked around the store. A handful of bikes were piled at the back of the store and chained to a steel post. "Anyone here?" Donovan called out.

They waited and listened, then heard movement from the back room. "Hello!" Kyle called as he wandered around the damaged and empty display racks. Something caught his eye and he turned towards Donovan, noticing a red dot on Donovan's forehead. "Raise your hands over your head right now!" Kyle ordered as he lifted his own arms in the air.

Donovan looked quizzically at Kyle, but did as he was told.

"We're not here to steal anything. We just came to talk to you about a bicycle!" Kyle shouted as his eyes darted from the dot on Donovan's face to an open door leading to the back of the store. Kyle held his breath as the dot slowly descended down Donovan's front and hit the floor.

"What are you looking for?" a voice called from through the doorway. "Obviously I'm not open for business."

Kyle heard footsteps, and an older man of about fifty years emerged from the doorway holding a tan AR15 that was loaded with lasers, night scopes, and flashlights, and looked like it weighed more than the slender man carrying it. The man's eyes darted between Kyle and Donovan, and his finger hovered over the trigger, ready to fire at the smallest provocation.

"Pardon the weapon, but you can see business hasn't been the best the last couple of days." He stayed on the far side of the shop, his back to the wall, fidgeting nervously with the strap around his neck.

"I'm guessing that has something to do with the window?" Donovan asked as he lowered his hands.

The man nodded, his head bouncing quickly. "Shot a kid yesterday. There was a group of them broke out the window about four in the morning. Shot at them as they were riding away and hit one of them. I expect they'll be back at some point. Why are you here?"

"I'm trying to get home, and a good bicycle would help."

"Where's home?" The man assessed Kyle as he asked the question. "And when's the last time you rode a bike?"

"Western Montana, and I haven't ridden since high school, closing in on twenty years now."

The man let out a squawk. "Why don't I just shoot you now and save you the trouble. It will save you dying a painful death in the middle of nowhere."

"You don't think I can make it?"

"No thinking required, pal. Unless you're Lance Armstrong, I know you can't make it. What's the furthest you've ever ridden?"

"I don't know. Maybe ten miles."

"As a high school kid, right?"

Kyle nodded.

"I get dreamers like you all the time. It's usually men who hit forty and need to prove they're as fit as they were at twenty. They've been sitting behind a desk for fifteen years, decide to ride to California, usually, and they come in and buy the most expensive bike I sell, train for two weeks, and then give the dream up before they leave the city limits. One poor guy actually made it to Colorado on his way to Alaska before a car hit him and paralyzed him from the waist down."

"How much for a bike?" Kyle wasn't willing to give up on being home before October.

"Everything I sold went for between fifteen hundred and four thousand dollars. I just have high-end stuff, but you're wasting your time here. I'm not sure what I'm asking now, but it would be suicide for you to attempt it. Trust me."

Kyle slowly pulled out the handgun they'd acquired on the highway in Texas and held it up with two fingers. "Do you have anything you'd give me for this? We don't have any ammo for it, but the gun works."

The man's shoulders sagged. "You said you're trying to get home to your family?"

Kyle nodded.

"I admire your heart, but you need to get real. I used to race professionally, and my sponsor did this promo to have our team ride across the country. There were four of us, and we had all raced in Europe. Two on the team had even made the US Olympic team. We'd all ridden for years, had a van loaded with equipment that trailed us, stayed in motels, were monitored by doctors and dieticians, and bought supplies along the way. Even with that, only two guys made it, and that was with cheating a little through Nevada. I made it to Missouri before my right knee swelled up so big I had to give it up. But that was better than the other guy who dropped out. He got an infection in his crotch that almost made him sterile. I'm sorry, but you're too old, too weak, and too inexperienced."

"What do you suggest then."

"Walk. It aint glamorous, but humans are designed for it. You've been training your whole life, and you can carry a whole lot more walking than you can on a bicycle."

Donovan cleared his throat. "I was thinking we could possibly build a cart for him, to haul stuff in. Do you have anything that would help us with that?"

The bike shop owner thought for a minute. "Just wait here," he said before disappearing into the back room.

"I'm sorry," Donovan said, giving Kyle a consoling smile. "I guess you were right about walking. Hope you're not too disappointed."

Kyle shook his head. "No. It was nice to think about getting home that quick, but I didn't have a good feeling about it."

"What do you think?" the man said, offering two bicycle wheels. "I was servicing a trade-in bike in the back. The tires are solid and have really good hubs that might actually last as far as you're going. I'd be willing to trade them for your handgun and some food, if you have any."

"We do. Let me get it," Donovan said, then exited the store to retrieve the case of food they'd brought just in case. He returned in a hurry carrying the food, just as the jeep started up. "Here you go. But I think your friends from yesterday might be on their way back. There's a group of people coming down the street."

The man handed the two wheels to Kyle and shoved the handgun in the front of his pants. "Good luck with your trip. Y'all better get out of here. No sense in you getting mixed up in my business."

"Thank you," Kyle said as he hurried from the shop right on Donovan's heels.

They jumped into the Jeep, and Ed threw it into gear, chirping the wheels as he pulled away from the curb.

Kyle's head swiveled at the sound of gunshots behind him. Through the back window, he saw the shop owner standing outside his store, barrel pointed in the air as he shouted at the approaching youths.

Tuesday, September 6th
Boston, Massachusetts

Senator Christine George lay on the floor outside the men's room of the eighteenth floor common area. She was sure her right leg was broken. It was discolored and swollen, and every time she attempted to stand up, the pain was so intense that she nearly blacked out, making it impossible to do anything other than slide along the ground.

Two and a half days of lying in helpless solitude had followed Christine's failed attempt to escape the high-rise perch from which she'd watched the chaos unfold below her days earlier. Early Saturday morning the streets had appeared safer and mostly clear, and so, still tired and sleepy after a fitful night on the reception area couch, she'd attempted to exit down the unlit emergency stairway.

After descending twenty floors using the light from her cell phone, it had finally faded to black, and her heel had caught on a step and sent her careening head over heels down the stairs in the inky black darkness. She'd only fallen a single flight, but blind in the darkness, it had seemed like she'd tumbled all the way to the parking garage. As she lay on her back, winded, hurt, and groping for support, a deep burning sensation just above her right knee had impressed itself on her mind, to the exclusion of all her other injuries. She'd probed the area with her fingers and found, to her horror, an unfamiliar angle to the bone and shooting pains with every hint of movement.

It had taken her five hours filled with pain so intense she almost lost consciousness to get down to the next landing and the door to the 18th floor. By late Saturday afternoon, she was in too much pain to use a toilet and had soiled herself as she lay in the hallway fighting back tears, mortified, but confident then that no one would know what the always perfectly-coifed politician had been reduced to. A fever had set in sometime Monday, and now she noticed red streaks shooting out from the dark bruises around her knee.

As she lay on the floor, reeking of urine and feces and reduced to drinking water out of the toilets, Christine thought long and deeply about her own mortality. Before her fall Saturday morning, she hadn't thought much about dying, but she was thinking about it now, and this certainly wasn't how she had hoped it would be. She would have liked to die in her own bed, surrounded by family and friends, certainly not crippled, helpless, and alone on the floor outside a public bathroom. She knew, however, that even under normal circumstances, her chances of dying so comfortably and so beloved were small. Her husband was fifteen years her senior, and her only child, whose visits home rarely seemed to fit into his busy San Francisco schedule, had no plans to give her any grandchildren. And if the people she represented paid their respects, they certainly wouldn't mourn her passing.

Christine had resigned herself to the fact that there would be no rescue and no grand funeral. Twice on Sunday she'd heard people going down the stairs and had even managed to get the attention of one of them, but that was more than forty-eight hours ago, and the frightened Asian cleaning lady who had heard her cries, but whose English consisted of only a dozen words, was an unlikely candidate for heading up a rescue effort. Now Christine just wished she could write a note, to leave some kind of farewell, but she couldn't even do that since her purse was up one flight of stairs and impossible to retrieve in her condition.

She wondered how long it would be until the end came and how long until someone found her body? Would they know who she was and that she had powerful friends and a burial plot already paid for? Her emotions tapped out, Senator Christine George, sixteen-year senator and chairman of the Senate Intelligence Committee, lay her head on the floor and waited to die.

San Angelo, Texas

With dinner over, Kyle and the Davis family sat in the living room, their conversation uncomfortable and forced. Kyle was on the floor with the items he planned to take on his trip piled in front of him. As he inspected the meager stacks, he wondered if he was making the right decision but didn't have a better plan and was much too anxious to delay his departure any longer.

After the trip to the bicycle shop, the decision had been made to go with Donovan's idea, which was to construct a cart that Kyle could pull behind him, much like pioneers had done a century and a half before. Using Donovan's half-stocked work-shop, the men had worked all day Monday and until just past noon on Tuesday, mustering enough wood, nails and screws to cobble together the cart. Logan and Cheyenne had made the ultimate sacrifice, having donated the wooden ladder from their swing-set to be used for the arms that extended forward for the cart's handle. The finished cart had a bed approximately four feet by three and a half feet, with three sixteen-inch tall sides and a back that was twenty-four inches high, giving Kyle a comfortably sized wooden box for his supplies. The two wheels from the bike shop had been attached to the sides, and the side pieces from the playground ladder were secured to the box, extending four feet beyond the front of the cart with a shovel handle attached between them, leaving a small space for Kyle to walk in while pulling the cart.

When they had finished, Kyle had been both relieved and embarrassed by their efforts – relieved that the cart worked and was sturdy enough to carry far more weight than he himself could carry, but embarrassed by the crudeness of the construction, a result of using simple handsaws, screwdrivers, hammers and nails.

Worried that he would forget something important, Kyle once again inventoried the items in front of him, most of which he had taken from the Wal-Mart on Saturday, but the list remained the same: four changes of clothing, unopened bags of underwear and socks, a new pair of hiking boots, a blue back-pack, a case of water, three boxes of food, a sleeping bag, a thin jacket and a sweatshirt, a hunting knife, a .22 Marlin rifle, and two boxes of bulk ammunition. Donovan had also contributed several items to the pile: a small tent, a frying pan, a hatchet, matches, a leather canteen, a first aid kit, a half-full can of mos-quito spray, an old pair of tennis shoes, an extra blanket, and a dozen trash bags.

"Doesn't look like much for such a long trip, does it?" Ed said, summing up Kyle's thoughts succinctly.

Kyle shook his head. "No, but I'm not sure what the right amount is. The more I add, the slower I'll go."

Virgie put her hand on Ed's knee. "I still think we should have tried to find a horse, like I suggested, to save poor Kyle from so much walking."

"Who's going to give up a horse right now? Besides, he'd need a camel to get through the northern part of the state this time of year. This isn't a great option, but it's the best one he has under the circumstances, honey."

"My heart's breaking for you, Kyle. You've got me scared to death."

"I'll be fine, Virgie, and I appreciate the concern."

"Are you sure that peashooter is going to be enough?" Donovan asked. "I have a real rifle, if you want to take it."

Kyle laughed. "I think I'll be good. I won't be hunting big game, just rabbits and raccoons, maybe an armadillo or two. Besides, I've got a thousand rounds of ammunition for this little .22, which should give me more than enough opportunity to get some food."

"But what about for protection?"

"I'll just be careful and avoid dangerous situations as much as I can, besides, the more armed I appear, the more likely someone will shoot first and ask questions later. I know things are bad, but I'm not planning to shoot any big game, or any people for that matter, so the .22 should do. Besides, the six of you need more protection than I do, don't you?"

Donovan looked uneasy. "I suppose. I guess I just still think you're crazy to try and walk. The offer to stay here still stands," he said, shaking his head slowly.

"I know, and I appreciate that," said Kyle, "but I'd go insane sitting here even one more day. These past four have been hard enough. At this point, I'd much rather die trying."

Wednesday, September 7th
San Angelo, Texas

The sun glowed a bright orange on the eastern horizon, and a hint of the early morning coolness still hung in the air as Kyle made the final adjustments to his load.

Ed, Virgie, Donovan and Wendy watched Kyle, not knowing what to say.

"You ready for this?" Ed asked finally.

"Ready as I'm ever going to be," replied Kyle. "I certainly wouldn't be this ready if it wasn't for all of you."

"You saved my life; it's the least we could do. Sending you off on foot sure doesn't seem very gracious though. I wish I could drive you home."

Virgie stepped forward and wrapped her arms around Kyle. "Once we get through this, you'd better come back with your family to visit," she said. "We need to tell them what kind of a hero you are."

Donovan extended his hand. "It was great getting to know you. Thanks for helping my dad, Kyle. Good luck with your trip."

"Thanks. Don't forget, I owe you a bike, and Cheyenne and Logan a ladder. Please be sure and thank them again for me." Kyle shifted his weight from foot to foot, the fear of heading into the unknown resting heavily on his mind. "Guess I'd better get on my way, before I chicken out."

Kyle stepped behind the handle of the cart, picked it up, and started to walk down the driveway, his pace slow. "I feel like I'm pulling a rickshaw," he joked. "Anyone want a ride?"

The four Davises laughed. "I don't think I trust the cart," said Ed. "I know who put it together."

Kyle laughed and waved. "Wish me luck," he called over his shoulder as he approached the front street.

Virgie dabbed at her eyes. "I'll be praying for you, Kyle," she called out. "Please watch out for yourself!"

"Good luck, Kyle!" Ed shouted, his voice breaking with emotion. "Be careful and Godspeed."

Kyle gave a half-hearted smile as he once again said goodbye, then turned onto the road and headed off. He forced himself not to look back. They had been through a lot over the past few days, and Ed and Virgie had come to feel like family. Walking off into the heart of an America he was no longer sure he knew was more difficult than Kyle had expected it to be.

To keep his mind off of his emotions, Kyle forced himself to think about the task at hand. Twenty-five miles a day was his goal, at least to start, and three miles an hour was the pace he was striving for. That meant eight to nine hours of walking, not including breaks, meals, and sitting out the hottest part of the afternoon, if needed. If he could cover twenty-five miles on the good days, and fifteen to twenty on the tough ones, Kyle estimated he would be back home before Thanksgiving.

What he was confronted with still didn't seem real. A week ago he was scheduled to make the trip in a few hours with minimal effort, the only concerns being making his connection and finding the right souvenirs for his kids. Now he was setting out on a trek in excess of fifteen hundred miles, pulling a homemade cart in which, he hoped, he was carrying all the items he needed to survive. He was stepping into the unknown: no guaranteed shelter, no guaranteed food, and no one who would know where or how he was.

Kyle approached the first corner and turned back to take one final look at his friends. Ed and Donovan stood in the street watching him. Kyle raised an arm over his head and waved in a long sweeping motion. Ed and Donovan returned the gesture, and he could faintly make out their shouts of encouragement over the breeze blowing through the trees.

His throat tightened, and he closed his eyes, then turned back to face the road. He glanced at the map Donovan had drawn showing the quickest way to the highway while avoiding the city, a detour that had been planned after Wendy had come home Tuesday afternoon with frightening tales about the chaos at work.

The situation at the hospital had been reasonably calm through Sunday, but on Monday, safety and order had rapidly deteriorated. A gang fight early Monday morning had resulted in a number of wounded people, accompanied by friends with weapons, demanding treatment and threatening the staff and other patients. Without police or any viable security, the staff, which was short-handed to begin with, had started to walk off the job, one after another. To compound the hospital's troubles, their supply of drugs had been robbed, the generator powering the hospital had only enough fuel for maybe another four days, and the condition of their patients was becoming more desperate by the minute. Finally, after a nurse had been shot and killed during a brawl in the emergency room, the hospital director had called the staff together and ordered them all to go home.

Wendy had resisted, but without any hope for power, medication, or food, and no guarantee of safety, she had come to realize she would only be postponing the inevitable while risking her own life. The hospital staff had been encouraged to help where they could in their own neighborhoods, then they quietly exited through a service entrance. Wendy knew that some of the staff who had no families to go home to had ignored the order and stayed, but she had ridden her bike home in tears, struggling to come to grips with abandoning her patients and knowing that most wouldn't make it, but seeing no way to change the outcome.

The city of San Angelo lay to the east, and Kyle could see a large column of smoke rising from a warehouse that was on fire and burning furiously. He took a long look at the city and wondered if he would ever make it back to visit the Davises and, if he did, how different things would be.

CHAPTER ELEVEN

Wednesday, September 7th
Deer Creek, Montana

Jennifer sat on a hard wooden kitchen chair pushed up against a wall in Doug Jarvis's unfinished basement. It was apparent to Jennifer that Doug wasn't in the habit of hosting large groups as the seating was an eclectic mix of kitchen chairs, a rolling office chair, mismatched metal folding chairs, and a half dozen cheap, green, plastic patio chairs. Regardless of the improvised nature of the furnishings, after days of anxiety it was a relief that things were being done to organize the community.

The previous meeting, with no strong voice to direct it, had gotten out of hand, and Jennifer hoped this one would go better. At the last meeting, people had barely had twenty-four hours to digest the fact that their lives had been irreversibly upended, and rationally discussing how to spend the next several months had been too much for many. Most people had still been trying to wrap their mind around the fact that there would be no more trips to the grocery store, no more daily work routines, no more turning on the TV or surfing the web or contacting your family. It was now five days removed from what was being referred to as "the event," and Jennifer hoped that people would be able to be more reasonable.

For her part, the adjustments were ongoing and far from over. With simple things she was managing adequately, although she still found herself flipping the light switches when the sun went down, fighting the urge to check for emails, reaching for the phone when she thought about her mother, and going to the fridge for food. On an emotional level though, Jennifer had a long way to go. She thought about Kyle on an hourly basis, sometimes more often than that if there was nothing to keep her busy. The two weeks that he had been gone prior to "the event" had been much easier, and she remembered, with some guilt, that he'd only crossed her mind occasionally during those days. Now, knowing that he should be home and wasn't, and that she had no idea where or how he was, thoughts of Kyle were never far removed.

Jennifer watched people filter into the meeting and wondered what situations they were dealing with. Who else might be missing a spouse? Who had kids away at college? Who needed medical care? The questions were endless. She tried to read people's expressions, but most wore masks that revealed little beyond the fact that they were scared. As she surveyed the room, Jennifer recognized a few people from her street and some from school events, but most in attendance would have been complete strangers had it not been for the meeting three days prior.

An older woman walked over and sat down beside Jennifer just as Doug, dressed in his uniform, stood up in front of the group of about sixty people. "I want to thank you all for coming this afternoon," he began. "I realize the circumstances we are in are less than ideal, but I really think if we work together we can make it through this. For those who weren't able to hear the President's broadcast today, he warned that rioting had broken out in a number of cities and he encouraged us to be calm, but also to prepare to protect ourselves. He said the government wouldn't be deploying the military domestically because of threats that require him to keep the troops where they are and that we need local law enforcement to fill the vacuum."

Doug looked around the room, his confidence seeming to grow. "Just so you know, folks, as a member of the Sheriff's Department, I can tell you that we won't have official law enforcement out here, at least not anything organized by the county. The county is too big, and the department is just too small, so this is going to be up to us. The President didn't say much else, just some more patriotic crap, if you'll excuse the expression. I just find it frustrating because we're not going to learn anything the government doesn't want us to know. Someone could nuke New York City tomorrow, and we wouldn't know about it unless the President decided to say something. Anyway, on that happy note, we need to get some things figured out. I propose that we get some kind of council going so we can get organized and use the skills of the people in the community to help each other. Does anyone disagree or have a better idea?"

He looked around the room and saw most people shaking their heads. "Okay, that was easy. I guess we'll need to start with a chairman. Who would be interested in that position? And just so you know, I'd like to be the director of security, not the head of the council, so I'm hoping someone else will volunteer for that job."

Jennifer looked around the room and saw a few hands go up. "Good," said Doug. "If we could get you to come up and introduce yourselves and give us your background, then we'll have a vote."

Four men and one woman made their way to the front of the room and took turns telling about themselves. After the impromptu campaign speeches, the candidates and their spouses were asked to leave the room. Jennifer's options included a junior high school vice principal, a self-employed plumber, an attorney, an architect, and a county inspector. With the candidates out of the room, those left behind debated the merits of each person. The plumber's neighbor stood up and went on and on about his neighbor's virtues, swinging Jennifer's vote in his direction, and when the voting was complete, the results showed the plumber winning with the architect a close second.

Doug invited the individuals back downstairs and announced the results. Gabe Vance, the plumber, stood in front of the group. "I appreciate your trust," he said. "I'll try not to make you regret it. If it's all right with you, I'd like to have Cheryl be the vice chairman, or second in charge, whatever we want to call it. She had the second most votes and seems like an exceptional lady. Is anyone opposed to that?" He looked around and, seeing no one dissenting, continued. "Thank you. Now we're going to need more people than just Cheryl and me to make this work." Almost like magic, Gabe took control of the room, exhibiting a confidence and warmth that engaged everyone in attendance. "Is there anyone who is organized and experienced with taking notes that could help us out?"

Without thinking, Jennifer raised her hand, followed by two others. Gabe pointed to Jennifer. "I would sure appreciate your assistance. Would you be willing to do that, miss?"

Jennifer looked back at Gabe, wishing she hadn't been so impulsive and wanting to say no. She didn't like to speak out, had three kids and no husband at home, and just wanted to be told what to do to survive. "Sure," she heard herself say. "If you need the help, I can do it."

Gabe nodded. "We're going to need everyone's help. I see you've already got a notepad. That's great. Why don't you come sit up here so you can hear everyone better for taking notes."

Jennifer stood slowly and walked to the front. She wasn't sure why she'd volunteered. Maybe it was that Gabe had a certain confidence she was drawn to, and he reminded her of her father with his folksy charm. Gabe was older, probably late fifties, with short, dark, gray-streaked hair, and was one of the few men who was still cleanly shaven. He was a little on the heavy side, and his cheeks sagged a little, but his face radiated a confidence and wisdom that put her at ease. Gabe grabbed the plastic lawn chair he'd been sitting in and set it at the front of the room for Jennifer.

"Thank you, Ms…?"

"Tait. Jennifer Tait."

"Thank you, Ms. Tait. If you could write some things down, that would be helpful." He turned back to the group. "We'll need some form of law enforcement, as was mentioned earlier. Doug's been great with things so far. Is anyone opposed to him leading out in that area?" Again, people shook their heads. "That's good. I was also thinking we'll need a person with some medical experience for our team. Do we have any doctors here?"

Everyone turned to survey the room, hoping for a hand to go up, but none did. After a few seconds of silence, a woman near the back of the room stood. "I'm a veterinarian," she said, looking around. "I realize we'd all prefer a regular doctor, but I do have a fair bit of the same background and training."

"Well, a vet beats a plumber," said Gabe smiling. "I think you'd be of great service. Are there any objections?"

A few whispers rippled through the room, but no one voiced any concerns. "Looks like you're hired. What's your name?"

"Carol Jeffries."

"Welcome, Carol."

In like manner a gardening expert, an education coordinator, and a sanitation director were selected. "I think we've enough people on the council, at least for the time being," said Gabe. "I'd like to meet with the council tomorrow, but for the rest of the time today, I wondered if the rest of you would let us know what kinds of issues you see that we can work together to resolve. And please remember, we're pretty limited in our resources, so we'll only have each other to rely on."

A number of hands were raised in the air, and Gabe pointed to people while Jennifer took notes. "I have no clean water." "My kids are missing out on their education." "Our family is almost out of food." "My child was in Seattle visiting his dad for the long weekend, how do I get him back?" Jennifer wrote furiously to record all of the issues. "My toilet doesn't work." "Someone is stealing fruit from my trees." Jennifer heard an older woman's voice and looked up to see the lady she had been sitting next to speaking. "My husband is on dialysis," she said. "I can't get him to the doctor, and I don't know what to do so he won't die? He's not doing well." The room went quiet and all eyes turned towards the woman.

"I'm not sure, ma'am," said Gabe softly. "Maybe Carol could visit with you after the meeting. If anyone has experience in that area, if you would also please stay."

After enough issues were raised to fill three pages with notes, the meeting was wrapped up and the following Sunday set for the next meeting with the community. Jennifer was amazed at the difference between this and the previous gathering. Whether it was the fact that people were adjusting to the situation or Gabe's reassuring personality, this meeting had been conducted without the bickering and acrimony that had marred the first one. Jennifer noted that even her own mood had improved since the meeting began. Having someone like Gabe, a person who could lead naturally without intimidation or force and who seemed sincere and able to make wise decisions, made things feel much less desperate.

Jennifer shook Gabe's hand as she prepared to leave. His grip was firm and she could feel thick calluses on his fingers. "Thank you so much for helping us," he said with a smile and a wink. "It's quite a challenge we've got, isn't it?"

Jennifer nodded. "It is, but I'll do whatever I can."

CHAPTER TWELVE

Thursday, September 8th
Deer Creek, Montana

Jennifer wheeled David's bike out of the garage towards the front street just as the sun began to peak over the eastern horizon. It had been years since she had ridden a bicycle, but after a few blocks she was pedaling comfortably down the street on her way to Missoula. She wore a sweatshirt to keep warm in the unseasonably cold weather, and with no activity in the streets, she rode in near silence, the only sound being that of a squeaky wheel and the rocks that crackled under the tires.

On her back, she wore David's school pack filled with a handful of sturdy bags that she hoped to load up with supplies. Her plan was to try and find some food in Missoula and see what the situation was. At yesterday's meeting, a few people had commented on their forays into the city, and Jennifer was anxious to see for herself how things were. Her family's dwindling food supply was worrying her, and while it would still be awhile before they were down to nothing, anything extra she could find would be welcome.

Pedaling steadily, Jennifer covered the fifteen miles into town faster than expected. It had only been six days since she'd driven this road, and she was shocked to see such a big change in so short a time. At the early hour, the ride into Missoula was like a scene from a disaster movie – abandoned cars littering the streets, no one emerging from their home, no farmers working their fields, no radios blaring, no airplanes overhead. It was unsettling, and Jennifer's nerves were on edge the entire trip.

An hour after leaving home, Jennifer arrived at her regular grocery store and was surprised to see that the parking lot was half full of vehicles, then she realized those cars were abandoned as well. She rode up to the front of the building, leaned her bike against a lamppost, and chained it up. Glass was broken out of one of the front doors, and she carefully pushed against the frame. The door resisted, the motor for the automatic door fighting her efforts, but allowed her to enter.

As she stepped inside, the sound of the door closing behind her echoed ominously in the empty store. The only illumination in the building came from the sun streaming through the front windows in a dozen shafts of blazing light. Nervous, Jennifer paused and listened, then looked behind her to see if anyone might be following her before taking a deep breath and walking further into the store. She looked down the first aisle and was greeted by a gut-wrenching sight. Shelves that had been packed full with groceries a week before were empty, stripped of everything but shelf labels and sale signs. Jennifer walked up and down each aisle hoping to find just a few items, but with each step she became more certain there would be nothing left for her. She noted as she passed the greeting card and magazine racks that even those had been emptied.

Removing a small flashlight from her pack, Jennifer searched through the back room, finding only a few packages of spoiled meat and several boxes of ice cream that had long since drained their contents onto the floor of the warm freezer.

Jennifer walked slowly back to the front of the store, her feet heavy, the squeak of her shoes on the tile floor sounding louder and louder with each step. Back outside, she shielded her eyes from the bright sunlight and walked dejectedly to a bench near her bicycle. Jennifer felt tired and helpless, and even though the day had warmed, her body felt cold and weak. The weight of the situation was oppressive – children who needed to eat, Kyle gone, no contact with her family, and her world turned upside down. It all seemed to squeeze her like a vise, pressing the air from her lungs and the hope from her heart.

Sitting alone on a bench in front of the empty grocery store with no one to talk to and not knowing how tomorrow would be, Jennifer felt as helpless as she ever had in her life. Tears started slowly but were soon cascading unchecked down her cheeks. She pulled her feet up onto the bench, wrapped her arms around her knees, and buried her face in her legs. Oh how she wished Kyle was there, to hold her, to put his arm around her and reassure her that things would get better, to protect her, to make everything alright. Her friends described her as a strong, capable woman, and she felt she was, but after sharing fifteen years of her life with Kyle, it was like half of her was missing, and she desperately wanted to be whole. She missed everything about him, the touch of his hands, the smell of his cologne, the sound of his voice, the feel of his lips, the way he smiled at her when he came home at night, and even just the simple comfort of knowing he was there. Jennifer closed her eyes and tried to picture him. What would he do? How would he handle the situation?

Jennifer heard a sound and looked up to see a young girl, maybe eighteen, pushing a stroller towards her. The girl had shoulder length hair that was either blonde with dark streaks or dark with blonde streaks, bad acne, and was wearing a white t-shirt and well-worn blue jeans. A baby wrapped in a thin blanket lay in the stroller, sleeping peacefully as the stroller rattled along. Jennifer wiped at her tears and runny nose and tried to compose herself, embarrassed by emotions she couldn't quite manage to control.

The girl barely acknowledged Jennifer as she passed by, her eyes locked on the doors of the grocery store.

"There's nothing inside," Jennifer said, trying to sound calm.

The girl stopped. Jennifer could tell the girl was busy processing the information. "Are you totally sure?" she asked, turning towards Jennifer, sunlight reflecting off a metal stud in her nose.

Jennifer nodded. "I am. I just finished searching the store. I even brought a flashlight to search the back room, but it was empty too."

"Isn't there even anything, like salad dressing, or ketchup, or something?" the young girl asked, undisguised desperation in her voice.

"I'm sorry. It's empty," Jennifer answered, holding up her empty backpack as proof. "Even the shampoo and dog food are gone. There's nothing but empty shelves."

The girl let out a long, heavy sigh and slowly turned the stroller around. She walked back the way she'd come, and Jennifer could see that she was crying as well. "Hey, you gonna be okay?" Jennifer called out.

The girl shook her head. "I don't know," she managed to say, the tears audible in her voice. "We're real hungry, especially my little boy."

"I have a couple of granola bars," Jennifer said as she unzipped a side pocket on the pack. "Would you like those? I don't need them."

The girl turned back, eyeing Jennifer suspiciously. "You mean that?" she asked, wiping her face with a dirty hand.

Jennifer nodded. "I have some more at home," she lied. "I'll be alright."

The girl stepped towards Jennifer and stretched out her hand, her eyes hungry and anxious. Jennifer handed her the granola bars and smiled. "I know it's not much, but I hope it helps."

The girl tore one of the packages open and bit into it. "I haven't eaten for two days," she said between bites. "I'm starting to think we really are going to starve to death."

"Don't you have someone who can help you?"

The girl shook her head. "It's just me and Austin. We just moved here, plus my parents and I don't get along."

"What about Austin's dad?"

"He's not around. I haven't seen him since before Austin was born." The girl finished off the first bar and looked at the remaining one in her hand. "Do you think he can eat one of these?" she asked, pointing to her baby.

"Does he have teeth?"

She nodded. "A few. He's teething, which doesn't make things easy."

"It's not what a doctor would recommend, but I think if you break it into tiny pieces, he'll do okay with it. Just make sure they're real tiny."

"I will. Thanks. Thanks a lot, Mrs?"

"I'm Jennifer. You can just call me Jenn. What's your name?"

"I'm Cassidy. Nice to meet you, Jenn."

"Well, Cassidy, I hope I've helped. Do you think there are any other stores around we could go try?"

"No," Cassidy said. "My neighbor went to the big Wal-Mart, and she said it was wiped out. I walked two miles to get here. Thought with it being on the edge of town it might have some things left. I guess we were both wrong, huh?"

"I suppose so. I rode fifteen miles in on my bike to get here. I was afraid it would be empty, but I came anyway. You know, it's funny in a way. I was here last Friday afternoon, probably an hour before the event, and everything was fine. No indication whatsoever that anything bad was about to happen. If it had happened an hour earlier, my car would be out in that parking lot with the rest of them."

"Guess you had luck on your side, didn't you."

"I suppose. More luck than the people who owned these cars at least. I wonder how many of them were unlucky by just a few minutes."

Cassidy shook her head. "I'm sure a few."

Jennifer looked at the cars. "You know, Cassidy, I bet there were a few that already had their groceries when the bomb went off. I bet there are a couple of cars out there with food in them. Do you want to look with me?"

A flash of hope lit Cassidy's face, and she nodded.

They found some shade beside a van for Austin and started to work their way across the parking lot, searching each vehicle as they went. Most vehicles were locked, but they could see through the windows of the trucks, vans and SUV's, which were all empty. Two sedans were unlocked, but their trunks had nothing.

"Our luck hasn't been so good," Jennifer observed, leaning against a white Taurus. "There are only four cars that we haven't been able to open or see inside. Should we try and get in, or give up?"

Cassidy's expression had gradually fallen as the search yielded nothing, and she now looked thoroughly hopeless. "I think people came and got their stuff. It won't get us anywhere," she said, turning towards the parked stroller.

Jennifer could see the blanket moving and heard Austin crying. Retrieving her bike, she pushed it over to Cassidy. "What are you going to do?"

Cassidy shrugged her shoulders and broke off a tiny piece of the granola bar to put in Austin's mouth. "I don't know," she said, her voice lacking any life. "I just don't know."

"You should try some of the local churches," Jennifer suggested. "They might be able to help you. Just don't give up, okay, Cassidy? You've got your little boy to live for. He needs you to stay strong."

Cassidy nodded but didn't speak.

Jennifer gave Cassidy a pat on the shoulder and smiled at Austin, who was busy trying to chew on the piece of granola bar, his arms and legs kicking excitedly. "I've got to go, but please don't give up."

"I'll try," Cassidy responded weakly.

Jennifer pedaled away and was about to turn onto the street when a wine colored car near the back exit of the parking lot caught her eye. She stopped and looked at it, noting that the car was facing towards the exit. She pedaled over and peered through the windows. The seats were empty, but the rear passenger door had a big dent in it that kept it from closing tightly. Jennifer tugged on the door and managed to pull it open after a couple of good yanks. She opened the driver's door and lifted the latch for the trunk.

Hurrying to the back of the car, Jennifer opened the trunk and stared at a dozen plastic bags filled with groceries – pasta, canned vegetables, a dozen or so cans of tuna fish, crackers, and plenty more. She removed her backpack and quickly filled it with food. A foul odor came from one of the bags, which held a package labeled as chicken thighs but was now a putrid, dripping, brown mass. Holding her breath, she tied the bag of rotting meat shut, finished loading her bags, and climbed onto her bike.

Jennifer rode around to the front of the building where she had last seen Cassidy, but Cassidy was gone. She rode to the other side of the building and looked both directions, spotting Cassidy pushing the stroller down the street and away from the store. "Cassidy!" she shouted as she hurried to catch up. "Cassidy! I found some food!" Startled, Cassidy turned to see Jennifer holding out a bag. "There was a car on the other side of the building. The trunk was full. I grabbed this for you, but there was more for you to take if you go back."

Cassidy's eyes went from Jennifer, to the bag, then back to Jennifer again. She reached out and took the bag, but her expression didn't change. "I don't know that I should."

Jennifer nodded. "Go ahead. I have as much as I can carry on the bike. I just wanted to find you and let you know."

Cassidy shook her head. "What's the point, Jenn? So we get some food. That just prolongs the inevitable. Now we'll die in two weeks instead of one. It doesn't change the reality."

Jennifer stared at the young mother, shocked. "What are you saying? That you're giving up?"

Cassidy looked away from Jennifer and didn't respond.

"I can't believe you," said Jennifer, her anger rising along with her voice. She struggled to find the right words. "You're a mother. You should be ready to kill for your child, not sentence him to death." Jennifer felt her hands shaking, and she clenched the handlebars of the bike. "You should be ashamed. I've heard of mothers fighting wild animals to save their children, and you're just going to give up?"

Cassidy turned back around and started to push her baby away from the store, the single bag of food hanging from the stroller.

"You need to think of Austin," Jennifer called to her. "He deserves a chance at life, not a death sentence. The car is by the far exit if you change your mind, but the food won't last long." As a few people nearby took Jennifer's directions to heart and ran for the unclaimed groceries, Jennifer watched Cassidy walk away, feeling madder than she had in years.

Jennifer jerked the bike around and had just started to pedal when she felt something tug on her bicycle. She twisted her head around and saw a man with unkempt, curly red hair holding onto the cable of the lock she had wrapped loosely around the post of the bike seat. The sight of him holding her back frightened her, and Jennifer pressed harder on the pedals, trying to break free of his grip.

"What do you want?" Jennifer shouted as he pulled her to a stop. Her heart was racing and her legs shaking so much she had a hard time keeping her balance.

"You said you have food. I want it," the man demanded.

"Please, I have three children. I need it."

The expression on the man's face didn't change. He was young, probably in his mid-twenties, and his face was covered with freckles, giving him an especially youthful look, but his eyes were set hard, and Jennifer could tell by his expression that he was completely serious. "I don't care about your kids. I have my own worries. Give me your food!"

Jennifer swallowed hard, trying to stay calm. She could see Cassidy monitoring the situation over her shoulder, but hurrying in the opposite direction and making her escape while she still had a chance. "Please," Jennifer begged. "Please, I really need the food."

The man jerked on the cable, pulling the bike and nearly knocking Jennifer to the ground. "Just shut up and give me the food. I don't want to hear about it."

Jennifer swiped at a tear on her cheek and had started to slip the backpack from her shoulders when she heard another voice from across the street. "Let go of her!"

Both Jennifer and the man holding her bike turned in the direction of the voice. An older man wearing boxer shorts and an undershirt that was once white was striding across his lawn with an aluminum baseball bat raised threateningly above his right shoulder. He had a determined expression and was making a beeline towards them.

"Stay out of this, old man," the red head snarled, looking back at Jennifer. "This is none of your business."

"I've seen enough to know this is my business, you little punk. Let go of the lady. I don't want to have to get your blood on my bat. You understand?"

The young man nodded slowly and released his grip on the cable, the lock falling back against the frame of the bike with a metallic clang. "Leave now!" the man with the bat ordered, looking at Jennifer.

Jennifer wasn't totally sure who he was speaking to, but didn't really care. As soon as she was free, she pushed her bike away and reached with her foot for the pedal. Once up to speed, she turned to look back at her protector. Just as she turned she saw the red head lunge towards the older man, and the baseball bat swing around in a heartbeat, catching the red head on the side of his head and dropping him to the ground like he'd been shot.

The violent act shocked Jennifer and she almost lost control of the bike. Catching herself, she weaved the bicycle in between a couple of abandoned cars and turned back to where the two men were. This time the older man was kneeling on the ground, checking the younger man for signs of life.

She let out a horrified gasp and didn't stay stopped long, too frightened to spend any more time in the city.

CHAPTER THIRTEEN

Sunday, September 11th
Northern Texas

The Eastern sky glowed yellow as the sun began its daily ascent. Kyle tied his shoes, then rolled up his sleeping bag and squeezed it back into its designated place in the cart. After a few hours of pulling on Wednesday, he had stopped and adjusted the load every mile or so until finding just the right balance. Now his challenge each morning was to repack the cart without upsetting the carefully earned equilibrium.

With his bedding repacked, Kyle stepped into pulling position, grabbed the handle, and set off for a fifth day. His legs and shoulders ached, but not as much as they had the day before, gradually becoming accustomed to the demands of pulling.

North Central Texas was forgivingly flat, and heading north from San Angelo, Kyle had made better time than he expected. Wednesday, his first day, he had pulled until well after dark, making it most of the way to Sterling City before stopping. A grassy patch had been his first bed site, but bugs, noises, worries and the hard ground had kept him from getting much rest. The second day started early, and he had walked to just north of Sterling when an old pickup passed him by. One thing that had surprised Kyle as he walked was the number of vehicles still operating. He had expected the roads to be devoid of any traffic, but on Wednesday, eight vehicles had passed him, and the pickup was the second one on Thursday.

Most drivers just waved as they sped by, and Kyle had been expecting the same from the pickup, especially since the truck bed had been loaded with boxes and bags, but it pulled over and a young couple jumped out.

"Where are you headed to?" the driver asked.

"Montana," Kyle answered with a grin. "I don't suppose you're headed that way?"

The man's eyes widened, and he looked at his wife. "No," he said, "but we could help a little if you want. We're heading to family in Hobbs and could save you a few miles."

Kyle had eagerly accepted their offer, and the three of them loaded the cart in the back of the truck. There were no ropes to secure the cart, and three small children were wedged on a narrow bench behind the driver, so Kyle had sat in the back, perched on top of a box and clinging to his cart like a mother holding a newborn. The miles had sped by without incident, and within two hours they had arrived in Lamesa, where Kyle's cart was unloaded and they parted ways, with Kyle thanking the couple profusely for saving him three days of walking.

From Lamesa, Kyle had continued towards Lubbock, thrilled to already be so far ahead of schedule and only stopping at night once it got too dark to continue walking. Camp that night had been set up on the shoulder of the road. Friday he had been on the go again at dawn, anxious to stay ahead of schedule, but before he could get very far in the day's journey, aching muscles and joints had conspired to slow his progress. This setback surprised him since he was in relatively good shape, having hiked dozens of miles in the mountains around Missoula every summer. He was quickly finding out, however, that none of that was preparation for the punishment he was currently inflicting on his body.

A little after noon, Kyle found a shaded area by a small creek, ate lunch, and managed to get in two good hours of sleep. When he awoke he washed himself in the creek, refilled his water bottles, and continued on his way, walking for only three hours before stopping for the day.

Saturday, blistered, sore, and tired, Kyle only managed to pull a couple of hours before stopping for the day to give his body a break. By Sunday morning, nine days after he had expected to fly home, he was approaching Lubbock, two days ahead of schedule on his new timeline. Despite the aches, the satisfaction of making good time helped keep him going, and he noted with grim satisfaction as the numbers on the mile markers slowly count up.

Over the past four days he had met others who were in a similar predicament, although he had yet to meet anyone with as far to travel as he did. In these limited interactions, it was apparent that people were scared, struggling, and lacking the resources to cope. The few reports he'd heard about the federal broadcasts had a similar theme, with no hope of immediate assistance being offered beyond limited government food stockpiles that they were unable to deliver and a few emergency air shipments of food that were more symbolic than useful. The man who had given that information to Kyle had agreed that three hundred million people weren't going to be helped much by the arrival of a handful of cargo planes full of food.

As Kyle approached Lubbock, a haze hung over the city that made his eyes water and his lungs burn. He could see evidence of fires in multiple locations, but he trudged warily onward, worried about the danger of the city. Residents eyed Kyle suspiciously, rarely waving or offering words of encouragement like he'd experienced in the small towns when he'd begun his journey. Part of it was probably because the homes here were set further back off of the highway, but there was still a different feeling, a sense of wariness and fear that he hadn't felt in the towns he'd passed through earlier.

Kyle waved at a man sitting on the back steps of a house and shouted "Good morning!" to him. The man sat quietly, eyes locked on Kyle, then, after much deliberation, responded with a slight dip of the head before disappearing into his home.

From the position of the sun, Kyle estimated that it was just before noon, and he stopped briefly to eat a power bar and take a drink. The water was warm, but it quenched his parched throat and helped lessen the hunger pangs. It had been six days since he'd had an official meal, and a drink with ice was well over a week removed. He thought about some of the things he missed, simple things he'd taken for granted his entire life – cold drinks, hot food, mattresses, air conditioning, showers, cars, clean clothes, a phone call. Until a week ago, he'd never given those things much thought. Now they were unattainable luxuries that crossed his mind incessantly.

Kyle capped the water and stowed the jug, then resumed pulling. As he walked, his thoughts once again drifted to his family. What is Jennifer doing? How are they getting along? Are they safe? Hungry? Scared? Worried? These were the same questions he asked every day, and he still didn't have any answers. He tried to reassure himself that Jennifer was strong and that she could handle it, but it hurt beyond description to not be with her and the kids.

As Kyle pulled his cart into Lubbock, gloom hung in the air like the smoke that blanketed the city, creating a feeling that enveloped him and made his cart feel heavy and his legs weak. The further into the city he ventured, the thicker the smoke became and the stronger the uneasy feeling grew.

At the top of an overpass, Kyle was close enough to watch a fire burning through a neighborhood. The homes were close together, and the fire was spreading from one home to another. Kyle stopped and watched as people on the roofs of the homes nearest the fire, with shirts pulled over their faces and armed only with blankets, tried to stop the flames from spreading. Cinders from the burning houses dropped onto the roofs of neighboring homes, and panicked homeowners rushed forward to beat at the flames, then retreated, driven back by the heat.

Kyle was drawn in by the drama and wanted to help, but knew there was nothing he could offer beyond what was already there. The scene was pitiful, no fire trucks or even garden hoses to fight the fire with, just people, blankets and sweat. He shook his head in sympathy as he picked up the handle of his cart and continued on his way.

Deer Creek, Montana

Jennifer was attempting to take notes, but with all of the arguments, the meeting was going nowhere. It was easy to understand why Gabe was reluctant to bring too much up for discussion. Education and food had already run their course. Now the subject was generators. Of the just over one hundred homes in their community, so far only six generators had been identified. Everyone assumed that there were more, but they knew of just the six.

"We just need to confiscate them!" a woman shouted from the back of the room as the argument raged. "I need water, and I bet most of you do, too." A couple of people voiced their agreement.

Gabe raised his hands, trying to regain order. "Folks, I know we need them, but we can't just take them."

"Why not?" yelled a man. Jennifer recognized him as the attorney who had wanted to be the council chairman. "It's for the good of the community."

"I know that, sir, but that doesn't give us license to do it." Gabe looked around, trying to garner support. "We have no authority to do something like that, nor do I have the desire."

"There are more of us than there are of them. What more authority do we need?"

Chuck, who was attending his first meeting and was obviously exasperated with the proceedings, rose from his chair near the front of the room. "Folks," he began, "my name is Charles Anderson, and I'm new to these meetings, but I need to say something. I know this is a frightening time, and we've all got our own worries, but there are some things that we just can't do. I put my life on the line in Vietnam to fight for liberty, and that's what America stands for." He looked around the room, his expression serious but warm. "I know we're just one small group, but if we start taking things from other people just because we want them or need them, then we're giving up on those principles that made this country great. We'll be just like the people I fought against. What's right isn't decided with a vote. It's what we all know in our hearts, and taking something from someone else isn't right if you ask me." He paused and looked around the room. "We're not Hitler's brownshirts; I'm sure we can figure out something better than force. That's all I have to say." Chuck smiled politely and sat down.

Jennifer caught his eye and gave him a wink; he smiled back at her. She could hear mumblings in the group, some rejecting what Chuck said, but most seemed to agree.

"What if it's a life or death situation?" demanded a woman standing in the back. "This council is a joke if it can't even solve a little problem like this." She looked down at her husband who was glaring at Gabe. "Come on; we're done here," she ordered as she grabbed her husband by the arm and pulled him to his feet. They squeezed past an older lady sitting beside them, then stormed from the room.

Gabe silently watched the couple leave, then shook his head. "I have to agree with Mr. Anderson, who just spoke. We just can't take things from people. I know there are a couple of owners, Mr. Patel being one of them," he motioned to a man sitting in the middle of the room, "who have been willing to share and try and make things work for other people. We'll talk to the other folks with generators and see if we can make arrangements for them to be made available to more people. I'm sure something can be worked out. One thing we all have to remember, folks, is our group is voluntary and not everyone has chosen to participate. We don't have any authority, so we have to rely on people choosing to cooperate, which makes things much tougher.

"This meeting has gone on too long already. Lets meet again on Wednesday. Those of you who volunteered for the school committee, please see if you can have some schedules worked out by then. The council will see what can be done with the other items we've discussed today. Does the same time work for everyone?"

People nodded their agreement and rapidly filed out of Doug's basement, heading off on foot, bicycle, or horse, leaving just the council members behind.

"Aren't you all glad you signed up for this?" Gabe asked, shaking his head. "Looks like we've got some work to do. Can you meet Tuesday?"

"What else is there to do?" asked Carol Jeffries, the vet.

"Probably not much, but I hate to assume. Lets plan on Tuesday at my house. Same time."

Jennifer was heading for the door when Doug grabbed her arm. "Could you stick around for a couple of minutes? I want to talk to you for a second."

"Sure, no problem," she replied and sat back down.

Doug spoke with the others as they left, then sat in a chair close to Jennifer. "I hope I didn't say anything that offended you during the meeting today. I get worked up sometimes. Guess I'm a little hot-headed, but some people just say stupid things."

"My dad was a truck driver, and occasionally I rode with him during the summers. I learned from those experiences not to let things people say offend me."

"That's a relief. Listen, I wanted to see how you're doing with your situation. It's got to be tough taking care of your kids alone."

"It is, but we're making it. David's a big help, and we're starting to get routines figured out."

"I'm really sorry about your husband," Doug said, his face solemn. "I heard what happened to him"

Jennifer felt her breath catch in her chest at the mention of Kyle. "What do you mean by that?" she shot back defensively.

"Well, I heard he was flying when the attack happened, and I've heard what was said about airplanes. I suppose I assumed the worst."

"We don't know anything, Doug, just that he's not here." Jennifer could feel herself getting angry, and she stood to leave. "I hope you're not implying that he's dead, because I don't believe that."

"I'm sorry." Doug stood up and put a hand on her shoulder. "Really, I didn't mean to hurt you. I'm just trying to be a friend and wanted to tell you that I admire how strong you're being." He stepped closer to her, putting an arm across her shoulders. "And I want you to know that if you need anything, you can ask me. I'll be there for you."

Jennifer wiped at her eyes and pulled away. "Thanks for the offer. I'll make a note of it." She walked across the kitchen, fighting her emotions. "I've got to get home to my kids," she said as she walked out the door.

"I'm sorry, Jennifer," Doug called out, catching the door before it shut. "If you need anything, let me know. I'd like to help."

Lubbock, Texas

Kyle pulled his cart through the heart of Lubbock, his senses on high alert for any signs of trouble. The freeway dipped under the cross streets, and Kyle found it easier to take the level frontage road to avoid the constant rising and falling of the freeway.

Lubbock was far different from what he'd experienced in the small towns. There was more activity in the streets, and when the occasional car passed by, its occupants studied him closely. After weighing his options, Kyle concealed his rifle in the cart, hoping not to appear threatening, but picked up his pace in an effort to get through the city as quickly as possible. Signs of looting were everywhere, and though he worried about his dwindling food supply, he was far too anxious to stop and search for any.

The streets were filled with cars that had been abandoned where they died, which meant that pulling the cart required a steady dose of winding through frozen traffic and occasionally up onto the sidewalk. The scene was similar to his drive through Houston with Ed, but walking in broad daylight through a city that had literally been stopped in its tracks was a different experience. All makes and models of cars were abandoned in the streets, a few with windows broken out. Some had been pushed to the side of the street, but for the most part they just sat as they were nine days before.

As he walked past a line of vehicles backed up at an intersection, Kyle wondered what it would have been like to be sitting in your car when everything stopped. He imagined sitting at a traffic light and suddenly the car dies. You look around and see that people in the cars surrounding you are also experiencing problems. Then you notice that the traffic lights are out, and cross traffic has rolled to a stop. Eventually you climb out of your car, not sure what to do. Ironically, your cell phone doesn't work either. The radio might work, but stations aren't broadcasting, so all you get is static. Everything around you is dead, but there is nothing to indicate a problem – no flashes, no explosions, and no violent impact that would explain the dramatic change.

How long, he wondered, would people have sat there before they decided to leave? How hard would it be to abandon your car? He noticed that most of the cars were locked, indicating the owners were expecting to come back and retrieve them, preferably in one piece. As he passed cars with license plates from out of state,

Kyle wondered how those drivers were dealing with the situation. Perhaps they accounted for some of the walkers he'd met. He'd been fortunate to have Ed, but what would he have done if there hadn't been someone to help him? What if a family was traveling? Where do four or five people go when you don't know anyone, and everyone is desperate? How do you survive?

His mind weaved around those topics as he weaved around the frozen traffic, the faint sounds of the city playing in the background. He passed block after block and was lost in thought when the sound of footsteps caught his attention. Kyle turned and noticed three men a block behind, walking the same direction he was. There was nothing threatening about them, but he felt a spark of fear shoot through him.

Kyle picked up his pace, but knew that if it came to it, he wouldn't be able to outrun the men with his cart in tow. He also knew he couldn't abandon his possessions and still hope to make it to Montana. He told himself that he was just being paranoid, that in another block or two they would turn off on some side street and he would again be alone. He glanced over his shoulder, hoping they had turned, but instead saw that they were closing the gap. He picked up his pace even more until he was almost at a jog, the blisters on his feet throbbing with each step, but he ignored the pain and pushed himself as hard as he could.

Looking over his shoulder once more, he saw the men angling across the street towards him at a run. He glanced around frantically for some kind of protection, but the area was commercial, and it wasn't as if shoppers were wandering the sidewalks or police were on patrol. He'd passed a few people several blocks back, but none of them had looked like anyone to approach for assistance. Kyle looked back. The men were close now.

Kyle slowed to a walk and tried to catch his breath. The sound of their footsteps got louder, and he momentarily considered trying to grab his gun, but decided against it. Maybe he was just overreacting, he thought, and what if they were armed? One against three wasn't very good odds. Maybe, he hoped, they weren't going to do anything. Maybe they were just curious. He desperately clung to those thoughts.

"Hey, amigo. What's the hurry?" one of the men called out as they approached.

Kyle didn't answer. He just kept pulling.

"What's wrong?" asked another. "We're the Lubbock Welcoming Committee. You look like you're from out of town, so we need to welcome you. Maybe we could be of assistance." The two others laughed at this line, finding it immensely funny.

Kyle spoke over his shoulder as he pulled. "I'm doing fine," he said. "Just passing through town, but I appreciate the offer."

The men had now caught up to Kyle and were looking over the sides of the cart. "Glad to hear you've got things under control," the third man said. He was closer to Kyle and appeared to be the leader. "I guess we'll just collect our toll, and you can be on your way."

"I don't have any money," Kyle said. "I lost my wallet last week, but I'd give you my cash if I had any."

"What do we need cash for?" the man asked. "Cash isn't any good to us. We'll take a look and tell you what we want."

Kyle could feel someone tugging on the cart. He lurched forward and pulled the cart free.

"Hey, slow down, buddy," the leader said. "No need to make this difficult. We're reasonable guys."

"Sorry," said Kyle. "I've got a long ways to go, so I'm going to need everything. Maybe next time." He could feel someone pulling on his cart again and strained to break it free. As he pulled, Kyle felt a hand grab his arm. His heart was pounding, and his hands and legs trembled as adrenaline rushed through his body.

"I told you that I need what I've got," Kyle said, jerking his arm free. "Just leave me alone. I've got a family to get home to."

He pulled harder on the cart, but the three men were too strong. They forced the cart to a stop, and Kyle finally gave up the tug of war. Two of them held the cart, and the third started to rummage through the contents.

"Give us your food, and we'll let you go," the leader said. "This can be really easy."

Kyle dropped the handle of the cart and watched the men dig through his things. He felt completely impotent as his possessions were carelessly tossed on the ground.

One of the men handed the leader a bottle of water. "Hector," he snickered, "I think this guy is going to start crying." Then he burst out laughing.

"See, I told you this would be easy," Hector sneered at Kyle as he tossed the tent out of the way. "You'll figure something out. We need stuff too, you know. Besides, why hurry home? Your wife's probably busy sleeping with the neighbors for food, and I bet she's got the pantry stocked. Probably thinks you're dead or something."

The two holding the cart burst out laughing. One of them started making sounds of pleasure. "Oh baby, faster, faster," he moaned.

The second one chimed in with a comment about how much she was charging and sent the three men into hysterics.

Kyle stepped in front of the cart, watching them take what he needed to survive while trying to ignore their taunts. He could feel rage mixing with his fear, tightening his chest. The two holding the cart joined in the search and continued badgering him with vulgar comments about his family.

They were drinking his water, eating his food, and talking about his wife doing group sessions when Kyle snapped. He lunged for Hector, whose head was turned, and punched him hard, catching him on the back of the head. Caught off guard like that, Hector's head snapped to the side, and he stumbled away. Kyle followed and swung again, this time hitting Hector with a blow to the chin, but lost his footing and stumbled into Hector, knocking him to the ground. Kyle caught himself and kicked at him, catching him in the stomach just as he was tackled to the ground from behind.

Kyle and his tackler tumbled and twisted on the hot asphalt, the rocks grinding into their arms and legs. The man held Kyle tightly around the waist, but Kyle managed to twist towards the man and pummeled him around the eyes and nose with five or six sharp blows until the man released his grip.

Kyle rolled over and scrambled to his feet, but as he turned back towards his assailants, the third man was on him, his fist connecting hard with Kyle's cheek. Stars exploded in Kyle's head and he staggered backwards, struggling to stay on his feet. He turned to the source of the blow and raised his arms in front of his face, but a second blow caught him square in the stomach and knocked the wind out of him. Kyle doubled over and dropped to a knee, fighting to catch his breath.

Another punch connected with the side of Kyle's nose, causing a loud popping sound, followed by a stream of blood flowing from his right nostril. The man stepped back as Kyle finally caught his breath and took in some big gulps of air, choking on his blood. Kyle regained his footing and retreated lamely towards a blue pickup on the far side of the road. The first two men were back on their feet and walking towards Kyle as the third man circled to his right. One man's nose pumped a steady crimson stream, leaving large red stains on the front of his shirt. They were all angry, and Kyle knew there was no way he was going to be able to talk his way out of the situation.

The man closest to Kyle lunged at him and pushed him towards the truck. Kyle flailed his arm out to catch himself, hitting the hood of the truck as the back of his head cracked against the side mirror. He rubbed his head and wiped blood from his face while shuffling back along the truck and watching his attackers close in on him, no longer interested in his cart.

Desperate, Kyle spun to his left and started to run, hoping the men would let him be and just take the things in his cart, his desire to survive outweighing everything else. He sprinted down the street, barely able to see through his swollen, watery eyes, furiously pumping his arms, not knowing where he was headed, but just wanting to get far away. A half block down the road, he looked over his shoulder, praying the men had given up, but found instead, that Hector and his cohorts were in full pursuit, with Hector only a few steps behind Kyle and closing. Kyle veered to the left and tried to slip between two vehicles but lost his footing and collided heavily with a minivan.

Hector skidded to a stop and grabbed the back of Kyle's shirt and shoved him face first against the hood of the van. "Where you going, tough guy?" he yelled. "You did a bad thing, now you're going to pay." He leaned in close to Kyle's ear, panting from his run. "Hope the Mrs. isn't too particular about how her man looks, 'cause she might not recognize you, if you make it home."

The other two caught up and Hector barked out orders. "Grab his arms!" he yelled. "Turn him around so I can see his face!"

They yanked Kyle away from the van and turned him towards the center of the street, bending Kyle's arms painfully to keep him from struggling. Hector swung at Kyle with a sweeping right hook, landing it on the left side of Kyle's face and wrenching Kyle's head violently to the side. Blood and saliva flew from Kyle's mouth, splattering the man holding Kyle's right arm. The man cursed as he wiped the fluids from his face. Another punch connected, hitting Kyle in the eye and snapping his head backwards. As the adrenaline wore off, the pain became overwhelming, with every nerve in his body simultaneously firing signals of distress. A punch to the stomach caused him to retch.

Kyle kicked feebly at Hector, who was standing close by after the last blow, and managed to connect weakly with his thigh.

"Get him on his knees," Hector demanded as he stepped back and wiped blood from the corner of his mouth. "I'll show you how a kick is supposed to feel. I wasn't going to get this rough, but you don't know how the game works."

The men holding Kyle forced him down on his knees, laughing at Kyle's vain attempts to resist. Kyle saw movement to his left, a fourth man running towards them. He didn't want to die five days into his journey on the streets of Lubbock, but he resigned himself to that fate.

A boot connected with Kyle's cheek and everything around him began to spin. His head rolled forward limply, and the bright afternoon sunlight dissolved to black as the hands holding him let go and he collapsed forward onto the blistering street.

Deer Creek, Montana

"I don't think he thought about how it would come across," said Grace. "Guys don't clue in on those things."

Jennifer had left Doug's and gone straight to the Anderson's house. During the past week and a half, now that phone calls to her mother and sister weren't an option and her social network had been disrupted, Jennifer had found herself at her neighbors' quite often, and Grace had become her sounding board.

"I know he probably didn't mean for it to sound like it did, but the way he said it hit me hard. Do you think Kyle's dead?"

Grace smiled in her grandmotherly way. "Does it matter what anyone else thinks?"

"No, but maybe it would help me know what to expect when I talk to people. I think Kyle's alive, and I've just assumed everyone else thinks the same. Does that make people think I'm in denial?"

"Of course not, dear. There's no reason not to think he's alive. That would be far worse than holding out hope. I think he's alive. And one of these days, when you aren't expecting it, he'll come walking through your door and wrap you up in his arms. Trust me."

Jennifer smiled. "I hope you're right. I just wish he'd get here soon, because I really need that right now."

"Just you be patient, sweetie," said Chuck from the other room. Jennifer looked at Chuck, who had been reading. "I don't mean to listen in on your conversation, but it was more interesting than my book."

Jennifer laughed.

"Well, like I said," he continued, "you just be patient. For all we know, he's going to have to walk here from Texas. That's a long way and a tough journey, but any man worth his salt would do it for his family. I don't know your husband that well, just spoke to him a few of times, but if he's smart enough to marry a woman like you, I'm sure he's smart enough to figure out a way to get home. He's probably on his way, and I bet he can't wait to get here."

"Thanks, Chuck," Jennifer said as she wiped her nose. "Kyle is a good man. I'm not going to give up."

"Now another thing," Chuck said as he leaned forward. "Watch out for that Doug fellow. I don't trust him."

"What do you mean? The sheriff? He's harmless. I'm sure he was just trying to be nice."

Chuck got up and came into the room. "Maybe, but you still need to be careful. I've worked with too many guys who are just like him. They act all nice and stuff but are after one thing, and once they get it, they brag about it like they've conquered Everest. It used to make me sick."

"I'll be careful, Dad," Jennifer said teasingly. "Thanks for worrying about me."

"He misses his daughters," Grace said to Jennifer. "Before the event, he called them up every Sunday to check on them. It was sweet when they were young and single, but they're over forty now, and he's still doing it. Calls his granddaughters too, and they're starting to have kids. He's got a soft spot for his girls, and it looks like you've been adopted." Grace gave Chuck a look and a knowing tilt of the head, like a mother would a child she was gently reprimanding.

Chuck grinned proudly. "Guilty as charged. It's just the way I'm wired. You should be used to it by now. We've been married for fifty years."

"Oh, I'm used to it, and you know I appreciate it," said Grace. "I'm just warning Jennifer about what she's in for if you start treating her like a daughter."

"Don't worry about it," Jennifer said. "I'm flattered that you're concerned."

Lubbock, Texas

Kyle felt something cold and wet wipe across his face. His head throbbed, along with the rest of his body, but at least with the pain he knew he wasn't dead. A chair scraped loudly and unexpectedly on the floor, and he swung his arms up to shield himself.

"It's okay. You can relax," a woman said in a soothing voice. "We're not going to hurt you."

Kyle cautiously lowered his arms and tried to open his eyes, the swelling in his face making it difficult. His left eye was stuck shut, but his right opened a crack and, in the darkness, he could faintly make out a figure on a chair near where he lay.

The last thing he remembered was being beaten by three men in the street, but that was around noon, and now it was dark. He tried to piece the day together but drew blanks.

He attempted to sit up, until a hand on his shoulder gently pushed him down. "Don't get up," the woman said. "You need to rest. You've had a rough day. In the morning you'll feel a little better."

Kyle relaxed and lay back on the bed. "Where am I?" he asked, his voice barely audible.

"You're safe," the woman answered. "My dad brought you home, and we're going take care of you."

"What about my stuff? Did he get my stuff?"

"I think so, but I'm not sure. I'll ask him in the morning. It's almost midnight and he's asleep. You go back to sleep. We'll talk tomorrow."

Kyle inhaled deeply and felt sharp pains in his ribs. He slowly exhaled and closed his eyes. "Thank you," he said. "Thank you for helping me."

CHAPTER FOURTEEN

Monday, September 12th
Deer Creek, Montana

Jennifer laid in her bed, drifting between sleep and consciousness, the sunlight warming her face as she lay there thinking about the new day. The house was cool, and with nothing on the schedule until later, she resisted getting out of her cozy bed.

Hearing a faint noise at her front door, she sat up and listened. Again she heard the noise, a soft but distinct knock. Jennifer quickly put on her robe and ran to the door. Looking through the peephole, she saw Doug standing on her porch.

"Doug, what are you doing here?" she asked as she opened the door. "Is something wrong?"

"Hi, Jennifer. No, nothing's wrong. I was thinking about what I said yesterday, and I know I made you upset. I just wanted to apologize. I seem to be doing a lot of that lately."

"Don't worry about it, Doug. I know you didn't mean anything by it."

"Do you mind if I come in a minute? I don't want to let your warm air out."

Jennifer hesitated. "I guess," she stammered, "but just for a minute. The kids are still sleeping."

Doug stepped inside and closed the door behind him.

"You've got a nice house," he said, looking around.

"Thanks. I'd offer you some coffee, but I can't seem to get the machine to work," she said in a half-hearted attempt at humor.

"That's fine. I'm learning to live without it. That and donuts, you know how cops are."

Jennifer laughed. "Guess we're all making sacrifices, aren't we?"

Doug nodded. "I also wanted to see how your family is doing. You've got, what, four kids to take care of?"

"Three," corrected Jennifer, "and we're doing pretty good. My oldest son, David, has been helping the crew at the Shipley farm south of here and has been bringing some food home. Between that and the Anderson's garden next door, we're doing okay. We miss the meat, but we're not starving."

"Let me know if you need anything else," offered Doug. "There's a group of us going hunting on Friday. And Jacob May, the guy with the truck that runs, he's been hitting the semi trucks on the freeway. Sometimes he comes back with big loads of food. Found a beer truck not too long ago and was pretty pleased with himself."

"We heard his truck the other day and walked over to his house to visit. It was exciting to see a working vehicle. What does he want for what he finds?" asked Jennifer. "I don't need the beer, but if he has food, I could obviously use that."

"Gas is the big thing. He says if a person helps with gas, he'll give them part of his load. If you sent your oldest boy, was it David?"

Jennifer nodded.

"Anyway, if you sent him along to work, he might give you a bigger share."

"Thanks, Doug. I appreciate the information. We'll have to see what gas we can come up with."

"If you want, I can help you drain the gas tank of your car. I've helped a couple of people with that, and I'm getting pretty good at it. Just let me know."

"That would be nice. I'll check to see how much gas I have and let you know."

Doug was standing by the door trying to find something else to say when the basement door swung open and Spencer came wandering down the hall, rubbing his eyes. He saw Doug and stopped, eyeing him suspiciously, then walked over to Jennifer and hid behind her.

Doug spoke after an awkward silence. "Well, I guess I'd better get going. It's been nice visiting with you." He reached for the door and pulled it open. "Will you be at the meeting on Wednesday?"

Jennifer struggled to stifle a yawn. "I plan to be."

"Good, I'll see you there then."

Lubbock, Texas

Kyle awoke to the sound of a pot clattering to the floor in an adjoining room. He slowly opened his swollen eyes, cracking them enough to allow some light in which brought on sharp, dagger-like pains in the back of his head, causing him to moan. He shielded his face with his arm and lay motionless on the bed as he waited for his eyes to adjust. Gradually the pain eased until he was able to take a look at his surroundings. He lay on a single bed in the corner of a small room. A desk pushed against the opposite wall was adorned with a lamp, a jar of pencils, and a digital clock with a blank display. The window above the desk was draped with simple, pink curtains that waved in the breeze and gave the room a rippling, pink tint.

Kyle pushed a yellow flowered sheet to the side, carefully swung his legs out of the bed, and eased into a sitting position. The pounding in his head was intense enough to make the room spin, so he moved slowly and deliberately. Once able to sit up, he leaned forward and rested his forearms on his knees, letting his body adjust to being upright. His neck was stiff and sore, and his arms were scratched, bruised, and spotted with patches of dried blood. A quick inspection of his clothing showed that they were torn and dusty, and that the sheets of the bed were soiled with dirt and dried blood.

Using the wall beside the bed for support, Kyle stood up when he thought he was strong enough, but immediately felt the blood rush from his head, making him dizzy. He staggered across the room and grabbed the back of the chair by the desk to steady himself. When his balance returned, he stepped away from the desk, groaning as muscles he didn't know existed called attention to the punishment they'd received.

Kyle slowly hobbled towards the bedroom door, holding the wall as he carefully stepped over blankets and a sleeping pad lying on the floor. He could hear voices on the other side of the door and was both curious and nervous to find out who they belonged to.

He twisted the handle and eased the door open, then held himself steady in the doorway. No more than a dozen feet away, at a simple kitchen table, three faces turned to watch him.

A burly, middle-aged black man spoke up. "Good morning. How are you doin'?" he asked in a booming voice.

Kyle thought a second. "I guess that depends on how you look at it," he said. "Thanks to someone, you I suppose, I'm doing a lot better than I might otherwise be, but I really feel like crap, if you'll forgive the expression." Kyle spoke slowly and with great effort.

The man got up from the table and went to Kyle. He put an arm around Kyle's waist and helped guide him towards the table. "My name's Elijah," he said. "It's nice to finally be able to visit with you."

The two men shuffled slowly across the kitchen floor. "I'm Kyle Tait. It's a pleasure to meet you, although I can't say much for the circumstances."

"These are my children," said Elijah. "That's my daughter, Diana, and my son, Stevie." He motioned to the girl and boy sitting at the table. "Stevie, get out of your chair so our guest can sit. You go get one out of your bedroom."

The boy jumped up obediently and dashed from the room. Elijah helped lower Kyle into the empty chair, and Stevie returned seconds later dragging a metal folding chair behind him. "Don't drag that chair, Son. You'll scratch the floor," said Elijah with a look of exasperation. "You should know better than that."

Stevie lifted the chair and carried it the remaining few feet before setting it down beside Kyle at the table. "Sorry, Dad," he said with a slightly masked grin on his face. "Didn't mean to mess up our lovely kitchen floor," he continued, looking at the tired, worn linoleum. His sister laughed and smacked him on his arm.

Elijah looked at the two of them and frowned. "Don't be mocking me in front of our guest," he said. "You could at least pretend to have some respect for your father."

Kyle smiled along with the children, who could barely contain their laughter. He estimated Stevie to be about fourteen years old. His sister was older, probably nineteen or twenty. Both kids were neatly dressed, and by the look in their eyes, Kyle got the strong impression that they were fond of their father.

"Are you the one who took care of me last night?" Kyle asked Diana.

She nodded, embarrassed. "Yes, sir, I am."

"I guess I need to thank you then," Kyle continued. "It looks like you gave up your bed for me too."

"It was no problem, sir," she replied. "I'm glad I could help."

Kyle turned to Elijah. "Thank you for bringing me into your home. I probably owe you my life."

Elijah waved his hand in front of his face in a kind of "it was nothing" dismissal. "I was just in the right place at the right time," he said. "That's all."

"I think it was a little more than that. I was getting worked over pretty hard. Not sure at what point it was you found me."

"Dad used to be in the Marines," blurted out Stevie, "before he became a preacher. So first he kicked those guys' butts, and then he brought you home. It was kind of like Jesus in the temple and the good Samaritan, all in one." Stevie's eyes twinkled as he summed up the story, smiling broadly at his father and obviously proud of what had transpired.

"Stevie's a little dramatic in his storytelling, but I guess that's the gist of it," said Elijah with some embarrassment. "You must be hungry Kyle. Diana, get Mr. Tait some food, would you?"

Diana got up from the table and went to a small camp stove set up next to the kitchen window. "Do you like oatmeal?" she asked from across the room.

Kyle nodded and soon there was a bowl of oatmeal sitting in front of him. "So was that you I saw running towards me when I went down?" he asked Elijah.

Elijah nodded. "Stevie and I had just walked one of the ladies home from church. She was scared to be out alone; things have gotten a little rough, as you might have noticed."

"Yeah, I got that impression," Kyle said as he gently probed a swollen eye.

"Anyway, we were heading home when I heard some noises and saw the three of them picking on you. Tried to get there before they did too much damage, but I've slowed down in my old age."

"Did they hurt you?" asked Kyle.

"No. One of them threw a punch, but the old marine training came in handy. A couple of those guys already had a fair bit of blood on them. Looked like you had done some damage before you went down."

"Maybe a little, but not enough," Kyle said, then explained what had happened before Elijah's arrival.

Elijah and his kids listened intently to Kyle's story. Stevie was quite excited by the description of the fight. "Do you fight a lot?" Stevie asked.

"No." Kyle said, shaking his head stiffly. "Not since I was in high school, and then just a couple of times. Do you know what happened to my cart?"

"It's around the side of the building," said Stevie. "My dad had me pull it home."

"I figured it was something important," said Elijah. "After your friends left, you kept mumbling about it. Couldn't understand what you were saying for the most part, but I could see your cart down the street, and you kept going on about it, so I figured it meant something to you."

"Yeah, it does. I'm heading to Montana, and I kind of need it to haul my things."

Elijah whistled. "Montana's a long way away," he said. "I guess that cart would be helpful."

"We've been to Montana," said Diana. "We went up that way the summer before Mom died. She wanted to see Yellowstone Park. I don't remember it too well, but we've got lots of pictures."

"It's a pretty part of the country. A lot more mountains than around here."

Elijah burst out laughing. "That's an understatement if I've ever heard one. Around here we call any hill over twenty feet a mountain. It sure was pretty country up there, but I'm guessing you're not headed that way for the scenery."

"No. My family's in Missoula, Deer Creek, actually."

Elijah nodded. "I figured that was it. I'm guessing there are a whole lot of displaced people right now, not knowing what to do. Where'd you start out?"

Kyle told them about his experience on the airplane, about traveling with Ed, and then leaving from San Angelo.

"Sorry things went bad for you here," Elijah said when Kyle finished. "Lubbock's a good town with good people. Don't let those idiots you met yesterday make you think otherwise. I was born here and came back after I left the military. I expect I'll probably die and be buried here as well."

"Well, my first impression of Lubbock wasn't so good, but it's gone up considerably since then."

"Good job, Daddy," Diana teased her father, patting him on the back. "You should join the Chamber of Commerce, maybe make a commercial for the city."

"See what I get to put up with?" Elijah said, giving his daughter a look. "She's just like her mother. Makes fun of everything I do. Seriously though, you should be careful. People are scared and desperate and are doing some crazy things. We were all used to jumping in our cars and running to the store to fill up our refrigerators. All that went away in an instant, and we weren't prepared for it."

"You seem to be doing alright," said Kyle. "How are you getting by?"

"I was in the military," said Elijah. "I visited some pretty destitute countries and experienced some miserable things. I promised myself I'd be ready for anything if I made it home. We'll be good for a few more weeks, but we've already talked about heading out of town to an uncle's place. He works on a farm east of here."

"Why are you waiting?"

"I've got a congregation that I need to get situated before I go," said Elijah, matter-of-factly. "The preacher can't just take off and abandon his flock. What would the Lord think?"

"Hadn't thought of that," said Kyle. "How is your flock doing?"

"Scared and hungry, at least the ones that I know about. I've got a lot of older people, and they're not managing so well. Two of them have already passed away. Did one funeral on Saturday, and I've got one tomorrow. Another lady will probably be gone in a few days, so it's been a tough week." Elijah's voice broke as he spoke, and he wiped at a tear with his hand. "Excuse me for getting emotional," he said. "But it's kind of like losing family."

"Anything I can do to help?" Kyle asked. "I owe you my life. There must be some way I can repay you."

Elijah shook his head. "No. I appreciate the offer, but you've got more important things to be doing, like getting on your way back to your family. Speaking of which, you need to eat and get cleaned up. How are you feeling?"

"Like I got run over. I don't think there's any part of me that doesn't hurt. How do I look?"

"Real bad," Stevie said. "Like you got run over."

Diana smacked her little brother on the head. "Shut up, Stevie. That's not nice," she whispered.

"But it's true," he retorted, rubbing his head and looking to his dad to scold his sister. Elijah just shrugged and gave him a "you deserved it" look.

Kyle swallowed a mouthful of oatmeal. "I'm sure you're right, Stevie. I can tell by the lumps on my face that I look pretty bad."

When he finished his food, Kyle excused himself and headed to the bathroom to clean up, armed with a bucket of water and a couple of washcloths that Diana had supplied him with.

Kyle closed the bathroom door and turned to the mirror. Staring back at him in the dim light coming through a small window over the toilet was a puffy-eyed, broken-down, old man. It took him a minute to catch his breath, and then he started to cry. Kyle dropped down onto the toilet and let the tears run. I've only been on the road five days, he thought, and I'm already a mess. How am I ever going to make it?

He heard a tapping on the door, and Diana called to him, "Are you alright in there?"

Kyle shook his head to clear his thoughts. "Yeah," he called back, "I'm fine, just getting cleaned up."

Kyle sat on the toilet pondering his situation for some time before standing in front of the mirror again. He dipped a washcloth in the bucket, wrung it out, and began to wipe away the grime. Starting with his forehead, he scrubbed the dirt out of his hairline and gingerly worked his way down his face. Dried blood stuck in wounds and creases and places that Diana hadn't wiped the night before. He worked tenderly around his eyes, both of which were swollen and various shades of purple and blue. The left eye was worse then the right and hurt intensely as he cleaned it.

Kyle took his shirt off and washed his neck and chest. Both arms were missing patches of skin that had been rubbed off on the street, his right shoulder having gotten the worst of it. He washed it tenderly, picking out small pieces of gravel as he went.

Another knock sounded at the door. "Dad said to bring you some clean water," Diana's muffled voice came through the door.

Kyle opened the door and took the bucket from her.

"Here's our first aid kit. I thought you might need it as well," she added, handing him a shoebox-sized plastic container. "It's kind of messy, but there are probably things in it you could use."

Kyle thanked her, then shut himself back in the bathroom and continued to wash.

He emerged from the bathroom thirty minutes later, bandaged and cleaned. Elijah sat at the kitchen table reading, and Stevie was in the living room drawing on a pad of paper, a magazine propped open to a picture of a helicopter in front of him. "You look a little different," Elijah said, looking up from his Bible, his black reading glasses perched on the end of his nose.

"I feel different," said Kyle. "I feel better now that I'm cleaned up, but you might want to burn those washcloths you gave me."

Elijah chuckled and set his glasses down on the table beside him. "We might not use them right away, but I don't think we'll be burning anything for the time being. You never know what might come in handy."

"Who's your barber?" Stevie called from the other room. "I hope you didn't leave him a tip."

Kyle grinned. "Found some scissors in your first aid kit. Figured I'd be better off with a little less hair. I didn't go for the bald look, like your dad. Us white guys don't have such nicely-shaped heads."

Elijah rolled his eyes. "If you lived here long enough, you'd learn to ignore my son. Sometimes his mouth engages before his brain fires up."

"He's fine," said Kyle. "I've got a son about the same age, so I'm used to it. Helps keep a smile on your face."

Kyle sat down at the table across from Elijah. "So I need to know, how could you leave a nasty-looking, homeless bum, who you don't know, in the same bedroom with your daughter? Weren't you worried?"

"Not really," said Elijah. "I was in the next room, and Diana's pretty tough. She wants to be a nurse, even works as a nurse's assistant at the old folks home part time, and I thought taking care of a corpse would be a good experience for her. And to be honest, you were so messed up my grandmother could have taken you, and she's closing in on one hundred."

Kyle laughed. "I suppose. But I was pretty scary looking. I really want to thank you for not leaving me in the street."

"Truth be told, I wasn't planning on bringing you home, I just wanted to stop the beating. But you kept mumbling about your cart, and you didn't strike me as a bum. I guess I had the impression you had someplace important to get to. Maybe the Holy Spirit whispered to me."

"Whatever the reason, you were right," said Kyle nodding. "That place is important, at least it is to me."

"How soon till you think you can get back on the road? Not trying to rush you, but I'm sure you're anxious to move on. Winter starts early up there, doesn't it?"

"Depends on the year. Sometimes we get snow in September, sometimes not till January, but I'm sure the mountains will have some by the time I get north. I'd like to get going in the morning, if you don't mind me staying another night."

"Sure, that's no problem. Are you sure you're up to leaving that quickly? I wasn't expecting you'd be ready to go that soon. You are welcome to stay longer if you need to."

"I think I'll be alright. My legs are in pretty good shape, just a few bruises. I might have a couple of busted ribs, and maybe my cheek, but nothing to stop me from moving along. I'll probably scare anyone I meet, but maybe that will keep trouble away, and I don't want to waste the good weather."

"Well then," said Elijah, "lets go take a look at your cart and see what you're missing.

CHAPTER FIFTEEN

Tuesday, September 13th
Lubbock, TX

The ringing of an alarm clock in the next room woke Kyle up. He swung his feet out of bed and stiffly twisted his head from side to side. His neck was tighter than yesterday, but at least his legs still felt good. He could hear movement in the next room and then a light knock on his door.

"Kyle?" Elijah's voice called through the door.

"I'm up," Kyle replied. "Be out in a minute."

He put on his clothes and joined Elijah in the kitchen for breakfast while Diana slept soundly on the living room couch.

"You sure you're ready?' Elijah asked, studying the bruises on Kyle's face.

Kyle nodded as he finished eating his cereal. "I'll be alright. I need to get moving."

"Sorry we don't have milk," Elijah said as he gathered up their bowls. "Haven't been to the store for a few days and haven't found any good deals on dairy cows."

"You're forgiven," said Kyle. "Water does the job."

"Did you remember that notebook you asked me for?"

"I did. I packed it last night. I appreciate it."

"Don't mention it. The kids started school a week before this all went down, so we had a few extras around. I don't think school will be starting back up for awhile, do you?"

"No. I think it's going to be a long time, two or three years at least, before traditional schooling starts again."

"You certainly are optimistic, aren't you," said Elijah, chuckling. "What d'you need the book for anyway? You going to be doing some sketching in your spare time?"

Kyle laughed, then got serious. "No. I want to keep a journal. After getting beat up Sunday, I realized there's a good chance that I might not make it home. I figured I'd keep a record of my trip, then if I don't make it, maybe someone will find my journal and forward it to my family. That way Jennifer will find out I didn't forget about her. Plus, it'll help me keep track of time and know where I'm at in my schedule."

Elijah nodded. "Hopefully you can deliver the notebook in person, but if I don't hear from you when things come back together, I'll send your wife a note too, assuming my kids don't get hungry and eat me first."

Kyle wiped the crumbs off the kitchen table and walked outside with Elijah. The eastern horizon was just starting to brighten and the day wasn't unbearably hot yet. Elijah sniffed the air. "Smells like rain," he said. "Still want to head off today?"

Kyle nodded. "Rain will keep the temperature down. Besides, the longer I wait, the harder it will be to get started."

"Help me spread these out before we leave," Elijah said, grabbing some buckets stacked beside the house. "If it does rain, I want to collect all the water I can."

In no time, the buckets were spread out, and Kyle and Elijah, who had insisted on walking with Kyle to the outskirts of the city, headed out in the gradually brightening dawn.

After walking a few blocks, they turned onto a street Kyle recognized, and he felt himself tense up. "Are we going to be safe here?" he asked, scanning the street for danger.

Elijah nodded confidently. "It's too early for trouble. The gang bangers you ran into the other day will be sleeping, and I don't even think they're from this part of town. They probably followed you for a while, waiting to jump you someplace with less people around. We'll just make good time and get you out of the city, and there shouldn't be any problems."

"But how about you? Will you be okay getting back home? People will be up by the time you come back through."

"I'm not worried. I know the areas to avoid better than you did. Besides, you looked out of place and had a cart full of stuff, so you were an easy target."

"I suppose. I'll really have to try and avoid the cities, won't I?"

"Probably best. People are going to be desperate where there's no easy way to get food."

"One of the reasons I love Montana is that there aren't as many cities, and the hunting's good too."

"I enjoyed my visit there. If it wasn't for my family all being in Texas, I could move there pretty easily I think."

"How long ago did you visit?"

"It was eight years ago last June, six months before Tasha died."

"Tasha was your wife?"

Elijah nodded.

"I'm sorry for your loss."

"It was a tough time, but we got through it. At least we were able to say goodbye."

"It wasn't sudden?"

"No, we had some time to get ready. That's why we went to Montana. She picked all these places she wanted to see before she passed: Yosemite, Old Faithful, Mt. Rushmore, Statue of Liberty, and a few others. We took that last summer and saw them all. It was one of the happiest summers of my life." Elijah radiated peace as he talked about the trip and his wife.

"Were you in the ministry at the time?"

He shook his head. "I was in Iraq. Tasha was diagnosed in early April, so I got leave. When she died, I received a discharge. Couldn't very well raise kids alone from the other side of the world."

The sun had fully risen above the horizon, the temperature climbing enough to make Kyle sweat. "So how'd you end up becoming a minister?"

Elijah thought as they walked, the stillness of the city interrupted only by the sound of their footsteps and the wheels of the cart. "Well," he began slowly, "dealing with Tasha's death forced me to think about life. You know, what's it all about? Is there really a God? I just couldn't accept it all being for nothing, and I wanted some answers. Tasha always believed, ever since she was a little girl. It was easy for her, but I struggled with it. Faith is a tough thing to come to grips with; it was a lot easier to not think about it, because then you never have to feel guilty about anything. Then when she passed... her body... I can't explain it, but it wasn't her. It was her body, but it was like her skin had just been something she was wearing, and the real Tasha was gone. I guess I made up my mind then that we weren't just highly evolved monkeys and that we had a soul, or a spirit, or whatever you want to call it. After I came to that conclusion, things kind of fell into place. Maybe this is where God wants me."

Kyle didn't respond. He just listened and walked, pulling his cart along behind him.

Elijah looked at Kyle and laughed. "Sorry, Kyle. I guess it doesn't take much to get me into preacher mode anymore."

"No, don't apologize. You're good. I was just thinking back on the past week and a half and everything that's happened. I know I should believe in God, that's how I was raised, but watching how quickly people fall apart, I don't know. I mean, why would God create people who would do what they did to our country? I bet thousands of people have died in the last week that wouldn't have under normal circumstances. It just seems we're a lot closer to animals than we are to anything holy."

"I can see where you're coming from, but that's part of life – seeing how we deal with what's put in front of us. I don't claim to know how God thinks or why he lets happen the things that he does, but I believe he's there. Doesn't mean that somebody else isn't going to do horrible things. It just means that I need to treat people the best way I can. Heck, if we're just a chance grouping of cells, then why haul that guy off the airplane? You weren't expecting that it would do you any good. Why go back to your family when it'd be a whole lot easier to just start a new life here? Name one animal that would go to half the lengths you have for a breeding partner or their offspring. If we're all products of the 'survival of the fittest' heritage that the scientists proclaim, then we should be living an every-man-for-himself lifestyle. From a non-theistic standpoint, there's no explanation for why we care about others or try and do good."

The highway ahead of them was littered with cars and trucks, paralyzed in the full swing of activity, and with most of the city behind them, Kyle knew that Elijah would soon return home. He stopped and turned towards Elijah. "You've given me a lot to think about," Kyle said with a grin. "We should have started this conversation yesterday. It gives me a little more hope for mankind. Not a lot at this point, but some."

Elijah's broad smile spread across his face again, and his eyes sparkled in the early morning light. "I'd have loved to talk about it; it's one of my favorite topics, but you slept most of the day." He winked at Kyle and laughed. "You know, Kyle, you do believe in God. It's just that your brain gets in the way and screws everything up. But think about your life, how you live, how you treat other people. Ask yourself why you do things that help others at your expense, whether it's your kids, or your wife, or someone you don't even know. Why do you care about going home? That's the spiritual part of you, the divine spark at work. There's your answer."

"I'll think about it, Elijah. I'm sure I'll have some time for thinking in the next few weeks."

Elijah stepped forward and embraced Kyle. "Sunday school's over. You need to get moving; you have a long ways to go. Take care of yourself. It's not going to be easy."

Kyle wrapped his arms around Elijah, trying not to grimace in pain as Elijah squeezed his bruised ribs. "Thanks for everything. You promised to come to Montana when this is all over, and I'm going to hold you to that. Tell your kids thanks, too."

Deer Creek, Montana

"Meeting adjourned," Gabe said as he ran his hands through his thinning hair, frustrated with everything that wasn't getting done. "Let's work on those issues and try to come up with some more ideas for our next meeting," he added as the first of the committee members headed to the door.

Jennifer finished writing her notes, stuffed her pad in her handbag, and got up to go. The meeting had been difficult for the council. The weight of what they had to deal with was becoming more and more apparent. There had already been one death in the community, and the number of people going hungry was mounting. The committee was discovering that those who were more prepared were the ones who avoided participating in the group, leaving them with the people who needed the most help but had little to offer.

Jennifer recalled learning about when the pilgrims first came to America, how half of them had died in the first year, and then it was a number of years before survival rates improved much. Considering the helplessness of so many in their community, she worried that they might experience similar losses. Jennifer was caught up in her thoughts and jumped when a hand touched her arm.

"Mind if I walk with you?" Doug asked.

He was dressed in his sheriff's uniform again, and while Jennifer thought he overplayed his security role, it seemed to make Doug feel important and didn't really hurt anything. Besides, who was she to be critical of a person's appearance? Her routine of a daily shower had devolved to the occasional sponge bath, and she had only washed her hair a handful of times since "the event," if you counted a quick rinse in cold water as washing. Consequently, Jennifer wore extra deodorant and perfume to mask body odor, and guessed, from the potpourri of scents in the room, that most of the people on the council were resorting to the same tactics. Even her clothes had seen little soap over the same time period. With water being such a precious resource, two rainstorms had been the extent of their laundry. When the first storm had rolled in, she had been unprepared for the sudden opportunity and barely managed to get their clothes wet. The second time it rained, she and the kids had rigged clotheslines in the backyard and hurried to get their clothes out and hanging before the rain quit.

"Doug! Sorry for jumping. I was kind of lost in my thoughts. Um, I'm a little out of your way, aren't I?"

"Oh, just a little, but it's no big deal. Besides, the walk will go by quicker if you have someone to chat with."

"I guess that's okay," Jennifer answered, making a point not to show any enthusiasm.

"Great. I was hoping you wouldn't mind." Doug offered to carry her bag, then held the door for her as they bid Gabe goodbye.

"So, Doug," said Jennifer, Chuck's words of caution ringing in her ears, "I don't know much about you. Are you married?"

"Nope," he replied. "I was engaged once, but it didn't work out."

"Sorry to hear that."

"Probably for the best. I don't think she liked that I was in law enforcement. Said I was too authoritarian." He said the last word in a mocking tone and made quotation marks with his fingers.

"So no kids then?"

"No. Well, not with her at least. I've got a son with a girlfriend from a few years back, but I'm not even sure he's mine. I didn't really trust her while we were together. I think she just wanted to get some money out of me."

"Does your son live close?"

"Spokane. At least that's where they were when I last heard from her. What's with the inquisition?"

"Sorry. I didn't mean to pry. Just trying to make conversation. What should we talk about?"

"I don't know. How about you? How are you doing, you and your kids?"

"Still as good as one could hope, all things considered. We're trying to stretch the food out, so always a little hungry. Guess I'll be losing the weight I've been trying to drop for the past five years."

"You don't need to lose any weight," Doug said, stepping back to take an exaggerated look. "I think you look good. Hope you don't mind me saying that."

Jennifer's breath stuck in her throat. She mumbled a "thanks" and tried not to give any reaction beyond a brief, forced smile, wishing she'd kept the conversation from taking a personal turn. After a long pause, she changed the subject. "So, how are things going on the security front? Have you found anyone to help you with that yet?"

"That's going fine," he answered. "Not a lot happening with it really. One of my neighbors gave me a bike, so now I can get around a bit more, but it's uncomfortable and making me sore, if you know what I mean. Once I get used to it, it will be good transportation."

"That was nice of them. I'm sure it will make things easier."

"Yeah, I suppose so, at least until winter. Then I'll really be wishing my patrol car worked."

"Hard to believe how much we relied on our cars, isn't it? I feel totally helpless without mine. If anything happened to the kids, I couldn't rush them to the doctor, if there was one, and I can't run to the store, or go see my friends. You can't do anything except on foot or bike anymore, or a horse if you have one. It's been a tough adjustment."

"There's that one truck that I told you about that belongs to Jacob. He would probably give you a ride in an emergency, but I don't know where you'd go. On the radio the other day, the President said that a few hospitals still had some services, but who knows where they're at or what's there. Did you talk to Jacob about helping you find some food?"

"I did, on Monday. David managed to get some gas out of our car and we took that over. Jacob came back with some stuff that evening. I have to say, I feel bad about just taking things out of trucks. It doesn't seem right."

"I know what you mean. Usually I'd arrest people for doing that, not suggesting it in the first place," Doug said, chuckling softly. "Times are pretty desperate though, and all that food will just spoil if it sits there. I don't know what else can be done."

"I thought about writing down what we get and from where, so somehow we can make it up, but I don't know how that would ever work."

"Honestly, Jennifer, I wouldn't worry about it. People are just trying to survive. I bet there've even been shootings for food, especially in the cities, and the situation is probably going to get a lot worse before it gets better."

"I hope it doesn't, but I do worry about my kids. Did you have any success hunting the other day?"

"No, we saw a couple of deer a long way off, but it's still warm, and they haven't come down very far. Another month or so and we should start to see them. We were just scoping out areas as much as anything."

"Well, I'm sure that will be helpful. David says they're going to start butchering cattle at the ranch this week. It will be good to have some meat again." Jennifer looked up and saw her street. "It looks like I'm about home. I can walk from here."

"Oh, I don't mind," said Doug. "I'm the security guy. I'll just make an early patrol of the area."

Jennifer offered a lukewarm smile and resigned herself to his continued companionship.

Doug motioned to a brown two-story home on the other side of the street. "Have you noticed anyone at that house? I've stopped by a few times but haven't found anyone there."

"I haven't seen anyone. Why?"

"Well, the other day when I was on patrol, I was thinking about these three houses where it's obvious people have lived in them, but no one is around now, and I bet there's food inside, if someone hasn't already stolen it. I figured I should wait awhile to see if the owners show up, but there's no sense in people starving if we have some food this close. I think maybe this week I'll try and get inside."

"You're probably right," Jennifer mused, "but this seems kind of weird. Now I'm talking with the sheriff about breaking into my neighbor's home."

Doug laughed. "Think of it as survival. If they're not going to use it, we should."

As they approached Jennifer's house, Doug reached out and took her hand, which she yanked away reflexively.

"Hey, easy, Jennifer. I'm not trying to hurt you," Doug said while reaching for her again. "I just wanted to tell you how much I like you, and I thought maybe we could be there for each other, you know. We have no idea how things are going to turn out. It would be good to have someone to be with and talk to, someone who's looking out for you."

Jennifer shook her head and took a step back. "Doug, I'm sorry, but the last thing on my mind right now is finding some-one. I've got myself and my three kids to worry about, and I'm married, in case you'd forgotten. No offense, but romance isn't on my to do list."

"Look, Jenn, I know you're married, and if your husband comes back, fine, I understand. But if he doesn't, or until he does, we can be there for each other."

"Doug," Jennifer said, searching for the right words, "I know the world's changed, and I think you're trying to be nice. So in a way, I'm flattered, but…," she stammered, "but no. No! We can't 'be there for each other.' I'm sure you can find someone else, if that's what you need, but I'm not the one. Please understand. Okay? I need to go." She turned abruptly and hurried to her house.

Doug stood in the driveway with his hands on his hips, watching her walk away. "I'll see you at the next meeting, Jenn," he called out as she disappeared into her house.

CHAPTER SIXTEEN

Wednesday, September 14th
Northern Texas

The sun was low in the western sky as Kyle pulled his cart to the side of the road. He was two days removed from Lubbock and healing little by little, but still carried many painful reminders of the city's unofficial "welcoming committee." The warm, clear evening showed no sign of rain, so Kyle left his tent in the cart, found a soft spot of ground, and unrolled his sleeping bag. With some light still left in the day, Kyle pulled out the notebook Elijah had given him and began to write.

Day 12

This journal is the record of Kyle Tait. If it comes into your possession, I ask that you please send it to my wife and children who live at 324 Deer Falls Trail, in Deer Creek, MT. Their names are Jennifer, David, Emma, and Spencer. It is a record of my attempt to return home after the EMP attack of Sept. 2nd.

Jennifer, if this notebook gets delivered to you, it more than likely means that I've failed in my efforts to return home. Please know I tried. If nothing else, this notebook gives me a chance to say goodbye and let you know that being with the four of you was more important to me than life itself.

It has been 12 days since the attack, and by various means, I have managed to travel from Houston to a point just south of Dimmit, TX. Without a calendar or a watch, the days just blend together (which isn't all bad, because now I don't have to dread Monday mornings, though in a way, every day seems like a Monday). I've reverted to my caveman heritage and have simply started counting days since the attack instead of trying to figure out dates, as that seems to be the easiest way for me to keep track of time. With next to no transportation available, I have resorted to walking but am fortunate enough to have a small cart, which I use to haul my supplies. If things go as planned, I expect it will take me between 70 and 80 days, putting me in Deer Creek towards the end of November.

Jennifer, how do I write something that you will probably only read if I'm dead? I want you to know that I love you. Looking back, I'm sure I never told you enough, and as I think about the possibility that I might never see you again, it completely rips my heart out. I know I took you for granted and never really took the time to think about what you meant to me. Thank you for being my wife, my love, my friend, my support, my partner. I want to see you so badly, to hold you in my arms, to kiss your face, and simply hold your hand. The thought of not being with you is almost unbearable. I know there's a good chance I won't make it, and if I don't, please move on with your life and find someone else who will love you and make you happy.

David, you're a son any father would be proud to have. I probably wasn't as patient with you as I should have been, but I was a rookie dad, and I hope you know that your father loved you. I'm not sure under what circumstances you might see this notebook or how old you'll be, but please promise me you'll live a good life and not let circumstances make you bitter. Take care of your mother, and be there for your sister and brother. They'll need you. The world will need good people for leaders. Be one. Things may never be like they were before, but take on your challenges, stand up for your family, and continue to make me a proud father.

Emma, you've always been my beautiful and sweet princess, just like your mother. I've missed your hugs and smiles; my days haven't been nearly as bright without them. Your heart has always been especially tender, and I worry about you every day. Please don't let the way things are keep you from living a happy life. I've realized in the past few days that we don't need much to be happy, just good people to be with. Please know that I loved you more than you can understand. Keep smiling and save some hugs for your dad.

Spencer, it breaks my heart to think I might not get to see you grow up and become the man I hope you'll be. You probably won't remember me, but know that your dad loved you enough to try to walk across the country to be with you. We named you after my grandfather, your great-grandfather. He was a good man. Do his name proud. You're smart and determined, full of energy and innocence. Do good things with your life. One way or another, I'll be there to watch you grow up, if not as your father, then as your guardian angel. Help take care of your mother. She'll need you to be strong.

My trip has been and will likely continue to be more difficult than I expected. People are scared, supplies are scarce, and it's a long ways to walk, but I think I can do it.

I love you all.

The light was nearly gone when Kyle put his notebook away and lay down for the night. He felt a small weight lift from his shoulders, knowing that if he didn't make it home there was a chance his family would know some of what happened to him and how he felt about them. He closed his eyes and quickly drifted off to sleep.

Saturday, September 17th
Northern Texas

Kyle set his cart down in the shade of a semi-truck emblazoned with the powder blue Werner Enterprises logo. It was sometime in the early afternoon, and a light breeze blew but did nothing more than circulate the hot, stale air. During the month he'd been in Texas, he'd grown more accustomed to the heat and humidity, but still longed for the cool, dry air of Montana.

He pulled out a jug of water and took a long drink, then rolled out his sleeping bag on the ground for a pad, hoping to get a few minutes of rest in the shade of the truck. With a rolled-up pair of dirty jeans for a pillow, Kyle closed his eyes and was just drifting off when he heard a strange noise. In his semi-conscious state, he dismissed the unfamiliar sound, until he heard it a second time. The third time he heard the noise, his eyes popped open. Propping himself up on an elbow, he strained to listen and finally heard a soft moan coming from somewhere close by. Kyle rose to his knees and looked around, trying to spot the source of the moan, sure that it wasn't coming from any of the animals he had become familiar with over the past two weeks.

Kyle put his hands to his mouth and yelled, then heard the sound again, this time louder. He jumped to his feet and scanned the surrounding area more thoroughly. As he looked around, he thought to himself how everything he loved about Montana, this area of Texas lacked. Instead of mountains, trees, rivers, and lakes, it was flat, barren and had just two prominent features: scrub brush and brown dirt. As far as the eye could see, scraggly, waist-high scrub brush dotted an ocean of brown dirt, and he had grown sick of it. When the wind blew, it got in his eyes, his ears, and his nose, and he seemed to taste it all of the time. Even in his dreams he saw and tasted the same never-ending, brown dirt.

Puzzled by the strange noise, Kyle continued to scan the area, but could see nothing that would account for it. Then he heard the sound again. He walked to the edge of the road and noticed a dry wash, thirty feet from where he stood, that connected to a culvert running under the road. He ran to it, knelt down on a knee, and peered inside.

Not a dozen feet from where Kyle knelt was a tiny, frail old lady, starring back at him from the shelter of the culvert. She lay on her left side with her back against the side of the culvert, as if someone had simply pushed her over. She looked at Kyle and smiled weakly, her white teeth a stark contrast to the dirt that covered her face. "Can you help me?" she whispered through cracked lips, barely able to form the words.

Kyle knelt in front of the tunnel, momentarily stunned by his discovery. He scrambled forward into the cool shade and put a hand on her shoulder. "Are you hurt?" he asked, leaning his face in close to her ear.

"No," she said, shaking her head slowly. "I'm not hurt." She paused, then struggled to speak again. "I'm thirsty...and hungry." She swallowed with great effort. "I don't think I'm going to make it much longer." She reached out, put her hand on Kyle's arm, and looked intently into his eyes. "Did you come to save me?" she asked.

"Let me get you some water." Kyle crawled out of the culvert and ran back to his cart. He grabbed his last jug of water and returned to the tunnel where he set the jug down before helping the woman into a sitting position. Bracing her upright with his shoulder, Kyle lifted the jug, held it to her lips, and slowly poured the water into her mouth.

She drank in deliberate, careful swallows. Some of the water spilled down her cheeks and onto her blouse, leaving muddy brown spots. Kyle assumed the blouse had originally been white or beige, but it was now nearly as brown as the dirt that surrounded them.

"Thank you," she said, pulling her head away. "I've been so thirsty."

Kyle nodded and offered her the water again. She took another long drink, then held up her hand, and Kyle set the jug on the ground beside her. "Wait here," he said without thinking. "I'll be right back."

Kyle ran to his cart, and then quickly returned to the culvert again with a handful of food that he dropped onto the ground beside the woman. "What would you like?" he asked.

She scanned the items and motioned to a package of donuts. Kyle tore the package open and fed the donuts to her. When they were gone, she ate a package of Twinkies followed by a chocolate bar.

The woman ate slowly and said little. Finally, after about a half an hour of eating and drinking, she rested, her arms hanging limply by her side.

"Can I get you anything else?" Kyle asked.

She shook her head. "Who are you?" she asked.

"I'm Kyle, " he responded. "Who are you?"

"Louise Kennedy."

"How long have you been here?"

"I don't know," she answered after some thought. She spoke slowly and formed each word carefully, as if she had just awakened from a deep sleep. "My car quit. That was more than a week ago."

"Why didn't you go somewhere for help?"

"I was afraid. I thought that someone would come to help, but no one did." Her voice trailed off as a tear slowly ran down her cheek, turning to mud before it reached her chin. Louise reached feebly for Kyle's hand. "By the time I decided that I should go, I was already out of food."

"How long since you last ate?" he asked, patting her hand.

"I'm not sure – four, maybe five days." Her voice was tired and lifeless. "I was going to see my grandkids and had some treats for them. I didn't want to eat them, but I was so hungry."

Kyle patted Louise's hand. "Did you have water?"

"I had a little with me, and there's a truck that I've been getting some from. When the driver left it, he told me that I could help myself. He tried to get me to go with him. I think he thought I was crazy when I wouldn't, but it's too far for me to walk. I guess I should have tried, but I didn't know I would be here so long."

"Don't feel bad. It's hard to know what's best right now. I don't think anyone knows how to act." Kyle let go of her hand. "I'll be back in a few minutes," he said and shuffled out of the dark tunnel, the sunlight blinding him as his eyes once again adjusted to the bright afternoon sunlight. He scanned the road and saw the truck Louise had mentioned, a red Coke delivery truck about a half-mile to the North. There was a faint path worn in the dirt leading from the culvert to where the truck had stopped.

Kyle walked back to his cart, his mind wrestling with the situation he was in. He was anxious to get moving and wanted to make good time, at least as good as he could in the condition he was in. Winter could hit Montana at any time in the fall. There might even be snow in the mountains already for all he knew. Under normal circumstances he would've simply made a phone call and waited for an ambulance. He thought again. Under normal circumstances he'd be in Montana and Louise would be back home. What if he hadn't stopped to rest where he did? What if he'd noticed the Coke truck further down the road and simply continued on to that point? Then he'd know nothing about Louise and wouldn't be faced with this dilemma. He wondered how many other stranded people he had unknowingly passed.

None of those "what ifs" mattered now. He had stopped where he had, and her life was in his hands. It would be easy to load up his cart and go. There would be no way for her to stop him. Could anyone blame him for leaving her, as old and feeble as she was? His food and water were limited, and his body was sore from walking and pulling, let alone the bruises and cuts that were still healing. Would she even be able to walk if he took her with him? She was weak and no doubt slow. How far would his obligation run? Where would he take her, and who would take her in? Were there even any shelters operating?

His other option was to leave her. In a day or two, the heat and hunger would get her, if the animals didn't first. There would be no real consequences for him if he left. Other than Louise, no one would know he'd been there. If he did leave, it would likely be years, if ever, before anyone discovered what happened to the old woman. There were probably thousands of people like her who had or would die on the side of the road, most probably younger than she was. No, he decided, he wouldn't really be guilty of any crime if he were to leave Louise behind. The only thing he'd have to deal with would be his conscience.

Kyle felt sick to his stomach. Life and death decisions weren't supposed to fall into his hands. They were the domain of doctors and judges and soldiers, people who had been trained to deal with those matters. He was a simple power company field supervisor. The decisions he made were easy, like who to schedule for what job, or whether to run overtime on a project, not whether someone was going to live or die. Kyle sat down on his sleeping bag in the shade of the truck. The sun was on its downward arc, and the line of shade had shifted noticeably since he had stopped. He knew there were still several hours of daylight left, and he could travel a long ways in that time, at least he could if he was traveling alone.

Kyle leaned back against the wheel of the semi and thought of his family in Montana, without him. As he did dozens of times each day, he wondered how they were doing. He'd give anything for a one-minute phone call. Pulling a handcart gave a person too much time to think.

Sucking in a deep breath and letting it out slowly, Kyle got up, quickly repacked his handcart, and pulled it towards him, the handle chattering noisily on the ground as he did. He lifted the handle and started to pull. Every nail and screw in the cart seemed to protest in unison, screaming loudly across the barren landscape.

From the culvert, he heard the faint voice of an old lady. "Kyle?!"

CHAPTER SEVENTEEN

Sunday, September 18th
Deer Creek, Montana

Jennifer sat at the council table, trying to focus on the group's conversation. Despite Gabe's best efforts, the discussion had again gone off on another tangent. This time the conversation had drifted to the subject of what had happened to the people in prison and whether or not they were free and a threat to the community. Jennifer felt it was a useless topic to discuss because there had been no issues with any outside threats so far, but Doug spoke animatedly about forming some kind of militia, and the council was hearing him out.

Doug's infatuation with her made listening to him difficult. He had stopped by everyday since the last meeting with the excuse "to check on them," but to her the visits were obvious attempts to win her over, and his comments made his intentions all too clear. Before the meeting, he hung around her like a dog in heat while she did her best to avoid him. That seemed to upset him, so when the meeting began she waited for Doug to find a seat, then sat as far away from him as she could, only to find that every time she looked up he was staring at her.

The meeting dragged on for another forty-five minutes, with Jennifer too distracted to contribute to the discussions but trying hard to focus on taking notes. As the meeting concluded, the thought of possibly having to walk home with Doug tightened her stomach. She looked around and noticed Carol Jeffries, the community's "doctor," about to leave.

"Carol!" Jennifer called out. "Mind if I walk with you?"

"Sure," said Carol. "That would be nice."

Jennifer grabbed her bag and dashed out the door, catching a glimpse of Doug visiting with Gabe and unaware of her hasty departure.

"So," Carol said as Jennifer caught up with her, "how are you guys dealing with all of this?"

Jennifer filled Carol in on her family's routine, and soon the two women were chatting like old friends.

As they walked, Jennifer glanced back regularly to see if Doug was following them, but he was nowhere to be seen. The longer they walked, the more she relaxed, and by the time they arrived at Carol's house, her anxiety was mostly gone. The two women chatted easily at the end of Carol's driveway for twenty minutes, then bid farewell.

The day was warm and sunny, and after two days of cold, windy weather, Jennifer enjoyed the change. She walked with the sun on her face, and her mind shifted from worrying about Doug to worrying about Kyle to worrying about to how she and the kids were going to handle the coming winter. Extra shirts and socks at night had worked so far, but when winter hit, she knew there would be some major adjustments.

Jennifer turned the corner onto her street and stopped to visit with a neighbor who was trying to alleviate his boredom by cutting his grass with hedge trimmers. After a short visit, she continued on to her house.

When she walked through her door, David was in the kitchen searching for something to eat. "Hey guys! I'm home. How is everyone?" she asked as Spencer's laughter drifted in from the living room.

"Hi, Mom. We're good, but we've got company," David said, motioning towards the living room.

Jennifer gave him a curious look and stepped around the corner. Sitting on the couch, with one arm perched casually across the back, was Doug. She noticed dark patches of sweat in his armpits, along with a half-dozen white rings where sweat had previously dried since the last time he'd washed his uniform. The sight of Doug sitting in her living room, smelly, unwashed, and playing with her son, made Jennifer sick to her stomach.

"Hi, Jenn," Doug said, a big smile on his face. "I missed you after the meeting. Figured I had better stop by and see how things were." He reached out and grabbed for Spencer, who giggled loudly as he dodged Doug's hand.

Spencer was thrilled that someone was willing to play with him and made repeated feints towards Doug before darting out of reach and laughing hysterically.

"I appreciate the concern," Jennifer replied dryly. "We're doing just fine. Thanks for stopping by."

"Glad to hear it," said Doug. "It sure makes my job easier when things run smoothly." He paused and looked around, while Jennifer just stared at him. She wasn't sure how to deal with the situation. She had never allowed him to come so far into her house, and she certainly didn't want to do anything to make him feel welcome.

"Say, would it be possible to get a glass of water?" he asked. "My throat's a little dry."

"Just a minute," Jennifer replied. She walked into the kitchen where David was still searching for food. "How long has he been here?" she asked under her breath.

"I don't know, about ten, fifteen minutes. Not too long, why?"

She avoided answering with a shake of her head, then grabbed a worn paper cup from a stack on the counter and the jug of drinking water out of the fridge, which no longer worked but was a handy place to store food and keep it away from the flies.

She filled the cup and returned to the living room. "Here you go," she said, handing it to him.

Doug drained the cup in three loud swallows, then crushed and set it beside him on the couch as he wiped a drop of water from his chin with the back of his hand. "Are you avoiding me?" he asked, his eyes locked onto hers.

Jennifer was startled by the bluntness of his question and struggled to gather her thoughts. "I, uh, I think 'avoiding' sounds a little strong," she answered, her voice wavering a little.

"Then what do you call it?" Doug asked, hurling the words at her.

The situation felt like an interrogation and Jennifer forced herself to stay calm. "I don't know that I call it anything," she replied. "I guess I'm just trying not to do anything that makes you think we're more than just acquaintances."

From across the room Spencer darted towards Doug, continuing the game they had been playing when Jennifer got home. Doug stuck out his arm to stop Spencer but sent him tumbling to the floor. Jennifer could see that her son was stunned and struggling not to cry.

Doug ignored Spencer and stared at Jennifer, his face expressionless. "Why don't you like me?" he demanded.

"I don't want what you want, Doug," Jennifer said, gathering her courage. "Like I've told you, I'm not looking for a relationship. I'm married. I have three kids. I'm waiting for my husband to get back. Our world has been turned upside down, and I've got more important things to think about. I don't even know if I'll have enough food for us to get through the winter, and you want me to have some relationship with you? Why are you doing this to me?"

"I offer to be around for you and help with stuff, and now it's me who's doing something to you?" he shot back.

"It's not the help that I have the issue with, Doug. It's what you expect in return. Everyone needs help, myself included. I just don't want to sleep with you for it. Is that clear enough?"

Doug glared at her, his jaw muscles working, but he didn't say anything. His eyes drifted from her face and slowly scanned down her body. The t-shirt and blue jeans she wore were certainly nothing that made her feel alluring, but it didn't seem to matter. Jennifer crossed her arms in front of her chest and turned to block his gaze. Doug ignored her attempt to shield herself, and continued to leer at her.

Spencer, having recovered from his tumble, resumed his game, darting towards Doug again and grasping Doug's arm in a wrestling hold. Doug shifted his attention from Jennifer and grabbed Spencer just above the elbow, holding him out at arms length. Spencer laughed and pried at Doug's fingers, trying to break free.

Jennifer could see the muscles in Doug's forearm tighten, and Spencer's laugh changed to a whimper, his mouth open in a silent cry, but Doug didn't let go.

"Mom?" Spencer managed to say, his eyes pleading for her help.

"Let go of him, Doug!" Jennifer ordered. "He's five years old, for heaven's sake."

Doug's face was filled with contempt, and he gave Spencer a hard shove towards Jennifer.

Spencer's legs tangled as he lunged for his mother, and he fell in a heap at her feet. He immediately started to cry. Jennifer scooped him up and put his head on her shoulder. "You need to leave," she said. "We have nothing else to talk about."

Doug looked at her, an arrogant smirk on his face. "It doesn't need to be so difficult. Most women find me quite likable."

"Then go find some other woman," Jennifer snapped. She lay Spencer down on the loveseat and stepped to the side to allow Doug to pass.

Doug stood, smiling like he had been when she'd gotten home. He spread his arms out, as if to give her a hug. "Let's be friends," he said and stepped towards her.

Jennifer took a step back and stuck out her hand. "No. But if you want to just be friends," she emphasized the word just, "I'll shake on that."

"I'd rather hug. It's so much more enjoyable," Doug said as he reluctantly took her hand in his, his eyes drifting down her body again.

Jennifer jerked her hand away, wishing she could run and wash it. Doug stopped in front of her and put his hand on her shoulder. She could tell he was trying to come up with something to say. "A guy's got needs, you know," he said at last.

She looked at him, disgusted. "I can't help you with that."

Doug turned, and as he stepped towards the door, he dropped his hand from her shoulder and rubbed it across her breasts. "I think you could. I bet you'd be great."

Jennifer knocked his hand away. "Get out of my house, you pig!" she spat, no longer disguising her disgust and anger.

Doug laughed as he showed himself to the front door. "Thanks for having me. I'll stop by again to check on things. Don't forget to call if you have any problems."

Jennifer didn't reply, she just watched the door close behind him.

"Are you okay, Mom?" David asked his mom as she walked into the kitchen. He sat at the kitchen table, chewing on a piece of dried spaghetti. "You look upset."

"I'll be fine. It's just Doug. He's having a hard time dealing with things, and that worries me."

"Do we need to get a hold of the police?" David asked, a grin on his face.

"He is the police, Son," Jennifer replied, her eyes on the door. "That's a big part of the problem."

Tuesday, September 20th
Northern Texas

Kyle awoke to the sound of wind whistling around the cab of the truck. The weather had turned stormy the night before, forcing him to call it a day earlier than he would have liked. Luckily there had been a semi truck close by on the side of the highway, and Kyle had been able to force it open and get out of the weather. Now he lay on the top bunk, listening to the wind as he drifted in and out of sleep. An unfamiliar sound caught his attention, and he sat up in the bunk and listened. The sound grew more intense, until finally he realized it was rain.

This was the first significant rainstorm of his journey, and Kyle was not about to waste it. He put on his shoes, climbed out of the truck and, in the near blackness of the early morning, hurried cautiously to where his cart was stowed under the trailer. He dug out empty water bottles and positioned them around the truck to catch the runoff, then stripped to his underwear and washed his body and his clothes in the downpour. It had been forever since he'd showered, and with the rain pouring over him, he could feel the layers of grime washing away.

Feeling clean for the first time in weeks, Kyle grabbed a clean set of clothes from his cart and climbed back in the cab of the truck. Cold and wet from the impromptu shower, he pulled a blanket off of the bunk and wrapped it around his shivering body, then dropped into the passenger seat. The chattering of his teeth accompanied the steady drumming of the slowing rain, and with his knees pulled up to his chest, Kyle rubbed his arms and legs in an effort to warm them.

The sun was just starting to lighten the sky on a day that looked to be cold, wet, and gray. As Kyle warmed up, he took in the world around him through the rain-streaked windshield. In addition to the mud, crops, and streams of water, he was relieved to see the city of Dalhart in the distance, a city he had originally planned on passing through early the day before.

Kyle put his feet down and dried his hair with the blanket, then dropped the blanket onto his lap and inspected his injuries from Lubbock. The bruises were fading but still felt tender when pressed. The visor mirror showed that the purple around his eyes was turning dull gray, and the cut on his cheek was still slightly swollen, but the scab was starting to wear away. Kyle laughed at his reflection. With his beard, bruises, and self-inflicted hair cut, he'd have no chance of passing as the man in the picture on his driver's license.

He unwrapped the blanket and dressed, putting on the last of the new clothes he had looted with Ed back in Houston. It had only been sixteen days since that excursion, but it felt like a lifetime ago as he thought about everything he had been through since then.

Kyle climbed into the driver's seat, pulled out the set of keys he had found the night before, and inserted the key in the ignition. He hit the power button on the radio and once again tried to coax some life out of the unit but met with no success. He'd only listened to one presidential broadcast since leaving Donovan's, and as one accustomed to reading the news two or three times each day, he was anxious to know what was going on. Frustrated with his failure, he turned off the radio and threw the keys back on the dash.

He looked to the west, where the sky was gray and threatening as far as he could see. The rain had slowed to a steady drizzle, the steady sound of it almost lulling him back to sleep. Shaking his head to stay awake, Kyle reached into the back of the truck for a case of CD's he'd noticed and, flipping curiously through the mix, was delighted to find a disc that had been a major part of his childhood years.

Kyle slid the disc out of its case and held it tenderly in his hands, memories from thirty years earlier flooding his mind. He scanned through the song list on Eddie Rabbit's Greatest Hits and immediately spotted the first song he had any memory of, I Love A Rainy Night. Kyle's thoughts drifted back to his childhood, to the family car trips when his mother would pop in their Eddie Rabbit cassette and crank that song up every time it started to rain. Having grown up in the Pacific Northwest, Kyle had heard the song a lot. He was quite young, maybe five or six years old, when the song had stuck in his memory. At that age, he had loved to sing along with his parents and older brother as they barreled down the freeway, all of them singing at the top of their lungs. The tradition continued as he got older but gradually became a symbol to him of how un-cool his parents were, until every time the cassette was slipped into the player, Kyle and his brother, Kurtis, would moan and groan and refuse to sing along.

Reflecting back now, he was sure that his mother had continued the tradition to get a rise out of her sons, but also to instill a memory, as every other cassette, and eventually CD, had been switched out of the car with the exception of Eddie's. It had even gotten to the point that Eddie Rabbit became the family peacemaker. If Kyle and Kurtis got to fighting too much in the backseat, their mom would threaten to pop Eddie into the player, usually eliciting promises of improved behavior followed by peace and quiet for a good twenty minutes.

As he relished these memories, Kyle's fingers began tapping out the song's beat on the steering wheel, and with the rain outside providing background percussion, he soon found himself singing the song he'd grown to love to hate. "Well, I love a rainy night. I love to hear the thunder, watch the lightning, when it lights up the sky..."

He was on the chorus following the second verse, singing "I wake up to a sunny day" at the top of his lungs and drumming enthusiastically on the steering wheel and dashboard, when a boney hand reached out and grabbed him on the shoulder. Kyle jumped violently in his seat, throwing the case of CDs in the air and banging his thighs sharply against the steering wheel. He spun to his right and looked into the face of Louise Kennedy.

"Pipe down! I'm trying to sleep!" she shouted at him.

Kyle exhaled slowly, his heart pounding in his chest like a jackhammer. "Louise. Sorry. I forgot you were back there," he said. "I guess I got carried away."

She gave him a dismissive look, then crawled back into the lower bunk and turned her back to him, pulling the blanket tight around her narrow shoulders.

Kyle watched Louise as his heart slowed to its normal rate, then turned back to the front and picked up where he'd left off, minus the drumming and earsplitting vocals, with memories and worries about his parents and brother and wife and children filling his mind.

Louise and Kyle waited in the truck until a little after noon, when the sky finally started to clear and the wind died down. Together they left the shelter of the semi behind, with Louise perched carefully in the cart and Kyle straining against the handle. Kyle's joke with Ed about pulling a rickshaw no longer seemed nearly as funny. When the unlikely pair had set off three days before, Kyle had tried to have Louise walk, but that had worked for only about a half mile before it became apparent that because of her age and condition, she would only be able to walk a few minutes at a time before becoming too exhausted to continue. So, a half hour and a half-mile into their journey together, Kyle had been forced to repack his cart to make a place for her to sit. And there she rode, while he strained at the handle.

"It sure is muggy," Louise said from the cart, the first complaint coming less than three minutes into their day's travel.

"I know Louise. It rained," Kyle answered, trying to sound pleasant but no longer caring very much if he did. "It will probably be muggy like this for the rest of the day." He had grown numb to her ability to find the cloud that belonged to every silver lining, and while he wasn't expecting a reward, at the very least he didn't want to hear her constant complaints: the food, the heat, the wind, the uncomfortable cart, how slow he was walking, not enough food, the smelly truck, nothing to read, and on and on. By this point, each new whine had become something of a joke to him.

Dalhart was about eight miles ahead and, to Kyle's inexpressible relief, was where Louise was headed when the attack had occurred and where Kyle would soon be able to deliver his passenger to her family. The temptation to abandon Louise on the side of the road the first night had been strong, and had she been headed much further north, he would have left her somewhere in Texas without a second thought, or at least that's what he told himself. However, because so many people had been willing to help him, he had decided he could put up with a cranky old lady for a few days.

Six hours later, and three days after finding Louise, Kyle halted the cart on the north side of Dalhart in front of a cream-colored, stucco house adorned with a gray, armadillo-shaped welcome sign that hung to the side of the front door. He knocked, waited, and was about to knock again when he heard footsteps. A short, heavy-set, teenage girl cracked the door open and peered through the narrow crack. Kyle wondered to himself what she must be thinking to find a strange, bruised and bearded man on her doorstep. The girl eyed Kyle and seemed poised to slam the door shut when Kyle spoke up.

"This is the Kennedy home, correct?"

The girl nodded. Kyle could see a man, likely the girl's father, coming towards the door from a kitchen, his face wary.

"I found your grandmother on the side of the road. I brought her here."

The girl looked past Kyle to the street where Louise was gathering what few possessions she had brought. "Daddy!" she called, turning towards her father.

The man had heard the comment, pulled the door open wide, and looked out to the street. "I don't believe it," he said to no one in particular, then stepped past Kyle and ran to his mother.

The girl called for her mother and older brother, and the family hurried outside to help Louise with her things. Kyle watched from the sidelines, musing that normally if a woman who'd been missing for two weeks had been found and returned, the family would've been overcome with emotion and barely able to contain themselves, an event worthy of a live CNN broadcast. This celebration was reserved. They hugged and talked, but there were no tears and no big displays of emotion. It was almost business-like in manner, as if they were actors in a play that no one really cared about.

Louise's son approached Kyle. "I need to thank you," he said. "We've been worried about Mom for the past two weeks, but I didn't know how I could find her, and…"

Kyle interrupted him. "Look, it's been rough for everyone. You don't need to explain anything. I'm glad I could do it." Kyle extended his hand to Mr. Kennedy, who embraced Kyle's hand with both of his.

"I'd offer you something, but we don't have much," he said, assessing Kyle's cart.

"I don't need anything. Besides, you have more people to feed than I do." Kyle started to walk towards his cart, and Mr. Kennedy followed along behind. "You know, I could use a hammer though; my cart needs some repairs. And, if you've got a way to get me to Montana, I'd take that as well," Kyle said over his shoulder. "Otherwise, I'd better get on my way."

The man shook his head soberly. "I don't have any way to get you to Montana, but I do have a hammer. Give me a minute." Mr. Kennedy ran off to look for the hammer, and Louise hobbled over to offer her thanks and say goodbye, then walked to the house with a grandchild under each arm just as her son returned, leaving the two men alone in the street.

Mr. Kennedy handed Kyle the hammer. "Go ahead and take this with you. I have another one. Good luck on your trip. We'll be praying for you."

"Thank you. Good luck to you too. Things are tough."

The man nodded in agreement, his anxiety apparent.

As he swung his cart around and headed back towards the highway, Kyle wondered if he'd done the family any favors, giving them one more mouth to feed. With conditions already bad, maybe they would have been better off without Louise, as cruel as that sounded. He trudged towards the edge of town, hoping he hadn't made the family's predicament worse.

Staying near Dalhart for the night was an option that would have fit his schedule, as tired as he was, but everything about the town unsettled him. It had been a week since he'd passed through any big towns, and in comparison the overall mood in Dalhart was much bleaker. There were no children playing in the streets or in the front yards, and despite the rain, even the grass and trees seemed lifeless and wilted. Instead of the friendly waves and words of encouragement that had been offered earlier in his trip, people eyed him suspiciously and retreated towards their homes when he approached, much as the people in Lubbock had done.

Walking gave Kyle plenty of time to think, and the hopelessness of the Kennedy's stuck with him for a long time. They were hungry and fearful, like so many other people, perhaps even his own family. With those thoughts haunting him, Kyle walked on into the night, wanting desperately to be home, not stopping until long after the sun had set and the darkness had fully engulfed him.

CHAPTER EIGHTEEN

Wednesday, September 21st
Oklahoma Panhandle

Day 19

Covered good ground today. I'm traveling alone once again after finding an old lady 3 days ago who, by some miracle, had survived for two weeks in the middle of nowhere. Yesterday I delivered her (Louise Kennedy) to her family, but their reunion was not the joyful experience I expected. Her granddaughter's eyes have haunted me all day. She reminded me of the children from Africa you see on the late night TV commercials, hopeless and starving and waiting for someone to save them. The father's expression wasn't much better. I feel like rather than saving one life, I've endangered four others, or at least consigned them to more severe hunger than they would have experienced without Louise. It made me worry about how you are surviving. The biggest problem with walking is no longer the physical demands (not that my feet and legs don't ache), but the time to think and worry and not know. Just the chance to get any news would be worth so much. This afternoon I met a man who had a ham radio that was working. He said he'd been anticipating something like this for 20 years. I gave him a message to try to send but have little hope it will get to you. I will keep my fingers crossed.

Food is an issue, but there have been generous people along the way, especially some of the farmers. I have new respect for the toughness of the pioneers. Can't imagine doing this on dirt roads. I'm in Oklahoma tonight and hope to be in Colorado tomorrow night. I wish all five states I need to cross were as easy as Oklahoma's panhandle. Getting through Texas feels like a big accomplishment. Just wish I wasn't celebrating alone.

I love you all.

Saturday, September 24th
Southern Colorado

Day 22

I'm sitting on the banks of a large reservoir, trying to catch my lunch. The weather has been good so I've been pushing hard, but my legs are feeling it. David, I wish I had you here with me. You've always had a knack for catching nice, big fish every time we'd go fishing, and I'd love a big fish today. I bet I've lost at least 15 pounds since I started walking, but it's not a diet I'd recommend.

I visited with another walker (that's what I call people like me) for a while this morning. He's a truck driver, really a nice guy, and was heading to Albuquerque from South Dakota, a lot closer to home than I am. Kind of made me jealous. He just had a duffle bag and made me a little nervous as he eyed my cart. He's hopeful that he'll make it but has had a few bad run-ins; it's sad how some people have become violent and threatening. We had a nice talk, and it made me realize how much I miss that. Since I dropped off Louise (the old lady in Texas), the longest I've visited with another person has been about 30 minutes, and then I never see them again. Even though there are a few people around, the loneliness is pretty strong. Jennifer, I know I never talked with you as much as you'd have liked, but I sure miss that now. When things get fixed, I'm not going to buy a TV; I'm going to spend more time with you and the kids, and with other people.

My face and arms have gotten pretty dark. I know you'd get mad at me for not wearing sunscreen, but that's not really an option. I went swimming this morning, so I feel a little cleaner. I think it had been 5 days since...

A slight tug on the line alerted Kyle, and he set his journal down to watch for more movement. Another tug, this time a little firmer, and he poised himself to haul in his catch. With another tug, he pulled his arms back and felt the firm resistance of something on the line. Grabbing his shirt off the ground, Kyle quickly wrapped the shirt around his hand, then the fishing line around that. He began to back slowly up and down the bank of the reservoir, his legs acting as the reel while he coiled the fishing line around his hand, watching while the water near the shore began to churn.

Kyle waited for the thrashing to stop. When he felt the line slacken and could see the fish calm, he pulled the line and lifted the fish into the air, landing it a couple of feet in front of him. He leapt forward and grabbed at the fish with his free hand, while corralling it with his other arm to keep it from flopping back to the water. With the fish secured, Kyle found a rock and clubbed his catch until it quit moving.

After two previous failures, this fishing success buoyed his spirits. Kyle carried the fish to the top of the slope that surrounded the reservoir, stopping where he'd left his cart in a cluster of trees that offered shade and fuel for a fire.

Kyle pulled out his knife and a box of matches and ignited the wood he had gathered earlier, then cleaned and prepped the fish while feeding wood into the fire, coaxing the blaze until it was large enough to cook with.

Despite the crude cooking environment, the fish cooked up beautifully, and Kyle thoroughly enjoyed his lunch. A little seasoning and an even larger fish would have improved the meal, but after more than two weeks on the road, the fish tasted as good as any he could remember eating.

With his stomach full, Kyle carefully wound the fishing line back around the spool it came on, a treasured gift from a talkative farmer back in Oklahoma. Kyle had found that many of the people he met were decent and helpful, especially those who were more isolated, as they seemed as hungry for fresh conversation as he was. Several families had given him extra produce from their gardens, and one kind woman had cooked him the most delicious omelet he'd ever eaten as she pumped him for information about the things he'd seen as he traveled.

Kyle kicked the fire down, then doused it completely with water from the reservoir, aware that there would be no way to contain an out of control fire like the one he'd witnessed in Lubbock. He wondered how bad fire season had been in the mountains, and how many towns and homes had been lost without the equipment and manpower to fight them.

Kyle finished his journal entry, packed the cart, and pulled onto the highway. The past few days he had pulled hard and was now well into Colorado. Yesterday he had pushed hard and gone just over forty miles, ten more than normal, but he felt it in his legs today. The terrain had worked in his favor so far, with most of the roads still flat and easy to walk. There were the occasional dips and rises, but nothing severe, and nothing that slowed him down much.

On the western horizon, however, loomed the Rocky Mountains, their peaks already capped with snow. Even from this distance, they taunted him with their size. As he got further north, Kyle had noticed that the nights were getting colder, and the days were growing noticeably shorter. He knew that in another month he needed to be ready to contend with snow, and the thought of that, even on a warm, sunny day, sent a shiver down his spine.

CHAPTER NINETEEN

Monday, September 26th
East Central Colorado

Day 24

If I've been accurate with the tally marks I'm scratching on my cart, then today is our anniversary. Happy 15th, Jennifer. It's a gloriously beautiful morning, which is fitting for what this date means to me. I want you to know that I didn't forget our anniversary, and that my heart is with you, even if I'm not. I wish, with all of my energy, that I could be with you instead of stuck in the middle of Colorado, but it's not meant to be. I hope you know you're still the girl I dream about every night.

Writing's not going to get me any closer to home, so I'm going to get on the road. If you read this, I want you to know that my first thoughts today were of you.

I love you Jenn!

Deer Creek, Montana

Spencer was playing with a bucket of Legos in his room, and with David off working at the farm and Emma attending her second week of community school, the house was quiet and peaceful. On most days, Jennifer tried not to dwell on Kyle's absence, but today she planned on getting emotional. She needed to have a happy cry.

Finding the photo album she wanted, Jennifer got comfortable on the couch and flipped the cover open.

She smiled as the faces of two happy, love-struck, young people glowed innocently from the first page of the album. The picture had been taken in the reception hall of her childhood church, a last minute change in plans when Mother Nature had decided to interrupt their outdoor group photo session with a bone-rattling thunderstorm. Kyle, in his tuxedo, and Jennifer, in her wedding dress, were surrounded by both of their families and the wedding party, all crowded between dinner tables at the end of the narrow hall.

Lightning had struck nearby a half-second before the picture was taken, and the expressions on the faces of their loved ones had been so fresh and alive that the picture had been Jennifer's favorite and ended up displayed at the front of the album. The thing she liked the most about the picture was that, despite every car alarm in the parking lot blaring outside and the bridesmaids being in full shriek, Kyle's eyes were riveted to her like nothing else in the world existed, and the biggest, warmest, most in-love smile she'd ever seen on a man's face was spread across his. In the early years of their marriage, when they'd had a disagreement or when Kyle hadn't been as attentive as she'd have liked, she'd pull out the album and take a peek at this photo, just to remind herself that he really did love her.

Jennifer flipped slowly through the rest of their wedding album before moving on to the others that crowded the bookshelf, reliving the nearly seventeen years since she'd first met Kyle. The first picture she had of Kyle was from her freshman English class, taken with a friend's new digital camera to show her roommate the cute guy who kept asking her out. The photo, showing Kyle as he was about read a paper in front of the class, had been tacked up on her dorm room wall for the final two months of the semester. It would have been a perfect photo, had it not been for her purse strap blocking part of the shot as she'd attempted to conceal the camera. After taking the picture, Jennifer and her friend had laughed so hard they had distracted Kyle, ruining his concentration as he kept checking his zipper, probably costing him a letter grade.

Other albums were filled with memories of vacations, birthdays, kids' sports, and school programs. Jennifer loved to look through her albums, but this was the first time she had opened them since Kyle had been gone. Every picture of him was another reminder of his absence, filling her heart with loneliness until it was saturated and overflowing.

Spencer walked into the room, noticed her tears, and came over and gave her a big hug and a kiss on the cheek, then headed back to his room to play. Jennifer choked out a teary "thank you" as he walked away, then opened up the last album.

The most recent photos she had printed were from this year's Father's Day camping trip and showed Kyle packing up their tent as they got ready to head home Sunday afternoon. His face was sunburned and mosquito bitten, and his elbow was bandaged from a fall the day before, but despite his injuries, he was still mugging for the camera, with Spencer clinging to his back while David chased Emma with a grass snake in the background. Jennifer lingered on this picture for a long time, reliving the weekend over and over in her memory and wondering if they would ever have another day like that again.

Jennifer stroked Kyle's cheek in the photo, then closed the book and hugged it to her chest. "I believe in you, Kyle," she whispered. "However long it takes, I'll be here."

The front door swung open and a book bag dropped loudly to the floor. Jennifer heard Emma's voice calling out to her. "Mom, I'm home. What's for lunch?"

Thursday, September 29th
Central Colorado

Day 27

Stopped early for the day. Stomach is not feeling good. Will try and get some extra rest and hopefully be off again in the morning. I'm on I-70, so lots of vehicles. Found a nice truck to stay in. The evenings are getting colder, so the shelter's appreciated. Jennifer, I wish you were here to take care of me (I really wish I was there to take care of you). I hope this stomach bug isn't too serious. I've been lucky with my health so far. I can see the mountains out the window, and they worry me.

I love you all.

Friday, September 30th
Deer Creek, Montana

Jennifer sat in the living room, the sun having set an hour before and the room now too dark for reading. The kids were in bed and asleep, their schedules having adjusted to follow the sun's – in bed at sundown and up at sunrise.

Tired from a long day of hauling water, canning with Grace next door, and teaching her assigned hours of school, Jennifer got up and headed for her bedroom. As she passed into the kitchen, there was a sharp knocking on the door, which made her jump. She stopped and stared at the door, her heart beating rapidly, not sure what to do. This was their first nighttime visitor since the event, and with no lights, the thought of opening the door scared her. After a second knock, she moved closer to the door and called out nervously. "Who is it?"

"It's Chuck," answered a voice.

Jennifer twisted the deadbolt and pulled the door open. "Chuck, is everything okay wi…," she began, and then realized it was Doug, not Chuck, standing in the darkness grinning at her. "Doug? What are you...you lied to me!" she fumed and tried to slam the door shut, but Doug blocked it with his foot. "What do you want?" she demanded as she pushed the door against his foot. "You know how I feel. Why don't you just leave me alone?"

"Why don't you like me?" Doug asked, ignoring her questions. "You've been alone for four weeks now. I'm really sorry, Jenn, but your husband would be back by now, if he was coming."

"Quit saying that!" she spat at him. "I don't care what you think, Doug. And whether he's coming back or not, I don't want to be with you. Why can't I get that through to you?" Jennifer could make out a smirk on Doug's face and could hear him breathing loudly. She tried to force the door closed again, but his foot was still blocking it. "Doug, my kids are asleep. Please go away."

"Jennifer, I've been totally alone for four weeks. It's almost been a month. Can you believe that? Our world's been screwed up now for four full weeks, and we don't even know how long it's going to take to fix it. I was wondering, Jennifer, would you do me a favor?" His speech was slurred, and she could smell alcohol on his breath as he leaned in close to her in an attempt to whisper.

"What do you want, Doug?" she replied, still trying to force the door shut.

"Would you just give me a hug?"

"What?"

"I want a hug, some human contact. Do you have any idea at all how hard it is to be alone so much? I want to feel like someone cares about me."

"What are you talking about? You're drunk. Go home and sleep it off, before you do something stupid."

"I'm not drunk. I was telling you, I'm alone. The girl I was dating, she lives on the other side of Missoula...I can't call anyone...I don't have kids to give me a goodnight kiss or a dog to sit beside me on the couch...I can't even get online anymore. The only contact I have with people is at our stupid community meetings or when I walk around the town, and all that is is business. No one cares about me. I know it sounds stupid, but it's just 'Hi, Doug', 'Thanks, Doug', 'Goodbye, Doug'. There's always a goodbye. I hate that word; they may as well be saying 'get out of my life.' Jennifer, it's been more than four weeks since I've had physical contact with anyone, at least beyond a stupid handshake."

"Why me, Doug? There has to be someone else."

"There isn't, and I like you. You're nice, and you're really pretty, and with your husband away...you know...I thought we could help each other out."

Jennifer wanted to slam the door and be rid of him, but she knew she wasn't strong enough to take him on, if it came to that, even if he was drunk. A part of her was touched by what he said. As much as she hated to admit it, she believed him. It had been a long time since she'd felt the feelings Doug was talking about, of having someone who cared about you, just because you were you. As much as she'd come to loathe Doug over the past couple of weeks, his words managed to stir her compassion. "If I give you a hug, will you go home and leave me alone?" She could feel her heart pounding and was sure Doug could hear it in the silence of the evening.

"That's it. Just a hug. Then I'll go home. I promise."

Jennifer hesitated, then released her grip on the door. "Don't come in my house," she warned as she stepped forward.

Doug stepped away from the door to let her come outside.

For a brief moment, she thought about slamming the door, but worried about how he'd react to that in the coming days and weeks, let alone that night. Jennifer closed her eyes in resignation and stepped onto the front step.

"Thanks, Jennifer," Doug said, sounding sincere.

Jennifer opened her arms, and Doug stepped towards her. "Remember, this is just a hug," she reminded him. "Stop when I tell you to."

Doug nodded and bent down, put his arms under hers, and squeezed her tight, lifting her up onto her toes and pulling her towards him. Jennifer's arms draped limply over his shoulders, and she gave him a light squeeze in response.

In the cool night air, his warm breath down the back of her neck made her shudder, and the smell of alcohol on his breath, mixed with the days-old stench of body odor and sweaty clothes, nearly made her gag.

"Okay, Doug, that's it," she said after what seemed like minutes but was likely only a few seconds. Between his smells and her nerves, she struggled to maintain her composure. "I'm tired. I want to go in."

He continued to hold her, choosing not to hear.

"Doug!" Jennifer said, her voice rising. "Doug, I'm done! I need to go in."

He didn't respond, just continued to embrace her. Jennifer put her hands on his shoulders and tried to push him away.

"Doug! That's it! Let me go!"

There was still no reply. She felt his hips pressing against her stomach and could tell he was aroused. Doug turned and nuzzled her neck with his whiskery cheeks, then pressed his cold, fleshy lips against her skin. Jennifer pushed as hard as she could against his shoulders, trying to break free.

"Doug!" she shouted in desperation. "Stop it. Now!"

"Please, Jennifer," Doug whispered. "Don't make me stop. You don't know how good this feels." He pushed her backwards against the house, pinning her there with his body. His hands slid down from her back and began to massage the back of her thighs. Jennifer struggled against him but could barely breathe; she was pressed so tightly against the house. She struck Doug on his back with her fist, but it had no effect. Struggling, she fought to hold back the tears while he continued to trap her between the house and his body, massaging her with one hand and pinning her arm with the other.

"You feel so good," he whispered, continuing to kiss her neck, then moving his lips roughly to her ear.

Jennifer stopped struggling and forced herself to calm down and breathe while she pushed against his shoulder with her free hand. She regained her composure while Doug continued to stroke her and kiss her neck passionately. When he didn't feel any more resistance, Doug loosened his hold on her, and Jennifer, catching her breath, leaned her head in towards him. Aware of the change, Doug pulled his head back and looked at her quizzically, his eyes barely visible, but full of desire. Jennifer met his gaze and didn't turn her head away, so Doug leaned in cautiously and kissed her lightly on the mouth. Jennifer hesitated for a long while, then gently kissed him back. With some excitement, Doug kissed harder, pressing his mouth firmly against hers, his breaths coming more rapidly. Releasing his grip on her arm, he moved his hands back to her body, found the bottom of her sweatshirt and slid his hands underneath. His fingers were cold and rough, and the feel of them against her skin made Jennifer flinch.

As he worked his hands steadily upward, Doug pushed his tongue against her lips, hoping for entry. Jennifer slowly parted them, and Doug excitedly pushed his tongue into her open mouth. He pressed hard against her, consumed with his lust. As his fingers fumbled to unclasp her bra, Jennifer bit down on his tongue as hard as she could.

Doug screamed and grabbed for his mouth, the new feeling an obvious contrast to the sensations that had been coursing through his body. He pulled away from her, and Jennifer brought her knee up, catching him squarely in the groin with a strength and accuracy that surprised even her. Doug collapsed to the ground, the wind rushing loudly from his lungs. Jennifer lunged for her door, spitting his blood from her mouth and wiping his vile saliva from her face.

Doug reached out and grabbed her ankle but was unable to hold on. She jerked her foot away from him and fell inside the house, kicking the door shut behind her, then scrambled to her knees and latched the deadbolt. She slumped with her back against the door, expecting to cry, but instead, it was an intense anger that found her, anger aimed at Doug for what he had done and at herself for being so easily manipulated. "Go away, Doug!" she shouted through the door. "Go away and don't ever come back here again!"

Jennifer sat with her back against the door until she felt like she was in control of her emotions. She couldn't tell if Doug had left, but it didn't matter. With the aid of an old flashlight, its dim beam providing barely enough light to see by, she went down to the basement and straight to Kyle's gun safe. She dialed the safe's combination, her hands shaking so much it took her three times to get it open, then felt around inside until she found Kyle's handgun and the ammunition for it. Returning back upstairs, she spent the remainder of the night on the floor in front of the door, the loaded gun at her side.

CHAPTER TWENTY

Saturday, October 1st
Central Colorado

Kyle knelt in the grass on the edge of the highway, hands braced on his knees. A thin strand of saliva trailed from his mouth to a green pool of vomit in the dirt in front of him.

Exhausted, he waited for the heaving to resume but was instead granted a reprieve. He sat back on his heels and took in his surroundings as a cool breeze dried the sweat on his forehead. To the east, the prairies rose up to meet the mountains. To the west, the city of Denver was visible with the snowcapped Rockies towering far above it, as if nature was mocking man's pathetic attempt to create something grand. He'd looked at this same scene through the same windshield for two days, but this was the first time since stopping that he'd felt well enough to appreciate it.

There was no way to determine the exact cause of his illness, but Kyle felt certain it was food poisoning since contact with other people had been too limited to catch anything that way. He'd narrowed down the likely culprits to either a raccoon, eaten three days prior, or water drunk from a slow moving stream. And while none of that particularly mattered at this point, Kyle had had plenty of time to think and found reflecting on the source of his illness to be much less discouraging than worrying about the time he was losing and the task that still lay ahead.

Using his rifle for support, Kyle pulled himself up and walked back to the truck that had become his recovery room. Ever since reaching the freeway he'd kept his rifle close at hand instead of buried in the cart. His first day on the interstate, which was 26 days after the attack, he'd crossed paths with 6 other walkers, most looking more desperate than he felt, and that made him wary. For the week prior to reaching the freeway, all through southern Colorado on the back roads, he'd encountered only 9 others traveling like he was, and this sudden surge in the number or walkers had him on edge.

Before climbing back in the truck, Kyle inspected his handcart to make sure his belongings were secure. He inventoried his food rations and determined that if he was careful he would have enough food for at least six more days. From a supplies standpoint, the interstate had been good to Kyle, with a considerable number of trucks waiting to be plundered and his conscience long since over any aversion to stealing. Survival and arrival, as he now termed his objectives, were his only concern, and whatever helped him meet those goals was now acceptable. In pre-EMP life, it had been easy to worry about those kinds of things, but now that everything had changed, Kyle was operating under much broader constraints.

Satisfied that he was adequately situated for another day of convalescing, Kyle pocketed some food and climbed back into the cab of the truck. By his estimation, distance-wise he was almost halfway home from Houston. Time-wise, he wasn't sure. The terrain had been easy to this point, but it was going to get much more difficult with the mountains ahead.

Kyle's mind drifted to his home in Montana. Twenty-nine days had passed since he should have been there, and two weeks prior to that was the last he'd seen his family. The day he'd left had been typical, the kind that would be easily forgotten under normal circumstances. He had read the news on the internet as he ate breakfast, then packed his bags while the rest of the family got ready to go into town for back-to-school shopping. Few words had been exchanged, just the routine conversations families have during the course of a morning. He hoped he'd told Jennifer that he loved her, but couldn't even say for sure that he had.

He did remember giving the kids hugs, although he had gotten after Emma for texting and not helping Spencer. David had worn his earphones most of the morning, avoiding any interaction with the family, and Spencer had tried to help Kyle pack his suitcase but was ushered out of the bedroom under protest after knocking a stack of shirts onto the floor. Hurrying, Kyle had overreacted and brought Spencer to tears. Now those shirts he had been so concerned about were a long forgotten pile of ashes, and Spencer was hundreds of miles away without his dad.

Jennifer had been frustrated with the kids, and after everyone had given dad the requisite hugs and kisses goodbye, his family had piled into the car and hurried off to shop, more concerned about new clothes and backpacks than seeing dad off. That night after the kids had gone to bed, Jennifer had called and left a message on his phone, apologizing for her mood and the rush, but Kyle was working long hours repairing hurricane damage and hadn't returned her call for several days. By the time he did, all was forgotten, and the events of their days apart had filled the conversation. They had talked every couple of days after that, with a brief visit the day before he was to return home, but hadn't spoken for very long, expecting to see each other soon.

Reflecting on his family and their life together, Kyle could think of countless things he'd do differently. He teared up thinking about Jennifer, the way she was with the kids, her strange affinity for yellow flowers, the way she got giggly after reaching her one beer limit, and her devotion to him through their years of marriage. Kyle knew he took his wife for granted and that their happy marriage was more a reflection of her patience and efforts than his. In many ways, his need to make it home was driven by a desire to put his whole heart into doing something for her. His first inclination, that first day at the airport when he thought the problems might be related to an EMP, had been to wait and let things get back to normal, or at least close to it, then return home the easy way. It was a fact he admitted to himself with a great deal of shame because he knew Jennifer's first impulse would have been to get home right away, whatever the price.

Kyle ate most of the food he'd gathered from his cart, then reclined his seat and closed his eyes, with thoughts of his family playing on the stage of his mind. The warm sunshine drew out what little energy he had, and after two days of vomiting, Kyle quickly drifted off to sleep.

As he slept Kyle dreamed about his family more intensely and more vividly than he had at any point in his journey. He dreamt that his wife and children were trapped outside their home during a violent thunderstorm. That Jennifer, climbing into the house through a broken-out-window, cut herself and lay bleeding on the kitchen floor while the children cowered outside, surrounded by a lightning induced firestorm.

Kyle awoke from the dream panicked, with his heart racing and sweat running in streams down his face. Relieved to discover it was only a dream, he laid his head back and began to relax again, then closed his eyes and drifted off, this time sleeping more restfully.

After a couple more hours of sleep, Kyle felt better and more rested than he had since getting sick and was anxious to get on the road again in the morning. He finished off his water and climbed down from the truck, hungry for something to eat. The setting sun bathed the surrounding area in a golden glow, and Kyle realized he'd slept longer than he'd expected to. He ducked under the trailer where he had left his cart and stopped dead in his tracks

The cart was gone.

Kyle spun around frantically and looked in every direction, but saw nothing to indicate where his cart might be. He ran to the side of the road hoping, perhaps, that the cart had rolled into the ditch, but it hadn't. He scanned the freeway in both directions, but between the volume of dead vehicles and the rolling of the road, he could see little. He cursed the interstate as he pulled at his hair in frustration.

He remembered that the last time he had vomited had been mid-afternoon, but wasn't sure when he'd fallen asleep. At most, whoever took his cart had a four-hour head start, but in what direction had they gone? He peered up and down the freeway again, praying for a clue, but could see no sign of the cart. His head swam and his legs felt weak. Everything he needed for his journey was in that cart--his clothes, food, blankets, and tent, and he was sure it would be next to impossible to make it home without it.

Kyle forced himself to try and calm down and think. He needed to make a decision, but it needed to be the right one. If he went the wrong way, he would never find the cart. Pacing on the side of the road, Kyle reflected back on the last two days. In the hours he'd been awake, he'd seen more people heading west, their travel, for the most part, mimicking the way cars normally traveled: westbound walkers on the north side of the road, eastbound walkers on the south.

After a final survey of the road to the east, Kyle slung his rifle over his shoulder and set off at a run towards Denver. In his weakened condition, he struggled to maintain the fast pace for more than a few minutes at a time and was forced to slow down and walk ten minutes for every five that he ran. All the while, his mind raced ahead, trying to figure out what he could do if he'd made the wrong decision and his cart was heading towards Nebraska. With the exception of his rifle and the clothes on his back, everything he had was in the cart, and the chances of replacing the other supplies were slim at best.

He'd only been hunting for his cart for about five miles, but Kyle's legs felt like rubber, his lungs burned, and the rumblings in his stomach reminded him that he'd kept little down for the past two days. In the descending darkness, he came to a rest area filled with at least a dozen trucks and knew it was a good place to spend the night. He searched the parking lot for his cart but didn't see it anywhere, then found an empty berth and retired for the evening, weak, hungry, and terrified he might not make it home.

Sunday, October 2nd

The first hint of sunlight found Kyle feeling better and more determined than ever to find his belongings. The morning air was brisk, and he rubbed his arms as he climbed down from the truck and got his first look at the parking lot in daylight. A further search confirmed that his cart truly wasn't at the rest stop, but there was a grocery truck that had gone unnoticed the night before. He hurried to the truck, the steady rumblings of his stomach setting his priorities, and pulled open the back doors, flooding the trailer with light. Most of the trailer was knee deep in empty boxes, but Kyle could see that there were still full cases of food stacked to the ceiling at the far end.

"Hello!" Kyle shouted while climbing inside the trailer. There was no reply so he moved forward. He had just started kicking his way through the debris when a mound of boxes only a few feet in front of him erupted, and a figure sprang out.

"What do you want!?" shrieked a thin, young woman, the desperate look on her dirty face more animal than human.

Startled by the unexpected figure, Kyle jumped back. "I just want to get some food. I didn't know anyone was in here."

The woman backed further into the trailer. She eyed Kyle suspiciously as she moved, her gaze jumping from Kyle's face to his gun as her hands tugged at a dirty blanket wrapped tightly around her shoulders. Kyle watched her move away, reading the nightmare her life had become in the lines of her face and the fear in her eyes. Her matted hair, swollen cheek, and piercing, wild eyes spoke volumes about her struggle for survival.

"I'm not going to hurt you," Kyle insisted. "I've been sick. I just need to get some food." Kyle could see that his gun made her anxious, and his rough appearance likely didn't help either, but he wasn't about to put down the only protection he had, meager as it was. "Did you see anyone pulling an old wood cart made with bicycle tires last night?"

The woman shook her head almost imperceptibly, then backed against the wall of the trailer and slid down until she sat on her heels amongst the empty boxes, her eyes still locked on Kyle.

"Anyone else in here?" Kyle asked as he passed by her.

Refusing to speak, the woman shook her head. Once Kyle was past her, she scurried to the door of the trailer, jumped to the ground, and disappeared.

Intent on finding something to ease his hunger pangs, Kyle scanned the wall of boxes in front of him before noticing a half-empty case of soup on the floor. He pulled a can out of the box and read the label. Cream of Mushroom. It was a soup he hated, but he was starving. Quickly pulling the tab on the can, Kyle tossed the lid to the side and tipped the can back, gagging as the cold, slimy soup slid down his throat. It was better than nothing, and he swallowed it all, even scraping the can with his finger to salvage every glob. He emptied another can and then began searching through the stack of boxes.

When he was done rummaging, Kyle had a decent-sized stack of food haphazardly piled at the back of the truck. He ran to a nearby moving van, dug around unsuccessfully for a bag of some sort, then grabbed a large blanket that was wrapped protectively around a dresser. He tied the corners together to fashion a crude sling, then looped it over his head and returned to the truck to fill the sling with the food he'd collected: a dozen cans of soup, two jars of peanut butter, a case of tuna, and cans of olives, corn and mushrooms. Kyle wished he had his cart with him so he could have loaded up a couple of week's worth of groceries, but he didn't. That was his next item of business.

With a fuller stomach and an improved outlook, Kyle hurried towards the freeway, his eyes scanning the road in front of him for his cart. He looked back to the east, in case he'd missed the cart the night before in the dark, but saw no sign of it. Kyle walked down the ramp towards the freeway and scanned the road. In the distance he noticed a man's head bobbing along on the far side of a flatbed trailer. Kyle's pulse quickened as something about the man's gait didn't seem quite normal. Kyle focused his gaze under the truck and saw what appeared to be wheels rolling closely behind the man. Elated but unsure, Kyle stared, hoping for confirmation, then ran to the side of the road to get a better view and wait for the stranger to emerge from behind the truck. After several long seconds, the man appeared, followed by a familiar wooden cart.

Kyle's heart skipped a beat, and a huge wave of relief swept over him. He'd found his cart. With the cans of food clanging about in the sling at his side, Kyle took off at a quick trot, the fastest he could move with his load. The sling of food was cumbersome and slowed him down, but it was too valuable to leave behind, so he wrapped his arm tightly around the bundle and continued to trot, the gap between him and his cart gradually shrinking.

Kyle's mind raced in unison with his feet. How would he approach the man? Would there be a confrontation? Was the stranger armed? Kyle had been warned by other walkers about the lawlessness of the highway, and their words haunted him as he considered his options. Wanting to stop the man and retrieve his cart before getting too close to Denver, and guessing there was still a good mile between them, Kyle picked up his pace.

The terrain was fairly level, but the road was full of vehicles, giving Kyle the cover he needed in order to stay out of sight until he was ready to confront the stranger. The man with the cart traveled mostly on the left side of the freeway, so Kyle stayed to the right, moving quickly from vehicle to vehicle. Fifty minutes after first spotting the man, Kyle closed the gap to within thirty yards. He set his sling down behind a silver Chevy and trailed along until a semi-truck that was pulled well over on the right shoulder provided him with good cover. Waiting until the stranger was out in the open, Kyle took one last nervous breath, then stepped out from behind the truck and fired a shot into the dirt on his side of the road, just as he'd scripted it in his mind. Immediately he had the man's attention.

At the sound of the shot, the stranger dropped to the ground, his head pivoting from side to side to see where it had come from. Kyle stayed close to the semi-truck with his gun held ready at his side. "Put your hands where I can see them," Kyle yelled, "and get away from my cart."

The man crawled behind the cart for protection, one hand raised in the air. "What do you want?' he yelled back. "Why are you shooting at me?"

"I want my cart. You stole it from me yesterday. I want it back."

"This is your cart?" the man asked incredulously, his head peering up from behind it. "I thought you were dead. I didn't think you'd need it. I swear."

"Well I'm not dead, and I want my cart."

With both hands raised in the air, the man stood up from behind the cart. "I don't want any trouble," he said. "I'm just trying to get back home."

"I don't want any trouble either, but I need my cart." Kyle lowered his gun slightly in a show of good faith.

"Okay! You can have it back. Just don't shoot again." The stranger took a step away from the cart, his eyes fixed on Kyle. Kyle appraised him as the tension of the moment began to ease.

The man appeared to be older than Kyle, maybe forty, and was physically bigger – taller, and broader in the shoulders. Like most guys Kyle had met on the road, the man had a full beard and a thin, dirty face. Unlike most, a tattoo of what looked like a dragon extended from below his right eye, disappeared under his beard, and continued down below the collar of the man's sweatshirt. A well-worn Pittsburgh Steelers hat covered his head, and long, dark hair escaped from underneath it.

Kyle kept his gun pointed in the man's general direction, maintaining his control.

"You can put the gun down," the man shouted as he slowly lowered his hands and stepped back over to the cart. "I just need to get my stuff."

Kyle lowered his gun a little more and took a cautious step away from the protection of the truck. He could feel perspiration forming on his forehead in sharp contrast to his mouth, which was so dry he could barely swallow. Standing in the middle of the highway, gun drawn, facing down a stranger, Kyle was unsure how the situation was going to play out, especially knowing there would be no one to step in and help if things went badly.

The man hesitated, then slowly pulled a green duffle bag from the cart and tossed it on the ground beside him. As Kyle watched the bag tumble to the ground, the man turned casually away from Kyle and seemed to be scratching his stomach before he spun back around a split second later, a handgun drawn and a wicked sneer on his face. Kyle dove back towards the truck as two shots rang out, one of the bullets shattering the truck's headlight and showering the ground around Kyle with pieces of glass.

Kyle frantically gathered himself behind the truck's tire, a slight groan escaping his lips as the sound of the man's cold laughter carried across the freeway. Clutching his rifle in his trembling hands, Kyle climbed onto the step of the truck and peered through the window. The man in the Steelers cap was kneeling behind the cart and rummaging with one hand through his duffle as he watched for Kyle.

"I just want my cart!" Kyle called out. "I don't want any trouble!"

Through the window of the truck, Kyle saw the man stand up, smiling as though he were holding three aces in a game of poker. The man was now carrying another handgun, this one with a longer barrel, and after checking his weapons, the man crouched and began to circle wide around the front of the truck that Kyle was using as his shield. Kyle tugged on the door of the cab, but it wouldn't open. Panicked, he ran along the step of the truck towards the rear of the tractor, grabbed the rail at the back, and swung himself around to stand on the back tires of the rig. On the back of the cab was a rack that was used to hold chains. Kyle quickly scaled it, then peered over the fairing for his assailant.

A hundred and fifty feet in front of the truck, the man knelt on the pavement and scanned under the truck. Kyle, his heart pounding so forcefully he worried it might shake him from his perch, ducked back down and tried to calm himself. He had shot a deer or an elk almost every year for as long as he could remember, he'd even hunted bear once, but he had never shot at another human being. His older brother had been in the service and one night over beers had opened up to Kyle about the horrors of combat, but Kyle never imagined himself being in a situation where he might have to actually shoot a person.

Kyle reached down and grabbed his rifle from where he'd propped it while doing the math in his head to figure out how many shots he had left. He was pretty sure he had at least four, maybe five, but couldn't remember exactly when he'd last filled his clip, nor how many bullets he'd used since reloading. With one hand holding tight to the top of the truck, Kyle slowly rose up and looked over the fairing again, pointing his gun towards the spot where his assailant had been kneeling. "I don't want anyone hurt," he yelled with undisguised desperation.

The man had moved and was now crouching in the grass on the north side of the road. At the sound of Kyle's voice he rolled sideways and fired in Kyle's direction. Kyle squeezed off a wild shot and dropped down as two holes exploded in the fairing beside him, peppering him with shards of fiberglass. He leapt down from the top of the truck, then jumped onto the road on the south side of the truck in a desperate attempt to flee. With the man in the grass on the opposite side of the truck, Kyle, using the semi as a shield, raced towards the median. He slid into the meager shelter of the vegetation and rolled onto his stomach, his gun shouldered and ready to fire if the opportunity presented itself.

Holding his breath and praying that he hadn't been spotted, Kyle strained to see any sign of movement. The grass around him had grown unchecked for at least a month and provided some camouflage, but Kyle knew the thigh high grass wouldn't stop any bullets if he was spotted. Feeling agonizingly vulnerable, he edged eastward on his stomach while watching under the truck for his pursuer.

A flash of movement caught Kyle's eye, and he saw the legs of the man moving towards the back of the trailer, bringing him frighteningly close to where Kyle was hiding. Kyle instantly jumped to his feet and sprinted across the median, an eastbound pickup truck about thirty yards back to the west became his goal. Covering the distance in record time, Kyle ducked behind the truck just as a shot rang out and a bullet struck metal, hitting a foot or two from where he'd taken shelter. A second shot echoed, and the windshield of the truck exploded, sending glass bouncing in every direction.

Clutching his gun to his chest, Kyle swung around to the back of the pickup and popped his head up just long enough to catch a glimpse of the man standing half-exposed at the back corner of the semi-trailer. Another shot rang out and whistled by somewhere overhead. "You can have the cart!" shouted Kyle from his shelter. "I don't want to die... and I don't want to hurt you!"

"I don't think you're in a position to negotiate," the man shouted back. "You took a shot at me when I had my back to you. You think I'm going to let that go?"

"I didn't shoot at you!" Kyle protested as he scrambled towards the front of the pickup on his hands and knees. He looked under the pickup in the direction of his attacker, but the westbound roadway was ten feet higher than the eastbound side and made it impossible for Kyle to see beyond the median from under the truck. Stopping at the passenger door, Kyle cautiously raised his head until he could peer through the broken windows towards the semi. The man still stood at the back of the truck with much of his body exposed, almost daring Kyle to take a shot. Kyle looked to the west to assess his chances of escape, but it was at least a hundred yards to the next vehicle. To the east, the closest vehicle was maybe fifty yards away, but if he ran in that direction, it would take him directly in front of the shooter, giving the guy an easy shot.

"I can't shoot you!" screamed Kyle. "I have no argument with you. I'm just trying to get home. Please, just let me go. You keep everything." The fear of dying alone on the freeway in the middle of Colorado weighed on him, almost pinning him to the ground. To die like an animal, with his journal in the cart heading to some unknown destination, would mean that Jennifer and the kids would never know what happened to him. His body would rot on the side of the road until animals and nature had their way with it. Then, if he was lucky, he'd be tossed into a grave along with other unidentified bodies. He couldn't let that happen.

Kyle squatted behind the pickup, still struggling to breathe, listening for what seemed like an eternity for an answer to his plea. His hands and knees shook uncontrollably, and he forced himself to take some deep breaths. He held onto the side of the truck to steady himself and rose to take another look. The man hadn't moved but was no longer pointing his guns towards Kyle.

Instead, his arms were pulled back and resting against his body, his elbows bent with his hands up by his shoulders, pointing the guns at the sky.

Kyle stayed crouched behind the truck and tried to come up with a plan while still watching the man, hoping he would give up and leave. When it became obvious his attacker was willing to wait him out, Kyle summoned his courage and raised his head and both hands slowly into view. The man stepped closer to the trailer but didn't make any threatening movements. Kyle continued to rise, his eyes locked on his assailant, watching for any hint of danger, but the man made no attempt to move. His face was blank – no fear, no anger, no murderous rage, just a placid look that wouldn't have been out of place at a children's ballgame. Kyle was now exposed from the waist up, holding his rifle by the barrel in his left hand with the stock against his arm and pointed unthreateningly in the air. The man still didn't react. Kyle forced himself to move his legs, shuffling them clumsily towards the back of the pickup, his eyes still locked on the figure across the highway. Reclaiming his cart was no longer his goal. It was now survival.

Kyle reached the back of the truck, knowing that in just a few more steps he would be fully exposed. "I'm going to move along. You can have the cart," he shouted. Kyle gave the man a look, as if to ask permission to continue, but the man didn't respond, his face seemingly carved in stone. Kyle held his breath and tried to move, but his legs resisted, as if they had a mind of their own and were refusing the assignment. With a forced step, then a second, and then a third, Kyle slowly emerged from behind the truck until he was out in the open. Still the gunman didn't react. Taking courage, Kyle took a breath and another few steps.

Once Kyle was ten steps from the back of the pickup, the man's expression changed. A grin spread across his face, freezing Kyle in mid-step as he tried to interpret the look. Time stood still, each man assessing the other. In the next instant, the man extended his right hand forward and fired. Kyle spun to his right and dove back for the cover of the truck as multiple gunshots rang out. Twisting in the air, Kyle felt a bullet strike his left arm, knocking his gun from his hand and tossing it in the air. He screamed as he dropped to the ground behind the truck, the sound of his rifle clattering on the highway ringing loudly in his ears.

Panic stricken and wounded, Kyle lay behind the back wheel of the pickup. He could see the blood flowing down his left arm as it pumped from a wound three inches above his elbow. He squeezed his fist and saw that, despite the pain, his fingers worked.

Kyle heard the shooter laughing at him across the highway and could see, as he peered underneath the truck, that the man was coming across the median towards him, walking with a bounce in his step, almost a sense of excitement. Kyle knew the man had heard him scream and had seen his rifle knocked away. As he lay on the ground bleeding, the faces of Jennifer and his kids flashed across his mind.

His rifle lay fifteen feet away from him, its stock splintered where a bullet had struck it. Blocking out the pain, Kyle scrambled for his gun, staying as low as he could. He expected to hear a shot and feel a bullet tear through him at any moment, but he reached his rifle unscathed, grabbed it, and scrambled back to the cover of the truck. Glancing under the truck again, he saw the feet of his assailant in the other lane, approaching the front of the pickup. Kyle, still crouching, scurried to the front of the truck.

CHAPTER TWENTY-ONE

Central Colorado

Stan walked victoriously across the median towards the red Ford half-ton that shielded his newest victim from view. For him, taking a life was sport, not anything that affected his conscience. The truth was his conscience had died a long time ago, probably back when he was spending time in jail instead of finishing high school. A fight at a party one weekend had ended with a kid dead. Stan, no stranger to violence, had used the leg of a chair to beat to death a football player from a rival school who was flirting with his hoped-to-be girlfriend. His memory of the event was vague, clouded by a haze of drugs and alcohol, but the weeks after the killing were clear, with judges and lawyers hustling around him. On the weekends, friends from school had visited him in jail and regaled him with tales of his growing reputation, and he, a trouble-making, fifteen year old, freshman punk that no one had ever noticed before, had been the talk of the school. He liked it.

His appointed lawyer, an ambitious climber who was more focused on padding his resume than seeking justice, had convinced Stan to avoid trial by pleading guilty, and Stan's youth, combined with the judge's sympathy for his having been raised in a broken home by an alcoholic mother, had resulted in a sentence of thirty-four months in a juvenile detention facility. On his eighteenth birthday, six months before his friends graduated from high school, Stan had been released from jail with a clean record.

By twenty-one, Stan was in jail again, this time for trafficking drugs, although it could have been worse had the grand jury indicted him for murder two, the crime he'd been arrested for in the first place. With no weapon, and unreliable junkies as the only witnesses, the DA had decided to prosecute Stan for the lesser charge, the one that would guarantee a conviction. That was the first in a series of offenses that had kept Stan behind bars for fifteen of his next twenty years.

He had been two years into a twenty-year sentence for rape and torture in a facility near St. Louis when fate had smiled on him in a big way. The prison had lost power, and for four days the prisoners were locked in their cells like animals, with little food, smelly toilet water to drink, and a rapidly dwindling number of guards to monitor the inmates. A hundred hours into the ordeal, with only a handful of staff left at the prison, Stan's cell had been unlocked by a conscience-racked corrections officer, and Stan had wasted no time in evacuating the facility. The last thing Stan remembered before leaving the prison was the screams of that softhearted guard as ungrateful prisoners repaid him for their years of incarceration. Whether the entire prison population had been released or some had been left to die in their cells, Stan didn't know and didn't care. He was free and in an environment in which he excelled, a place where strength had become the law of the land.

During his most recent years in prison, Stan had missed the company of women, his girlfriend never even paying him a visit, and once free he'd wasted no time in leaving a trail of devastated lives as he made up for this lost time. Stan was on his way back to Vegas, the last place he had heard his girlfriend and son were living, and after acquiring weapons from acquaintances in St.

Louis, the trip had been relatively easy. So far he had found the people he met along the way to be most cooperative, the lack of any effective law enforcement a huge factor in their compliance. Stan prided himself in so completely overwhelming his victims that the only things they could offer in their defense were screams and unheeded pleas for mercy.

There was one woman he'd let live though. After killing her husband, he hadn't felt right about killing the two small kids, babies really. Children were Stan's soft spot, his one real weakness he'd decided, so after spending a few hours with the mother, he'd left without taking her life, knowing the kids wouldn't be able to fend for themselves. She would have been quite easy to kill, especially since she'd cried too much and hadn't given him the satisfaction he desired, but he'd just given her a good beating and moved on.

This newest victim would mean nothing to him beyond the fact that this guy was the first one who had made it somewhat interesting and managed to get some shots off at him, a fact that irked Stan as this silly game played out.

Stan realized now that he should have killed this latest pain-in-the-ass yesterday. He'd found the guy's cart parked under a truck with trash blown up against the wheels and would have left it, but at the last second had decided that the cart would be useful in some of the more deserted areas he'd be traveling through. He'd even looked through the window of the cab, seen this guy on death's doorstep, and figured he didn't need to waste the ammunition. Now, as this pathetic game of cat and mouse was about to wrap up, he was ready to invest some extra bullets.

Stan appreciated the man's guts, the way he stood out in the open and begged for mercy. Handguns were far too unreliable from a distance, especially against a rifle, so exposing himself like that had been a great help. He thought it was his second shot that had hit the guy, but it didn't matter. The fool no longer had his gun and was injured, possibly already dead if his squeal was any indication. Now it would just be a matter of finishing him off if he was still breathing, probably in a slow and painful manner, and then continuing on to Denver.

Looking forward to having some fun, Stan walked towards the front of the truck, his guns hanging loosely at his side.

Kyle sprang up from behind the pickup, acting on instinct, fear, and rage. He didn't know how many shots he had left, but he planned on using all of them. As soon as his rifle cleared the hood of the pickup, he began to squeeze the trigger. The hollow grin on Stan's face morphed from businesslike indifference to shocked surprise with the first crack of the rifle.

The first shot hit Stan in the chest, spun him slightly to his left, and knocked him back a step. Kyle was pulling the trigger as fast as the semi-automatic would allow, and with his target standing less than ten feet away, he knew he wasn't missing. On the third shot, Stan dropped his guns, and the fourth shot finally brought him down, sending him toppling backwards onto the freeway where he struck his head on the ground with a sick, hollow thud. Kyle pulled the trigger once more as Stan fell and heard the metallic click of an empty chamber.

With no shots left, Kyle ducked behind the pickup again, scared that somehow the man had survived the barrage and would be coming after him. As Kyle leaned back against the front wheel of the truck, his hands started shaking, and his rifle slipped from his fingers and clattered to the ground once again. Kyle gasped for air, unsure how long it had been since he last took a breath. The smell of gunpowder hung in the air and a thin, blue haze from the gunfire slowly drifted away to the east.

Kyle waited for what seemed like a lifetime, listening for movement, but heard only the sounds of birds and insects coming back to life now that the shooting had ceased. He circled around the back of the pickup on his hands and knees and slowly approached the man, every sense on alert for any signs of danger, but the man lay motionless in a pool of blood that was spreading towards the median. Kyle, still frightened, rose to his feet and braced himself, prepared to flee, until at last he got to a spot where he could look down at the man's face. Although the rise and fall of the man's chest was barely perceptible, to Kyle's surprise, the man's eyes were open and followed Kyle as he moved. The dying man's guns lay by his feet, and Kyle kicked them away.

Turning back to face the body, Kyle felt himself growing numb. If not for the pain in his arm, he wouldn't have felt anything at all. Stan's eyes still followed Kyle's movements, and Kyle returned the gaze, wanting to say something, but not knowing what he could say that would mean anything. Emotions tumbled around inside his head: pity, anger, fear, isolation, but none of them moved him to speak. At his feet lay a man – a man who minutes ago had tried to take Kyle's life, but was now himself dying. There was no ambulance to call or aid to administer, no police to wait for, and no family to contact. There was just Kyle and this stranger whose life was draining away, together on an empty stretch of interstate in the middle of Colorado.

Stan's breathing became more shallow, and an occasional wet cough sprayed blood on his face. Kyle walked over and recovered his own rifle, then gathered up Stan's guns. He thought he should end the man's suffering, but to take such overt action against a human life, without active fear and rage to motivate him, was beyond Kyle's capabilities. Kyle watched the man, whose life was slowly ebbing away, with questions flooding his own mind that he knew would never be answered. Who was he? Who did he leave behind? Why did it have to end this way? The man coughed loudly again, then his chest quit moving and his eyes lost their focus and stared into space.

Kyle turned and walked away. He crossed over the median, forcing himself not to look back at the body that lay on the ground behind him. He walked to his cart, then sank to his knees and held onto it, shocked by the sense of security the touch of the cart brought him as the price paid to reclaim it ran through his mind. Kyle stood up, his shaking legs and aching stomach reminding him of his weakened condition, the adrenaline from the morning's events no longer carrying him along.

Searching his cart for food, he found that what had been there yesterday was now mostly gone. Kyle rifled through the duffle bag that had belonged to the dead man and found a change of clothes, a box and a half of ammunition, a bloodstained hunting knife, and a few pieces of gold jewelry, but no food. He wanted to discard everything associated with the man, but instinct told him to hold on to all of it.

Kyle walked back along the highway and retrieved the sling of food he had left on the side of the road. He carried it back to the cart, sat down and ate, then did what he could to bandage his arm with the supplies from his first aid kit. His arm ached, but the wound was less severe than he feared. Upon inspecting his rifle, Kyle found that it had been the stock of his rifle that had deflected the bullet. The slug had only passed through his flesh while thankfully missing the bone, avoiding more serious damage to his arm.

Kyle loaded his cart with the contents of the duffel bag and his cans of food, then turned to take one final glance at the body in the road. Magpies had already found the corpse and were picking at its face, their black feathers shining in the sun as they scavenged and tore away pieces of flesh. Kyle fired a shot in the direction of the birds and scattered them, but he knew they would soon return as soon as he was gone.

Monday, October 3rd
Northern Colorado

Day 31

It's good to be alive. Today the sky seems bluer and the air fresher than it ever has before. Denver is in my rearview mirror, but Colorado is a state I will never forget. I'm over my illness, having experienced an unbelievably quick recovery, and am fairly well stocked with food. I've even acquired a couple of new guns that might come in handy. The area ahead of me is a little more populated, which always worries me. Not a lot of farmland around, so I hope people are not too desperately hungry.

Kids, I just want to say again, I love you. I know I wasn't a perfect dad, but I hope you know that I tried to do what I thought was best. Jennifer, you are probably tired of me writing this all the time, but I love you. If nothing else, please know that you are the best thing that ever happened to me.

There are a lot of things that make a person think about mortality, and some of the people you meet really make you think about it. If something happens to me before I make it home, please know I'm glad I've lived the life I have. Sure there are regrets, but I know that I had it good, and I hope it doesn't have to end yet. I've seen a lot of fresh graves, and people tell me that hospitals are shut down. It's been over a month since everything stopped, and I guess without power, drugs, and people willing to work, even simple things like infections and sickness are proving fatal, let alone the hunger and lawlessness.

Being this close to the mountains reminds me of home. I sure wish I was there.

I love you all.

CHAPTER TWENTY-TWO

Wednesday, September 28th
Deer Creek, Montana

Jennifer sat quietly at a large wooden table in Connie Bolan's dining room. With Gabe sick, the location of their weekly council meeting had been moved, and Connie, as the council's new Vice President, had agreed to host the meeting. Connie's large house was decorated in an old-fashioned, country style with lots of mauve and country blue, a soft contrast to the hard, aggressive personality that was evident after just one week on the council.

As she waited for the meeting to begin, Jennifer watched the door for arrivals. It had been a rough few days since her encounter with Doug, spent under a self-imposed house arrest with Kyle's handgun as a constant companion. Sleep had been fitful and hard to come by, and she had found herself losing her temper with her children far too easily.

Jennifer wanted to bring up her run-in with Doug at the meeting, but wasn't sure what, exactly, to complain about. "Doug kissed me, pays me too much attention, thinks I'm nice, and copped a feel of my boobs," she imagined herself saying. It wasn't something she could call the police about under normal circumstances, and besides that, he was the police. She continued toying with the idea of bringing it up but decided against it after an extended, internal debate. She was an adult and would handle it herself. Besides, maybe Doug had gotten the message this time. She hadn't seen him since Friday's encounter.

Five minutes after the hour, Connie brought the meeting to order. Doug was still absent, and Jennifer was pleased that she wouldn't have to face him. As Jennifer pulled out her notes from the last week's meeting, Connie veered from the regular agenda. "I have some unfortunate news to relate," she began, her tone somber. "Some of you have likely already heard this, but the Klein family was found dead two days ago."

Jennifer's jaw dropped, and the room went silent.

Connie continued. "Their neighbors hadn't seen any activity at the home for a couple days, so they checked on the Kleins and found the bodies. Doug is pretty sure it was a murder-suicide, probably two or three days before they were found." It was evident from the shocked looks that most in the room hadn't heard the news. Jennifer didn't know the Kleins, or even where they lived, but the news still hit her hard.

"Do we know why it happened, or anything about the family?" asked Craig Reider, the community sanitarian.

Carol Jeffries spoke up in a shaky voice. "Mrs. Klein had been sick for awhile and seemed to be getting worse; she was in a lot of pain without her medications. I went over a couple of times at her husband's request. I couldn't do much for her, but I sure didn't expect something like this to happen." Carol leaned back in her chair and wiped at her eyes.

"How many kids?" asked Jennifer.

"Two," answered Connie. "Both boys. Ten and six. Doug said they had been smothered in their beds, same as their mother, most likely in their sleep. Mr. Klein was found hanging in the basement."

Nobody spoke for a long time. Jennifer guessed that Emma probably knew one of the sons from school or the bus and wasn't sure if she would tell her daughter about the deaths.

Craig Reider broke the silence. "What about burial?"

"That's already happened," said Connie. "Doug helped Mr. Tanaka, the neighbor, bury the family yesterday in their backyard." She paused and then added, almost as an apology, "We don't have a morgue or a cemetery and needed to take care of things quickly."

The meeting was interrupted by a noise at the door as Doug let himself in. Jennifer's loathing for Doug softened somewhat, knowing what he had dealt with over the past few days, but her stomach still knotted at the sight of him.

"It looks like you're discussing the Kleins," Doug said as he approached the table. "It was a sad thing. Sorry I'm late. It took me longer to get here than I expected." Doug sat down in an empty chair across the table from Jennifer and smiled at her as she turned away. Out of the corner of her eye, she could see him watching her, but she avoided any further eye contact.

The discussion of the Kleins continued, with Doug filling in details that Connie hadn't known. Finally, they moved on to more mundane subjects. During a discussion on heating homes, Jennifer noticed Doug bend down under the table, and just as his head disappeared, she felt a hand on her knee. She immediately clamped her legs together to try and stop his hand as it slid up her leg, but he persisted. She kicked blindly at him and felt her foot connect with some part of his body, followed immediately by the sound of his head banging against the underside of the table.

The noise caught the attention of the group, and conversation paused. Doug emerged from under the table, making a show of placing a pen on the notepad in front of him and rubbing his head. "Excuse me," he said, with a shrug of his shoulders and a goofy look on his face.

The group turned back to Connie and the discussion resumed, with no further thought given to the disruption.

Jennifer was dumbfounded, unable to believe Doug's audacity. Shaking and on the verge of tears, she clenched her fist and placed it in front of her mouth, forcing herself to breathe slowly as she struggled to gain control. Doug joined in on the discussion, carrying on as if nothing had happened.

Jennifer felt a hand on her arm and jumped. She turned to Carol who was sitting beside her, and Carol gave her a puzzled look.

"Are you okay?" Carol mouthed.

Jennifer nodded while blinking her eyes and trying to stymie the tears. Carol pressed further. "Are you sure?" she whispered.

Jennifer nodded again and held up a hand to reassure her. "I'll be fine," she mouthed back. She forced herself to pick up her pen and take notes on the discussion, but each time Doug spoke, the memory of him forcing himself on her, and his odors, and the kiss made her want to gag.

Finally, the meeting wrapped up and the council began to disperse. Jennifer stalled until she knew Doug was gone, then thanked Connie as she handed in her notes from the meeting and let herself out of the house. Jennifer crossed the street and waved to Craig and Carol who were visiting on the sidewalk. "See you next week," she called to them.

Carol motioned to Jennifer. "Wait for me, would you?" she called.

Jennifer stopped, unsure if she wanted to be questioned but not wanting to just walk off on her friend, a friend who she needed right now. She could see Doug a block ahead, methodically making his way home. At least waiting would give her more separation from the jerk, she thought. She waited while Carol and Craig said goodbye and Carol walked over to join her.

"Sorry to make you wait," Carol said.

"That's fine. Beats walking home alone." Jennifer hoped that she sounded more sincere than she felt.

"So what's going on?"

"Oh, just the usual. Trying to find food, taking care of the kids. You know."

"That's not what I meant, and you know it," said Carol. "What got you so upset at the meeting?"

Jennifer walked along, deciding if she wanted to talk about it. She watched Doug up ahead, scanning the houses as he walked, acting all official-like.

Carol followed Jennifer's gaze. "Something happen with Doug?"

Jennifer pursed her lips and looked at the ground. "I guess you could say that." Her voice trailed off as she spoke.

"Don't be too hard on yourself, Jennifer." Carol said, putting her hand on Jennifer's shoulder. "Things happen. Times are tough. No one is going to blame you. He seems like a nice guy."

"What? No. Wait." Jennifer glared at Carol, pushing Carol's hand off her shoulder. "You think I did something with him? With that creep?" Her eyes bugged wide, and tears welled up. "I can't believe you'd think that. I thought you were my friend." Jennifer turned and walked away.

"Jennifer! Jennifer!" Carol called, hurrying to catch up. "Please. I'm sorry. I guess I got it wrong. I didn't mean to upset you." She caught Jennifer by the arm, turning her around. Jennifer wiped at her nose and turned her head away.

For a moment, they silently stood on the side of the road while Jennifer composed herself. Jennifer didn't know Carol all that well but had felt a connection with the older woman from their first conversation. Carol seemed like someone she could relate to, and right now Jennifer needed to talk.

"I didn't sleep with Doug," Jennifer said firmly. "Although it would probably be easier if I did."

"What do you mean?" Carol asked, puzzled.

"Well," began Jennifer, "Doug has made it pretty clear that he wants to be more than acquaintances. I don't want anything to do with him, and the more I resist, the worse it gets, but he won't take no for an answer. The other night he showed up drunk at my house. I think he would have raped me if I hadn't gotten away from him." Jennifer started walking again as the events of the past couple of weeks tumbled out, finding it a great relief to finally be able to open up to someone about her problems with Doug.

Carol walked beside Jennifer, her arm draped supportively across Jennifer's shoulders. "I'm so sorry, Jennifer. I had no idea."

"Don't apologize, Carol. I shouldn't have gotten so upset. There's no reason you would have known."

"But still, I should have given you more credit. I guess it says something about our society when everyone's first guess is that the sex happened, not that it didn't."

"Yeah, I suppose. I think it's my dad's fault."

"What does your dad have to do with Doug?"

Jennifer shook her head. "He doesn't have anything to do with Doug. He's why I reacted so harshly when you thought I had sex with Doug."

"Was he a preacher or something?"

"A preacher?" Jennifer laughed. "There's a funny thought – my dad a preacher."

Carol laughed along with Jennifer. "I'm not sure why that's so funny, but at least you're smiling. So fill me in on the joke. How's your reaction related to your father?"

"My dad is a truck driver."

"I don't get it. Was he really protective of you, or something?"

"No, I wouldn't say that." Jennifer was quiet as they walked, trying to figure out how best to explain her family dynamics to Carol, and Carol just waited, willing to listen. Finally Jennifer had her thoughts collected. "Dad would be gone for weeks at a time. My mother was, correct that, my mother is a wonderful, pure woman. It was her doctor who clued her in on the fact that dad was unfaithful."

Carol nodded. "I see."

"I was just twelve at the time, so I didn't understand everything that was going on. My sister, she's four years older than me, she explained everything to me when I was in high school. All I knew before that was that mom and dad didn't love each other anymore. I had spent three weeks riding with dad that summer and thought it had something to do with me, or at least that I should have been able to fix things."

"You don't still hold yourself responsible for their marriage breaking up, do you?" Carol asked.

"No, I realize the problems were theirs, not mine. But I'll always remember how what my father did affected my mother. It was months before I didn't hear her cry anymore at night; she was such an emotional wreck that she even lost her job as a teacher. My mom was beautiful, and not even forty, but she refused to date anyone let alone get serious with anyone, because she didn't ever want to pass along to someone else what dad had given to her."

"How long did it take you to get over it? That would be tough on a young girl."

"I'm not sure that I ever fully have. I was right at that age when girls start to think about boys and here I was, passionately hating the most important man in my life. It took me a long time. I dated a half a dozen times in high school, but I never let myself get close to any boys. I didn't want to allow anyone to do to me what my father did to my mother."

"Well, you're happily married now, so you must've gotten past that."

"I've gotten over it for the most part, but Kyle doesn't even know the whole story. It's just mom, my sister, and me that are in on the family secret, a skeleton mom wants buried with her. I'm surprised I even told you."

"Your secret's safe with me. I am sorry, again, that I assumed what I did."

"It's fine. It's been over twenty years since my parents divorced, so the wound's healed over for the most part; there's just a lot of scar tissue that doesn't want to disappear."

They arrived at Carol's house, and Jennifer finished telling Carol about her troubles with Doug while they snacked on apples picked from a tree in Carol's backyard.

"So what are you going to do?" Carol asked when Jennifer seemed talked out.

Jennifer shook her head. "I don't know. On different days I have different feelings. If he had tried to get in the house last Friday, I was so mad I would have shot him and not thought twice about it. Then today, before his little stunt, I was thinking, hey, he's not such a bad guy. I bet he just got carried away and things will be civil between us. But then he got handsy under the table, and I wanted to shoot him again." Jennifer ran her hands through her hair as she spoke then dropped them to the table in exasperation. "What do you think I should do?"

Carol absentmindedly wiped at smudges on the table with a dishtowel. "I don't know what to tell you," she said. "I've never had to deal with a situation like this."

"Sometimes I ask myself if it wouldn't be easier to just give Doug what he wants. I mean, if I do, who's going to know except for him and me and now maybe you? Maybe then he'd get bored with me and go away. Like he says, I don't even know if Kyle is still alive, so what am I saving myself for. But, if I do it," Jennifer paused, trying to swallow the idea. "If I do it, I've still got to live with myself."

"Jenn, men will never understand, and a lot of women don't either, but sex can never be a casual thing for us. For guys it can, apparently, but not us; it's tied in too closely with our emotions, and it messes with our feelings. My second daughter had to learn that the hard way. She dated this boy for about six months, and at some point things got sexual. Then something happened, and he moved on, but she couldn't. As far as I know, he never gave her a second thought, but she was depressed for weeks, even started thinking suicide. These naive kids think that a condom eliminates all of the residual effects of sex, but it doesn't. It might prevent a baby, but there's so much more to it than what they're told to expect. I guess that's what happens when you get your information at school or on TV." Carol looked at Jennifer and chuckled. "I'm sorry, I don't mean to climb up on my soapbox and lecture, but after a couple months in therapy with my daughter, I got pretty opinionated on the subject."

"Don't apologize, Carol. I spilled my guts to you, it's only fair you get to vent a little, too. Besides, I feel the same way, and it's nice to hear someone else confirm my thoughts. I honestly don't think things would be better if I slept with him. He might be happier, but I know I wouldn't be. What do I do though? What he did today was tell me he's still there; I'm sure of it. It's not like he was expecting that I was going to crawl under the table and let him take me on the floor. He was telling me that last week wasn't the end, that he's not afraid of me."

"Do you think the council could do anything?" Carol asked. "He seems to feel important there. Maybe we could lean on him a little bit."

Jennifer shook her head. "I don't think so. What could the council do anyway? We can barely even get people to share their generators and food. How's anyone going to stop the guy with the biggest weapons from coming on to me? There isn't even a jail, for Pete's sake. And for that matter, I'm not even sure that what he's done is illegal. I can promise you it was heading in that direction, but nobody gets locked up for kissing, not even if they've got a record."

Both of them thought about the problem, Jennifer picking at her last piece of apple and Carol twisting the towel she held, but there was no easy solution. Jennifer finally spoke. "Do you think one of the towns around here has a functioning police department? Maybe someone Doug worked with could talk to him."

Carol shook her head. "I don't think so, Jennifer. From what I hear, our little community is doing pretty good."

Jennifer looked at Carol quizzically. "What do you mean?"

"I was talking to Craig after the meeting. Earlier this week he rode his horse to Missoula to visit a brother. Said things are pretty bad there. Apparently, at first people just looted from stores and suffered along with what food they had. But after a week or so they realized that nobody would be stepping in to fix things any time soon, and the new furniture and the nice TVs they'd taken weren't going to keep them alive. That's when people started getting desperate, forming gangs and stuff. Craig said his brother's scared and is going to bring his family out here as soon as he can get their things together, hopefully before it gets too much worse."

"How bad is he talking?" asked Jennifer.

"Well, he didn't have a chance to say a lot because I wanted to catch up to you, but it sounds scary. People getting shot for food, suicides, lots of people dying, and no morgues or cemeteries operating. There isn't really any kind of functioning police force, even there; it sounds like borderline anarchy."

"Guess I shouldn't complain, should I?"

"All it means is we've got to deal with our own problems, not that we don't have any. No one is going to come out here and save us. Just be glad we don't live in New York or Los Angeles or some other big city. I can't imagine the desperation in those places right now."

Jennifer shuddered. "Looks like I'm going to have to deal with this on my own. I wish he would just lose interest. Maybe if I shaved my head and let him see my hairy legs it would turn him off."

Carol laughed out loud and patted Jennifer's hand. "We'll figure something out," she said. "Try not to let it get you too down."

CHAPTER TWENTY-THREE

Thursday, October 6th
South of Cheyenne, Wyoming

Day 34

Cheyenne lies a few miles ahead of me. I would pass through today, but I'd rather not go through in the daylight. Going through cities at night, even with the darkness, scares me less than facing the people in the daytime. It's a helpless feeling, knowing that if I run into trouble, I'm on my own. I carry a handgun in my belt, but that doesn't provide much comfort. In the past when I saw a policeman, it always made me a little nervous. Now a real-life cop would be a welcome sight. I've met a couple of sheriffs in some small towns. They were on foot and were nice enough, but pretty interested in me passing through in a hurry.

I'm in Wyoming, and it's exciting to think I'm in a state neighboring my own. Seems kind of juvenile, but does help keep the motivation up. I'm over halfway home and close to being on schedule. The weather has been great. I'm not sure how long my luck will hold out, but I think I'll be home before winter. Emma, you'd enjoy the colors in the mountains. I know how you like fall and the way the leaves change. I'm seeing a lot of red and gold, and it's been really pretty, just wish it didn't mean that cold weather's on the way.

I love you all.

Tuesday, October 11th
Central Wyoming

The muscles in Kyle's legs burned as he trudged towards the top of the hill. The gradual rises and dips of the western prairie had given way, over the past week and a half, to the steeper slopes of the foothills, and he was feeling it. Reaching a level area near the top of the hill, Kyle braced his cart and dropped to the ground in the shelter of a maroon suburban that had been carefully pulled off to the side of the road. It provided a good break from the chilling wind that whistled in from the west as well as a place where Kyle could sit and catch his breath.

Once rested, Kyle stood up and walked the remaining distance to the top of the hill. It was only a few hundred feet further along, and walking without the cart was easy and felt good. At the crest of the hill, he surveyed the surrounding area. To the north, the highway trailed off in the distance, rolling over and around and behind the hills that stood in his way. To the east, the foothills gave way to the rolling, brown expanse of the prairies. South of where he stood, Kyle assessed the miles of road he'd covered that day, road that had been difficult and had slowed his progress considerably. Cheyenne had disappeared from view early yesterday morning and was now miles behind him, another city he could cross off his well-worn map.

To the west, the mountains rose in a growing crescendo, reaching their climax with the rocky, snow-clad peaks far off in the distance. He studied the scene, trying to put to rest his nagging doubts about the route he had taken. He had chosen to take the interstate from Fort Collins to Casper instead of the shorter looking route through Laramie, hoping that the roads to the east would be less hilly and easier to cover. Having strained over numerous hills since making that decision, however, Kyle wondered if his choice had been the right one.

Still second-guessing himself, Kyle returned to his cart, pointed it north, and took up his journey.

Houses in this part of Wyoming seemed further and further apart. Sometimes he walked for hours without seeing a house, giving him a sense of complete isolation. Only the interstate, littered every few hundred yards with abandoned vehicles, kept him from feeling as if he had been dropped in the middle of another planet.

As dusk descended, Kyle picked out a semi a mile ahead for his evening lodging and, with a goal in sight, picked up his pace. Twenty minutes later he was sheltering his cart under the trailer. Finding the side window broken and the truck's door unlocked, Kyle called out and knocked on the window, then climbed inside when he was sure the cab was empty. In the fading light, he set up a bed in the back, then returned to the front seat to watch the final few minutes of sunset and the nightly unveiling of the stars. He'd come to appreciate sunsets on his journey, both for their beauty and as a confirmation that he had survived another day, and each day survived meant he was another day closer to home.

The last of the daylight seeped slowly from the sky and revealed another dazzling display of stars, more vivid at the higher elevation and in the blackness of the night than anything he'd ever seen in his life. As he watched the constellations appear, Kyle noticed a cabin a couple miles up a hill, partially concealed by trees but with light coming from its windows. Something about it seemed strange. He focused on the cabin and saw a light flip on in an upstairs window, and then, a few seconds later, it flipped off. He swallowed hard, not believing what he was seeing, and strained to see more details of the house, picking out another light on a post in the yard.

Kyle hadn't seen electric lights since coming across a few houses running off generators weeks ago. He scanned the horizon to see if other homes were lit up as well, but the surrounding hills blocked his view and shrouded him in darkness, other than that one glowing point of light.

He climbed out of the truck, his eyes focused on the lights in the distance. Leaving his cart behind, he buttoned his thin jacket to keep out the chill and hurried towards the cabin. A small lane a quarter mile from the truck led from the frontage road towards the home, and Kyle followed it in the darkness, the light drawing him in like a moth. He tried to temper his hope, but his mind raced through all the possible explanations. He hadn't heard a radio broadcast or spoken to anyone about anything important for weeks. Were things getting fixed faster than expected? Maybe the EMP hadn't done as much damage or affected things this far north. If the mountains of Wyoming had power, then surely other cities would too. Jennifer and the kids might be safe. With electricity, it wouldn't be long before cars and planes could be made operable again. If that was the case, he wouldn't need his cart and could abandon it, and then he'd be able to get to Casper much faster, maybe in a day or two. From Casper, a bus or a plane could have him safely home in a matter of days.

If power lines had been repaired, then that meant there was a good chance that phone lines were working as well. Assuming there was a phone in the house, he could be talking to Jennifer in just a couple of minutes. It had been almost six weeks since they had last spoken, and he had so many questions. Was everyone safe? Did they have enough to eat? How had they survived? Did they think he was alive? The questions tumbled around his brain in a burst of unbridled excitement.

Kyle reached a gate at the edge of the property where an electric bulb on a post bathed the yard in a pale white glow. He paused and stared at the light, laughing to himself with excitement. For everything it might mean, that light was the most glorious thing he had seen in a long time. Racing across the yard, Kyle leapt up the porch stairs three at a time, halting briefly at the top to catch his breath. From inside the house, Kyle heard music and voices. His heart pounded as he knocked sharply on the door. "Hello!" he called out.

The voices stopped instantly, and the music was silenced. A dog began to bark, but nobody answered.

Kyle knocked again. "Hello? Can you help me?" he shouted through the door.

Footsteps approached the door, and he heard someone clear their throat. "Just a minute, please," a woman called hesitantly.

Kyle waited on the porch, the prospect of talking to Jennifer filling his mind, but the door didn't open. He stepped back and tried to look through the window, all the while bouncing on his toes to keep warm as the cool night air seeped through his sweaty t-shirt.

As he was about to raise his hand to knock again, Kyle heard a voice from the far end of the porch. "Raise your hands above your head!" it ordered.

Kyle turned and saw, in a shadow to the side of the house, a glint of light reflect off of the barrel of a rifle.

"I told you to raise your hands!!" a young man shouted in a voice that was firm but laced with fear.

Kyle held both hands out in front of him and slowly raised them over his head. He could see that a second gun was also pointed in his direction, but the guns' owners were both obscured in the darkness. "I saw the lights. I thought you could help me." Kyle said, his eyes on the guns.

"Why would we help you?"

"Your electricity," Kyle said, confused. "You've got electricity. Do they have things fixed?"

"What are you talking about?" demanded the person who had been issuing the orders. Two figures emerged from the shadows, and Kyle could see that his captors were two large teenage boys. The bigger one seemed to be in charge and looked about seventeen years old. His companion, likely a brother based on the resemblance, looked two or three years younger.

"Are you talking about the government?" the older one asked, the expression on his face showing how utterly preposterous he thought Kyle's question to be.

Kyle nodded, embarrassed to have let his judgment become clouded by hope for what he now knew was impossible.

"The government screwed everything up, and you think they're going to hurry and fix it for us? They're living comfortable and safe in their shelters, shelters they built using money they stole from the people they were supposed to serve. Why would they be in a rush to get anything done? The longer they wait, the fewer of us there'll be and the more they'll be able to take." The young man walked towards Kyle, shaking his head like someone scolding a puppy. "Get off our porch!" he ordered,

"Please don't shoot me," Kyle pleaded as he backed down the steps. "I'm not dangerous at all."

The older boy watched Kyle carefully, his gun aimed at Kyle's chest. "Put your hands behind your back!!" he ordered when Kyle reached the bottom step. He turned to his brother. "Stand over there," he said, indicating a spot by a tall tree a few feet away. "If he tries anything, shoot him!"

The younger boy nodded and backed away towards the designated tree. Kyle watched the boy and could tell by the way he held the gun that he knew how to use it. In contrast to the older boy, Kyle didn't sense any fear in this one, just a calm, steady gaze and a finger poised by the trigger.

Kyle's hands were jerked backwards, and a rope was wrapped around his wrists. "I'm not trying to hurt any..." Kyle protested.

"Shut up!" ordered the older boy. "I don't want to listen to you."

The rope was pulled painfully tight, cutting into Kyle's wrists. "Listen," Kyle pleaded, "if you just let me go you'll never see me again. I'll be gone. I promise."

"I told you to be quiet. Now get on your knees."

Kyle dropped to his knees and another rope was wrapped around his ankles.

"What's this?!" the boy demanded.

"What's what?"

"This!" yelled the boy as he pulled up the leg on Kyle's pants, revealing the large hunting knife strapped to Kyle's leg. "What did you plan to do with that?"

"I carry it for protection."

"You bang on our door late at night, and you think you need protection? I should have shot you like my dad told me to do if any strangers came around."

"Look," said Kyle, "I understand you're scared. I am too. That's why I carry the knife. If I hadn't thought that the power was back on, I never would have bothered you. I've got a pistol stuck in the front of my pants. It's loaded, and I have an extra magazine in my back pocket. I'm not trying to hide anything."

A hand patted Kyle's back pocket, and the clip was removed, then the boy stepped cautiously in front of Kyle and pulled up Kyle's shirt, revealing the handle of the gun. "Just trying to get some help, were you?" the boy mocked, pulling the gun from Kyle's pants.

"Please," Kyle said, "I know this seems bad. If I were in your place, I'd probably be doing the same thing. But I just want to tell you, if you hurt me, you'll be hurting an innocent man."

The boy tugged again on the knots that secured Kyle's limbs, then walked to the door and pounded on it with his fist. "Mom!" he called out. "Open the door."

Kyle heard the deadbolt slide and watched the door swing open. A middle-aged woman stepped onto the porch. "Are you okay, Daniel?" she asked in a soft voice.

The boy nodded. "He didn't fight. Said he just wanted some help, but I found these on him." He held out the knife and gun he'd taken from Kyle.

The woman looked at Kyle, her expression hidden by the shadows cast from the light in the yard. "What are you doing here?" she asked as she stepped into the light.

Kyle studied the woman before answering, trying to find anything that might give him something to relate to. She wore jeans and a simple white, cotton blouse, and her long, dark hair was pulled neatly into a ponytail. Her face was plain, with a prominent nose and narrow cheeks, and her skin was dark, like she'd spent much of her time in the sun. Her eyes sparkled in the light, and Kyle could tell by the way her eyes moved back and forth between her boys that she was obviously concerned about her sons.

He cleared his throat before answering her question. "I'm going back home, back to Montana. I was in Texas when the attack happened, and I've been walking for five weeks. I haven't had much contact with people lately, so when I saw your lights, I thought that maybe things were fixed. I thought I might not have to walk all the way home." Kyle's voice trailed off, and he tried to keep the emotions he was feeling from showing in his voice. "I have a wife and three kids that I need to get back to. I'm sure you understand…"

The woman watched Kyle, her eyes searching his as he spoke, and then she turned to her sons. "Bring him inside."

"But, Mom," Daniel protested. "Remember what Dad said? I'm supposed to look out for the family. We can put him in the barn until Dad gets back. We'd be safer that way."

"I know you were instructed to protect us, Daniel, and you are. But I said to bring him inside. It's cold. He'll freeze if we leave him outside."

Daniel gave his brother a look. "Come and give me a hand, Joshua."

Daniel handed his gun to his mother, then the two boys picked Kyle up and carried him into the house, setting him roughly on the floor in front of a well-worn couch. A cast iron, wood-burning stove in the corner of the room near where Kyle had been dropped gave off plenty of heat, and after being outside in the chilly fall air for so long, a shudder surged through Kyle's body.

The woman sat down in a recliner facing Kyle. She sat silently, studying him intently. After five uncomfortable minutes she spoke. "My name's Emma. You've met my sons, Daniel and Joshua." She motioned in the direction of the two boys, who were now sitting on stools in the kitchen, still anxiously gripping the guns they had greeted Kyle with. "My daughters are Rachel and Rebekah. They're in their rooms. You've put quite a scare into them. I guess we've all been scared lately," she added, "but they just show it more."

"I'm truly sorry to have frightened you," said Kyle, looking at the boys and then back to Emma. "When I saw your lights, I guess I just wanted everything to be back to normal, and I wasn't thinking clearly. I've been alone and walking for such a long time..." he trailed off, his emotions again rising to the surface. "I have a daughter named Emma," he said, changing the subject. "It's a good name. My name is Kyle Tait." He paused and looked around the brightly lit room. "I didn't hear a generator. How do you have power?"

"My husband installed solar panels and wind turbines years ago," Emma answered. "It's all hooked up to batteries and grounded some special way to protect it, plus he's kept extra equipment in case something went wrong. When the batteries are full we're able to use as much power as we want. We don't like having to rely on anyone else, and my husband has never trusted the government, so we've done what we can to take care of ourselves."

"It seems to be working," Kyle said as he admired the brightly glowing lamps. "Emma, I'm sorry to have scared your family. I'm sure you don't get many visitors this far out, but I really don't mean you any harm." He looked her in the eye. "If you would let me go; I'll be on my way, and you'll never see me again."

"Mom," Daniel said, rising from his stool. "Remember what Dad said when he left? He said he'd kill the next person who stepped foot on our property. Said everyone's a liar and a thief, and that we can't trust anyone."

Emma looked at her son. "Daniel, we're not going to shoot him, you know that, and neither will your father. He was just mad when he said those things."

"What if this is the guy who took our chickens?" asked Joshua. "Dad would kill him for sure if he was."

"Why would the person who took our chickens knock on our door?" asked Emma.

Daniel turned his head to the side, his bottom lip clenched between his teeth and a flash of anger showing in his eyes. "Why did this guy come here with a gun and a knife then? When Dad left I promised him that I wouldn't let anyone hurt the family. He'll be back in a couple of days. Why don't we let him decide what to do?"

"And what do we do with Mr. Tait in the meantime? Hold him hostage? Daniel, he's another human being."

"Dad put me in charge," Daniel retorted. "I've got to look out for you and the girls. You know the sheriff isn't going to come here and help. He's only been by once in the last five weeks. We've got to take care of this ourselves."

Emma frowned and considered her son's argument.

Kyle listened to the discussion, watching Emma and Daniel. "Could you at least untie my hands?" Kyle asked. "My fingers are numb."

Emma shook her head, but didn't look at him. "No, Mr. Tait. I'm sorry, but I have four children to protect. In the past five weeks we've had one of our dogs shot, half our chickens taken, and our home has been broken into twice. Things have settled down lately, but who knows how long we'll have to deal with this mess. I'm not sure what we're going to do about you, but I will not have you in my home without some way to protect my family."

She looked at her sons. "Help Mr. Tait up onto the couch," she directed them. "There's no need to make him sit on the floor."

Kyle sat uncomfortably on the couch listening to the fire in the woodstove burn itself down, his arms and shoulders throbbing from being bound behind him. He wiggled his hands, trying again to loosen the rope, but found no more success than he had in his previous attempts. Joshua sat in the kitchen keeping watch over Kyle, his eyes tracking Kyle's every movement. Daniel and Emma had retired to a back room, and from the snippets of conversation he could hear, Kyle had no doubt that he was the subject of their discussion.

The clock on the wall showed 10:35. Kyle was anxious to find out what decision Emma and Daniel came to but was exhausted from the day's events and losing the fight to keep his eyes open, so he lay down on the couch and rested his head on a musty, velvet pillow. The couch was soft and the room was warm, and despite the aching in his arms, he quickly drifted off to sleep.

Kyle was sleeping deeply when a hand shaking his shoulder roused him from his sleep. He forced his eyes open, trying to remember where he was. Emma knelt beside the couch. "Don't make any noise," she whispered, placing a hand softly on his mouth. Kyle blinked, then nodded to indicate he understood. He tried to wipe his eyes, but his hands were still restrained behind his back. In the dim light cast by a small bulb in the hallway, Kyle could see Daniel in the kitchen, his head on the table and his rifle leaning against him. His breathing was deep and marked by shoulders rising and falling in a steady rhythm.

Emma grabbed Kyle's shoulders and helped him into a sitting position, then she leaned forward and gave him instructions in a barely audible whisper. "I'll loosen the ropes, then you do the rest. Once you're untied, you leave. I've got my shotgun, and if you do anything other than leave, I'll shoot you. Do you understand?"

Kyle nodded his agreement, marveling at how straight forward this woman was in promising to kill him.

Emma reached behind him, and Kyle felt her tugging on the ropes. After a brief struggle, the knot loosened, and the blood rushed back into his hands and fingers, causing an intense tingling sensation. Emma stepped away from Kyle and picked up a gun that was propped against the wall, then watched as Kyle tugged on the ropes, finally managing to free a hand. With one arm free, Kyle brought his hands in front of himself and pulled the rope from his other wrist. Once both hands were freed, he rubbed them together and stretched his arms stiffly in front of himself, trying to restore the circulation.

"Hurry!" Emma whispered, glancing nervously at her son.

Kyle untied the rope from his legs as quickly as his stiff fingers would allow, then massaged his ankles. When the circulation returned to his feet, he stood up slowly, holding onto the couch for balance, then stepped carefully towards the door. Emma and her gun trailed a few steps behind.

At the door, Kyle turned to Emma. "Why are you letting me go?" he asked in a hushed voice.

"It's the right thing to do," she whispered. "Daniel's a good boy, but everything is black and white to him. He's a lot like his father." She paused a moment, then continued. "I believe you're a good man and have a family to get to, so I won't stop you from getting there. I've put a loaf of bread on that shelf for you," she pointed to a shelf over some coat hooks with a loaf of homemade bread on it. "Take it to help you get to your family. If you were lying to me, then you will have to live with that, not me. I'll watch to make sure you leave. If you do anything to threaten my family..." She gave her gun a firm shake.

Kyle smiled at Emma as he reached for the bread. "I understand, and thank you. You won't see me again. I promise." He turned back to the door and pulled it open without a sound, then stepped out into the cold air of the early morning.

"You need to hurry," Emma whispered. "I'll wake my son in a few minutes and tell him you're missing, if he doesn't wake before then."

Kyle nodded and tiptoed down the front steps, then hurried away from the house in a slow trot, gradually picking up speed as the sensation in his feet returned to normal. It was downhill to the truck where he'd left his cart, and he made it there in a little less than fifteen minutes. Kyle hastily dug through his cart in the dim light of a cloud-covered moon. He found a sweatshirt at the bottom of the pack and pulled it over his head before heading off into the night, towing his cart behind him.

CHAPTER TWENTY-FOUR

Wednesday, October 12th
Central Wyoming

Day 40

    My head is still spinning. Last night when I stopped for the evening I saw a home all lit up like how things were before Sept. 2nd. I hadn't seen electric lights for a month and my feet got ahead of my brain. I got so excited thinking that everything was fixed and I'd be able to get back to you quicker and maybe be able to talk to you on the phone. But that's not how it turned out. It was a bitter disappointment, making today one of the hardest days so far. I didn't cover many miles, and it was hard to motivate myself to keep going, especially with the never-ending hills. Sometimes I wonder if I'll ever make it. Right now you all seem so far away. If I knew that you were safe, it would lift a huge weight off of my shoulders. I have to think positive and hope for the best.

    I love you all.

Deer Creek, Montana

After checking on the boys, Jennifer closed the door at the top of the stairs and started down the hall to her bedroom when she heard a noise coming from Emma's bedroom. She stopped and slowly pushed the door open, peering inside for the source of the sound. Emma rolled over in bed and looked towards the door. "Hi, Mom," she whispered.

"Hi girl. Why are you still awake? You went to bed an hour ago."

"I can't sleep," she whimpered.

"Are you crying?" Emma didn't reply, but Jennifer could hear her sniffing. "What's wrong, Em?"

Emma rolled back over and faced away from the door, so Jennifer tiptoed in and sat down on the edge of the bed and rubbed her daughter's shoulder. "Sweetie? What is it?"

Emma started to sob and turned back to her mother, who lay down on the bed and wrapped an arm around her. "It's okay, Emma. I'm right here. What's going on?"

Jennifer heard Emma take in a deep breath and then let it slowly out. "I don't like the nights, Mom."

"You don't like the what?"

"I don't like the nights."

"What do you mean, you don't like the nights?"

"I don't. I hate them. I want the sun to shine all the time."

"But that's impossible, Emma. You know that. How come you've started hating nighttime so much?"

Jennifer could feel Emma shrug her shoulders. "I don't know. I just do. It just gets so dark now. It's like I'm lost in a cave that I can't get out of. I had a dream the other night, and I woke up and I was scared, but it was so dark I didn't even know if my eyes were open."

"Why didn't you call me? I'm just down the hall."

"I was scared. The dream was about you – that you left, and it was just me and David and Spencer here, and there was something in the house. I didn't want to make any noise." Emma started to cry again, and Jennifer pulled her daughter tight against her.

"Oh, Emma. I promise I will never leave you. If you have a bad dream again, just call me. Okay?"

"Can I have a candle in here? So it's not so dark?"

"No, honey, you can't. We only have a couple left. And even if we had a lot, it would be too dangerous to keep it lit while we sleep. Do you want me to sleep in here with you tonight?"

Jennifer could sense Emma nodding, so she pulled the blankets back and slid under the covers. "I already had my pajamas on. This'll be good. Just the girls, huh?"

Emma laughed softly. "Thanks, Mom."

"I remember when your Aunt Tracy and I used to share a room. Sometimes we'd stay up past midnight talking. She was a good big sister, and we always had a lot of fun."

"Can I have a sister?"

"You want a sister?"

Emma laughed again. "I do. I'd be a good big sister."

"I know you would. You know, Dad and I tried to have more kids, but I had some medical problems, and the doctor said I couldn't have any more after Spencer was born. He even said Spencer was a miracle. Maybe we could steal a little girl though, what do you think?"

"Mom, don't be silly. We can't do that, and Spencer is no miracle; he's a pain in the neck."

It was Jennifer's turn to laugh. "I thought you said you'd be a good big sister."

"I meant for a girl, not a boy."

"Oh, I see how it is. So if he was a girl, you'd like him more?"

"Probably. Cause he'd be nicer if he was a girl."

"Well, just be glad you've got him. Things would be awfully quiet if he wasn't around." They laughed some more and talked about the things they missed most since the event, until finally Jennifer saw a sliver of moon peek through the window.

"I can see the moon, little girl. We should probably go to sleep."

"Do you think tomorrow will be the day?" Emma asked, ignoring her mother.

"What day is that?"

"The day Dad gets home. Do you think tomorrow will be the day?"

"I don't know." Jennifer swallowed hard. "I hope so…but I don't know."

"I think that's what I hate about the night the most – that Dad didn't come home. As long as the sun's up, I tell myself he might still come home. But when it gets dark…" Her voice trailed off and Jennifer heard a sniffle.

"I hate the night too, Emma. I feel the very same way. Maybe tomorrow will be the day. Pinky swear with me that you won't give up on your dad?" Jennifer felt the bed jiggle as Emma nodded her head. Their hands found each other in the darkness, and they linked pinkies and shook. "I love you, Emma. Let's go to sleep and dream some happy dreams. Okay?"

Friday, October 14th
Deer Creek, Montana

Six weeks after "the event," life for Jennifer had been reduced to a steady diet of predictable drudgery punctuated with regular doses of spirit-draining anxiety. Seven days a week most of her waking hours were spent pursuing survival – trying to locate and store enough food to last them a day, a week, a month. In addition to the hunt for food, there was also the struggle to secure the fuel to cook the food and to keep the family safe and warm.

With bedtime commencing at sundown due to lack of light, many mornings Jennifer and the kids would wake up well before dawn but stay in bed and savor the warmth and security of their blankets while waiting for the sun to rise and the daily rituals to begin again.

The first item of the day was getting dressed, which too often required putting on the same clothes that had been worn for the past two, or three, or sometimes more days. Having clean clothes every day was a luxury that was now a distant memory. Instead, laundry was done by hand every couple of weeks at a makeshift laundromat set up in the community using a large tub of water heated on an open fire and with just barely enough soap to make suds.

Breakfast was the next item on the agenda and, thanks to the Andersons next door, theirs was better than what most people in the community enjoyed. The menu varied from day to day but might consist of a small portion of fresh berries, sometimes canned peaches or applesauce, or a few fresh vegetables. They ate oatmeal once or twice a week, and when David was paid for working at the ranch, which he did most days, payment was made in grains, eggs, meat, and the very occasional container of milk, which was always a welcome treat.

The Anderson's garden was nearly at the end of production, but with a delayed first frost there was still an abundance of produce that Grace was harvesting, allowing for tomatoes, peas, lettuce, and other vegetables to account for a good portion of their diet as well. Lunch was similar to breakfast, and dinner consisted of any meat they had as well as any food that Jacob May might have collected during one of the scavenging trips in his truck. For filler, Jennifer made up simple whole wheat biscuits and cooked them in the old Dutch Oven she'd retrieved from their camping supplies. All of the family had lost weight, but they weren't starving, and they had adjusted without too much complaint to their new routine.

Beyond their search for food, Emma attended school four days a week, Spencer and Jennifer had playgroup three times, David did his work at the farm, and council and community meetings usually occupied three or four of Jennifer's afternoons. A community lending library, with a variety of books available to borrow, had been started, along with game groups, dance groups, craft groups and a number of other venues that gave people a chance to get together in the evenings. On Sunday mornings, two different families hosted church services, and while attendance was rumored to be increasing each week, Jennifer hadn't yet felt compelled to participate.

Late evening was the loneliest time of day for Jennifer because it ended any opportunities to socialize and made her feel like her family was being held hostage to the demands of darkness. No longer could the night be held at bay with the flick of a switch, or loneliness salved with a phone call or a visit to a friend. With batteries and candles exhausted, for all intents and purposes, and Jennifer too afraid to experiment with any kind of flame for light, the coming of night forced the completion of each day whether she was ready for it or not, and each day was ending a little earlier than the one before.

Jennifer had found that if she started getting the kids off to bed when the sun hit the horizon, there was usually enough light for her to get them bedded down and still have a few minutes of time to herself before all of the light disappeared. Spencer typically went down first, although lately Emma was beating him, sometimes thirty minutes before the sun set. David preferred to stay up, but with the hard work he was doing at the ranch, the cooler weather setting in, and his energy tapped, he was usually ready to head to bed at dusk without much prodding.

As part of her nighttime ritual, Jennifer sat next to Spencer on his bed and tucked the covers around him. She leaned down and kissed him on the cheek. "I love you, big guy," she whispered in his ear.

"Love you too, Mom," he replied, raising up to wrap his little arms tightly around her neck. He gave a grunt as he hugged her, then fell back onto his bed. "Mom," he said, his blue eyes gazing up at her, innocent and wide. "When will dad be here?"

Jennifer flinched. Over the last few weeks, he had gradually quit asking about his dad, and Jennifer had been relieved that

Spencer wasn't thinking too much about Kyle's absence. "I don't know, honey. Why do you ask?"

"He said he wasn't going to be gone so long, but it's been lots of days."

"Dad didn't know he'd be gone this long, hon, but some stuff has happened to make him late. No airplanes or cars are working right now."

"How's he going to get home?"

"Well," said Jennifer, "how would you get home if you couldn't use an airplane?"

Spencer considered the question, and then smiled. "I'd ride a horse, like a cowboy."

"Well, you're dad is probably riding a horse, just like you would."

Spencer laughed. "But Dad's not a cowboy."

"I bet he'd learn, so he could get home to you."

"Do you think he's still mad?"

"Why do you think he's mad?" Jennifer asked, surprised.

"He got mad when I knocked his shirts on the floor, and I didn't say sorry."

"Spencer, don't you worry about that. I know your dad loves you, lots and lots." She started to choke up. "I bet he doesn't even care at all about those silly shirts. He just wants to get home to his kids."

"Mom, tell him I'm sorry when he gets back."

"I think he knows, Spencer. I'm glad you're thinking about him."

Spencer grinned broadly "See you in the morning, Mom," he said, then turned on his side and closed his eyes, still smiling.

Jennifer kissed him again, then walked up the stairs as she thought about Spencer and wondered where Kyle might be. In the living room, David was sitting on the floor playing solitaire with a well-worn deck of cards. "Time for bed, Son," she said. "It's almost dark, and you're not feeling well."

David coughed hoarsely and raised a hand in the air. "Just let me finish this game," he choked out between coughs.

"Are you going to be able to go to work tomorrow? You sound pretty bad."

David shrugged. "We'll see," he said just as another coughing fit struck. "I hope so. We need the food."

"Well, if you're sick, you're sick. I'm going to help the Andersons get most of the vegetables out of their garden this week. Grace is worried about frost and doesn't want to lose anything. She said she'd share as much as they can spare, and they have lots of carrots and potatoes stocked in their basement, so don't worry too much about missing a day or two at the farm."

"But I've been getting us meat, and I'd rather not be a vegetarian."

Jennifer laughed at her oldest. "We can get by on vegetables if we need to. Mrs. Anderson has a wonderful garden, so you'd better be grateful to her."

"I am, Mom. You know I'm just kidding. Has Mrs. Anderson ever said why she has such a big garden? The thing takes up most of the yard around their house. It's huge!"

"Grace says it's a hobby she enjoys. She likes to try out new varieties and techniques, plus they do a lot of canning and usually share it with their kids. We're extremely lucky that they live next door."

David nodded and finished his card game while he visited with his mother, then wished her a good night and headed downstairs to his bedroom.

Jennifer straightened up the house before settling in on the couch with a borrowed book. The evenings were getting cooler, and she wrapped a blanket around her legs and positioned herself to catch the last of the fading light, reading until the words on the pages could no longer be deciphered. Finally she folded down the corner and set the book on the floor.

Lately with the cooler evenings, it felt like fall, and Jennifer worried again about how they would stay warm through the winter. The propane fireplace would provide some heat, but they only had a quarter tank left, and she had no idea how long that would last, especially if temperatures got down below zero.

She worried, as she always did, about Kyle, and seriously wondered for the first time, if he was really alive, and if he was alive, where he might be. She worried about their food, but hoped that between the Anderson's generosity and David's work at the farm, they would scrape by. She worried about Doug. He was a constant, nagging stress she carried with her everywhere she went. She'd seen him around recently, but thankfully he'd avoided any contact with her. Maybe her message had been received after all, but she doubted that. His actions at the last meeting told her that was unlikely.

Jennifer worried about the community. The death of the Klein family seemed to have broken things open, and a dark cloud had settled over many of the people she talked to. Some now talked openly about dying, and many were no longer participating in the community activities. Occasionally she cranked up the radio to listen to the President's radio broadcasts, but the hope and optimism portrayed there contrasted so sharply with what she saw around her that she had simply dismissed the broadcasts as propaganda and quit listening. According to others, the President had reported that some power had been restored in Washington D.C., but rather than finding that encouraging, the news had depressed her more than she would've imagined. Going on five weeks, she thought, and that's all the progress they can report?

She worried about her kids, wishing they could have typical childhood experiences like attending a real school, visiting relatives, going to the zoo, or just watching TV. She hated that they were worrying about whether or not they would see their dad again and that they had to work for food or help with the burial of a neighbor. Emma struggled the most, and Jennifer didn't know what to do. Their night together had helped some, plus Jennifer had tried playing games and reading books with Emma and even going on mother-daughter walks, but she was still having limited success in helping her daughter cope with their new way of life. David was becoming a man, having matured rapidly in the past few weeks, but Jennifer worried about him too, that he was being forced to grow up too quickly. His work at the Shipley farm was tough, but the milk, meat, and other food he was earning were a huge help to the family, and David knew the value it had for them, which added to his pressure and responsibilities. Spencer, on the other hand, was young and taking everything in stride, not worrying about things too much, just innocently accepting the situation for what it was. Still thinking about her kids, Jennifer drifted off to sleep where she dreamed about easier times.

Jennifer slept peacefully until a noise broke through her dreams and abruptly woke her. Without moving from the couch, Jennifer tried to regain her bearings as she listened for the noise to repeat. A neighbor's dog barked in the distance, and comfortable that she'd identified the disturbance, Jennifer relaxed and drifted off to sleep again. Just as she lost consciousness, she heard muffled footsteps in the house. Her mind focused immediately and she sat up. "David?" she called out and waited for an answer. The noise stopped, but no answer came. "David, is that you? Are you feeling okay?" The house was eerily still.

Darkness surrounded her, the dim glow of the moonlight barely illuminating the windows let alone the rest of the house. Now sitting on the edge of the couch, she held her breath and leaned forward, straining to hear the sound. She heard the neighbor's dog again but was certain that wasn't the noise that had awakened her. The silence was thick and heavy, and Jennifer listened and waited, but still nothing.

After a tense minute, she exhaled slowly and leaned back against the couch. Her heart raced, but she tried to dismiss the noises as "night-sounds" amplified by her stressed-out situation. Too wound up to go back to sleep, Jennifer felt with her feet for her slippers, then got up and walked into the kitchen for a drink of water. A cool breeze drifted across her ankles, covering her legs with goose bumps. She looked for the source of the breeze and saw that the front door was open with a narrow wedge of moonlight illuminating the gap.

Jennifer's mind raced. Had she closed and locked the door earlier in the evening? She was positive she had. Had one of the children wandered off? Emma had been so unsettled – was it her? Filled with dread, Jennifer ran outside to the porch and scanned the street in front of the house. She saw nothing and hurried back inside, her heart pounding like a piston. She walked as quickly as she dared in the darkness down the hall towards Emma's room.

Passing the open door to her own bedroom, Jennifer sensed movement. She stopped and turned. "Emma?" she said in a hushed voice. "Are you..." she started to say before being silenced by a shape, much too large to be Emma, moving rapidly towards her from inside her bedroom. Petrified, she stood in front of the door wanting to scream, but only a dull gasp escaped her lips. She tried to pull herself away from the door, but her legs wouldn't respond. She raised her hands in front of her for protection just as the intruder, in his attempt to flee, collided with her and sent her careening backwards into the wall of the hallway. Her arms flailed behind her to find the wall and catch herself, but the impact was too violent and she only managed to knock the pictures that were hanging there to the floor with her as she fell.

As the intruder dashed towards the front door to escape, his legs tangled with hers and he fell with a loud crash to the ground, then quickly recovered, scrambled for the door, and was swallowed by the darkness of the night as he fled through the front door.

Jennifer lay on the floor, stunned and trying to make sense of what had happened. As she began to pick herself up, a sound came from the basement stairs and terror took root again. Jennifer crawled silently into her room as the footsteps approached the top of the stairs. She reached under the mattress for Kyle's gun, her heart skipping a beat when she heard a hinge on the basement door squeak as it opened.

Who else was in her house? What had they done to her children? Rumors of gangs had spread through the community in recent weeks, but so far there hadn't been any problems locally. Was she the first victim? Jennifer's fingers found the cold, reassuring steel, and she quickly pulled the gun from under the mattress. With her hands shaking, Jennifer tossed the holster to the floor and turned back towards the door.

Images of David and Spencer butchered in their beds in the basement terrorized her. What had happened to sweet Emma? Was it too late to save any of them? She could feel her heart pounding, then her fear dissolved into a rage more intense than she had ever felt in her life.

Jennifer held the gun tightly with both hands and pointed it towards the open doorway. She had shot the gun a few times in the past and knew how to use it, if she needed to. Aiming the gun at chest level, she pressed her right index finger lightly against the trigger, ready to squeeze as soon as the intruder appeared. She listened, senses magnified, adrenaline pumping, exhaling in short, shallow puffs, her mind focused on the gun in her hands.

In her other life she would have called 911, but not now. Being able to call for help, or even just flip on a light was a distant memory. She longed for the sound of approaching sirens and flashing blue lights racing down the road to save her, but knew they would never come.

A loose floorboard produced a barely audible creak, but it echoed loudly in her head. She squeezed the grip of the gun tighter. In her head, she heard Kyle's instructions. "Squeeze the trigger, don't pull it." Jennifer's arms began to tingle from holding the gun extended, but she blocked the discomfort from her mind.

Her eyes straining in the darkness, Jennifer saw the dark shape of a hand placed carefully on her doorway. She tensed and waited, ready to fire, knowing that she would need to incapacitate the intruder before he could return fire. She felt the pressure of the trigger against her finger and braced herself for the recoil and sound of the shot, knowing it would echo loudly throughout the house.

As she waited and watched, poised to shoot, she heard a voice from down the hallway calling timidly for her. It was Emma. Jennifer wanted to scream out to her, to tell her not to draw attention to herself, but she was too afraid.

Jennifer forced herself to breathe, still watching the hand on the doorway. Something crunched and she knew the intruder had stepped on glass from one of the broken pictures. The hand pulled away from the doorway, and she heard a muffled noise. The noise came again, then again. A stifled cough!

Jennifer lowered the gun. "David?" she hissed, listening for a response, "David? Is that you?" she hissed again, more urgently this time.

"Mom?" came David's frightened voice. "Mom, it's me. Are you okay?"

Jennifer started to shake. She dropped the gun and crawled across the room to her bedroom doorway. "David, you scared me," she said, her voice choking off. Tears flowed down her cheeks as she envisioned herself shooting David and watching him die by her hand. She reached him and wrapped her arms around his head as he sat on the floor in the hallway holding his foot.

"Mom, be careful. There's broken glass," he said. "I cut my foot. I heard a crash, then someone running. What happened?"

Jennifer knelt on the floor embracing her son, barely able to think, completely unable to answer.

Monday, October 17th
Deer Creek, Montana

"Who is it?" Jennifer yelled through the closed door.

"It's Carol. What's going on in there? Are you okay?"

Jennifer cracked the door open, squinting in the bright afternoon sunlight and braced to slam the door shut if it wasn't her.

Carol, her head cocked to the side, looked quizzically through the narrow slit. "Jennifer?" she said. "What's going on? You missed our meeting today. I figured something must be wrong."

Jennifer opened the door wider. "I'm sorry Carol. I just didn't feel like going today. I should have stopped by to tell you."

"You're still in your robe. Are you sick? There are a lot of people down right now."

Jennifer shook her head. "David's been sick, but the rest of us are doing okay. Did I miss anything at the meeting?"

"No, just the usual depressing reports. Seems like everyone's hungry, and no one's sure how we're going to make it through the winter. Heat's also a problem of course, but that's not why I stopped by. You've never missed a meeting. Something's got to be up."

Jennifer stepped away from the door and let Carol in. "You want to sit down?"

"If I'm not intruding. You look horrible. You sure you're okay?"

Jennifer wobbled her head from side to side and shrugged her shoulders, then her eyes started to tear up. "It's kind of hard to talk about. Not even sure what happened."

Carol took her friend by the hand and led her to the couch. "Jennifer, what happened? Was it Doug?"

Jennifer shrugged. "I don't know. It might have been. Probably was, but I can't prove it," she choked out.

"Was he here?"

Jennifer nodded. "Someone was. I fell asleep on the couch and then woke up when I heard a noise. I thought it was one of the kids, so I got up to check and noticed the front door open. I was worried that maybe Emma had wandered off; she hasn't been dealing with things too well lately. When I walked past my bedroom door... to go check on her, I saw someone in my room, but it was dark... and I couldn't see a face, just a shape." Jennifer's crying got worse.

Carol put her arm around Jennifer's shoulder. "Oh Jennifer. That must have been terrifying."

Jennifer nodded. "I think whoever it was thought I was going into my room because he raced out and pushed me over. He fell, and I heard a grunt. It was a man's noise, but that's all I heard. He didn't say anything, just got up and took off. It scared me to death."

"Were you hurt?"

"Not really," Jennifer said, shaking her head. "Just a bump. But then I heard someone sneaking up the basement stairs, so I got Kyle's gun. I was so scared and mad I couldn't breathe, and I was going to shoot whoever it was. Turned out it was David. I came this close to killing my son," she said, holding up her fingers a quarter inch a part. "If he hadn't started coughing, I might have shot him."

"Is he okay?"

"Yeah, he cut his foot on some broken glass, but that's it. He doesn't know his mom almost blew him away. Carol, if I had shot him, I don't think I could've lived with myself. Looking back now, it was stupid not to realize it was David, but I wasn't expecting my fourteen year old to be sneaking around in the middle of the night. It was so dark, and I was so scared." Jennifer looked at Carol, searching for understanding in her eyes. "I'm so flustered right now I can hardly think. It's Doug's fault that I even have that gun in my room... and came so close to shooting my son... I couldn't stand to go to that meeting today, to see his smirk, knowing what he's doing to me."

"What are you going to do?" Carol asked. "Or, better yet, what do we need to do about this?"

"I don't know. I just don't know. My kids are worried. They think mom's going nuts, and they're probably right. It's bad enough that we're living like cavemen with barely enough to eat, using a bucket to flush the toilet, and having to walk a mile for water. Why does that man have to do this to me? Why can't he just leave me alone? He's such a, a..." Jennifer's voice trailed off as Spencer wandered in from the living room. Jennifer wiped at her tears and found Spencer a carrot to eat, then sent him off to play in the basement.

Carol reached out and rested her hand on Jennifer's shoulder. "I can't imagine having to deal with that jerk. Do you want to come stay with me? I have room at my house. You guys could stay in the basement, and you'd be safer there with more people around."

Jennifer shrugged. "Would I be safer there, or would I just put more people in danger? It's like we're living in a town with a crooked sheriff. How do you get rid of him?"

"We could have a council meeting. I'm sure there are other men who could take Doug's position. Craig's brother moved here this week. He sounds like someone who'd get involved."

"That doesn't get rid of Doug though. I feel like it's me that's the problem. No one else is having problems, are they?"

"Not that I know about. You think he might be bothering someone else?"

"I don't know. If he'll harass me, maybe he'd do it to someone else, too? But I'm also in a unique situation. As far as I know, everyone else has their husband around. I don't, so I'm an easier target."

"I'll ask around and see if anyone's seen anything. Do you think we should watch him in the meantime?"

"Maybe. I just want him to go away. My neighbor, Chuck, thinks I should just go shoot the bastard. Says there's no law right now, so I should just take things into my own hands. I'd rather just castrate the jerk."

Carol laughed and shook her head.

"You're the doctor, what do you think?" Jennifer continued.

"I'm a vet. I specialize in a different kind of animal."

"Can't be that different, can it?"

"I'm sure there are similarities, but I don't anticipate finding out."

Jennifer leaned back on the couch, rubbing her temples with her fingers. "The stress is wearing me out. I've had a headache for two days, and I don't sleep. What should I do Carol? Where do I go for help?"

"Let me talk to some people and see what they think. You just try to relax and not let him control your life."

"You think I'm not trying?" Jennifer snapped, then apologized.

Carol leaned over and gave Jennifer a hug as Jennifer struggled to hold back fresh tears. They visited a few minutes longer, then Carol left to find Craig.

A little before dark, another knock sounded at Jennifer's door. Her back instantly stiffened at the sound. She tried to control her fears, but every unexpected noise made her jump. As she crept to the door, a wave of relief washed over her at the sound of Carol's voice calling out.

Carol stood on the porch with a man that Jennifer didn't recognize but who seemed somewhat familiar. His dark hair, which, unlike most people's these days, looked like it had been washed recently, was cut short with no real attempt at a style and framed his square face and prominent forehead. The man wore a well-worn, brown leather jacket and faded blue jeans and was a good foot taller than Carol, so that even from his spot outside, Jennifer had to tilt her head back to look him in the eye. The man watched Jennifer study him and smiled warmly at her. His eyes were bright and conveyed a sense of confidence that Jennifer hadn't seen in quite some time. "Come in," Jennifer invited. "We don't have much light left, but come in."

Carol and the man walked into the house, and Carol made introductions. "This is Sean Reider. He's Craig's brother. I told you about him earlier."

"Nice to meet you," Jennifer said, shaking his hand. She led them into the living room where they all sat down. "What's up?" she asked, trying her best to sound cheerful and relaxed and hoping they wouldn't notice her shaking hands.

"Well," said Carol, "I went to talk to Craig about your situation. Sean was there, and we got into a discussion about things. Anyways, to make a long story short, Sean, Craig and I ended up going over to Doug's house to talk to him, to see if we could put an end to your problems."

Jennifer gasped involuntarily, quickly clamping a hand over her mouth to cut it off. "How'd it go?" she asked in a hushed voice through her hand.

"I don't know," said Carol. "I'm not sure what I expected, but it was just a conversation. Can't say whether it went good or bad. It just kind of went."

"Can I say something?" Sean asked, jumping into the conversation. Jennifer nodded.

"Just so you know, I was in the military for ten years and spent some time as an MP, so I've dealt with troublemakers."

"What's an MP?" Jennifer asked, interrupting.

"Sorry," said Sean. "Sometimes I assume everyone's familiar with military terms. MP stands for Military Police, the military's law enforcement. But anyway, I don't know this Doug guy, but sometimes if someone knows that what they're doing is no longer a secret, they change their behavior. So even if you can't catch them in the act, by confronting them you stop the behavior. I think under the current circumstances that might be the best we can hope for."

"Did he say anything when you talked to him?"

Carol shook her head. "Not really. Acted like it was all a surprise to him."

"Did he deny any of it?"

Sean spoke up. "He said you two were just friends, that you misinterpreted things. Said it was just taken wrong."

"What about the break-in?"

"He acted surprised. Claimed he didn't know a thing about it," said Carol. "Then he got kinda defensive and said there was no possible way for him to be able to police the entire area twenty-four hours a day by himself."

"I think he acted a little too indignant," said Sean. "To me, that show's guilt, but I have no way to prove anything, plus it was the first time I'd met the guy so I don't have any past references to go off of.

"What do you think I should do?" asked Jennifer. "It's not just me. I've got three kids that I'm worried about too."

"I think he's going to stop, or at the very least, cool it for awhile," said Sean. "He's a cop, so he knows better. If it was Doug that broke in the other night, maybe he just got carried away and will rein it in. There's also the chance that it wasn't him. Things were getting really bad in Missoula when I left. In the meantime, keep your doors locked at night, your eyes open, and maybe talk to your kids, at least your oldest, about things. Carol said your son's fourteen?"

"Yeah, David's fourteen."

"You can still come stay with me, if you'd like," said Carol. "You might feel safer at my place."

"I appreciate that, Carol," said Jennifer. "Let me think about it. Emma is having such a hard time right now, and I don't know how she'd react to another big change. Besides, this is our home. All of our stuff is here, and this is where Kyle will come back to when he returns."

Carol nodded and smiled. "I understand. I hope somehow we've helped. It's late, so we'd better get going."

Jennifer thanked Carol and Sean and walked them to the door and locked it securely behind them. She went straight to her bedroom and found her handgun, then checked to make sure it was loaded before tucking it back under the mattress where it would be easy to grab.

CHAPTER TWENTY-FIVE

Thursday, October 20th
North Central Wyoming

With yesterday's mishap still fresh in his memory, Kyle braced himself as he started down another hill, making sure his footing was secure and that he had a good grip on the cart. The day before he'd been heading down a hill, lost in thought, when he'd stumbled. As he fell, the cart had run up the back of his legs and tripped him, then cracked him in the back of the head before rolling over top of him. He had tried to grab one of the wheels as it rolled by but only succeeded in pinching his fingers between the cart and the tire, then watched helplessly as his cart raced down the hill. Halfway down, it veered towards the median where the handle caught in the dirt, vaulting the cart into the air and scattering its contents everywhere.

Fortunately, the damage to the cart had been limited to a slightly twisted box and the bottom of the handle being ground flat on the highway. Kyle's injuries hadn't been serious either, and the loss of time had been minimal, but now he tried to focus on the road more as he traversed one hill after another.

The scale of the map in the atlas he carried had made it seem like Wyoming would be a quick conquest compared to Colorado, and he hadn't given the difficulty involved in crossing it much thought, especially since he was more focused on the four hundred and fifty miles ahead of him in Montana. His initial estimate for crossing Wyoming had been that it would be a fourteen-day trek, but he was on day fifteen now and figured he still had a good week to go. Kyle also knew from the map that the elevation was increasing, and after each day's pulling, the sore muscles in his legs and the tightness in his chest from the thin air reaffirmed that knowledge.

As he looked around, Kyle noticed a threatening wall of purple-gray clouds to the west rolling slowly towards him. The wind had also begun to pick up in the last hour, slowing his progress and peppering him with a sandy grit that found its way under his clothes and into his mouth, and eyes, and ears. After two weeks of Wyoming, he was tired of the conditions and anxious to have the state behind him.

A number of semis had come to rest at the bottom of the hill, and he took shelter between them while he rested and drank some water, all the while eying the hill that loomed ahead and listening to the wind whistle around him. He put on another shirt as a shield against the cold, then continued on, anxious to cover a few more miles before stopping for the day.

The grade of the hill was steep and seemed to go on for miles, making it one of the hardest he had tackled to date. He lost his footing on the grit-covered road three times, nearly losing control of his cart, but each time he managed to hold on and avoid catastrophe. Finally, two hours after he began its ascent, he conquered the hill.

The ground leveled out at the top, and Kyle dropped to his knees, exhausted, legs feeling like Jell-O, lungs raw from sucking in the thin, cold air, which had developed an icy chill as he'd climbed. The wall of clouds he'd seen earlier was much closer and even more ominous than before, promising a change from the mild autumn weather he'd been enjoying over the past few weeks to the first blast of winter. Watching the front move in, Kyle knew his streak of good fortune was about to come to an end, a thought that greatly alarmed him, especially considering how far he still had to travel. As the storm approached, streaks of rain glowed in the mid-afternoon sun just a few miles west of where he sat.

Kyle climbed wearily to his feet, grabbed the handle of his cart, and after a long, deep breath, resumed pulling. The stretch of highway he was on seemed unusually barren, with fewer vehicles, no houses, and a complete absence of fellow travelers. A few miles ahead, Kyle could see a semi that he hoped would provide good shelter from the bad weather. There were a few smaller cars and a pickup closer, but past experience had proven that they would be too small and uncomfortable to wait out a storm, especially if it lasted more than a few hours. He scanned the horizon and spotted a couple of homes off in the distance, set back off the road, but there was no guarantee that the people, if there were any there, would be willing to help him.

The wind blew harder, and the temperature seemed to drop with each fresh gust. About a mile from the semi, Kyle felt the first hints of rain, tiny drops that stung his cheeks in the driving wind.

By the time Kyle reached the semi, he was in the middle of a driving rain, and his clothes were soaked completely through. Cold and shivering, his only thought was to get somewhere dry and out of the wind. The word "DEAD" was scrawled in large red letters on the driver's side door of the cab and struck Kyle as unusual, but he was too cold to care what it meant. After quickly stowing his cart under the trailer, he hurried back to the cab.

The door was locked, but the triangle window had been broken out, making it easy for Kyle to stick his arm through and pop the lock. Hurrying to escape the deluge, Kyle tugged the door open just as another gust of wind whipped up, catching the door and ripping it from his hand and knocking him from the step. He quickly recovered and climbed inside, then had to fight against the wind to get the door pulled shut behind him. Kyle was leaning back in the seat, shivering and wet, when an overwhelming feeling of nausea swept over him.

He twisted to the side and vomited onto the floor between the seats. Another heave wracked his body as he braced himself on the passenger seat for support. He took a deep breath and become instantly aware of a sickening smell and an unfamiliar buzzing sound. With a quick glance around the back of the cab, Kyle spotted a cloud of flies swarming over a dark object on the bottom bunk. Covering his mouth and nose, Kyle sat back up, fighting the urge to vomit again.

With his arms braced on both of the front seats, Kyle avoided his pool of vomit and stepped between the front seats towards the back. With his second step, he froze in his tracks. What had at first looked like a dead dog lying on the bed was instead a human corpse, gazing up through eye sockets filled with writhing maggots, its skin blistered, wrinkled and raw, and swarming with flies. He dropped to his knees and vomited again, heaving so violently that the bitter bile drained out of his nose. As he gasped for air, flies swarmed around the fresh, steaming vomit and up into his mouth. Doubled over, Kyle coughed and swatted at the flies, and felt his hand brush against a cold, meaty object. Revolted, he turned and saw an arm hanging from the bunk, its shriveled flesh hanging from the bone, the fingers resting in a dark, fly-covered stain on the carpet. Kyle's own hand seemed to burn from the contact with the decomposing flesh, and he wiped it feverishly on the back of the front seat.

Pulling himself to his feet, Kyle lunged for the door, rushing to escape the unexpected sepulcher before another bout of vomiting commenced. Desperate to get out, he fumbled with the door handle, opened it, then dove through the opening and crashed roughly onto the wet pavement. Dazed and ill, Kyle lifted himself onto his knees and crawled through the rain towards the back of the truck, heaving twice more along the way.

Huddled behind his cart, Kyle shielded himself as best he could from the bitter wind that whistled around him. Unable to purge from his senses the smells and images from inside the truck, he sat for a long time, vomiting until there was nothing left in his stomach but a clear, bitter liquid that burned his sinuses and hung in strands from his nose and lips. He had seen more dead people during the past seven weeks than in his previous thirty-seven years, but nothing to this point in his life had prepared him for this ghastly experience.

In the time that had passed since arriving at the semi, the rain had turned to sleet, and then to snow, and now the air was filled with thick, heavy flakes that fell more sideways than down and began to accumulate in the grass along the edge of the road in fluffy piles and in a thin, slushy layer on the road.

The wind had shifted from the west and was now blowing in hard from the north, biting sharply through Kyle's wet clothing. He pulled out his bag of clothes and dumped the contents in front of him on the cart, searching for something to replace his drenched clothing that provided little protection. The shirts left in his bag were wet in patches from where water had leaked into his duffle bag, but were drier than what he wore. He stripped off his shirts and put on the dry ones along with his thin, cotton jacket, all the while wishing he'd been able to find a heavy coat somewhere along the way.

He had hoped to make it home before the weather was too severe, but it felt severe already with the wind cutting through his layered shirts as he crouched under the trailer of the semi-truck. Kyle wrung out the shirts he'd removed and put them on over the dry ones to add layers. He took off his pants and put on a mostly-dry pair of sweats, followed by a drier pair of jeans.

He tried to get into the trailer, but a thick, round padlock kept it tightly secured, even after taking three shots at the lock with his pistol. With the semi offering no practical shelter, Kyle wrapped his sleeping bag around his numb body and stumbled down the road, looking for someplace to keep him warm and dry.

The sky had dulled to a charcoal gray, and as the temperatures and snow continued to fall, the slush on the road thickened to the consistency of oatmeal while the snow on the sides of the road accumulated to three and four inches, even approaching a foot in places where it drifted in the raging wind. Kyle spotted a sedan a mile away and trudged stiffly towards it. His feet, wet and cold from the slush, felt like cinderblocks tied to the ends of his legs.

When he arrived at the car, Kyle tugged desperately on the door, which, to his surprise, swung open effortlessly. Bending to climb inside, he saw that the seats were filled with snow that had blown in through a broken out window on the passenger side. He yelled in a fit of anger at his bad fortune and slammed the door shut.

Kyle jumped up and down in the driving wind and stomped his feet, trying to restore some of the sensation he had lost in them. His toes had quit tingling, and while he didn't miss that discomfort, he knew in the long run that no sensation was worse than the discomfort. Kyle weighed his options. He could curl up in a ball in the front seat of the car, or he could continue on. If he stayed in the car and the weather improved, he would be okay, but if it didn't, he knew there was a good chance he would freeze.

Kyle took one glance at the still darkening sky, shook the snow out of his hair, and plodded on. As he trudged through the snow, the misery compounded with each step. Snow melted in his hair, sending a trickle of icy water down his neck and back, while slush splashed up his legs, numbing them even more.

Kyle slipped in an icy patch of slush and fell to the ground. Frigid water soaked through his pants and seized his legs in a cold, steel vise. As he struggled back to his feet, he felt the freezing water running down his legs and into his shoes. "Damn you!!" Kyle cursed into the wind in a desperate sob. "I don't want to die!" He'd walked nearly a thousand miles and now he hoped desperately that it hadn't been in vain. He shook his arms and hands, trying to loosen up his fingers that seemed to have frozen around the handle of his cart. He stomped his feet and jumped in place to get his blood pumping.

He knew that to stop here would be suicide. Kyle looked at the cart at his feet. The thing that had allowed him to travel halfway across the country, and that he had killed for, had now become an anchor on the frozen roadway, slowing him to a crawl and threatening his survival. He pulled his sleeping bag from the cart and wrapped it around his shoulders, then, in an act of cold indifference, Kyle stepped over the handle and walked away, knowing his chances for survival right now were better without it than with.

Unencumbered by his cart, Kyle stumbled down the road, moving faster, but unsure of where he was headed. A mile up the road he came to a pickup and pulled at the doors, but they were locked. He pounded on the windows with his fists, succeeding in sending intense shocks of pain along his arms but doing nothing to the windows. He looked in the bed of the pickup and found a short 2x4 in a mound of snow. On his third swing with the 2x4, the side window shattered and glass exploded in every direction. Kyle clawed at the inside handle and opened the door, then struggled to climb inside, his frozen legs barely able to bend. Once inside, he slammed the door shut, slid across the seat, and huddled against the opposite door.

Kyle pulled his knees to his chest and wrapped his dripping sleeping bag around himself. Out of the wind, he started to warm up, but still couldn't control the shivering that racked his body. Pulling the sleeping bag even tighter around his torso and head, Kyle stared out through a narrow gap in the folds and watched the snow rush past in the howling wind and blow in through the broken window. His mind numbed by the raging storm, Kyle stared vacantly at the snowflakes that slipped in through the window, watching as they drifted softly down to the floor of the truck, free from the grips of the howling wind outside.

Kyle watched the snow for several minutes as his shivers subsided and his temperature slowly rose. Tired, sheltered, and warmer, he felt his head bob down as he started to drift off to sleep, a state he was afraid to succumb to. He shook his head vigorously, forcing himself to stay awake and assess his surroundings, trying to keep his mind active. Wet, cold, tired, and with no external heat source, Kyle knew his situation was terribly grave. Even the sleeping bag he was wrapped in, while it helped to keep the wind and snow away, was soaked and cold and far from an ideal covering. As a young man, stories of frozen hunters, hikers, and skiers had appeared in the newspaper every winter, making him so wary of the cold that he had always over-prepared for any kind of winter excursion and had become the butt of plenty of jokes at the hands of his friends. How ironic, he thought, that he was now stuck in the middle of a fall blizzard with next to no equipment and unlikely to survive for more than a few hours.

Kyle inventoried the truck for anything that might be useful. The dash yielded a couple of screwdrivers, and the glove box held nothing more than a dead flashlight and an owner's manual. Kyle reached behind the seat and felt a tire jack and some kind of cloth. He pulled hard on the fabric and, after a short struggle, pulled loose an old, grease-stained cotton jacket. Thrilled at this small bit of good fortune, he stripped off his wet shirts and replaced them with the jacket. It was cold and stiff, and had likely been in the truck for years, but it was dry and that was all that mattered at the moment.

With the sleeping bag removed, Kyle could see that his pants were soaked, but his legs were so numb that he hadn't known. With stiff fingers, he removed his shoes, then pulled off his pants and draped them over the seat with his shirts. He wrapped his sleeping bag back around his body, curled up on the seat, and tried to block out the sound of the blowing wind and the fear that gnawed at the back of his mind. Reaching down to rub his legs, Kyle felt the wet sleeping bag on the back of his hands and realized that it was nearly as wet as the clothes he'd removed.

Kyle shifted and found a drier section of the sleeping bag, and tried to keep that part closest to him, having to twist awkwardly to keep the wet areas away from his body. He lay back down on the seat, and tried not to think about the cold, but with every passing minute he felt it sinking deeper and deeper into his bones. A hard shiver shook him, nearly dumping him onto the floor of the truck. He pulled his wet clothes from the back of the seat and spread them on top of the sleeping bag, trying to add layers to block out the cold. Instead, his cold, wet shirt fell against his face, and snow drifted onto an exposed leg, all while the wind whistled even louder outside. A second hard shiver racked his body, and Kyle sat up, panic taking hold.

Trying again to clear his thoughts, Kyle shook his head and let out a fear-filled yell, the noise a distinct contrast to the steady drone of the wind. As Kyle looked out through the broken window at the swirling snow and pondered his predicament, he had an idea. He slid one of the truck's sun visors off its rod and wedged it in the opening of the broken window. He grabbed the second visor and repeated the process, successfully blocking off most of the opening.

Next Kyle used one of the screwdrivers from the dashboard to tear at the covering on the seat. If he could remove that, he decided, both the cover and seat padding would provide some protection. He slashed at the seats, his breath coming in deep, panicked gulps as he worked. The seat-covers resisted his efforts, and it was several minutes before he loosened an edge enough to get his hand under it. Rising up on his knees, he jammed his hand under the flap and pulled as hard as he could, finally hearing a rip and feeling the fabric give way, but as the seat cover tore, Kyle lost his balance and fell against the door, knocking the carefully placed visors out into the snow.

A gust of icy wind swept through the broken window and wrapped its cold fingers around his neck, then down under the collar of his jacket, around his face, and seemingly into every pore of his body. Shivering, Kyle fell onto the bench of the truck and pulled the sleeping bag down over himself, the cold, wet fabric like sheets of ice against the bare skin of his legs. Shivers coursed up and down his body, his teethed rattled, and tears of pain and frustration ran down his face.

Beyond discouraged, Kyle yelled out and shook his head to clear it again, trying to rouse himself to action, any kind of action, and knowing that if he stayed in the truck without a way to stay warm he wasn't going to last the night.

With great effort, Kyle dressed in his stiff, wet clothes, placing the driest layers closest to his body. He opened the door of the pickup, and an icy blast of wind hit him in the face, as if challenging his efforts to escape. Ignoring the affront, Kyle jumped to the ground. Pain shot through his frozen legs and up into his hips, but he disregarded the agony and forced himself to move forward, taking slow, painful steps. A dozen cold and difficult steps away from the truck, Kyle looked back and reconsidered staying in the truck to last out the storm, but the long, unbroken blanket of heavy, gray clouds extending beyond the horizon convinced him to move on.

With no good shelter behind him, Kyle moved forward towards a rise that was a half-mile north. From there he would determine the best course of action, whether to seek shelter in another vehicle or try to find shelter in a nearby home.

In his desperate state of affairs, moving gave Kyle purpose, and the flame of hope that had nearly been extinguished in the pickup flared again. With renewed determination, the wind didn't seem quite so cold, nor the snow so deep. Even his arms and legs somehow felt warmer. At the top of the rise, he scanned the area ahead of him, using his arms to shield his face from the wind. He could barely make out the snow-covered mounds of a few small cars close by and the hulking shape of a semi-trailer beyond them. Just past the truck and to the west of the highway was a house part way up a hill. To the east of the road and a little further along, lay another house which was sheltered by a windscreen of trees. Kyle thought he could see more trucks even further down the road, but with the wind, snow, and growing darkness, he couldn't be sure.

Neither house showed any signs of life, so Kyle set off for the truck, making his way as fast as he could in the ever deepening snow. By the time he reached the truck, his feet had lost all sensation, and he only maintained his balance by taking carefully focused steps.

As Kyle came around the back of the trailer, he looked up and stopped dead in his tracks. The vehicle he had pinned his hopes on for survival was a delivery truck, not a full semi, and the cab, which was even smaller than the pickup he had abandoned, had its passenger door wide open and was filled with snow. Desperate, he staggered to the back of the truck, unlatched the door and rolled it up, exposing an empty trailer. As the icy fingers of the storm clawed furiously at him, Kyle climbed stiffly inside to escape the wind and reconsider his plan.

Too tired to cry, Kyle looked out at the sky. "Why?! I want to live! I need to live!" he pleaded. Cold, hungry, and weak, Kyle dropped to the floor of the trailer and crawled to the side. He leaned his head back and closed his eyes, picturing his wife while the wind shook the trailer. "Jennifer, I'm trying, honey. I'm really trying…but I don't know…I'm so cold," he whispered the words as he held his frozen hands against his cheeks, trying to warm his skin.

Kyle stood up and leaned out of the back of the truck. The house to the west was on a hill that was much steeper than it had looked from a distance. To get to it, he would have to continue north and then hook back around. The house to the east looked like an easier journey and the better choice, especially since he was sure it would be his last chance for survival.

Kyle climbed down from the trailer and stepped into the wind. A gust caught him and pushed him to the side, almost knocking him down. Weak and unsteady as he was, he managed to maintain his footing, and he laughed defiantly at the storm, then tightening his grip on the sleeping bag still wrapped around his body, he pressed on. He climbed clumsily over a barbed-wire fence that lined the edge of the road, tearing a hole in his pants and gouging his leg, but the pain of the wound barely registered. The drifting snow almost came up to his knees in some places, and the soil underneath was uneven and slick, making his progress difficult and slow.

A small creek, about seven feet across, interrupted the way to the house. He couldn't tell how deep the water was, nor see an easy way to cross, so he backed up a few steps, lumbered as fast as he could towards the creek, and leapt. Under normal circumstances, jumping the creek would have been easy, but stiff with cold, he could barely get up to a run. His foot slipped on the bank as he jumped, and what little momentum he had wasn't enough to carry him across the water, landing him instead in the shin-deep creek a foot from the opposite bank. He took a quick step up the bank on the far side, but slipped and fell on his stomach, then slid towards the water. Frantic, Kyle clutched the soft, loose snow, which did nothing to halt his slide into the shallow creek. When he finally came to a stop, the right half of his body was submerged in the water, which felt warm compared to the bitter cold of the wind. As he sank into the creek, he considered rolling all the way in to escape the cold, but then the image of his dead body, frozen in a sheet of ice, flashed briefly through his mind and roused him back into action.

Clinging to tufts of grass buried under the snow, Kyle pulled himself up the bank and collapsed on the frozen ground, his spent body covered in mud, snow, and ice. He turned back to the creek and watched, not caring as his sleeping bag slowly floated away. On top of the bank, Kyle gasped as a fresh gust cut through his wet clothing, sending sharp pains through his chest like a knife being shoved between his ribs. He staggered to his feet once again and headed for the house, stumbling desperately across the field. He was aware of nothing but his goal – a house that was quickly dimming, both in the fading light and in his fading consciousness.

A hundred yards from the house, Kyle fell to his knees, exhausted. His clothing was nearly frozen stiff, hinging just slightly at his elbows and knees. He crossed his arms across his body and rested briefly then, with enormous effort, got back onto his feet.

Kyle teetered unsteadily, pausing to gain enough balance to put one foot in front of the other. The only thought he had was to get to the house in front of him, now maybe ninety yards away. Like an infant learning to walk, Kyle moved haltingly across the field, losing his balance and falling repeatedly, each time forcing himself to get up.

With just a driveway, a short rail fence, and a small yard separating him from the house, he fell again, too tired to rise. On frozen hands and knees, Kyle crawled across the road to the fence and used the horizontal wooden rails to pull himself up and over, where he fell to the ground completely spent.

Kyle eyed the house, which was now less than a hundred feet away. He needed to rest, he thought, just to regain a little more strength, and then he could make it. Sheltered from the wind by the fence and a few small shrubs, Kyle felt warmth spread slowly through his body. He looked down at his shirts. They were dirty and frozen, so he stripped them off and set them on the snow beside him. He leaned forward to untie his boots but gave up when his numbed fingers wouldn't grab the laces. Leaning back against the fence, he felt warm for the first time in three hours. In the shelter of a row of trees, the snow fell more calmly, almost peacefully, and Kyle watched as the flakes landed on his stomach, melting upon contact with his skin. Kyle, comfortable and warm, closed his eyes. He was tired and just needed a few minutes of sleep, then he'd have the energy he needed to be on his way again.

CHAPTER TWENTY-SIX

Friday, October 21st
Deer Creek, Montana

Jennifer stood at the living room window, shielding her eyes from the brilliant glare of the early morning sun reflecting off the fresh blanket of snow. Snow had fallen most of the day Wednesday, and now everything was covered in a thick, soft, as yet undisturbed, layer of white. She stared at the snow, fighting to breathe normally, her throat aching from suppressed sobs, streaks staining her cheeks.

"Kyle, where are you?" she whispered haltingly. "I'm so worried about you, and I need you. I don't know how I can do this alone."

She heard a door open at the end of the hallway, followed by the sound of approaching footsteps. Emma appeared around the corner, bundled in sweat pants, thick socks and a robe. "I'm cold, Mom. Can we turn the heat on?"

Jennifer wiped the tears from her face. "I'll go turn on the fireplace, doll. Did you sleep okay?"

Emma swung her head emphatically from side to side, a perturbed look on her face.

"Why not?" Jennifer asked. "I thought the three of you'd be warm in there?"

"It was warmer, but Spencer squirms around too much and kept pulling the covers off me."

"Sorry, doll. We'll try and come up with a better plan for tonight."

They walked into the family room together, and Jennifer turned on the fireplace. She pulled the couch up close and drew a blanket over their legs after they were settled on the couch.

"Are you okay?" Emma asked.

"Why do you ask?"

"You've been crying again. What's wrong?"

"Well, I guess I'm just worried about your dad. He's not home yet, so I worry. It's what moms do."

Emma looked at her mother and smiled. "I think he'll be fine. Grandma always tells me that I can pray about stuff, and God will take care of things. I've started praying every night for dad to get home, and I think God's going to hear me."

Jennifer gave Emma a hug. "You're sounding better. I think maybe I need to start asking, too, just so God knows I want your dad home as much as you do."

"Grandma said you don't like to pray too much, so I need to do it for the family."

"When did she tell you that?" Jennifer asked, taken aback.

"When she was here at Easter and took me to church. She said you hated to go to church and do all that stuff. But I liked it. It felt good."

"Well that was nice of Grandma to be talking behind my back like that."

Emma giggled. "It's true, isn't it?"

"I suppose," Jennifer stammered, "but it's not like I hate God or anything like that."

"Then why don't we ever go?"

Jennifer shrugged uncomfortably. "I went a lot when I was your age, but none of my friends did, and it always seemed like they were having more fun than I was. We had this really ancient minister. He was as deaf as could be, and having to listen to him shout the sermon every Sunday in his squeaky, old voice wasn't very exciting." Jennifer's eyes glistened again at the memory of Sundays with her mother and sister.

"Did you pray when you were my age?"

"I did when I remembered to, but I think I forgot to a lot. When Grandma and Grandpa decided not to be married anymore I prayed myself to sleep every night for a month…but God didn't listen, at least that's what I thought then." Jennifer found herself caught up in her memories. "I think that's when I decided that I really didn't like church anymore."

Emma gave Jennifer an innocent smile and snuggled in closer to her. "After breakfast can I go out and make a snowman? I'll take Spencer with me."

"I suppose, but I'm going to need your help. We're going to collect as much snow as we can today, and you and David will need to help. We'll fill the bathtubs, the sinks, and all the buckets I can find so we don't have to keep carrying water from the river, or from Mr. Patel's; he's really low on gas. Maybe the snow will help us get by for awhile."

"Okay, Mom. But first I want to make the snowman."

North Central Wyoming

Rose Duncan leaned forward in her recliner to once again check the unconscious man on the floor. He'd been in rough shape when she dragged him into the house the night before, and she hadn't been entirely sure that he was going to make it. The man had lain for hours without moving, then finally, a little before sunrise, he'd started to show some signs of life. Now that he was moving more, Rose got up from her chair and went into the kitchen. She retrieved a bucket of honey from the pantry, scooped three spoonfuls into a small pan, then added water. Returning to the living room, she placed the pan on the wood-stove that warmed the room.

The man moved again, and she turned to watch him. His foot slipped out from under the mound of blankets that covered him, and she noticed that, although his toes were still pale white, his skin was starting to regain a healthier tint. Carefully, she leaned down and placed a hand on his forehead, noting that his temperature had risen since she had last checked. She pulled the blanket back and put a hand on his chest. It felt warmer as well.

Gradually the man became more animated, until she noticed his eyes open just a crack.

"Good morning," Rose said. "How are you feeling?"

***

Kyle slowly drifted into consciousness. His body ached and his head throbbed, like someone had mercilessly beaten him with a club. He wanted to open his eyes, but the bright light in the room hurt too much. There was a voice saying words that his mind couldn't process, and he had a vague notion to sit up, but his body declined the request. He tipped his head to the side and forced his eyes open, squinting to take in his surroundings. The room came into focus and Kyle saw gray sky through a picture window and someone sitting nearby with a large dog curled lazily on the floor beside them. Kyle closed his eyes and let his head slump back down. He tried to piece things together in his mind, but the thick mental fog wouldn't clear. Soon he was drifting back to sleep.

***

Rose watched as the man came to and could tell that he was disoriented and confused. He hadn't responded to her greeting but did at least seem to recognize that she was there and that she had spoken to him before he drifted off to sleep again. His mind seemed to be in another place, reminding her of how confused she had felt a few years back when her horse had thrown her and she'd come to with her panicked son kneeling over her.

Rose was relieved that the man was coming around and hoped the steady progress meant he was returning to normal. She knew in cases of hypothermia that brain injuries were a possibility, and the thought of rescuing someone who wouldn't fully recover had been worrying her for the fourteen hours since she'd pulled him into her home.

Tired and anxious, Rose walked over to the window and looked outside. The storm had mostly blown over during the night and left the area blanketed in a heavy layer of snow. The trees behind the house were bent low, struggling under the heavy load of snow, and several branches had broken and were hanging to the ground. The light snow that was still falling was being carried by the wind, blowing around the fences, across the sidewalk, and behind the house, adding to drifts that were already over two feet high. Before closing the blinds to darken the room, Rose checked the outside thermometer and noticed that the temperature had climbed a couple of degrees, resting just below the 25° mark.

Rose found the book she'd been reading, opened it up to her bookmark, and stretched out on the couch with a favorite quilt pulled over her. It had been a long, fitful night with very little sleep, and after a few minutes of trying to read in the dimmed light, she gave up the fight to keep her eyes open. Rolling onto her side, she set her book on the floor and pulled the blanket up over her shoulders. From across the room, she watched the man on the floor, his chest rising with deep, steady breaths, his eyes shut to the world. She worried about him, this mystery man, as she too drifted off to sleep.

***

Rose had no idea how long she'd been asleep when a loud shout broke the silence and jolted her awake. Across the room, the man was still lying on the floor, but his eyes were open and panic stricken. She quickly crossed the room and knelt beside him, speaking in a soft, reassuring voice. "It's alright. I'm Rose, and you're in my home. You're going to be okay. Just try and relax."

***

Kyle looked at Rose and breathed deeply, but did not answer, his mind trying to figure out who this woman was and how he'd gotten inside her house. The last thing he remembered was standing in the back of a truck, trying to decide where to go. Now he was lying on the floor of a home he'd never seen, being tended by a woman he didn't know. Dim sunlight filtered in around the blinds, illuminating the room and its contents. There was a couch, a recliner, a coffee table stacked with books, and pictures and statues of horses and cowboys. The woman looked down at him, her brow furrowed. After a pause, she went to the woodstove and returned with a mug.

"Here, drink this," she said. "It's warm honey water. You need to get some warm liquids inside you."

Feeling as if he was in a drugged stupor, Kyle struggled clumsily to get into a sitting position so he could take the mug. Rose grabbed his arm and helped him sit up, then put the mug to his lips.

Kyle took a sip and swallowed it, feeling the liquid warm its way to his stomach.

"You had a close call last night," Rose said. "But I think in a couple of days you're going to be fine." Kyle watched her closely as she spoke.

She tipped the mug up again, and he took a few more swallows of the sweet, warm liquid. As the fluid settled in his stomach, Kyle felt as if the various systems in his body were being switched on one by one. A couple more sips and he reached up and took the mug from her, cradling it in his hands and drinking it slowly, enjoying the sensation of it warming his body.

"Let me help you to the bathroom," Rose offered when he finished the drink. "We need to be sure to get you in there regular the next couple of days. Your body has a lot of toxins in it that need to be flushed out." She stood and reached down to help lift Kyle. Kyle grabbed her hand and, bracing with his other hand against the wall, struggled to his feet. His legs were strong enough to support his weight, but were stiff and sore and his balance was off, so he held her shoulder as they shuffled through the house to the bathroom.

Rose helped him to the toilet, then excused herself when she was sure he wouldn't topple over. Kyle sat there, the haze that shrouded his mind continuing to clear like a fog gradually burning off with the morning sun. The memory of struggling across a field came to him, but he still couldn't place himself in the house.

Pulling himself back to his feet, Kyle paused in front of the mirror, curious to see his reflection. He held onto the countertop, steadying himself in his weakened state, and was astounded by his changed appearance. Returning his gaze was a frail, underwear-clad man with a bushy beard and cheeks that were weathered and red. His dark, tired eyes scanned from side to side across his body, taking in the skinny, discolored arms and legs that were more white than pink, leaving him dismayed by his withered physique.

He turned from the mirror, let himself out of the bathroom, and carefully made his way back down the hall.

Rose was arranging blankets on the couch and turned when Kyle entered the room. "You going to make it okay?"

Kyle nodded.

"I'm going to get you situated here on the couch. It'll be more comfortable than the floor. Tomorrow I'll get you a bed, but this room is warmer with the stove."

Kyle crossed the room, step by tender step, till he made it to his new bed. He lay back on the pillows Rose had piled at one end and pulled the blankets over himself. Rose refilled his mug and placed it on a table she'd pulled up by the end of the couch. "Here's some more honey water. You need to drink a lot of this. Your body needs calories to burn to get your temperature back up. Seeing as I can't get you to a hospital, this is the best I could come up with."

Kyle pulled up into a semi-reclined position and took a long drink. His head was clearing, but he still felt foggy. He was grateful that the headache that had plagued him earlier had eased to a dull ache. He set the cup down and looked at Rose. "Thank you," he said.

She smiled at him. "It's nice to hear your voice. You're welcome."

Kyle leaned back into the pillows, feeling exhausted. "I'm Kyle."

"Nice to meet you, Kyle. I'm Rose."

Kyle smiled at Rose in place of a handshake. "How'd I get here?"

"That's what I want to know," she answered. "I found you in my front yard. Beyond that, I can't say." Kyle looked confused, and she could tell he was trying to come up with an answer to the question she had implied. "Listen, Kyle. Let's get acquainted tomorrow. Today you just need to rest. You were pretty far gone when I found you, so just take it easy, drink lots of that honey water, and hit the bathroom every couple of hours. If you need anything else, just ask. Okay?"

"Are you a doctor?"

She laughed. "No, I'm a realtor, or at least I was. But I raised two boys in the Wyoming mountains who loved to be outside, and I learned to be prepared for a lot of different situations. I never had to treat my boys, but I guess it worked out well for you."

Kyle nodded, the fatigue growing stronger, his eyelids heavier. Even as Rose spoke, he let his eyes fall shut and was soon fast asleep. He slept most of the day and into the night, waking occasionally, drinking his honey water, and wearing out a path to the bathroom. Once when he woke up he found sweatpants and a t-shirt placed on the table beside him. A large German Shepherd kept guard on the floor of the living room throughout the night, his head perking up to watch Kyle every time he got up from the couch, but he never barked.

Saturday, October 22nd

Sometime early the next morning, Kyle awoke feeling rested and relatively good. He sat up, emptied his mug and, for the first time, looked around the room without the mental haze that had plagued him the day before. The pale moonlight provided adequate light for him to see a few more details of Rose's house, at least enough to tell that her home was decorated with a definite horse theme: horse pictures, figurines, a few trophies on a shelf over the woodstove, and a pair of spurs over the sliding door to the back yard. Even the furniture had a western feel to it, although it was too dark to make out the colors. He walked over to the window and peered outside. Seeing the snow brought back memories of the day before, and flashes of struggling towards the house came back to him. Shivering, he returned to his bed on the couch and lay down, pulling the warm blankets over him.

He was wide-awake when Rose walked into the living room an hour after the sun came up. "Good morning," Kyle said cheerfully.

Rose started a bit, then returned his greeting with a smile. "Good morning. Looks like you're feeling better."

He nodded. "I feel worlds better. It's amazing what thirty hours of sleep will do. My arms and legs still ache, but the rest of me feels remarkably good."

"You were in rough shape when you got here. I'm surprised you're doing as well as you are."

Kyle looked at Rose for the first time with a clear head. She had sandy-blonde hair, with a bit of natural curl to it, that was pulled back in a loose ponytail. A slender nose and prominent cheekbones adorned a face that was clear and tan. Her lips were a little on the thin side, and when she flashed her farm-girl smile, they revealed teeth that were a little too straight and a little too white. As to her age, Kyle estimated that Rose was in her early forties but knew he could be off by five years either way.

She wore a thick, white robe tied snuggly at her waist that seemed to hide a slender body with feminine curves. She appeared confident, not at all intimidated by having a strange man in her home. He watched as she walked over to the woodstove and tossed in some wood.

"I bet you're hungry," she said, turning back to Kyle.

Kyle nodded. "I am. I can't remember the last time I ate."

Soon Kyle was sitting at the kitchen table, eagerly feasting on a plate of scrambled eggs. "This is delicious," he said, wiping food from his beard when he was done. "I don't know how to thank you."

Rose took his empty plate to the sink, then sat down across from him at the table. "You don't need to thank me, but I would like to know who you are. I've been pretty curious this last day and a half."

Kyle cleared his throat. "Well, to make a long story short, I'm Kyle Tait from Deer Creek, Montana. It's a community just a little east of Missoula. I was in Houston for work on September 2nd, and I'm in the process of going back home. The snowstorm came in faster than I expected, and somehow I ended up here. That's it in a nutshell."

"You've walked here from Houston?" Rose asked, her eyes wide in disbelief.

Kyle nodded. "Well, I guess not from Houston, but from San Angelo. It's a little closer."

"Wow, that's amazing. I've met a few people heading in different directions, but no one from that far away. Most were just trying to get across the state or to Montana or Colorado. How many miles have you covered?"

"By my calculations, I'd say I'm right around a thousand miles, with close to six hundred to go."

"What's in Deer Creek?"

"My wife, Jennifer, and our three kids. What about you, Rose? Are you here alone?"

"Yeah, but I do have Max," she said reaching down to pat the German shepherd resting beside her chair. "I have two boys. Anthony's with the Air Force in Germany, at least he was last I knew, and William graduated from college last spring and took a job in Atlanta. I'd give anything to know how they're doing right now. My husband, Bruce, was back East on September 2nd, but I don't expect him to be showing up anytime soon. Your kids are lucky to have a devoted father like you," she said, with a note of sadness.

"Thanks," Kyle said. "I just pray everything's okay when I get back. Listen, there's one thing I want to know. I can remember walking in the snow for what seemed like forever, but I don't remember coming in your house. How'd I end up here? Was I just too cold and don't remember?"

Rose shook her head and motioned to her German shepherd. "No, Max saved you. I was about to crawl into bed when he started barking pretty crazy-like. He's usually quiet, as you've probably noticed. The last time I remember him barking like that was when we had a cougar lurking around. Anyway, I tried to get him to shut up, but he kept on, so I came out to the living room to see what was up. When I looked out the window, I saw a little bit of movement and realized there was a person in the front yard. After that it was just a matter of dragging you in, which took a little bit because you weren't exactly cooperative."

"Sorry," said Kyle. "I was a little out of it."

"You were more than a little out of it. Somebody must be looking out for you is all I can say. Max is starting to get old, and it takes quite a bit for him to get excited. He's even quit barking at the UPS truck. Why or how he noticed you is beyond me. Of course I'm kind of glad he did. It would have been really creepy to find a body in the front yard when the snow melted off."

Kyle laughed. "Maybe I'd have made good fertilizer. You could have had a nice patch of green grass come springtime. Seriously though, I owe you and Max my life. I really don't know how to repay that kind of a debt. Thanks just doesn't cut it."

"I'm sure you'd have done the same thing. That's just what people do."

"Well, not everyone," responded Kyle, "but that's another story." They sat in silence at the table before Kyle spoke up again. "How long do you think the snow will last?"

Rose looked out the window at the sky. "It's hard to say. This is pretty early for winter, even in Wyoming. It'll probably warm up in a day or two and start to melt off, and then most of it should be gone in five, maybe six days at the most, especially in the areas where it hasn't drifted."

"I'll get out of here as soon as I can. If you like, I can even leave today. I'm feeling pretty good. The cart I've been pulling is just a couple of miles back, and with the better weather, I'm sure I can find some shelter. Then once the roads are clear, I can keep going. Your husband would probably worry about you if he knew I was here."

"Oh, I don't think he'd care too much. You don't seem to be too threatening, and I've got Max to protect me. Besides, it's been pretty quiet around here for the last month and a half. You're welcome to stay until traveling is good."

"I appreciate that, and don't worry, I'll get out of here as soon as the roads are good. Maybe I can work off some of my debt while I'm here."

"I've been doing pretty good on my own, but I'll take a look and see if there's anything I need help with."

Rose cleared the dishes and sent Kyle back to the couch to lie down. With little to occupy him, Kyle spent the rest of the day napping, pacing the house, flipping through old magazines, and stretching the stiffness and aches out of his arms and legs. His body felt like it had spent twelve hours at the gym, which Rose, with her eclectic wealth of knowledge, explained was a build up of chemicals, a result of his muscles being short of blood and oxygen when he nearly froze. At her direction, he continued to drink the honey water mixture and, consequently, spent a lot of time in the bathroom.

Kyle watched the thermometer throughout the day, never seeing it rise above 30°. Water dripped from the roof, but the amount of snow on the ground didn't seem to change. In the distance, he could see the delivery truck he had briefly used for shelter, the last place he remembered clearly, and tracks in the front yard where Rose had pulled him through the snow, which were now mostly drifted over. Recalling the bitterness of the storm and noting the size disparity between the two of them, Kyle wondered at the effort it must have taken Rose to get him inside.

In the late afternoon, Kyle heated up some water on the woodstove and took a long, hot bath, reflecting that never in his life had bathing seemed like such a luxury. He scrubbed his body from head to toe three times and soaked until the water was cold and brown and his skin was shriveled. He rinsed with clean water, then climbed out of the tub and dried off, feeling truly clean for the first time in weeks. Rose provided him with deodorant, a toothbrush and toothpaste, and shaving supplies, and by the time he emerged from the bathroom, he felt almost human again.

Dinner was a simple meal of deer steak and potatoes with gravy, but was like manna to Kyle's still-recovering body. Dinner conversation started slowly, but gradually picked up momentum, revolving around their families and experiences since the attack. Between the two of them, they'd tallied just a few short hours of human interaction over the past six weeks, and this pent up need to share soon had their conversation flowing like a mountain stream in the spring, spilling haphazardly over its banks as it shed a season's worth of build-up.

Rose shared her story with Kyle, that she had grown up on a ranch, loved her horses, and done barrel racing as a kid, then eventually gone to college in Colorado and met and fell in love with a city guy. Bruce was into computers and could barely tell a horse from a cow, but love had won out and they'd gotten married. After graduation, they'd moved to Denver where he was successful, and she was unhappy. When their kids were six and eight, they'd bought the place in Wyoming and moved back closer to where she'd grown up. There she was happy, but he wasn't. Bruce had worked from home and traveled to meet with clients as needed, and that had been okay, but the last few years he'd needed to meet with clients a lot, she observed, which left her alone more and more often. She enjoyed her independence and the time it gave her to spend with her horses, as well as the less structured nature of her job in real estate, but in the rural setting, the work was more of a pastime with a part-time income, rather than a full-time occupation.

Kyle told Rose about the experiences he'd had on his journey, the highs and lows and the challenges he'd faced. It felt good to share his stories with someone, to talk about things he hadn't been able to talk about, except for occasional entries in his journal, some of which he would probably never share with his family. To talk about escaping death and taking a life, after mulling it over in his mind for weeks, was therapeutic. He bragged on his kids and the good people that had helped him on his way and voiced how he worried about his family and what they might be facing without him there to take care of them.

At sundown, Rose dug out a candle, and they talked and laughed and cried in a lavender-scented haze until the candle burnt itself out. Neither of them wanted the evening to end, the conversation being so welcome and humanizing, but candles were scarce, and the periods of silence grew more frequent.

The clock on the wall indicated it was well after midnight, so when Kyle struggled to stifle an extended yawn, Rose directed him to Anthony's bedroom, where he'd gotten some clothes earlier in the day. The room had been empty for over a year, Rose explained, but she had left it as it was when Anthony joined the service so that he would still have his room to come home to when he was on leave. In flickering candlelight, Kyle took a look around, noticing an assortment of posters on the walls ranging from the Swedish bikini team, to fighter jets, to Nickelback concert shots, along with a large Air Force logo painted on the wall across from the bed. On the desk was a framed picture of a young girl, who Rose identified as Anthony's fiancée. Other than the fact it was far too tidy, the room looked like the bedroom of a typical teenage boy.

Kyle wished Rose a goodnight and hurried to climb between the sheets in the chilly room, nestling deep under the covers, ready for a night of much needed sleep.

CHAPTER TWENTY-SEVEN

North Central Wyoming
Sunday, October 23rd

With blankets piled deep in the cold room and a bed that was soft and comfortable, Kyle slept through the entire night for the first time on his journey. When he awoke, the room was bright with filtered sunlight, and he could see clear, blue sky through the cracks of the blinds. Kyle heard Rose cooking in the kitchen, and the smell of food filled his senses as he lay in bed pondering his good fortune in going from nearly freezing to death to enjoying five-star accommodations. He crawled out of bed, put on a pair of jeans and a sweatshirt, and walked out to the kitchen.

"Good morning," he said with an energy he hadn't felt in weeks, the abundance of sleep and food having done his body good. "It smells wonderful."

Rose jumped before turning. "Oh! You surprised me," she said, pressing her hand to her chest. "I'm not used to having company. Good morning to you too. I was starting to wonder if you were ever going to wake up, but figured you needed your rest."

Kyle glanced at the clock on the wall. The hands showed 9:35. "Guess I still had some sleep to catch up on. I can't remember the last time I slept so well."

Rose smiled. "I'm glad to hear it. You need your strength. I hope you don't mind venison for breakfast. I ran out of bacon seven weeks ago and haven't come across any wild hogs to butcher."

"Venison is great. Can I help with anything?"

"No, I'm good. Just sit down. It's almost ready."

Kyle sat down at the table and glanced out the window. With the sun's intensity and the reflection off the snow, the scene was beautiful but nearly blinding. The thermometer showed 39°, and streams of water ran off the roof. "Looks like things are warming up."

Rose nodded. "I figured it would. Usually it's mid-November before we're done with fall. Too bad we don't have a weatherman to tell us how the rest of the week shapes up."

Kyle watched Rose as she finished preparing breakfast. This morning she wore a snug pair of Wranglers and a bright red sweater that clung to her nicely. Yesterday she had been a mother of twenty year olds. Today she looked like a well-put-together professional. Rose set a plate of food in front of him, and he caught the soft scent of perfume. As she walked back into the kitchen, he noticed the sway of her hips and that her legs were slender and long and joined just right with the pleasant curve of her rear end.

"Did I forget something?" Rose asked, looking at Kyle, a friendly grin on her face.

"What was that?" Kyle asked calmly, trying to bluff as he looked away but knowing he'd been caught.

"I wondered if I'd forgotten something. You don't seem interested in your food."

"Um...no. It's fine," he replied. "Do you have any salt and pepper?" he asked in a further attempt to bluff.

"They're on the table, right in the middle."

Kyle instantly spotted the large salt and pepper shakers, the only items on the table besides his plate. He looked back at Rose and wondered how red his freshly shaved cheeks were turning. "Thanks," he said, feeling foolish. "Guess I missed them." He picked up the salt, shook some on his food, and started to eat.

Rose returned to the table with her plate and sat down across from him. "Was there anything else you wanted?" she asked in an innocent voice.

Kyle inhaled some eggs and started to cough. "Pardon me?" he choked out. He had heard what she said but wasn't sure how she intended it.

"I just wondered if there was anything else you wanted, you know, for breakfast?" she said. Her head was tipped forward, and she looked up at him with big, blue eyes and a smile that made his heart skip.

"This is good," he answered. "I've eaten more in the last twenty-four hours than I have in a long time. You've been really good to me." He noticed her eyes for the first time, large and bright, a pretty shade of blue, with eyelashes that might stir a breeze if she blinked too fast. Kyle caught himself staring at Rose again, and turned back to his breakfast, concentrating on cutting his meat.

Thinking back over the last two months, he wondered how long it had been since he'd talked with an attractive woman around his age. His time in Houston had been busy with work, and since September 2nd, he'd met only a few women: Donovan's wife, the wife in the family that had driven him that second day of walking, the occasional housewife at farms he'd stopped at, and a walker here and there. Most of the people he'd met, let alone the women, had been scared, tired, hungry, and dirty. Many of these ladies would likely have been attractive, but conditions were such that hygiene and beauty routines weren't a priority, if even a possibility. It was survival that was the priority that topped everyone's list.

Kyle had last seen Jennifer in August, and now here it was going on November. It had been a long time since that part of his brain had stirred, and he was surprised it still functioned.

"Is the food alright?" Rose asked.

"Huh? Oh, the food? It's good. It's really good. If you keep feeding me like this I'm going to gain back all the weight I've lost."

"Okay…you just don't seem to be eating much."

"Sorry. Just lost in thought." Kyle looked away and wondered if Rose knew how much she was distracting him. There wasn't anything blatant in her manner or words, but there was something there that made him feel like she was toying with him.

Kyle took a few bites, and switched gears. "So, do you think your husband is alright?"

"Bruce? Oh, I don't know. He probably is. It's hard to say. He had a big project in Miami that he'd been working on for a year, so he got an apartment out that way. I've never been to it, but I'm guessing it would be safe. Of course, everyone you talk to seems to have a story about how bad things are in the cities, so I can't say for sure."

"You don't seem to be too upset by it. Don't you worry about him?"

"He's a big boy. He can take care of himself. We haven't been that close for the last few years. Neither one of us was happy in the other's world, me in the city, him out here. He's spent a lot of time away, and I think not all of it alone."

"Oh, I'm sorry. I didn't mean to bring up a touchy subject."

"Don't apologize. It is what it is. When you're young, sometimes you make decisions with your heart, not your head, figuring love will conquer all. He's always treated me well and taken care of my needs, so I can't complain. I've had a lot of time to work things out and have gotten all my crying done and over with. We were probably headed for divorce anyway, but now I guess we won't need to worry about it."

"What do you mean?"

"Well, if he hasn't survived, then he's gone. If he has survived, it will be years, maybe decades, until society's rebuilt to where it was. In the meantime, you can throw away your driver's license or marriage certificate and be anyone you want to be. Anyone in a difficult situation can just walk away."

"I guess I hadn't thought about the human part of all this," Kyle said as he played with his utensils. "I've just always thought about the technical aspect of the attack. Once we get all of the stuff fixed or replaced, I figured everyone would step back into the roles they were in before."

"I don't know, Kyle, maybe it won't be as bad I think. I hope that's the case. You seem like the technical type. How long do you think that side of things will take?"

"I think we're going to have to relive the last hundred and fifty years. We've got the blueprint and a lot of the physical assets, so it might only take us ten or fifteen years to do it, but we'll have to take the steps from a barter, to an industrial, to an information society again. We've lost at least a year of crops, let alone the equipment to manage it, harvest it, haul it, process it and everything else that our food goes through. Then there are the factories that'll need workers, drivers who'll need trucks, and stores that'll need cash registers and cashiers to run them. Plus there are the banks and money. How do you figure out what to do about all the missed payments and mortgages and abandoned properties? I just assumed that when things came back on-line, that people, at least the ones who survived, would be where they should be, doing the jobs and filling the roles they had before this mess."

"I agree with the technical side of things, Kyle, but go back to what I was saying. Don't you think it will be simple for people to just disappear? Say you stayed here in Wyoming, for example. You've got no I.D., no family here, and no one who knows you. You could pick a new name, get a job, find an empty house, and you'd have a new life. If only a couple of people do it, it might not work. But what if two or three percent of the population do it. That's ten million people, on top of all the people who have died. Our government can't find the people who overstay their visas or sneak over the border, even with all their systems working. How's a crippled government going to even care about getting everyone straightened out, let alone do something about it?"

Kyle let out a low whistle. "I hadn't thought much past getting home. We've been so conditioned to think that the government is always going to be there to fix things that we just expect everything to work out. But now that the government can't take care of us, we're almost too helpless to do anything for ourselves." The wheels of Kyle's mind spun as a whole new dimension to the disaster opened up to him. "So what are your plans? Are you just going to ride it out here?"

"What else can I do? My parents passed away a few years ago, which, thinking back on it, is probably a blessing because anyone in a care facility has probably died a long, slow death of neglect. My sister lives in Oregon, and we aren't very close. My sons are far away, and my husband's not likely to hurry back. A few of the neighbors and I keep tabs on each other, but no one is set up to take care of me. Besides, I'm pretty tough. As long as the creek doesn't dry up and the deer aren't hunted to extinction, I'll be alright, plus I've got Max to keep me company for a few more years. In a lot of ways, I'm actually in a perfect situation – no threats, no dependants, lots of resources, and just myself to worry about."

They continued their conversation as they cleaned up from breakfast. Kyle washed the dishes while Rose put them away. The ease of their conversation picked up from the previous night and veered from one topic to another. Rose giggled and laughed at all of Kyle's jokes, touched his arm and back frequently to make a point, and leaned into him with her chest when she reached to put things away in the cabinets around the sink. Kyle enjoyed the attention. It had been a long, long time since someone had flirted with him, and seemed like years since he'd looked at a woman with any sense of appreciation for their femininity. He tried to think about Jennifer and avoid certain subjects, but it was difficult because Rose was nice, and he enjoyed her company.

After breakfast, Kyle found a Louis L'Amour book and immersed himself in the story. When lunch was done, Rose took a nap while Kyle filled up her water containers from the nearby creek. With the water jugs filled, Kyle walked up to the freeway to take a look at the conditions and to work his legs, which were still stiff from his latest brush with death. The afternoon was sunny and warm, and the snow was melting quickly, but there were still several inches of heavy snow on the road, snow that could easily be cleared with snowplows but would now have to clear the old-fashioned way.

When he returned to the house, Rose was up and getting ready for dinner.

"What's for dinner?" Kyle asked.

"Deer and corn. Are you sick of venison yet?"

"No, it's fine. We hunt every fall."

"I hadn't eaten venison for awhile, but circumstances dictate otherwise now. Too bad you didn't show up a little later in the year. A neighbor has some cows, and he's going to share the meat but wants to wait until it's cooler so it will keep longer. You could have had some good angus if you'd timed it better."

"Those are the breaks, I guess. Next time I get hypothermic on your property I'll shoot for the end of November."

"That works," Rose replied cheerfully. "How'd the road look?'

"Still lots of snow. A couple more days like today and I should be good to go though. It looks like it's melting off quicker on the asphalt."

"Well don't take off too quick. You don't want to get in another situation where you get stuck in the snow. Might not find some-one as nice as me to take you in."

"That's the truth. If I was going to almost die in a snowstorm, I picked a good place to do it."

"Like I said, you have Max to thank for that, otherwise you'd still be sitting out in my front yard."

'You're right," said Kyle as he knelt down by the dog, patting him on the head. "I owe you one, buddy."

Dinner passed with conversation about who might have attacked the country. Kyle thought Russia was the likely power behind it, but speculated they'd done it through some terrorist group in order to be able to claim innocence. Rose's theory was that Pakistan was involved. Anthony, her Air Force son, had mentioned in some of his emails his concerns about Pakistan and its objection to lingering U.S. involvement in the region. Rose figured Pakistan had done it to force the military out of their part of the world and to get back at the U.S. for its threats to their autonomy.

After dinner, they talked some more and played checkers until the sun went down, with Rose winning four games to one and claiming, as her prize, a hug from the loser. Kyle conceded and good-naturedly opened his arms to her. Rose wrapped her arms around him, pressing herself tightly against him and resting her head on his shoulder. With her soft, warm body against his, Kyle felt sensations stir that had laid dormant for months and was briefly lost in the comfort of the moment as he held her.

"Thanks for everything, Rose," he whispered in her ear, the scent of her perfume filling his senses. "I don't think I'll ever be able to repay you for what you've done."

Rose's eyes were closed, and Kyle felt her warm breath on his neck. "Don't worry about repaying me," she replied in a contented whisper. "I'm glad I was able to help."

Kyle released his hold on Rose. "I'd better get to bed. It's late." Rose nodded and begrudgingly dropped her arms from around him. He wished her a goodnight, turned and walked down the hall, retiring to Anthony's room for a second night.

Monday, October 24th

Kyle woke up and rubbed the sleep from his eyes. The room was filled with the fresh, clean light of morning, and Kyle felt rested after another good night. He had slept well, even despite waking up in the middle of the night after dreaming about a woman other than Jennifer for the first time on his journey.

The sliver of sky he could see through the blinds was clear and blue, indicating another day of warm temperatures and good snow-melt. His spirits high in anticipation of another warm day, Kyle got out of bed and headed to the living room. Rose wasn't around, but the bathroom door was closed, and he could hear water splashing in the tub. Kyle tapped on the door. "Is there another bathroom I could use?" he called. "Too much water last night."

"Use the one in my room," Rose answered back, "but excuse the mess."

Her room was attractive and decorated with horses and western art like the rest of the house. The "mess" consisted of one side of her large bed being unmade and yesterday's clothes on the floor beside it. When he finished, Kyle headed back out to the living room, shouting "Thank you!" through the bathroom door as he passed by.

Rose's voice called back to him. "Kyle, could you bring me the pot of water on the stove? My water's beginning to cool off. There's a towel on the chair closest to the stove that you can use to grab it."

Kyle stopped by the door, not sure how to respond.

She continued. "I'd get it, but you're up, and I don't want to get my towel wet if I don't need to."

"Yeah, no problem," he answered hesitantly.

He found the towel, grabbed the large pan, and brought it back down the hall. He tapped on the door. "I've got it. Should I just slide it in?"

"Just bring it in if you would. It's alright, I'm decent."

Kyle set the pot down, opened the door, then carried the water into the bathroom. Rose was in the bathtub, and he turned towards her while averting his eyes. "What should I do with it?" he asked, struggling not to look directly at her.

"Just pour it in behind me."

Kyle could see Rose out of the corner of his eye, sitting towards the front of the tub with her knees pulled up and her body leaning forward against them, her head resting on her arms, which were folded across her knees. Rose's head was turned towards Kyle, her eyes closed and her face relaxed.

"Pour it in slowly, would you?" she murmured, her lips barely moving. "I'm not sure how hot it will be." Her skin glistened with droplets of water, and her shoulders lifted with each long, deep breath, giving her the appearance of being asleep.

"Okay," Kyle mumbled hoarsely. He lifted the pot up and tipped it forward slowly, but the pan slipped and a large wave sloshed forward, splashing into the tub. Rose jerked up and let out a slight gasp.

"Sorry! You alright?" Kyle asked. "The pan shifted more than I expected."

"I'm fine. It just startled me." She gave him a reassuring smile, then laid her head back down on her arms as it was before.

Kyle braced the pan and slowly started to pour the water in again. As he poured, his eyes drifted from the pan in his hands to a tattoo of a dainty, little butterfly on Rose's back, just below the water line. He watched as droplets of water rolled down her back, noticing that her body was slender and toned, more so than he had previously realized. His eyes wandered to her side, where her right breast was pressed against her thigh and seemed to be slowly slipping out. Captivated by the voyeuristic circumstance in which he found himself, Kyle's breathing grew shallow, and his heart thumped heavily as he watched, his eyes glued to her body, unable to tear them away.

"See anything you like?"

Rose's voice startled him, and he quickly turned his attention to her face. Her eyes were open a crack, and she was watching him with a look of amusement. Kyle quickly averted his eyes from her to the pan in his hands. "No, I mean…I just…" he stammered as he tried to find something to say that wouldn't make the situation any worse for him.

She giggled as he tripped over his words.

"I'm sorry," he said. "I guess the answer is yes, but I should go." He tipped the pan up, pouring in the last of the water, then turned to the door.

"You don't need to apologize," Rose said. "I'm flattered. It's been awhile since anyone has looked at me that way."

Kyle said nothing as he hurried out of the bathroom and almost ran down the hall, images of Rose, attractive and naked, playing over in his mind. He dropped onto the couch, his hands and legs trembling. She scared him, not because of any physical threat, but because she was attractive, and because he liked her, and because she liked him. He knew he loved Jennifer, but he was clearly in unfamiliar territory. When his legs stopped shaking, Kyle got up and walked back to the bathroom, swallowed hard, and tapped on the door.

"Come in," Rose beckoned.

CHAPTER TWENTY-EIGHT

North Central Wyoming
Sunday, October 23rd

As if to physically hold himself back, Kyle placed his hands on the doorframe. He closed his eyes and bit his lower lip. "No, that's okay Rose," he said after a moment's hesitation. "I just wanted to let you know I'm going for a walk. I'll be back in awhile."

"Everything okay?"

"Yeah. I just figured I'd better go get my cart before something happens to it. It's been sitting there for days."

Kyle put on a coat, left the house, and retraced his steps from the day before back to the freeway. The snow was wet and heavy, the air brisk and fresh, and the temperature rising quickly. Kyle guessed it was already in the mid-forties and thought it might hit sixty if the previous day's temperature was any indication. On the freeway, the water ran off the road in small streamlets through the slushy snow. Walking in it was messy and quickly soaked Kyle's shoes.

As he walked south towards his cart, Kyle thought about Rose. It was obvious that she liked him, and he certainly found her attractive and enjoyable to be with. Kyle was certain that if he were to pursue it, the relationship could easily become sexual. He thought about the last two months and realized it had been a long time since he had enjoyed any intimacy. Surely it would be forgivable if something were to happen. Of course, he wouldn't have to explain himself to anyone, because no one else would know. Ever. Just him and Rose.

He could really use some physical contact, a little bit of attention, he thought to himself, especially after everything he'd been through recently. In difficult circumstances like these, a person could certainly justify a little indulgence here and there. Didn't most people mess around? And they did it in situations that were far less trying than what he was in. Hell, that's what conventions in Vegas were all about. He knew plenty of guys at work who fooled around, and life still went on for them with no real consequences, and no one seemed any the worse off. Plus, he was in an ideal situation – no witnesses, and no way for anyone to know. Except for him.

Kyle's thoughts turned to Jennifer. He knew it would devastate her if she were to ever learn that he'd been unfaithful. Ever since they'd met, he'd wondered if maybe she was too pure, too perfect for him – that maybe he wasn't deserving of her. They'd been in a freshman English class together during winter semester, and her vibrant smile and energetic personality had intrigued him the first time he saw her. She was sweet and innocent, full of life and vigor, and stood out from the rest of the girls he knew on campus. Kyle had asked her out the second week of class, and with a flash of her bright smile, she had turned him down cold. He thought that maybe she'd had a boyfriend, but when he'd inquired, her friends had said she didn't.

Every week that semester, he had asked her out. And every week, she had told him no, but her "no's" didn't hurt because she would still smile, and talk to him, and treat him like he was her closest friend. It was worth it to ask, just to know that for a few minutes he'd be in her glow, and she'd be thinking about him and no one else. He had felt a connection with her, even though they'd never even gone on a date. Finally, the last week of school, she'd said yes, but there was only enough time for one date before school was out for the summer.

Kyle had gotten Jennifer's phone number and called her every week, at least three times a week, and by the time school started again in the fall, he was head-over-heels in love and thought maybe she was too. After dating steadily all of fall semester, they were engaged by early spring, and while all of his friends were bragging about how many different girls they had been with, Kyle had felt lucky just to get a goodnight's kiss. Jennifer had insisted on holding off on anything more than that until they got married, and he was content to go along because she made him happy just by being with him. Despite the incessant teasing of his roommates, waiting hadn't been a big sacrifice. That he was the one she had chosen to be with was worth more to him than any conquest he could ever have. Even with the harassment, Kyle had never been tempted to claim they'd been together, unwilling to do anything that might sully her reputation.

He vividly remembered how heartbroken Jennifer had been when she had learned about his past with Chelsea, his high school girlfriend, to the point of nearly calling off their wedding. Chelsea hadn't had the same values as Jennifer, and Kyle had experienced a lot of firsts in his young life with her. He had thought he loved Chelsea and expected that they would get married some day. When Chelsea went away to college, he had taken a year off to work and put some money in the bank so that they could take that step, only to discover during a surprise visit to Chelsea at college that she wasn't nearly as lonely as he was, leaving him disillusioned but wiser.

Once Jennifer came into his life, Kyle had forgotten all about Chelsea, but had nearly gone out of his mind when he realized that his past with Chelsea might cost him his future with Jennifer. Somehow, Kyle and Jennifer had weathered that storm, and never at any time since had Kyle regretted marrying her. David had been born a year later, and Kyle had had to quit school and get a job, but even then Jennifer had never made him feel like he was worth less because he hadn't finished college. If anything, her love for him seemed to grow stronger.

Their life together over the years had been good. Jennifer was a devoted and loving wife and mother, and they loved each other, but they were busy with life and children and work, and the flame didn't always seem to burn as brightly as it once had. Kyle wondered if Jennifer would ever cheat on him, then knew immediately that the thought was ridiculous, and that she would be devastated if she even thought he doubted her faithfulness. The fact that he was tempted to stray had nothing to do with Jennifer and everything to do with him. She was everything he could ever hope for in a wife, and more. He just needed to realize that. Rose was a good person, a miracle really, a woman who would have a place in his heart forever, but now that he was thinking with a clear head, Kyle knew that Rose was not someone he'd risk Jennifer for, no matter how sure he was that she would never know.

Kyle found his cart, filled with snow, on the side of the road where he'd left it. He scooped the snow out and examined his belongings. Everything was soaked through but salvageable if he could get the cart back to Rose's and dry it all out. He stepped into the familiar position behind the handle and started to pull, his legs protesting a little with the exertion. Despite the slushy conditions, Kyle towed his cart to Rose's without any problems and an hour after returning had his possessions drying by the stove.

"You planning on getting out of here soon?" Rose asked when the cart was empty.

"If the weather's good, I'll leave tomorrow. The longer I wait, the closer winter gets. I dodged a bullet this week, and I don't want to push my luck too hard."

"You know you're welcome to stay as long as you want to, don't you? I wouldn't mind the company, and traveling might be better in a couple of days."

"I know," he answered. "You've done so much for me already, Rose. I'll be forever grateful, but I need to get back home to my family. There's a big part of me that's missing."

"I understand," she said, her head hanging down and her hair shielding her face. Kyle thought he detected a sniffle, but wasn't sure. "You hungry?" she asked after a pause.

They ate lunch together, then spent the remainder of the afternoon gathering supplies. Rose went through Anthony's closet and found two old coats, a good pair of winter gloves, hats, and some thermals, along with extra changes of clothing. A pair of her husband's winter boots was added to the pile, and by dinnertime, Kyle was re-outfitted and packed, ready to go.

Dinner was quiet, the conversation continually grinding to a halt until Rose broke the silence once again. "How many days do you think it's going to take you to get home?"

Kyle thought as he chewed. "Hard to say. I've got over five hundred miles left, and the travel doesn't get any easier from here, still lots of hills. Probably four weeks, maybe a little quicker if the weather cooperates."

"Are you scared?"

"Of what?"

"Well, you know. It is getting to be wintertime. Maybe freezing, starving, wild animals, people. You never know what you might run into."

Kyle shook his head. "I'm not really scared. Concerned maybe, but not scared. I know there are risks, but I can't let that stop me. No matter what I do, there will be risks. If I wait until it's easy or safe, who knows if my family will be there? The longer I wait, the less of a chance there'll be of a happy ending."

Rose nodded but didn't say anything. Her head was bent forward, so Kyle could just see the top of her head. A tear rolled down the side of her cheek, which she tried to discreetly wipe away.

"You okay?" Kyle asked.

Rose nodded.

"Are you sure?" he asked again, leaning forward to look into her face. "I see a tear Rose. What's wrong?"

She let out a puff of air. "Don't worry about it, Kyle. I'm fine," she said as she turned away, wiping tears that were flowing more freely.

"Your fine seems different from most people I know. Usually it's not associated with tears. Maybe that's a Wyoming thing?"

Rose laughed. "Nope, not a Wyoming thing. Just a Rose Duncan thing." She got up from her chair and headed towards her bedroom.

Kyle got out of his chair and reached for her, but she pushed his hand away as she hurried past. He stood awkwardly by the table, not sure what to do, then gathered their dishes and took them into the kitchen.

He found a book and tried to read but couldn't concentrate. He and Jennifer occasionally had disagreements, but having been together as long as they had, he knew how to handle those and what he should and shouldn't do. He checked his bags that were piled by the door, went outside and inspected his cart, walked up to the highway to check the road, then came back inside. Rose still hadn't emerged from her room.

He went down the hall and knocked on her door.

"Who is it?" she called out.

"Fed Ex, ma'am," Kyle replied. "I need a signature for this delivery." He heard her laugh.

"Well, I guess you'd better come in then," she said.

Kyle opened the door and stepped into her room. Rose lay on her bed facing the ceiling, her tears long since dried. "Took you long enough," she said.

"Pardon me?"

"It took you long enough to come and check on me. How long has it been, one hour or two?' she asked, a slight grin showing.

"Sorry, I wasn't exactly sure how I was supposed to handle the situation. Some people like privacy, so I was torn."

"Don't worry about it, Kyle. Thanks for finally showing up," she sighed.

"So you're okay?"

Rose nodded. "Yes, I am. Sometimes I start to feel a little sorry for myself, that's all."

"What do you mean?" Kyle asked, sitting down on the opposite side of the bed.

Rose brought both her hands up and rubbed her face, then let out a deep breath. "Over the past four days, I've been on quite a roller coaster of emotions: worry, fear, helplessness, excitement, happiness. You name the emotion, and I've probably felt it. Before you came, even before the attack, there was just boredom and loneliness, day after day, so you can imagine the change you brought. These last couple of days, I've really liked being with you. I guess I was hoping you'd be around longer."

"If it means anything, of the past two months, the last two days have been my favorite."

"That's not saying much, is it?" she said, swatting at him with her hand. "I know your story. You've walked a thousand miles and almost died a half-dozen times, and that's the best thing you can come up with?"

Kyle reached out and grabbed her hand. "Well, it doesn't sound so good when you put it that way, but I've been very happy here, maybe too happy. I'm glad you found me, or I found you, however it happened. If I don't make it home, I want you to know that I'm still glad that I made it this far."

"Oh, damn you, Kyle. Don't talk like that!" she said. "You've started me crying again." Rose sat up and wiped her tears on her shirtsleeve. "Don't even think that you're not going to make it home, or else don't go tomorrow."

"I'm just saying that it's been worth it to walk this far if all it meant was getting to spend these days with you."

"I know what you meant, and I appreciate it. But you can't seriously think you're not going to make it. I didn't save your life so you could die trekking through Montana."

"Okay, I promise I'll make it."

"Good. I accept your promise."

"When or if things get back to normal, I'll send you a letter to let you know that I did make it."

"I'll watch my mailbox for it, so you'd better not let me down."

Kyle leaned towards Rose and wrapped his arms around her, holding her tight. She returned the hug and pulled him towards her. They lay back on the bed in silence, holding each other in the darkness of the night, enjoying the contact and the feeling of safety that being with someone offered. As the first stars appeared in the sky outside the window Kyle spoke. "I won't let you down, Rose," he whispered. She wiped her eyes on his shoulder, and the pressure of her arms relaxed, so he sat up to leave. "It's dark, and I want to get out at sun-up, so I should probably head to bed. I've got a lot of miles to make up."

Rose reached for his arm. In the faint moonlight, he could see that her eyes were soft and pleading, and her lips trembled as she tried to find the right words. "Stay with me tonight, Kyle, if you would."

Kyle took her hand in his and held it, staring into her eyes and feeling a storm of emotions. "I can't, Rose... I just can't." Her shoulders sagged, and he felt her hand pull away. "Don't think it's because I'm not attracted to you. It's far, far from that. This morning, in the bathroom, the second time I knocked at the door and you said to come in, with your voice so inviting and the image of you in the bathtub, like some Greek goddess, still fresh in my mind, it took every bit of willpower I had not to open the door. For the next hour I tried to find a way that I could justify being with you. I told myself that Jennifer would never be hurt because she would never find out. I know guys that would give their right arm to be in my shoes, and I could think of a dozen reasons why it wouldn't be so bad."

"And your answer's still no?"

He nodded. "It's still no."

"Can I ask why?"

"I don't know if my answer will make sense."

"Try me. I'd like to understand. Maybe I'd feel better."

"Well, these last six or seven weeks, without the constant distractions that I usually have to deal with, like work, and the TV, and the internet, you know, just the day to day things, I've had all the time in the world to think, and the thing I've realized, that really, finally, became crystal clear to me today, is that the only thing that matters, the only thing that I couldn't stand the thought of losing, was my family – my wife and our kids. I wasn't worried about getting the TV back, or even my job, or having a nice house to stay in. It's Jennifer and David and Emma and Spencer. With the distractions gone, you see it. I wouldn't deserve Jennifer's love if I would cheat on her if I could get away with it." He looked at Rose, her eyes were locked on his. "Jennifer wouldn't know it, but I would, and that would be enough to make me miserable. I've been faithful all these years just because I should, never thinking much about it. Now I know why. It all came together for me. She deserves someone she can trust, someone who loves her completely. I can't betray that."

"You know that sounds pretty old-fashioned, don't you."

Kyle nodded and smiled. "I do, but I think the older generations were on to something."

"Sounds like how my grandfather used to talk. He was married to my grandmother for sixty-one years. He died when she did; it just took his body six months to realize it. Guess I come across as quite the bimbo, don't I?"

"No. Now if you'd been under the blankets with me the first day I woke up, I might have thought so, but not with how things have turned out."

"You know, they say body heat's a good way to treat hypothermia."

"I've heard that, but it still would have been an odd way to meet."

Rose let go of him and lay back on her pillow. "I guess I'll be sleeping alone again tonight then."

Kyle lay down beside her and put his arm under her head. "If it means anything, I do love you. Not the passionate, physical, Hollywood kind of love. Just the true, human, I'll-remember-you-forever kind."

"I guess that's something," Rose said and laid her arm across Kyle's chest. "Your wife's a lucky lady."

Rose closed her eyes and sighed deeply as Kyle stroked her head. Within minutes, she was sleeping peacefully, and Kyle slid his arm out from under her, covered her with a blanket, and left the room.

Thursday, October 27th
Deer Creek, Montana

Jennifer trailed Spencer around the yard as he made the most of his first playtime outside in more than a week. The weather was sunny and warm, and most of the snow that hadn't been collected and saved in the house had melted off. It felt good to be outside. The air still had a cool nip to it, but it felt fresh and sweet. The birds were enjoying the sunshine as well, singing raucously and busily fluttering about. Jennifer noticed that the grass was long, but it looked like it was finally going dormant for the winter. She knew that if Kyle could see his yard, he would be disappointed. "He's worked so hard to get it in and to this stage," she thought. Kyle was always a stickler for keeping the lawn manicured and having things looking just so.

Being cooped up inside for a few days had left the family cold and a little on edge, and Jennifer worried about how her family would deal with being stuck in the house during the coming winter. David had been glad to get out of the house and back to work for the past couple of days, which surprised Jennifer. For a kid who wouldn't take the trash out without a protest, David's enthusiasm for work indicated just how sick he was of being stuck at home with the family. Emma was again withdrawing more and more but wouldn't talk about her worries, leaving Jennifer to wonder what, of the dozens of possibilities, the problem could be. Even Emma's instructor for her school group had been concerned. Spencer, of the three kids, still seemed to be the least affected by the changes. He missed his TV shows and movies and favorite cereal, but still found joy in simple things, like messing around outside.

"Good morning! How are the two of you?"

Jennifer looked up to see Grace waving as she walked towards her.

"We're surviving. How about you?" she called back and headed towards her neighbor. She tried to sound upbeat, but wasn't sure she'd succeeded.

"I'm good. Just coming out to see about harvesting the rest of the potatoes. It looks like the ground is still too wet. If the weather stays nice, I should have them in by the end of the week."

"You're pretty amazing, Grace. Are you going to need any help getting them in?"

"If you don't mind. Work always goes faster when you've got a friend to share it with."

"I'd love to help. You've done so much for us. I don't think we'd have made it this far without you. How's Chuck doing? You'd mentioned he was sick."

Grace's smile left her face. "Oh, not too well. It's his diabetes. His insulin has run out, and he's got me worried."

"You've never said anything about Chuck having diabetes. Is there anything I can do to help?"

Grace shook her head. "No. I don't know what anyone can do. You know how stubborn he is. He won't tell me how he's doing, but I can tell it's not good."

"How serious is it, Grace?"

"With the type he has, it's serious. I try not to think about it, and I try not to worry, but Jennifer, what am I supposed to do? Without his insulin, and at his age…I don't want to lose him."

"I'm sorry Grace. I had no idea it was like that. I can check with Carol to see if she has any suggestions, but I don't know."

"Don't let it get you down, sweetheart. Chuck wouldn't want that. He'd be upset if he knew I'd worried you about him, so let's not talk about that. Have you had any more troubles? Any more break-ins? We worry about you too, you know."

"No, there hasn't been anything else. I'm hoping that issue is history."

"We hope so too. We don't realize how much we depend on others, until there's no one there for you. But anyways, no sense dwelling on depressing things. I'll come knock on your door when I'm ready to harvest, probably by the end of the week. Alright?'

"Sounds good. Just let me know. I'll bring Emma over with me. It would be good for her to have something to keep her busy."

CHAPTER TWENTY NINE

Saturday, October 29th
Montana State Line

Kyle spotted the blue sign up ahead on the side of the road. He'd known by the mileage markers that he was getting close, but to actually see the sign sent a surge of adrenaline through his body. He picked up his pace and was close to a jog when he was finally able to read the words. Welcome to Montana. He stopped at the sign and set his cart down, then walked over to the sign and touched it tenderly, as if it was a long lost friend. Dropping to his knees, he raised his arms over his head and let out a victory cry. "I did it!" he yelled at the top of his lungs. "I'm in Montana!"

He knew he still had a long ways to go, 444 miles to be exact, but to be in the same state as his family, breathing the same air and seeing the same sky, seemed to make everything lighter. He stood, triumphantly, for a few moments, wanting to share this achievement with someone, but the only cheers he heard were the sounds of birds flying overhead, oblivious to his accomplishment. With the one-man celebration over, Kyle picked up his cart and once again headed north.

October 31st
South Central Montana

Day 59

Cold and windy today. The weather scares me now, so I'm hesitant to move along if there's a chance for storms. I waited for a couple hours in an abandoned Camry, then headed on before noon when the skies started to clear. Day ended up being a short travel day as the wind was too much, and I was tired. Passed Custer's Battlefield. Reminded me of our vacation just before Spencer was born. I remember that it was the last stop on our itinerary, and we made it home before dark. Now I've got more than 2 weeks to walk. Life has come full circle, even Custer would have made this journey faster than me, at least he would have before the Indians got him.

I'm not seeing many people on the road; in fact, I've only seen 1 other walker in the last 3 days. Not sure if it's because of where I am, or because people have already made it to their destinations, but things are quiet. Food is the never-ending challenge. Have killed and eaten a few rabbits, but hate to waste the ammo, plus I have to build a fire to cook them. Some canned food would be nice, as would a microwave, spices, something with flavor. My shoes are worn, but I think they'll make it. Just hope my feet and knees hold out. The clothes Rose gave me have kept me warm, and I'm glad to have them. The thought of walking through our front door now seems like more than just a dream, and being on familiar ground makes the days more bearable in some ways, tougher in others.

I love you all.

P.S. Happy Halloween, though I don't expect any trick-or-treaters stopping by.

Saturday, November 5th
Deer Creek, Montana

Jennifer closed the door to Emma's room, where David and Spencer were now sleeping, and walked down the hall to the living room. The dim moonlight through the windows gave just enough illumination for her to see her way around, and she moved comfortably without a flashlight. She checked the front door to be sure it was locked, found it secure, and went to her own bedroom. Removing her robe and slippers, she crawled into her bed, discovering that Emma had rolled over onto her side of the bed once again. Jennifer gave her daughter a push to scoot her to the far side but was glad that Emma had left a comfortably warm spot in the otherwise cold sheets.

As she always did, Jennifer lay awake with her thoughts, worrying about the kids, about Chuck next door, and wondering where Kyle might be. With Kyle still on her mind, she drifted off to sleep.

She was in the middle of a dream, a dream where she and Kyle were on a date at a fancy Italian restaurant, when an ice-cold hand clamped down hard on her mouth. Her eyes flew open and she struggled in the near darkness to see who was there. She reached to grab the hand and felt the cold steel of a knife blade press against her throat. "Don't resist, Jennifer," she heard Doug say in a harsh whisper. She stopped struggling, looked up, and saw his face hovering over hers. It was the face of a monster. His eyes were two dark sunken shadows. His cheeks were gaunt and covered in a wiry beard that had grown in since she'd seen him last. His lips were cracked and scabbed, and parted in an evil grin that revealed his crooked teeth.

Doug leaned in close, and she felt his hot, foul breath on her face. "I see you're not sleeping alone," he whispered in her ear. "If you don't do everything I tell you to, I'll cut her first," he said, nodding to Emma. "Do you understand?"

Jennifer nodded, terror filling her eyes.

"I'm going to remove my hand now. Don't make me hurt your daughter."

Jennifer shook her head, and Doug slowly removed his hand. "Please don't do this," Jennifer whispered as soon as his hand slipped off. "Doug, please. Not here. Not now," she pled, tears running down the sides of her face.

"Shut up," he spat back. "If you wake your daughter, things will get messy. Besides, you had your chance to do it your way. Now I'm doing it mine."

"Doug, please don't. I'll come to your house in the morning. I'll spend the whole day there. You can do whatever you want to me. I swear. Just don't hurt my daughter, or my boys."

"Shut up!" he said, his voice rising. "You think I'm stupid? You'll show up with ten armed men. It's every man for himself anymore, and I'm going to take what I want." He slid his hand under the blankets and caressed her breast, causing her to flinch. "We're going to do it right here, right now, and you're going to act like I'm your lover and do everything I want. Do you understand?"

"Please, Doug," she sobbed. "Not by my daughter."

"Your daughter's my insurance policy. This worked out well. If you don't do whatever I want, I'll hurt her first so you can hear it, and then you, and then maybe your precious boys down the hall. Got it?"

Jennifer nodded, another jolt of fear shooting through her at the mention of her boys and their location in Emma's room. "How do I know you won't hurt us even if I do what you want?" she asked, trying to control her voice.

"You don't, but I'm not a violent guy. I'm just sick of everything, and I like women."

"Why me, Doug. Why not someone else?"

"Why not you? You should have liked me. Your husband's dead, and you needed a man around. I would have been good to you. Everyone else is either old, nasty, or they have a husband at home. Who else was there?"

Jennifer's mind raced for a way out. "If I do what you want, then what? What happens tomorrow?"

"Tomorrow I'll be gone. I'm bailing. My friend's got a cabin in the mountains, and I'm going Grizzly Adams. People are going to start killing each other soon, even in our precious little community. I'm looking out for myself. I just wanted to say goodbye before I left. Now shut up! We don't want to wake your sweet little daughter. I hope she's a deep sleeper."

Doug stepped back from the bed and took off his shoes. As he slid his pants down, he glared at her. "You're not getting ready. It's our honeymoon, Jenn. You should be more excited. I'm sure you'll have the time of your life."

Jennifer lay frozen in bed, her eyes locked on Doug. She didn't see any weapons other than his knife, but it was a hunting knife with a long, threatening blade. If she could get to it, or her gun, she thought, she might win. But if she didn't, then all of them would lose. She started to slide her sweatpants down her legs.

"Wait!" hissed Doug. "It's my honeymoon. I'll take them off." He stood by the bed, now dressed only in his boxer shorts, and set the knife down on the floor by the foot of the bed. "Don't get any ideas," he warned before throwing the covers off of her. He grabbed the waistband of her sweats and slid them slowly down her legs.

Jennifer held her breath and turned her head away as she felt him running his hands across her legs.

"You have nice legs, Jenn," he said. "Your skin is soft and warm." He caressed her thighs with his cold, clammy fingers. "Sit up!" he ordered her.

Jennifer sat up, her eyes still closed.

Doug grabbed the bottom of her sweatshirt and started to lift it. "Open your eyes and look at me. I want to see the look of love in your eyes."

Jennifer took a deep breath and forced her eyes open. She turned and looked at Doug, his features more evil now than when the assault began. Jennifer's expression was cold and hard, her eyes boring into him.

"I guess that'll do," he said, continuing to lift her sweatshirt. He pulled it up over her head, revealing a thin white undershirt, then tossed the sweatshirt on top of her sweatpants. "You must get cold at night." Doug grabbed the neck of her shirt with both hands and, pulling them apart, tore her shirt in half, the violence and noise of his action terrifying her.

Emma stirred in the bed and both Jennifer and Doug froze until she was settled again. "Don't wake my daughter!" Jennifer begged, panicked. "Please don't wake her."

Ignoring her plea, Doug looked at Jennifer, who now sat in the bed in her panties and a sports bra. "You've got more layers than an onion, but I'm sure you taste much better," he said as he leaned down and kissed her shoulder and neck. "See, this isn't so bad. Even in the dark you look pretty good for having three kids." He nuzzled her ear, then threw her arms over his shoulders. "Act like you enjoy this!" he ordered.

Jennifer fought the urge to vomit and squeezed Doug with her arms.

"Say my name, like you want me!"

"Doug," she choked out.

He pulled away from her. "You sound like you're ill," he said disgustedly and shoved her away.

Caught off guard, Jennifer rocked backward and fell hard onto Emma. She held her breath as she looked at her daughter, praying that Emma wouldn't wake up, her heart pounding so hard against her ribs she was sure it would break them. Emma's head turned towards Jennifer, and her eyes opened a crack. "Mom?" Emma whispered.

"It's okay, baby," Jennifer whispered frantically. "Go to sleep! Please, baby girl, go to sleep! Everything's okay." Jennifer saw

Doug, holding his knife, step around to the foot of the bed. She cupped a hand over Emma's eyes to shield her view, but not before Emma noticed the movement and pulled her head back to see who was there.

At the sight of Doug with a knife, Emma let out a scream. Jennifer immediately slapped her hand over her daughter's mouth, cutting off the sound. As Doug moved towards them, Jennifer pulled Emma protectively under her and held her arm up to Doug.

"Baby, close your eyes, just close your eyes," Jennifer begged her terrified daughter. "Just think of this as a bad dream. Close your eyes and say your prayers. You know how you like to pray. That guy is someone mommy knows, so don't be afraid." Emma's panicked eyes darted around the room. "Do you understand me, sweetie?" Jennifer asked, her hand still clamped over Emma's mouth. "Can you do that, baby? Can you do it for mom?" Emma nodded, her eyes still open and terrified.

"Okay, good girl. Good girl. I'm going to slide you over to your edge of the bed. Lie on your stomach and don't look at anything. Close your eyes. Put a pillow over your head and hold it tight against your ears. Try not to listen. You understand?"

Emma nodded.

"Okay, good. Think songs, or prayers, anything. Just don't look, and don't listen. Promise?" Emma nodded again. Jennifer tenderly rolled Emma over to the edge of the bed, pulled the blanket up, and put a pillow over her head.

Doug stepped back around to the side of the bed and they stared at each other, neither one of them saying anything. "Do what you need to do," Jennifer whispered. "Then go to hell."

Doug set his knife down on the floor and stepped towards her. His eyes were steely and hard, and Jennifer knew that he was determined to get what he came for. She lay back onto her pillow, closed her eyes, and braced for it. As Doug's fingers reached inside the waistband of her panties, Jennifer heard a noise from the doorway. Her eyes flew open just as David lunged across the room and leapt onto Doug's back.

David grabbed a hold of Doug's neck and head and tried to pull the man away from his mother, twisting with every bit of strength he had. Doug stepped away from the bed, clawing at David's arms, trying to shake him loose. Doug balled up his fists and swung behind him, landing glancing blows, but David clung tight. Doug maneuvered to the doorway and repeatedly threw his body back against the corner of it, pinning David and knocking the air out of him with each blow. The third strike broke David's grip and he dropped to the floor. Jennifer dove onto the floor where Doug had placed the knife and grabbed it.

Doug turned back towards the bed. "This isn't how I planned this," he snarled. "No one was going to get hurt."

Jennifer stood against the far wall, clutching Doug's knife. "Get out! Get out now!"

Doug laughed. "I'm not afraid of you and some twelve year old. Tell him to go back to his room! I'm going to get what I came for!" Doug stepped towards Jennifer as she raised the knife and prepared to strike. Doug shook his head. "This is your fault, Jenn. It didn't have to be this way." He came towards her quickly, deflected her swing and grabbed her wrist, forcing the knife from her hands before roughly pushing her onto the bed.

As Doug bent to pick up the weapon, David tackled him from behind and knocked Doug headfirst into the wall with enough force that Doug dropped to the ground.

Jennifer scrambled across the bed and pushed Emma onto the floor, then thrust her arm under the mattress, searching for her gun.

"Stay away from my mother, you jerk!" David shrieked as he stepped back. His fists were raised in front of him and he rocked nervously from side to side.

Doug scrambled on the floor, searching in the darkness for his knife. He found it, stood up, and spun towards David who had backed across the room but was still threatening him.

Jennifer found the gun and raised it in front of her. "David, get out! Doug, back off! You get out of my house! I've got a gun!" she yelled. She could see well enough in the dark room to know she'd be able to hit her target.

Both of the men ignored her commands, and Doug lunged at David, who was standing near the doorway.

Jennifer pulled the trigger, but nothing happened.

David swung at Doug, hitting him on the cheek at the same time Doug's blade pierced his abdomen. As Doug pulled the knife back, David dropped his hands to his belly and found it warm and wet. He lifted a hand in front of his eyes and saw that it was covered in something dark, then wiped it on his shirt and raised his fists defensively in front of himself again.

Jennifer screamed in horror. She shook the gun in her hand. "Work!" she shrieked, and then she remembered the safety. She fumbled for the button, found it with her shaking fingers, and released it as she desperately raised the gun again.

Jennifer heard David's voice and could tell he was in a lot of pain. "I said stay away from my mother!" he repeated.

Doug stood back a few steps from David and could see the stain of blood spreading on the boy's shirt. The situation had spiraled completely out of control and he let out a gasp. "You're too brave, kid," he said. "You shouldn't have to die." As Doug dropped the knife and stepped towards David, he heard a gunshot and felt something hot strike him in the shoulder and throw him against the wall. He turned to where he'd seen the flash and saw another one, then a third.

Doug dropped to his knees, feeling like a mule had kicked him in the chest with both feet. He tried to speak, to tell Jennifer he was sorry, that no one was supposed to get hurt, but all he heard was a gurgling noise from his chest. Then his eyes closed, and he collapsed to the ground.

With the sound of gunshots still ringing in her ears, Jennifer discarded the gun under the bed and leapt across the room to David. He had dropped to his knees and was clutching his stomach with both hands. "David!" she cried out. "Oh, David! How bad is it?"

"I think he stabbed me, Mom. There's blood, and it hurts bad."

"Oh, sweetie," Jennifer sobbed. "Lay down and try to relax. I have to get Carol. She can help you. Keep pressure on it, okay, honey?"

David spoke through clenched teeth. "I'll try, Mom, but I don't feel so good."

Jennifer ran to Emma, who was still hiding by the bed with a pillow over her head, grabbed her by the shoulders and shook her. "Sweetie! You've got to stop crying! I need your help. David is hurt. Do you understand me?"

Emma nodded, her face twisted in fear.

"I'm going to get Mrs. Anderson next door, then the doctor. I need you to hold a shirt against David's stomach until I get back with them," she said as she yanked open her dresser. "You've got to help your brother. It's very important."

Emma nodded and took the t-shirt from her mother with trembling hands.

Jennifer found her sweatshirt and pants on the floor where Doug had tossed them, dressed, then stepped around Doug's nearly naked body and knelt on the floor beside her children. "Hold it like this," she instructed Emma as she folded the shirt over a couple of times and placed it on the wound, pressing down and making David flinch. "Emma, press hard and don't look around. Just look at David and talk to him. Whatever you do, don't let him fall asleep, okay? David, keep talking to your sister and make sure she doesn't look at anything but you."

Jennifer rushed into the hall, the smell of gunpowder burning her nose and reminding her of the nightmare she was living. At the end of the hall, Spencer was crying hysterically in his bedroom. Jennifer called to him as she ran to the front door. "Spencer, it's going to be alright. I'll be back soon."

Then she ran out into the night.

CHAPTER THIRTY

Saturday, November 12th
East of Butte, Montana

Day 71

I made a decision two days ago that I hope I won't regret. I left my cart behind so I can get through the hills and mountains easier. I've been second-guessing myself ever since, but so far, things have worked out. I think with the short distance I have left to travel, I can make a good hard push to get there. My backpack is all that I have, and I feel naked. As long as I can find shelter at night, I should be good. The last few days have been nice after some cold and snow. I'm so close now I can hardly sleep.

I love you all.

Monday, November 14th
Deer Creek, Montana

Day 73

I made it through Butte yesterday without incident, even got a hot meal at a church. People seem to have settled into some sort of acceptance of their condition, although hollow eyes and hungry faces are the norm. Some look like the walking dead. Even the children have little life in them. I only see the people near the highway, so I hope that they are the exception, but it's hard to tell. Yesterday the priest at the church said that the government's broadcasts don't offer much hope, that they often play the same message for 2 or 3 days in a row. I know lots of people don't have much hope, but I do. In three days, God willing, I'll see my family again. Words can't express how that makes me feel. On the other hand, the fear that something might happen to me after coming so far is a constant worry. I can't wait to touch your faces, hold your hands, tuck the kids into bed--all joys worth walking twice the distance for.

I love you all.

Thursday, November 17th
Deer Creek, Montana

The green mile markers counted down to Kyle's exit. For the past three days, he'd been walking on roads that he'd driven a hundred times before. Never had it looked so beautiful, and never had it taken so long to cover the distance. The anticipation of arriving home compelled him to push his limits, walking until well after dark, waking before sunrise to head off, and stopping for only a few minutes to eat what meager food he could scavenge. Without the cart, he was making better time but was having to adjust to the absence of the security the cart had provided.

The larger backpack Rose had insisted he take had proven immensely helpful, enabling him to carry enough supplies to make the final dash home, and now he was almost there. Mile marker 120. He imagined, for the five thousandth time, bursting through the front door, Spencer and Emma running into his arms, Jennifer, standing, waiting for him to run to her, David, acting cool and unimpressed, sauntering over to give him a one-armed hug…119…How had his family done without him? What had they eaten? Were they safe?…118…The fall colors in Montana were just as beautiful as he remembered, the mountains as majestic, the sky as blue…117…The businesses on the frontage road looked rough, most of them vandalized, with windows missing, and the insides stripped of anything valuable…116…The sun was setting. It was going to be late when he got there. He hoped the kids would still be awake…115…His stomach rumbled steadily with hunger, but he was unwilling to stop for the few minutes it would take to eat. The sign at the gas station at his exit was now in view…114…Just one more mile on the highway, the off-ramp now in full view…113.

Kyle walked slowly down the off-ramp of exit 113, his head swimming in ecstasy at all the sights that were so familiar to him: the gas station he usually filled up at, the road he drove everyday to work, the street going north to his friend's house, and the dark shadow of Missoula in the distance. He stopped for just a second at the bottom of the ramp and fought to hold back the tears. This was his home, where his heart belonged, where he would find his family. The last fingers of sunlight lit the scene for him, one of the most beautiful vistas he could remember. Kyle noticed the cars dead at the pumps and the doors of the gas station broken open. In the dim light he could see that the store was gutted and the diner across the street was likewise ransacked. The scene reminded him that suffering and chaos existed in his town too. He had somehow thought, or hoped, that the people in Deer Creek would be a little more civilized, a little more capable of handling the situation, but realized they too would do what was necessary to survive.

Kyle took his pack off his back and set it on the ground beside him. He tossed out his clothes, blankets, and maps, keeping only his food, journal, guns, and water. He shouldered his load again, cinched the waist strap, and headed down the home stretch. With his pack lightened, Kyle started to run. About a mile down this road, then across the bridge, and he'd be in the community of Deer Creek. A couple of turns from there, and he'd be home. There had been countless days of walking, and now he was thirty minutes from home. He ran as fast as he could. Everything was familiar, like it had been, kept alive in his memory for the past three months. It was dark when he made it to the first turn, and by then he was losing steam and had to slow to a fast walk. In the distance he could make out the big house that marked the corner of his street.

Breathing heavily, Kyle finally stood in front of his house, the sweat running down his back, his eyes wet with tears. The grass seemed a little long, but everything was what he'd remembered and envisioned for the past weeks. He walked to the door, trying to control his emotions, paused a second, then reached for the handle to throw it open, but it was locked. He pounded on the door with his fist and stood back and listened but heard nothing from inside the house. Concerned, he slowly walked through the darkness to the back of the house and tugged on the sliding glass door. To his relief, it slid open, and he stepped inside. "Jennifer?" Kyle called out as all his fears played out in his mind. He waited and listened. No response. He walked down the hall to his bedroom and scanned the room. It was dark and difficult to see, but he could tell that the bed was empty and messy, missing the sheets, and appeared not to have been used for a while. As he turned to leave, Kyle noticed dark spots on the wall, spots that, upon closer inspection, looked like blood, both splattered, and smeared down the wall. Then he saw large, dark stains in the carpet, and his heart skipped another beat.

Kyle's mind erupted in a panic. What had happened? He ran to the front door, threw it open, and ran across the field to the Anderson's. He pounded frantically on their door. "Charles! Grace! Open up!" he called out. There was no sound or movement from inside. He ran to the house across from them, trying to think of the people's names. He pounded on the front door and waited. Hearing nothing, he pounded again before finally hearing footsteps inside the house. As the steps approached the front door, Kyle heard a man's voice through the door. "Go away! I've got a gun!"

"I'm sorry, but this is Kyle Tait. I live across the street."

"I said go away!" the man snapped.

"I'm trying to find my family!" hollered Kyle back through the door.

"Go away! I'm not opening my door!"

"Please!" yelled Kyle in desperation. As he leaned towards the door, he heard the sound of a shotgun being pumped. "Okay, I'm going," Kyle shouted. He ran to the next house. It had been empty and for sale before he left and still had the realtor's sign in the front yard.

At the next house down, Kyle banged on the front door, then waited until he heard someone approach the door. "Who's there?" came a voice.

"My name is Kyle Tait. I'm looking for my family."

"They aren't here. It's just me and my wife."

"They," he started, then caught himself. "We live across the street, in the blue house. Do you know what happened to them?'

Kyle heard the deadbolt being turned, and then the door opened slowly. A man in his mid-50's wearing a white Budweiser t-shirt stepped out onto the porch, nervously holding a pistol in his hands. He pointed the pistol at Kyle and eyed him with suspicion. "I told you, they aren't here."

Kyle raised his hands and stepped back down off the porch. "I don't want any trouble. I'm just looking for my family."

"Who did you say you were?" the man asked again.

"I'm Kyle Tait. That's my house," Kyle said, pointing down the street towards his home. "I've been gone, but I'm back now, and my family isn't there. I'm just trying to find out where they are." Kyle was tired and scared and could feel himself losing control of his emotions.

The man thought a second, considering whether or not to tell Kyle anything, then shrugged his shoulders and began. "There was a shooting there a couple of weeks ago. The lady shot Doug, the sheriff guy. I don't know if you know him. Anyway, what I heard was that the kid caught Doug in the bedroom with his mother and tried to fight him. The boy ended up getting stabbed pretty bad, and then the lady shot Doug for stabbing her kid. At least that's what some people are saying, but you know how people talk. I'm avoiding everyone right now, so who knows what the truth is. I did watch them carry a body out of the house, so I know somebody died. It's all pretty nasty business. Everyone around here has been pretty scared now that Doug isn't patrolling and with the break-ins and stuff."

Kyle staggered back away from the man's house. Everything around him started to swirl, and he collapsed to his knees.

The man gave Kyle a look. "You all right?" he asked.

Kyle no longer heard the man. He dropped his head to the ground, losing awareness of everything around him. The horrible things the man had described resounded in his ears. A violent shudder seized his body, and he had a hard time catching his breath.

"Geez, buddy. You sick? You better not be contagious." The man hurried back inside his house and slammed the door, dead bolting it loudly behind him.

Kyle lay in the man's yard for several minutes, his body weak and his mind numb. Slowly he pulled himself together and staggered to his feet. Had Jennifer given up on him? Maybe she thought he'd died in a plane crash or somewhere between Houston and home. What happened to David? Why had Jennifer let that happen to their son? Where was his family now? Kyle stumbled across the road, struggling to place one foot in front of the other. He found his way back to his house, let himself in, and dropped to the floor where he lay motionless for hours, his mind tumbling from one thought to another, with nothing making sense.

Kyle started to shiver on the cold entryway floor. Slowly he got up and walked down the hall, past his room, to Emma's, where he pushed the door open and dropped onto her bed. Physically and emotionally drained, Kyle wrapped himself in a blanket and cried.

Friday, November 18th
Deer Creek, Montana

The bedroom was awash in sunlight when Kyle opened his eyes. Outside, the sky was blue, the air crisp, and a fresh new day had started, but inside, Kyle's world was cloudy and dark, as dark as any night he'd experienced on his journey. Kyle sat up in bed and shook his head, taking a moment to realize where he was, having slept in cars, trucks, or a tent for most of the last ten weeks. He picked up a picture of his daughter from the bedside table and held it in front of him. Emma stood at the edge of a creek holding a four-inch long fish she had caught on a camping trip back in June. In the background, Jennifer was helping Spencer cast his fishing line. Kyle studied the picture while the memories from the trip rushed painfully back, then set the picture down and walked out into the kitchen. The conversation with the neighbor from the night before replayed in his mind, breaking his heart once again.

Searching through the cupboards, Kyle found no food and assumed his family had taken everything with them, wherever they had gone. As he stood in the kitchen trying to figure out the best way to find Jennifer and the kids, his eyes caught sight of a single envelope stuck to the middle of the fridge with two happy face magnets. On the front of the envelope, written in large, black letters, was the word KYLE, with small hearts drawn on either side of his name. Kyle snatched the envelope off of the fridge, scattering the magnets, and hurriedly untucked the flap, half tearing the envelope before pulling out the paper inside. He unfolded the note and began to read.

Dear Kyle,

I live for the day that you read this note and will hold me in your arms again. The past months have been the longest of my life, but knowing that you'll come back, no matter how hard it might be, has given me the strength to make it through these difficult days. I'll wait 10,000 days for your return if I need to. We've moved to Carol Jeffries' house. She's taking care of David who was seriously injured while protecting me from an awful man who tried to hurt our family. David doesn't even complain despite not having anything to help with the pain. You will be so proud of him. He's become a man, and he reminds me of you. Spencer and Emma miss you terribly and will be so happy when their daddy returns. We come to our house every afternoon at 1:00 PM and wait until sunset, to see if you come home. It breaks my heart a little more every time I open the door and you're not here. If it's close to 1:00 when you get here, wait for us. If not, please come find us at Carol's house. She lives at 1272 Whitetail Lane. It's the green house across from the one that does the big Christmas display we always drove by when our house was being built.

I Love You!
Jennifer

P.S. Life seems fragile lately. Charles Anderson died 2 days ago from diabetes complications. If, heaven forbid, something should happen to me and I'm not here when you get back, please know that I've been madly in love with you since our first date. I've never regretted for a minute being Mrs. Kyle Tait. Hurry!

Kyle finished reading Jennifer's note through tear-filled eyes, then wiped his face on his sleeve so he could see to reread the address. The letter was dated November 17th. He saw, in the trash, crumpled notes from previous days. Kyle dropped the note on the counter and wept with relief, the pains of the last sixteen hundred miles washing away.

After dressing quickly, Kyle ran to the front door and threw it open, knowing exactly where the house with the Christmas display was. He sprinted down his driveway and into the street, his hair flying in the wind as he ran. Kyle waved joyously to the few people he saw as he dashed by. Neighbors who saw him had no idea who he was, nor that they had just seen the happiest man in America.

He rounded the corner onto Whitetail Lane. The house was about a half mile ahead on the left. He flew past door after door after door, registering the numbers as he went. 1112…1152…1192… He slowed to a walk just a few doors away and could see the green house. A little boy in a red sweater ran into the front yard from the side of the house, followed by another boy wearing a blue coat. Kyle recognized the blue coat. He had been with Jennifer when they bought it on clearance for Spencer early last spring. His son was two doors away. Kyle stopped and stared for a moment, his breathing no longer automatic. He began walking again, the lump in his throat that had been growing since he'd read Jennifer's note aching intensely.

Up ahead, Spencer saw Kyle and stared back at his dad. Kyle could tell by the look on Spencer's face that his son didn't recognize him. Kyle glanced down at his clothes, the well-worn blue jeans and the jacket Rose had given him, which Spencer had never seen. He had four weeks of beard growth, hair that hadn't been combed for a long time, and a face that had only been washed two or three times since Wyoming. It was no surprise that he was unrecognizable. Kyle looked back up at the boys. They were playing again, but Spencer's eyes kept returning to Kyle. Spencer again stopped and stared at Kyle, studying his face, seeming to recognize something, but unable to put the pieces together.

With tears streaming down his dirty cheeks, Kyle smiled at his son. The moment he did, Spencer's eyes flew open wide, and his head jerked upwards. He stopped running with his friend and stared at his father, his mouth hanging open. Kyle heard a woman's voice from around the side of the house. "Spencer, what's wrong?" Spencer stood frozen in place, then raised his arm and pointed at Kyle. His mouth moved as if he was trying to say something, but no sound came out.

Jennifer came from the side yard where the two boys had emerged earlier. She knelt down in front of Spencer and tussled his hair, saying something that was lost in the wind. Her hair was a little darker and longer than he remembered, and she looked thinner than she had in August, but there was no mistaking his Jennifer. She was wearing blue jeans and a pale yellow sweater, and oh, how Kyle loved the way she looked in a sweater.

"Daddy," Spencer managed to call out.

Jennifer pulled her head back and looked at Spencer, who was looking over her shoulder. She turned and followed his gaze to where a strange man had stopped on the roadside in front of the neighbor's house. She turned back to Spencer, who was still watching the man. "Daddy!" Spencer said again, louder.

Jennifer turned and looked at the man again. He was now walking towards them, smiling. Her heart leapt in her chest. She knew that smile. She'd seen it a million times before, but lately only in her dreams. She rose to her feet, struggling to keep her balance. Her hands covered her mouth, and her eyes welled up. She took an awkward step towards Kyle, and then another. Then she started to run. She stumbled but caught herself. He was running towards her now too. "Kyle!" she cried out.

They came together in front of the green house on Whitetail Lane. Kyle grabbed Jennifer with both arms and swept her off her feet, spinning her around and around. His throat ached too much to speak, so he just held her, held her with all the strength and love and energy he possessed. He closed his eyes and shut out the world and just experienced the touch and feel of his wife tight against him.

They stopped spinning, and everything he'd gone through during the past three months flashed briefly through his mind: the airplane crash, Ed, Louise, his friends in Lubbock, losing his cart, Rose. All of it was there, and then it was gone. He was home. He was with his family. Nothing else mattered. The joy of that moment was worth every ounce of energy he had spent to get there.

"Daddy!" came a little boy's scream. Now that his mother had confirmed what he'd already known, Spencer was charging across the yard. He slammed into his daddy's legs, and wrapped his little arms around them.

Kyle let go of Jennifer and enveloped Spencer in his arms. He picked his son up off the ground and squeezed him tight. Spencer wrapped his arms around his dad's neck and hugged him as tightly as he could, his face grimacing, his eyes closing to tiny slivers. Jennifer put her arms around the two of them, and they silently embraced for what seemed like hours, without saying a word.

In the midst of their embrace, the front door swung open, and a young girl squealed. Kyle turned to see Emma drop to her knees in excitement on the front steps of the house. He set Spencer down and ran to his daughter. Scooping her up off the steps, he kissed her cheek and carried her over to where Jennifer and Spencer stood watching.

Kyle swallowed hard. "I missed you guys," he said, finally choking the words out between sobs. "I sure had to walk a long way to get here… but you're worth every step."

"We missed you too, Daddy. We missed you too," said Emma, her grin spreading from ear to ear, nearly splitting her face in two.

Jennifer wrapped her arms around her husband, son, and daughter, rested her head on Kyle's shoulder, and closed her eyes. "I knew you'd come home, Kyle," she whispered. "I just knew it."

Kyle looked down at Jennifer, the love of his life, and gently took her chin in his hand, tilted her face up, and kissed her. Their lips pressed tightly together as their tears blended, the joy of their reunion still coursing through them.

Jennifer broke the kiss and looked into her husband's eyes. "Welcome home, Kyle. You have no idea how much we missed you."

Kyle smiled, every care in the world forgotten. "It's so good to be here." He looked at Jennifer, his eyes glistening. "There's one more person I need to see. I understand he's made his father proud."

Jennifer nodded and wiped the tears from her cheeks as she took Kyle by the hand and led him towards the house.

* * *

The following April, pallets of seeds from Australia and South America, along with instructions for planting and harvesting, were delivered by armed military vehicles to every community in the country.

By July, ten months after the EMP attack, partial power was restored to 10% of the residents within 100 miles of Washington, D.C. By November, 20% of East Coast residents reported between four and six hours of power availability a day.

In December, 20% of power was restored in Montana's three largest cities.

The following April, nineteen months after the EMP attack, mail delivery was reinstituted. It consisted of one day a week service and was limited to 4x6 postcards. Kyle sent out several postcards the first day of service. They read, simply:

I made it.
They were safe.
God bless you.
Kyle Tait, your friend for life.

Thank You

On behalf of everyone who has helped create this story, I would like to thank you for investing your money and taking the time to read this book. Taking a chance on an unknown author is a risk that is not always rewarded. Hopefully you feel your time has been well spent.

Speaking on behalf of independent authors, I would ask you to help increase our chances of finding success. Trying to break through as an author takes a lot of hard work, time, faith, and the support and encouragement of dozens of people, and even then, most authors find very limited success. In those instances when you read a story that you feel has been well written, is entertaining, and is worth the price of the book, please tell your friends about it, mention it on Facebook, or find other ways to spread the word about it. Independent authors have very limited advertising funds and most of us sell only a handful of books, so each new sale is exciting and motivating.

I would also ask you to consider adding a review on Amazon. The ratings help, the feedback is appreciated, and I can assure you that each review is read multiple times by the author, likely within hours of it being posted.

As far as the subject of EMP's goes, I sincerely believe the threat is real, and it is a subject that most people know little about and are terribly unprepared for. The fact that a rogue state or terrorist organization has the potential to bring our continent to its knees with a single nuclear bomb should keep our leaders up at night. However, seeing as our government is doing next to nothing to protect us, I strongly encourage the reader to take the initiative and do as much preparing as possible to protect themselves and their family.

Some of the resources I would direct you to are:

www.empactamerica.org – (the site with the best information on EMPs)

www.survivalblog.com – (an amazing site with hundreds of articles on preparedness)

www.mypatriotsupply.com – (a great resource for heirloom seeds and other items)

The Survival Podcast – (a daily podcast discussing various threats)

In addition, there are dozens of other books, websites, podcasts, and other resources a person can avail themselves to in order to improve their chances of surviving an emergency, whatever form it might take.

Thanks again.

Ray Gorham

Continue reading for a sample chapter from Ray's next book, Daunting Days of Winter

DAUNTING DAYS OF WINTER
BY
RAY GORHAM

Available soon on all major e-tailers

CHAPTER ONE

Friday, November 18th
Deer Creek, MT

Kyle gently stroked the back of Jennifer's hand. "I still can't believe I'm actually home. I've dreamed about this so many times that I'm terrified I'm going to wake up." Emotions remained close to the surface.

Jennifer laughed. "You keep saying that. We're real, Kyle. Believe it. Our family really is back together again." She grabbed his hand, squeezing warmly with both of hers and kissing the back of it. Spencer had fallen asleep on the couch between them with his head resting in Kyle's lap, and he stirred, mumbling something that neither of them could make out, then wiggled his shoulders and drifted off to sleep again.

"He's gotten taller."

Jennifer nodded. "You said the same thing about Emma and David. Also told us we all look skinnier. But you can say it again if you want. You can say anything at all, as long as you promise never to be gone again." She could feel tears bubbling up and dabbed at her eyes as her voice trailed off.

Kyle squeezed his wife's hand and rubbed her foot with his. He tried to make eye contact with her, but she was looking out the small window, staring at the sliver of a moon that hung in the night sky. "Don't worry. I don't ever plan on being away from you again. Besides, my legs are so tired from walking, I don't think I could go another mile, especially if it's away from you."

Jennifer let out a long, deep breath and closed her eyes, pressing Kyle's hand against her cheek. "Your hands are rough. I don't remember them being like this," she said, her voice soft and sleepy.

"You should have seen the blisters I had the first few weeks. I didn't realize how soft I was before all this happened."

"I like them. I know why they're rough; it means something to me." Jennifer tried unsuccessfully to fight off a yawn. "Have I mentioned how good you look with a beard?"

Kyle nodded. "A couple of times. I don't agree, but who am I to question your taste."

Spencer stirred again and moaned, then rubbed his eyes as he shifted positions. Emma sat on the other side of Kyle, leaning against the armrest with one leg draped over Kyle's leg and an arm behind his back.

"I'm tired," Emma said, yawning. "But I don't want to go to bed."

The fire in the fireplace cracked and popped and lit the room in a dancing, honey-yellow hue. "You can stay up as long as you want, Em. It's not every day your dad gets home after walking across the country. He'll be here tomorrow, too. Isn't that wonderful?" Jennifer paused, then continued in a halting voice. "So don't think you have to stay up all night."

"I won't stay up too late," Emma answered. "Just a little while longer."

Kyle turned as David pulled himself out of the recliner he was resting in. "The fire needs more wood," he said as he stood.

"I'll get it, Son. You sit down. Don't strain yourself." Kyle started to gently move Spencer off of him, but David protested.

"I'm fine, Dad. You're just like Mom and Mrs. Jeffries. They worry about me all the time. My wound doesn't really even hurt anymore. I can get the wood. I'm not a cripple."

"I know. I know. But if you tear it open, it could be dangerous. You know as much as anyone what the situation is."

David smiled. "Got it, Dad. You can go back to staring at Mom. I'll put more wood on the fire so there's enough light for you to see her."

"Maybe we don't want the lights on," Jennifer said playfully, her emotions temporarily back under control.

Emma made a gagging sound. "If you guys start kissing again, I'm going to be sick. I've never seen so much kissing in all my life."

"Emma, you're nine," David said as he placed a log on the fire. "I'm guessing you haven't seen much kissing, besides Mom and Dad."

"You're one to talk, David; you don't even have a girlfriend."

"How do you know I don't have a girlfriend? You follow me around all day?"

"Kids. Cut it out," Jennifer said, giving them a look. "Dad didn't walk all this way to listen to you fight. I'm sure he could have stayed in Texas and found some other kids to do that."

Kyle grinned. "This feels normal. Not you guys arguing, well, okay, I guess that is kind of normal, but just being together, talking, listening, touching. This feels normal. It feels right." Kyle choked up, and Jennifer's eyes glistened in the firelight.

"Mom cries a lot too. So don't feel embarrassed," Emma said matter-of-factly. "We've all gotten used to it. Didn't know it was contagious though."

"You're such a ditz, Emma," David said as he returned to his seat. "Mom, why couldn't I have had two brothers?"

Kyle reached out and pulled Emma into him, burying her face in his chest. "Don't say that about my only little girl, David. She might be ditz, but she's the only ditz I've got, so you'd better treat her well."

Emma let out a muffled yell.

"Am I smothering you?" Kyle asked, relaxing his embrace. "Or is my smell killing you?"

"A little bit of both, actually," Emma said as she leaned back against the armrest. "But you're not the only one who stinks."

Kyle laughed as he tussled her hair. Jennifer leaned forward and glared warmly at her daughter, her lips hinting at a smile.

"What? He does kind of smell."

"What's gotten into you, little girl? I can't remember the last time you had this much spunk. Are you feeling alright?"

Emma shrugged. "I'm just glad Dad's home."

"I'm sorry I smell so bad, Em. It's been a few days since I had a bath. For some reason the motels were all closed. Maybe I can get cleaned up a little better tomorrow. Hopefully Carol won't mind if I make an even bigger mess of her bathroom."

"You smell just fine to me," Jennifer said as she leaned back into the couch. "And Carol has repeatedly told us to make ourselves at home here.""I spit bathed with a wet towel a couple of times this week, but the river was awfully cold, so it was short and sweet. Those clothes I was wearing, they should probably be burned just to keep us safe."

"We're not burning any clothes. We make everything last. We'll set you up with a real bath tomorrow. There's a crew that brings water up from the river every morning. It's not our day for bath water, but I'm sure they'll make an exception. Your showing up here has really made a difference in the mood of the community. I actually saw a lot of people smiling for the first time."

"I think I met most of the community today, but I really don't know these people. How's it been?"

Jennifer shook her head from side to side in a slow and deliberate motion as she searched for the right words. "It's been difficult, but you seem to have given a lot of people hope who had lost it. You-- making it back from so far away--it's amazing. I still almost don't believe it. I've prayed for it and dreamt about it, thought about it every hour of every day, but I was losing hope, just like everyone else."

"I prayed for it more than Mom did," Emma interjected in a sleepy voice. "Every night before bed I said my prayers and asked for God to bring you home. Mom said I needed to do that every day."

Kyle rubbed Emma's leg. "I prayed to make it home, too, sweetie, and it had been a long time since I'd said any prayers. I guess God got tired of hearing from us, huh?"

Emma nodded, her eyes barely open. "But He listened, didn't He?"

Jennifer smiled at Kyle as he turned back to her. "Your daughter really missed you. I can see a change in her already." Emma's eyes closed. "This whole thing has been really difficult, Kyle. I know you've been through a lot, walking so far and somehow making it home. But being here every day, seeing our neighbors slowly die, being hungry most of the time, the weather getting colder, and the nights longer..." She shook her head. "It's hard. Sometimes you just want to give up. I think a lot of people had gotten to that point. We had gotten too used to easy; hard is taking some adjusting."

"Do you think we're safe here?"

Jennifer nodded. She glanced at the fire, watching the flames swirl and dance. "We're safer here than any place else I can think of. I think you're the miracle we needed, both for our family and the community. You've reminded us of what a person can do if something is important to them, if they don't let the impossible stand in the way."

"I didn't know what I'd find when I got here, Jenn. You can't imagine how I felt when I found blood in the house." Kyle wiped at his eyes. "But we survived. We're together, and we'll make it. I don't know what it's going to take, but we've got to promise that we'll never give up. Okay?"

"I promise," Jennifer said, her eyes still focused on the flames. "I don't know what it's going to take, but I promise."

"David, do you promise?" Kyle asked his son.

"I promise, Dad. If you can make it home, we can do this."

"How 'bout you, Emma."

Emma nodded, her eyes still closed. She mumbled faintly. "If David can do it, I can. I promise."

Kyle glanced down at Spencer, who was sound asleep and breathing deeply. "How about you, Spence? Are you ready to face whatever comes?"

40137848R00204

Made in the USA
Lexington, KY
26 March 2015